Two Hours to Darkness

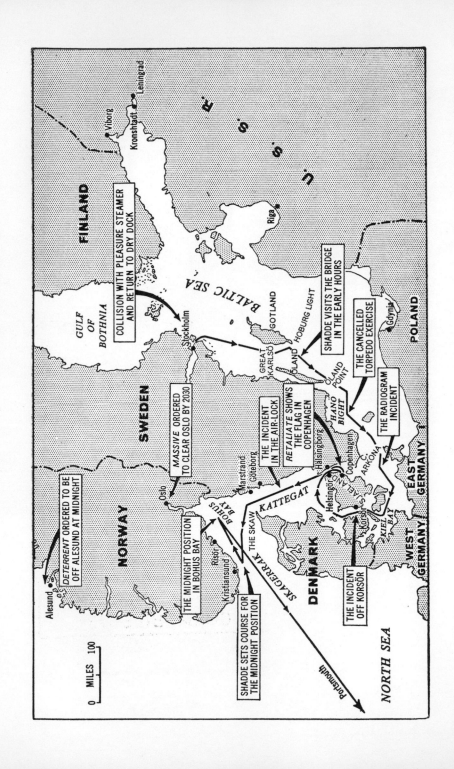

TWO
HOURS
TO
DARKNESS

by *Antony Trew*

RANDOM HOUSE   NEW YORK

Two Hours to Darkness

‖ I ‖

It was dark and cold and there was a fine drizzle. Pools of rainwater gathered in the dents and crevices on the chart-table screen, overflowed and splashed onto the steel deck. In the glare of the steaming lights the rain hung like fine muslin, green to starboard and red to port.

The sublieutenant called the bearings and Symington plotted them with cold and fumbling hands. Drops of water from his oilskins fell onto the chart and left dark smudges of damp. He dabbed at them with a towel.

"Once more, Keely."

In the forepart of the bridge the dark figure of the sub-lieutenant hunched over the azimuth ring. He swung it slowly, stopping on each bearing, the light from the gyro repeater accentuating the white, tense face.

"Great Karlsö one-six-eight; Västergarn zero-five-seven."

The voice was deep and sonorous, much older than his years.

"Bloody waste of time. Fixes by SINS. Fixes by loran.

D. F. fixes. The bloody lot. Why bugger around with this bow-and-arrow stuff? Lot of—"

"Shut up," interrupted Symington. "Can't think. Five point two. Five point two from Great Karlsö—making good sixteen point three—slight set against."

He transferred the position from the chart of Gotland to the general chart of the Eastern Baltic, switched off the light and moved across in the darkness to the voice-pipe. The dreaded moment had arrived. The sighting of the light must be reported. That might bring Shadde to the bridge, and that meant trouble.

"Captain!" He spoke quietly. There was silence; then Shadde's voice came back through the voice-pipe, cold, incisive: "What is it?"

"Sighted Great Karlsö light, one-six-eight, five miles, sir."

"What's the time?"

"O-one-sixteen, sir."

"Visibility?"

"Poor, sir."

"Weather?"

"Fine drizzle—light breeze—gentle swell." Hopefully, he added, "Very wet and cold, sir."

Another pause, then Shadde's voice again. "Very well, I'm coming up."

Symington moved to the forepart of the bridge and peered over the screen into the darkness. Fine on the port bow the blackness of the night was broken every thirty seconds by three tiny stabs of light from Great Karlsö.

"Skipper's coming up," he told the sublieutenant. "Tell the lookouts."

There was a call from the control room. "Captain's coming up, sir." The quartermaster's voice was urgent and conspiratorial.

"Very good." Involuntarily, Symington shuddered.

4

Shadde lifted his large, angular body up the conning-tower ladder—massive, anonymous and purposeful in his oilskins. From the upper hatch he stepped out onto the bridge.

The rain struck into his face, sudden, chilling. Eyes not yet accustomed to the dark, he felt his way past the periscope standards and along the bridge screen until he felt the canopy, lifted it and thrust in his head and shoulders. The light flicked on, then off. He moved to the foreside of the bridge.

"Symington!"

"Sir."

"Ah, Symington, there you are. Only one fix on the chart—why?" His voice was cold and challenging.

Symington stiffened, "In fact, sir, there are—"

"Don't 'in fact' me, Symington," Shadde interrupted. "I can assess the facts for myself. You've been officer of the watch since midnight. It's o-one-twenty-one. *Retaliate's* steaming at sixteen and a half knots. We're in sight of land. My standing orders require the officer of the watch to plot a fix every half-hour. There's only one on the chart. Why?"

Symington cleared his throat. "There are *three* fixes, sir."

Shadde's voice was cold, menacing. "Are you suggesting that I'm a liar?"

"No, sir, but . . ."

"But what?"

"You must have looked at the large scale chart, sir." He was quiet, deferential, anxious to avoid a scene. "I used it when we picked up the light. There're three fixes on the general chart. . . . Chart twenty-eight forty-two," he added.

"Where is it?" snapped Shadde.

"On the table, under the large scale chart, sir."

Shadde glared through the darkness at the younger man, fingers clenching and unclenching. Slowly, with an effort of self-control, he turned away and looked forward over the bridge screen.

"Symington, you're a lieutenant in the Royal Navy. You've done the long N course. Is it too much to ask you to see that the appropriate chart is always uppermost on the chart table when I come onto the bridge?"

Without waiting for a reply he turned and disappeared into the darkness. In a moment he could be heard going down the conning-tower ladder.

Keely broke the long silence. "Jesus, what a bastard!"

Then came Symington's nervous, unsure laugh. "That's the hangover from Skansen. Number One warned me. Said Shadde was after my blood."

"Always is, isn't he? Doesn't need you, does he?"

Symington nodded in the dark. "No. Can't think why. When my old man heard I was coming here he was very bucked. Said I was lucky. He said Shadde was first class."

"When did he know him?"

"In the war. In *Sabre*. Shadde was his Third Hand. Best he'd ever had, he said."

"Old boy should see him now. What a shit!"

"Admiralty don't think so. Wouldn't've got this if they did."

"He's a bastard," Keely muttered. "Unpredictable. All gay and jolly one moment, then chewing you out the next."

"I'm sorry for him. Can't be fun being like that. So moody. Makes himself a bloody fool. That display just now. What do the lookouts and signalman think? Vulgar. Bloody unnecessary."

They stood together at the bridge screen, isolated by the night; dark, rain-drenched shapes. Below them the casing stretched forward into the blackness, and the submarine pitched and rolled slowly in the swell from the southwest.

6

The wind sighed past the periscope standards carrying the noise of the sea creaming and curling at the bows.

Then they were caught up in the routine of the watch: the messenger with hot cocoa; reports from the lookouts; voice-pipes and instrument repeaters calling and chattering; ranges and bearings from radar and asdics; soundings from fathometers; sea and air temperatures; air analyses in compartments; position by ship's inertial navigating system, by loran, by D/F; signals from the W/T office; reports on the state of watertight doors; reports from the engine room, from the reactor-control and missile rooms.

There was an alteration of course before the watch ended. Symington reported it to Shadde, but he didn't come up to the bridge again.

By two o'clock in the morning it was still dark; the wind had freshened and they were steaming into a short, choppy sea. Näs Udden bore 106 degrees distant 12½ miles by radar, but the light there was not yet in sight. In accordance with the Captain's night orders, speed was increased to 20 knots.

Bustle and activity reached a peak as the watch changed; men came and went, and there was endless reporting and repeating of reports. Symington handed over to Cavan, the first lieutenant. Tired and wet, he and Keely went down the conning tower to the control room. They checked the various instrumentation fixes in the chart room and looked over the radar displays. Symington wrote up the logbook. Keely compared a line of soundings from the fathometer with those charted. Then they went down a steel ladder to the small cabin in the officers' quarters that they shared with Allistair.

They undressed. Symington knelt and said his prayers. Afterwards he switched off the light and climbed into the bunk below Keely.

The sublieutenant's last thoughts were of Anita. Gorgeous thing! Why hadn't her blasted girl friend pushed off? Would he ever see her again? He fell asleep.

Symington lay in the bunk below, tired and unhappy. Why did Shadde hate him? How long could he stand that sort of thing? He thought about the party at Skansen. That had triggered off this latest business. Whenever he thought overmuch about his Captain he ended up with a picture of Shadde's chin. It was with him now: a strong, outward-thrusting chin, deeply cleft. To the right of the cleft there was a longish brown mole—the sort that protruded. It was a strong chin, and somehow the mole lent it strength. And this was so even when it was topped by a tiny piece of cotton, which happened quite often when Shadde cut it shaving.

It was some time before Symington fell asleep.

‖ 2 ‖

The afternoon of the Skansen party they had gone to Salts-
jöbaden. Back in Stockholm that evening they had said good--
bye to the Swedes at the Skeppsholm Bridge.

Symington and the Doctor wanted to go into the old
city, but Cavan and Keely thought it too far, so they had
settled for Bern's.

Retaliate should have left Stockholm the day before,
but there'd been condenser trouble. She had been in harbor
for five days on a routine showing-the-flag visit. For security
reasons she was not alongside but at a buoy in the Strömmen.
She was closed to the public, but many people gazed out
curiously to where she lay, some furtively, others apprehen-
sively. There was something sinister about her, unwholesome,
an aura of death perhaps. But there was not much to see:
immense conning tower, hydroplanes sprouting like fins from
her sides; a long whalelike steel hull, sentries on the fore
and after casings, and an occasional sailor coming or going
through a doorway at the foot of the conning tower.

The round of official entertainment had ended the day before. On this unexpected extra day in Stockholm the submarine's crew were left to their own devices. Not that they were very happy about it. They'd done with Stockholm. They wanted to get on with the cruise, and back to Portsmouth, where they belonged.

It was pleasant at Bern's eating smorgasbörd, drinking schnappes, chasing the fiery spirit down with pilsener. The smoke, the noise, the laughter, the music, the women—Stockholm was an agreeable place.

Afterwards they left Bern's and went eastwards on Strandvägen where it flanked the harbor. It was May; a cold sea breeze blew in across the Strömmen. But it was still too early to go back on board.

They took a taxi and went out across the bridge to Skansen. For some time they wandered among the quaint collection of medieval farmhouses, mills and belfries, and looked in on some folk dancing; tired of that they made for the Solliden. It was packed. Keely went ahead to get a table. The headwaiter waved his arms desperately.

"Impossible! You can see."

"We're visitors from Britain."

The Swede shrugged his shoulders. "Everybody at Skansen is a visitor."

Keely reported his failure to the others.

The Doctor got up; he was Irish and his courage was running high, fired by the schnappes and pilsener. "Stand back," he said, "I speak Russian."

Cavan yawned. "Very dramatic, Doc. This is Sweden."

Dr. O'Shea went through the glass doors. In gruff, broken Russian he made his explanations. The political deputation was visiting Stockholm from Moscow; they were waiting in the foyer; they must have a table. He did not smile.

The headwaiter knew some Russian; he looked hard at the Doctor, speculating, his hands spread despairingly.

"A table? Where?" Pig of a Russian, he thought; there could be complaints to the ministry, then to the manager. Always trouble, nothing but trouble.

He found a table for them.

Half an hour later Shadde and Rhys Evans turned up. The Welshman was engineer officer of *Retaliate*. Aged thirty-nine Evans was the oldest man on board. He and Shadde had joined when she was building; they had commissioned her, put her through her trials and acceptance.

The two men liked and respected each other, though they were so different. Shadde, very much the product of Dartmouth and the Naval Staff College; Rhys Evans, still the quiet, stocky man from the Rhondda Valley, who had started as an E.R.A. and traveled the hard road of warrant and commissioned engineer to lieutenant commander.

The band stopped playing and the floor emptied. Keely came by with a Swedish girl. They walked arm in arm and she laughed gaily, happily shocked at something he said as they approached.

Cavan gave a heavy wink. The young man raised his eyebrows in affected disapproval. "Sir," he said coldly, and walked on with the girl.

Shadde was in high spirits. He talked endlessly and inconsequentially, racing from one subject to the other. Sometimes he laughed. Then they would laugh with him. Or was it at him? Cavan eyed him warily. How long would this mood last? Shadde heard they'd already ordered chicken sandwiches. He told the waiter to bring champagne. "Can't have the one without the other," he said.

How can he afford champagne? thought the first lieutenant. Not on his service pay. Must have private means or something. And why champagne, anyway? Showing off?

Shadde jerked his head towards Keely and the Swedish girl. "How does he meet these local beauties?"

"Pretty basic approach, I think," said the first lieutenant. "They seem to like it."

Shadde shook his head. "Beats me. He's such an oaf."

"She doesn't think so." Cavan pointed with his chin. "Look."

"Ah, well," sighed Rhys Evans, changing the subject, "We'll be on our way tomorrow."

The first lieutenant looked at him. "So the leaking cistern's fixed?"

Rhys Evans' eyes were angry for a moment. He turned away. "Condenser'll be serviceable by noon tomorrow, if that's what you mean." Why was the first lieutenant always ready to twit him? To make fun of his machinery? And forever patronizing him, as if it were everything to be first lieutenant but nothing to be engineer officer?

"Your reactor on heat yet?" asked the Doctor.

Cavan lifted his glass. "Don't be vulgar, the Chief's sensitive."

Shadde looked around the crowded room. "How d'you get the table? We couldn't."

"The Doctor speaks Russian."

Shadde frowned. "So what?"

They explained. Rhys Evans' voice was high and querulous. "And why give it to the Russians and not to us?"

Shadde looked at him sadly. "Swedes are scared stiff of the Russians."

"I'm sorry for them," said Symington. "Nice chaps with nasty neighbors. How'd you—"

"Pretty smug lot," interrupted Shadde. "Thrived on our wars. Traded with both sides. Don't blame them for fearing the Russians, though. Plenty to fear."

Rhys Evans shook his head and winked at the Doctor.

"Look here now, sir. Things are not so bad for them. They can count on the West."

Shadde's gaiety fell from him. His voice was cold. "You think so?" There was a pause. "I don't. The West's asleep. Had it too good too long. We're suffering from fatty degeneration."

The Chief was contrite, sorry now to have so changed the Captain's mood. "Maybe you are right, sir. But our side has brains and punch too."

Shadde shook his head. "Not enough. We need guts. Risks have got to be taken if we want to survive. Can't back your horse both ways."

"Meaning, sir?"

Shadde put his glass down and leaned forward, his eyes dark and gleaming. "We're afraid. Our politicians, I mean. Always trying to play it safe. Too cautious. Scared stiff. You don't get anywhere that way."

"The West can't just declare war on Russia like that. Be an awful shindy," said O'Shea. "That sort of thing isn't done any more."

Shadde looked at him suspiciously. Was he being supercilious? "Exactly," he said coldly, "the West can't. It's hamstrung by your 'it's not done' stuff. That's why we may go to the wall. Any bloody fool can see our choice."

"What choice?"

"Preventive war against Russia now, or submission to her later." Shadde leaned back in his chair. "Can you see the Commons or Congress solemnly debating that? Then voting for an attack on Russia? That'll be the day."

His voice had risen. People at nearby tables were watching.

Symington yawned. The gaiety had gone out of the party, elbowed out by the political discussion. He had heard Shadde on this subject before and it bored him. The Captain had a bee in his bonnet about Russia. Spoke an awful lot of tripe, really.

Cavan started. That tall girl in gold lamé. Same dark hair, high cheek bones. Could it be Susan? Would they be almond eyes? She turned, but the full face wasn't Susan at all. He sank back. This happened often. Silly, he knew, but he couldn't help it. Every tall dark woman had to be measured—measured against Susan. The band interrupted his thoughts.

"What's the tune?" asked Rhys Evans. "I believe I know it."

"I don't," said Cavan. "Must be pretty ancient."

Rhys Evans winced.

"Quite old," said Symington, " 'Que Sera, Sera'—lovely thing."

People were leaving their tables to dance. Symington stood up. "Going to see a man about a dog," he explained.

When he came back there were two familiar, uniformed figures at a table on the far side. He walked across.

"Hullo, Gracie! Hullo, Springer!"

Gracie was the submarine's chief P.O. telegraphist and Springer the chief electrical artificer. They began to get up, but Symington waved them down.

Gracie leaned forward. "Care for a beer, sir?"

"Love one," said Symington and sat down. "What sort of a day d'you have?"

"Fine," said Springer. "We've been doin' a Cook's tour. Ted's shot the place to pieces with his Leica."

Gracie nodded. "Got some good stuff, especially around about the Slussen. Top of that tower. Wonderful spot for pan shots."

"Katarinahissen," said Symington. "I was there yesterday—we'll compare results. I expect yours are better; they usually are."

.   .   .

Shadde saw Symington go over to the chief petty officer's table and the incident built up in his mind. First Symington's yawn during the conversation about Russia and the West, then his excuse to leave the table. Now this gesture to make it clear that he preferred the company of *Retaliate*'s chief petty officers to that of her Captain and wardroom officers. Shadde turned to the others. "Does Symington normally hobnob with our chiefs and P.O.'s ashore?" he asked.

Cavan looked at him doubtfully. "I don't quite follow, sir," he said.

"Look over your shoulder. He's sitting against the far wall. With Gracie and Springer. Drinking beer."

"I expect he's only being friendly, sir. After all, they *are* shipmates," said the Doctor cheerfully.

"Your naval experience is somewhat limited, O'Shea." Shadde's voice was ice cold. "It's not a custom of the service for wardroom officers to mix socially with chiefs and P.O.'s ashore. Not good for discipline. Both sides dislike it. Chiefs and P.O.'s particularly. They suspect patronage."

Shadde looked across at Cavan. "I take it you would agree with me, Number One." He said it with an air of finality. Clearly it was meant to be the last word on the subject.

Cavan failed to sense this. He didn't like Shadde; the man irked him. Always putting on an act. "I don't know, sir," he said slowly, "I don't think Symington patronizes anyone. He's too well bred. He and Gracie like each other. That's all there is to it."

Shadde turned slowly in his chair until he faced Cavan. The large, angular body seemed to overflow onto the table as he leaned forward, his mouth shut in a tight line. His hands were on the table, the fingers clenching and unclenching slowly, dark eyes smoldering as he glared at the first lieutenant. He stood up.

15

"Come on, Chief. Let's get back on board before I'm told I don't know how to run my bloody boat." His voice was thick with anger.

Cavan was taken aback. Before he could think of anything to say Shadde had gone, followed by the Chief.

The first lieutenant took the champagne bottle from the ice bucket. "Have some of the Captain's bubbly?" Without waiting for an answer he filled the Doctor's glass, then his own.

"Tell me," he said wearily, "did I say anything offensive?"

"Bit tactless. You might have left out the 'well bred' part."

"Think that was it?"

"You supported me, Number One. Not very bright. To Shadde, I'm a ruddy doctor from Dublin masquerading as a naval officer. You jump in and take my side when he's laying down the law about the customs of the Royal Navy."

Cavan made a gesture of impatience. "That bull about Symington and the C.P.O.s! Good God! This isn't the thirties! Why the hell shouldn't George sit down for a few moments and chat to them if he wants to?"

"I couldn't agree more," said the Doctor, "but Shadde's allergic to Symington. That makes a difference."

Cavan emptied his glass and took a long look around the room. Keely was dancing with the Swedish girl. She was laughing and her head was thrown back. For the first time he realized that she was very pretty.

"Oh, let's forget Shadde."

"Here comes Peter Keely with the body beautiful," sighed the Doctor. "Must have seen the champagne."

"Hullo!" said the sublieutenant. He and the girl sat down.

"Hullo, *sir*, you mean!"

"Sorry, *sir*. I saw the Captain go and thought you'd like to meet Greta Garbo."

The sublieutenant leaned towards the girl. "Greta," he said, "meet my chums." He poured her some champagne, then filled his own glass.

"He's silly," giggled the girl. "I'm Anita. Are all the English silly?"

"Yes," said the Doctor amiably. "They are."

Over by the band, the trumpeter started to play.

O'Shea jerked his head towards him. "How does he blow, Peter?"

Keely took his hand off her knee. "Not too bad. Quite good, in fact."

The girl lifted her glass with both hands, her elbows on the table. She looked up at Cavan. "You are very handsome," she said.

The first lieutenant's embarrassment was saved by the band. He got up and pulled her to her feet. "Stop talking nonsense and come and dance," he said. But the remark did his ego good.

When Symington came back, they told him of the Captain's outburst. He looked surprised at first, then worried, but he laughed all the same when he said, "Unbelievable." After that he changed the subject.

Anita produced a girl friend and gaiety returned to the party. They laughed and danced and talked endlessly, mostly about nothing, but it all seemed very amusing. At midnight they shared a taxi back to the square, but Peter Keely refused their offer to help him see the girls home.

"The kill," said Cavan softly to the Doctor.

"The what?" said Keely.

"Nothing. Just thinking aloud."

They said good night, and the taxi took Cavan, the Doctor and Symington back across the bridge to the naval base at Skeppsholm.

She was dizzy when she got up to go to the sideboard, and her face felt stiff, as if the muscles were frozen. Must be the whisky, she thought; she didn't really like whisky, but this was a very special occasion. She'd written the letter at last. That final, awful letter that had to be written.

When she got to the sideboard and put the glass down, it broke at the stem. "Silly Elizabeth," she said. "Shouldn't put it down so hard."

Lucky he wasn't there! That was the sort of thing that could spark off one of those awful rows. Well, there weren't going to be any more rows, because she wasn't going to be there any more. She took another glass and handled it with exaggerated care. But the screw-top seemed to fly off the whisky bottle; she heard it roll along the floor. She would pick it up later.

"Rather a big tot for you, Elizabeth," she said. "You're a wicked girl." She hiccoughed and giggled. I'm tipsy, she thought, funny feeling, isn't it? But I'm not frightened any more.

She poured some water on top of the whisky and walked unsteadily towards the armchair. As she rounded the table her heel caught in the carpet and she staggered; some of the whisky spilled over her blouse. "Damn," she muttered.

When she reached the little table, she put the glass down and felt her way carefully into the easy chair. On the table she saw the letter. "Handwriting looks awfully blurry," she said. Mouthing the words carefully, as if they were an elocution test, she read out the address: "Commander John Shadde, R.N., H.M.S. *Retaliate*, G.P.O. London."

She picked up the glass and drank. "John Shadde," she said unsteadily. Then again, "John Shadde." The corners of her mouth went down and she burst into tears; the glass fell out of her hand and the whisky made a dark pool on the carpet. She buried her face in a cushion and let her arms trail over the side of the chair. "My darling John," she sobbed, "what have you done to us? Oh, John! What have you done?"

She lay there sobbing, loudly at first, but afterwards quietly and at longer intervals, catching her breath now and then like a child crying herself to sleep. Pushing away the cushion, she got up and went to the bathroom and stood in front of the mirror. Look at my face, she thought, all swollen and puffy and blotchy, and those dreadful, bloodshot eyes. She shook her head. I used to be pretty once. Look at me now! My eyes! Mother used to call me Betty Twinkles— "because your eyes sparkle so, darling." Look at them now! Mournful orbs like lamps in a foggy cemetery. Oh, my God! To think it's come to this. She started to cry again and then managed to fight it down. She held a washcloth under the cold water tap and wiped her face with it, then brushed and combed her hair and tried to push and pat it into some sort of shape. After that she dabbed on some powder and did her lips. She made a mouth in the mirror. "Awful!" she said. "Awful!" She looked at herself for a long time and then hiccoughed again. "You sterile cow! If only you'd given him babies."

Back in the sitting room she looked at the envelope on the table. Some whisky drops had fallen on it. With a small handkerchief she wiped them dry. Before it was dark she'd go down to Dragon Street and post it. She sat down and thought about the letter. It would reach him in Copenhagen. What would he think when he read it? Then she realized that it didn't really matter. It was all over now. She had made her decision and there was no going back. Anyway, she didn't want to go back. She was thirty-three; any personality, any character she'd ever had he'd crushed and subdued. If she were to remain a person and have a life of her own, she had to get away from him. Now that she'd found the

19

strength to make the break she'd never go back. Pinkerton and Pillings were seeing to the legal end of things, and the passage to Australia was booked.

She sniffed and dabbed at her eyes with the crumpled, damp little handkerchief. But it was hopeless; she couldn't stop thinking of him. Tall, dark, immensely rugged and masculine. Inscrutable brown eyes that never really let you know what thoughts were going on inside. She remembered the night he'd proposed. It was coming back from a dance at Brockenhurst three weeks after they had met. Beyond Lyndhurst somehow or other they ended up in a funny little lane between high hedgerows. He said he'd lost his way. Months afterwards he admitted it was a fib.

When the car stopped he looked at her and smiled, "We're lost!"

She laughed. "Better turn the car and get unlost."

"Lots of time. Look at that moon."

"Where? It's all cloudy."

He pointed into the darkness. "Of course you can't see it. Just imagine it."

They both laughed. He put one arm around her and kissed her for the first time. Rather a timid kiss, and she remembered thinking he'd not had much experience.

Then he said, "Have you ever thought of joining the navy?"

"As a Wren?"

"No. As my wife."

Her heart had leapt. She was twenty-five. Behind her was a tedious, unhappy love affair—a hopeless, long, drawn-out tangle with a married man. And now this large, rather frightening but very attractive naval officer was asking her to marry him.

She put her hand in his. "If that's a proposal, John . . ."
She didn't know how to go on, so she leaned her head on his

20

shoulder. She felt his arms go around her, and she finished the sentence in a whisper. "I'd love to join the navy."

They sat there for a long time. She was blissfully happy and he made endless plans for the future.

But all that was long, long ago. She picked up the glass and drank from it. Funny thing about whisky. The taste was deadly but the effect terrific. But for it she would never have had the courage to write those letters. Neither the first one she'd sent to Oslo, nor this final one. He had written a rather shocked, contrite letter in reply to the Oslo letter. It told her how deeply attached he was to her, and how she mustn't make any decision until they had discussed things. She knew what that meant: a monologue. John laying down the law, and if she didn't agree there would be a ghastly row. No! There weren't going to be any more discussions or any more rows. The deed was done; the break was made. There was no going back.

She drank more whisky and some dribbled back from her mouth into the glass. She thought: I am terrified of him, and the whisky gives me courage. Yes, terrified! I'm broken and cowed. All my spirit's gone. Me, Elizabeth. And I used to be gay and bubbling. . . . God, look at me now!

For the first six years their marriage had been a success. Not an ecstatically happy affair, but a pleasant enough life with its quotas of fun and happiness and trial and tribulation. She had found from the start that he was a moody man. Down in the dumps and up in the air, but usually down in the dumps. In his good moods he could be gay and quite charming, but lately they had been few and far between. In the last two years he'd been more difficult, and in recent months quite impossible. Something had happened, must have happened. But she knew she would never know what. He wasn't a person who shared those deep, innermost thoughts.

21

The climax had come during that last dreadful leave in March. For days he sat and glowered. Some of the time he read; mostly he just sat there and brooded. Acutely sensitive, she supposed he sat and brooded about her failure to give him children.

When she suggested golf or walks or the pictures, or visits to the few friends they had, he would either not answer, or be rude and sarcastic. He would frown, an angry light would come into his eyes and he would say, "Please stop fussing! I can assure you that if I wanted to go for a walk I'd go."

"But it would be good for you, John. You've had so little exercise. It's been raining for days."

He would get up and go to the bookcase and take out a book, and she would wonder if he'd heard her.

"John, what's wrong? Why don't you answer?"

He would turn around, his mouth set in that hard, tight line and his eyes angry. "Nothing's wrong," he would say in a cold voice. "But for God's sake, stop prying into my thoughts. All I want is privacy. Surely you don't grudge me that?" Then he would go back to his chair, and she would go to her room and bury her face in the pillow in another searing bout of misery.

After a week of leave he went up to London for the day. He left in a black and desperate mood without saying goodbye or letting her know when he'd be back.

At nine o'clock that night she heard the Rover come into the garage. Fearful of his mood she went out to meet him, tensed for the inevitable row.

But the moment he said, "Hullo, darling!" and smiled at her, she knew he was in one of his tremendously good moods. He kissed her and they went into the house arm in arm. Then in the kitchen, before he'd taken his raincoat off, he looked at her and said, "Lisbet, I've got a surprise for you." He didn't often call her "Lisbet" nowadays, only on very special occasions. When he said, "a surprise," she didn't know whether to laugh or cry. The last "surprise" had been two months ago, when he bought the Rover and she had borrowed £500 from her mother to get them out of the financial scrape it landed them in.

Now she watched, smiling, but apprehensive. "What is it, John?"

"Spain," he said.

"Spain?" There was a catch in her voice.

"Yes! We're off to Spain. You, me and the Rover. We'll chase the sun. Get away from this bloody rain."

"John," she whispered. "How can we afford it?"

He laughed. "Don't worry about that, old girl. It's in the bag. Look!"

From his raincoat pocket he produced a paper travel wallet. "Here are the tickets and the bookings. Silver City to Le Touquet. Then we start motoring. First night at La Bouille. Then southwards to the sun." He flung out his arm dramatically and laughed.

He pulled another paper wallet from his raincoat. "Here's the A.A. itinerary. They say it's not necessary to book at hotels this time of year. We'll just jog along and stop where we like. Should be absolute heaven."

She looked at him doubtfully, compassionately. "Where's all the money for this to come from, John? We haven't got it."

He laughed. "Look!" he said, and showed her a sheet of yellow paper filled in here and there with words and figures in carbon.

"Installment-plan place in the Haymarket. They've paid for the tickets and given me hotel vouchers and cash for the balance. The whole thing'll cost us about a hundred and twenty pounds including interest. Pay it off over twelve months at about ten pounds a month."

Desperately, fearfully she had said, "But we can't remotely afford ten pounds a month, John. Think of what we owe already."

For a moment he looked puzzled, as if he'd not understood what she meant. Then he frowned and the veins on his forehead stood out, his eyes smoldered and his jaw muscles began to work. When he spoke his voice shook. "I see," he said thickly. "You're determined to be uncooperative. Your customary appreciation of anything I try to do." With a violent gesture he flung the wallets across the kitchen and they landed on the floor. "Very well, we'll stay and rot in this God-forsaken, rained-out bloody place."

With the noise of the slammed door still ringing in her ears, she heard him drive away. In the early hours of the next morning he came back, but for three days he didn't speak to her.

Now she picked up the glass and drank the last of the whisky, then she put on her raincoat and pulled the cape over her head. She walked over to the desk unsteadily. Through a mist of tears she saw the photograph in the silver frame. The strong, manly face with its rugged, familiar features was hopelessly blurred.

She started to sob. Then she picked up the letter from the table and let herself out of the front door. It was still raining and almost dark when she reached Dragon Street.

When Shadde and Rhys Evans got back on board the Captain suggested a nightcap in his cabin. It was more an order than an invitation, and the Welshman agreed, though he had no need of a drink.

They raised their glasses and drank, but Shadde said nothing. Dark and glowering, he sat hunched and withdrawn in an easy chair. Only the nervous tapping of his fingers betrayed that something was going on inside the man. The long silences worried Rhys Evans, but attempts at conversation brought only monosyllabic replies. Shadde's gloomy preoccupation so isolated him from the engineer officer that the two men might not have been in the same cabin.

When at last with muttered apologies Rhys Evans had gone, Shadde slumped back into the chair, knees drawn up, head sunk. For upwards of two hours he sat there until after one o'clock when he undressed and got onto his bunk.

It was going to be difficult to sleep, no doubt about that. This was one of those nights when your mind wouldn't let you rest. All his problems would come to him in the dark, one by one, pushing, jostling with each other, clamoring to be heard. The row with Number One at Skansen. How had that started? Over Symington. But that hadn't been the beginning. It was the flippancy and stupidity about Russia. Couldn't they see what was happening? Take the thing seriously. What did they think they were in *Retaliate* for? Why didn't they sense the danger as he did? In the darkness he felt his nostrils dilate and his heartbeat quicken. England was in mortal danger, he knew. The forces of darkness were gathering. The testing time was coming nearer. But the West was rudderless, drifting. England was soft, having it too good. People laughed when you told them of the dangers, of what was coming. High patriotism was needed. A man would have to come forward. There had always been a man to save England.

His thoughts went back to Skansen. Symington's offensive behavior. How dare Cavan oppose him and support the Doctor? What did he mean by the "too well bred" innuendo? For some time Shadde puzzled over this. Discipline in the submarine was not what it should be. He was sure of that. In the morning he would talk to Cavan about it.

Then with a sick feeling, he thought of Elizabeth. She had been his sleeping and waking thought for days now, and yet tonight, unaccountably, he'd forgotten that problem. Why hadn't she written? She knew how urgently his letter had demanded an answer. That incredible letter he had received in Oslo. How could she have written it? The veiled threat to leave him. He'd not taken it seriously at first. Not believed it for a moment. But slowly the truth had dawned on him. She was in earnest. She might really leave him. She might actually do that. It had been a shock to learn that she was unhappy. Why? Why? Because they had no children? The thought of losing Elizabeth terrified him. She was all he had. She alone understood him. Nothing in his life, not even *Retaliate*, was more important. She must know that. But what if she didn't? He turned uneasily in the bunk. He could never tell her. Those were things that couldn't be said. But they must be understood.

For years he had taken Elizabeth for granted. Not for any lack of affection on his part, but he had never really thought about their relationship. She'd always been there, somewhere in the background, and it never occurred to him that it might be otherwise. But now she was talking of leaving him, and the bottom seemed to be falling out of his world. It was ten days since he had replied to the Oslo letter, but still no answer had come from Elizabeth.

Tired and immensely depressed, he lay there for a long time in the darkness, torn by doubt and anxiety. The problems facing him seemed beyond solution. At last he fell into an uneasy sleep, the victim of jumbled, disquieting dreams from which Symington, the first lieutenant and Elizabeth were never absent.

‖ 3 ‖

At about the time that the officers from *Retaliate* found themselves in the Solliden restaurant at Skansen, Engineering Mechanic Ernest Kyle had found himself in another, more modest establishment in quite another part of Stockholm.

He had gone ashore with his fellow libertymen at 1800 that evening, but as so often happened these days, he was odd man out. His messmates had broken up into small cheerful parties, but they had not invited him to join them. And Ernest Kyle wasn't going to push himself onto anyone else. If they didn't want him, O.K. They were the losers. Poor lot, he reckoned. He'd just as soon be on his own. Or would he? Well, he wasn't going to admit that he cared, anyway. Of course he felt a bit fed up and lonely, but that was because he was in a foreign country. It was always like that in a foreign country. Foreigners were different. There was nothing you could talk to them about anyway, even if they understood your lingo. He wished he were back home in Southsea chatting with Mum in the kitchen. Always warm and friendly in there. Dad was no good; usually around at the pub boozing away his wages, or at home rowing with Mum and sometimes beating her up. But she was different, a real good sort. Bit irritable at times, perhaps, and always complaining that she was tired, but she understood a fellow. Always kind and helpful and pleased to see you. "You ought to find yourself a nice girl, you ought, Ernie," she'd say when he hung around the kitchen in the council house, kicking his heels and complaining that there was nothing to do, but in fact happy to be with her. "I don't want no nice girl, Mum," he used to say. "I've got you."

"Stop yer nonsense, Ernie," she'd say, but he could see she was pleased. They understood each other, that was it. Well, perhaps he'd take her advice, after all, and find a nice girl in Stockholm. He didn't know too much about girls, but he could always learn, and if he found one this evening it would help him to forget the submarine and all the lousy blokes in his mess; and Chief Shepherd, who made his life a flipping misery, always putting him in the rattle for something or other. He'd give Chief Shepherd something to worry about. Fix him if it was the last thing he ever did.

With these thoughts uppermost in his mind Ernest Kyle climbed onto a passing bus in the Hamngatan. He had no idea where he was going or what he was going to do. To get away from *Retaliate*—that was all he wanted. Near the front he found an empty seat and sat down, a slight, worried, young man with a pale and pimply face.

At about 2100 that night Ernie Kyle ended up in a tavern near the docks at Värtahamnen. He was feeling a lot better; Swedish beer had seen to that. Stockholm wasn't too bad a place after all. He didn't know who all these strange, noisy faces around him belonged to. Some of them seemed to speak English O.K. Funny accents though. Sven was a good chap—a sailorman, too, from a Swedish tramp steamer.

28

Didn't mind standing his round either. That reminded him;
how was the old money lasting out? He looked through the
imitation leather wallet. O.K. Still plenty there. He could
use the money he had been saving for Mum's present if
worse came to worst. With fumbling fingers he slipped it
back into his pocket. Things seemed a bit blurry, but what
the hell? All good fun!

"Sven ole pal, 'ave another pint." He slapped the Swede
on the shoulder.

The Swede shook his head. "Ach, ve hed enough; better
you stop now, Ernie."

"Balls!" said Ernie and giggled. "Not drunk, jus' bloomin'
well sloshed—tha's all pal."

As he slid clumsily off the stool his elbow knocked a
plate to the floor with a loud clatter. The bartender looked
at him with narrow, questioning eyes. He stood next to
Sven, swaying slightly.

"C'mon Sven," he insisted, "one fer the road."

"Ernie, you like meet that nice Swedish girl I tell you
about?" said Sven with a wink.

Ernie didn't believe there was any nice Swedish girl.
This was old Sven's trick to stop him drinking and break up
the party.

"Wassa name?" he said unbelievingly.

"Ingrid."

"Ingrid?" repeated Ernie. "Tha's a nice name." He
thought about it. "Look, Sven," he said confidentially, "you
think I'm drunk. Well I'm not, see. An' I don't believe
there's any Ingrid, see. You're jus' pullin' my leg," he said
sadly, and wagged his finger at the Swede.

"I go fetch her," said Sven, and disappeared.

To Ernie's astonishment Sven was as good as his word.
Five minutes later he was back with Ingrid—large, pink,
blond and friendly.

"Cor," said Ernie with undisguised admiration.

"Smashin'." He bought her a soft drink. He thought of Mum's advice. Got himself a nice girl now. They laughed and chatted and then Sven disappeared.

Ingrid complained of the noise. "Better we go to my home," she said in a low voice. "There we can talk and hear what we are saying."

" 'Tis noisy in 'ere, ain't it?" said Ernie. He looked around with a bleary eye.

"Do you like hit tunes?"

He liked the way she pronounced it: "Heet tunes."

"Yes, I do an' all."

"I have many at home." She smiled archly at him.

Ernie couldn't believe his luck. Meeting a nice girl like this and being asked to her home—and in such a short time, too.

It was dark outside. When they got into the taxi Ingrid spoke to the driver in Swedish. The journey seemed all twists and turns and Ernie hadn't the faintest idea where they were, but he had his arm around Ingrid and his nose in her hair, so he didn't much mind. Nice scent she's got on, he thought, and gave her a squeeze which she returned. The taxi pulled up and he paid the driver. They went down a small passageway and she stopped at a door and unlocked it with a key from her bag. The lights were on in the little hall. She put her finger on her lips and they tiptoed up the stairs. "Not to wake the others," she explained. Ernie nodded understandingly.

Now he was sitting on a divan in what seemed a bed-sitting room. Nice place, he thought. There were pictures of snow scenes, mountains and fir trees, all covered in snow. He stretched out his legs and lit a cigarette. He felt warm and comfortable and at home, like in Mum's kitchen at Southsea.

"I'll make some coffee," Ingrid said. "You wait." And she smiled coyly at him.

Soon she came back carrying a tray with the coffee things on it. But it wasn't the tray Ernie was looking at; it was Ingrid, and the blood went racing to his head. She had changed her clothes while she was out of the room. Now she was wearing a silky, pink affair. A sort of wrap, Ernie reckoned, like the movie stars wear in the pictures. As she leaned forward to put the tray on the low table in front of him, the wrap fell open and Ernie saw her breasts, pink, full and inviting. He experienced a sense of delicious shock. Quickly, roughly, he stubbed out his cigarette and pulled her down alongside him. She struggled, but not too hard. "No, no, you mustn't," she said. Afterwards she added practically, "Mind the coffee cups."

"Fergit the bleedin' cups," said Ernie thickly.

With a sigh she gave in and submitted to his embraces. Moments later, as waves of passion broke over him, Ernie was startled by the noise of the door opening and the sound of a man's voice.

He moved away from Ingrid and turned to see a large man standing inside the door.

"So," said the stranger softly.

Ernie thought he saw something in the man's left hand, and turned quickly to look at Ingrid. So it was a trap. She was standing there with nothing on, smiling at him in a strange way; and the man was smiling too. What had they got to smile about, thought Ernie? She's just as bad as me.

The man moved towards him slowly, still smiling, right arm extended as if to shake hands. But the left arm was rising as he came. Ernie wished that Sven were there to explain it all and help him. And then he panicked; he raised his arms to defend himself, but he was too late. There was a shattering, crashing sound and blinding white lights danced in front of his eyes.

|| 4 ||

Next morning Shadde breakfasted alone in his cabin. Leading Steward Miller had cleared away the plates and was washing up in the wardroom pantry. He nudged Target, the wardroom steward. "Bullseye," he said, "Skipper's in a bad mood—like 'e lost a bob and found sixpence."

"What's eating 'im, Dusty?"

"Don't ask me. You know what 'e's like. If it's not one thing it's the other. Waiting for a letter from 'is old woman now. Asks me if there's any mail every time the flipping bell strikes."

"Funny isn't it, what a woman can do to a man? And she's no oil painting neither."

"Well, I suppose she 'as 'er points." Dusty Miller blew on the glass he was polishing. "Nice bedside manner, p'raps."

"What time we sailing?"

"Fourteen 'undred."

"Not a minute too soon. Portsmouth for me."

32

The bell from the Captain's cabin buzzed loudly in the small pantry.

"There's 'is lordship again, Dusty—run along, me boy."

Miller put away the last cup and slipped on his coat. "Always on the flipping go," he grumbled, and hastened out of the pantry.

When the first lieutenant came in, Shadde was writing at his desk. He turned and nodded distantly. "Kyle still adrift?"

"Yes, sir. We're landing a patrol with Petty Officer Skinner at ten hundred to see if we can find him."

Shadde frowned. "Extraordinary business. Our people don't do that sort of thing. Can't make it out. Quite a good type, isn't he?"

"Not bad, sir. He's been in trouble once or twice. The Chief thinks he's all right. Shepherd doesn't. Says he's got a chip on his shoulder. He's surprised he was ever drafted to us."

Shadde shook his head. "Hope they find him. I don't like leaving a man behind. That's not happened to us before."

"I expect we'll get him back, sir."

The Captain seemed not to hear; he was suddenly pre-occupied, his mind on something else.

"Yes, yes," he said. "Now about those leave and training programs?"

Briefly they discussed them. Cavan watched him with a wary eye. He knew from Shadde's manner that all this was leading up to something.

"Got your program for Copenhagen ready, Number One?"

"Yes, sir, all lined up."

"Good. I'm glad to hear that." He put the pen down. The first lieutenant was standing just inside the door of the cabin, cap under his arm. Shadde pointed to the armchair.

33

"Close the door and sit down. There's something else I want to talk to you about."

Cavan sat down. Now we're coming to the point, he thought. Shadde offered him a cigarette, then turned so that he faced the first lieutenant, his big shoulders drooped forward, hands on his knees. The dark eyes narrowed as the cigarette smoke drifted across his face. When he sits like that, Cavan thought, he looks like an eagle that's just alighted, wings not quite folded. The freshly shaven chin with its deep cleft shone in the cabin lights. Cavan found himself concentrating on the mole. There was a small dried speck of blood next to it. Must have just nicked it, he thought.

Shadde looked at the first lieutenant for some time before he spoke. "Last night at Skansen." He paused and puffed at his cigarette.

So that's it, thought Cavan.

"I would have expected that as first lieutenant you'd've supported me when I explained the customs of the service to the Doctor. You know and I know that I was right. You know as well as I do that Symington behaved badly." Warming to the subject, he spoke faster. "Nothing wrong in greeting Gracie and Springer. Nothing at all. He could have exchanged pleasantries with them. That's fair enough. But he shouldn't have joined their table. Sitting there drinking with them! Apart from the fact that it's damn bad naval discipline, it was damn bad manners towards me." Shadde paused and glared at the first lieutenant. "And yet you supported him. Why?"

The younger man looked him straight in the face. "Frankly, sir, because I saw nothing wrong in what he did. Nowadays that's not—"

Shadde raised his hand. "I'm not interested in your views on what's right and what's not, Number One. I sent for you so that you'd be in no doubt about mine."

His eyes closed as he puffed at the cigarette. "There's

34

more to what happened than you probably realize," he said. "Symington's attachment to Gracie is undesirable. One's an officer in this submarine; the other's a chief petty officer. Because of their differences in rank, social standing and—er—background, the friendship is . . ." Shadde paused and looked away. "Well, to put it bluntly, it's odd."

"Odd?"

"Yes, odd. You've noticed, haven't you? Symington's effeminate. Gracie's a bit that way too—pink and boyish, you know. Damned good chief P.O. telegraphist—but he's only human, Number One. Symington's an officer; Symington's rich, socially secure, talented." Shadde's voice was mocking. "Very much a member of the upper classes, wouldn't you say?"

The first lieutenant's silence seemed to irritate Shadde. "Don't pretend you can't see what I'm driving at."

"Only too clearly, sir." Cavan's voice was measured and cool, and dangerously near to being insulting.

The Captain ignored the innuendo. "Don't like that sort of thing," he said. "Nasty smell about it."

Cavan struggled with his indignation. It was difficult to believe that Shadde was serious. "Do you really mean that, sir?" he asked.

"Yes, I do *really mean that*," Shadde mimicked him. "In fact, I think they're a couple of queers." He stressed the last word.

"I couldn't disagree more," Cavan said warmly.

"Couldn't you, Number One? Well, it may surprise you to know that in Portsmouth not so long ago I saw Symington and Gracie come out of the W/T office together—"

"Anything particularly wrong with that, sir?"

"Yes. Yes, indeed. When they come out of a darkened W/T office"— Shadde paused to let it sink in—"looking hot and bothered, tousled hair, the lot."

Cavan's contempt for these insinuations was plain, and

his temper was rising. "Everybody knows they're keen on photography, sir. They use the W/T office for developing films and . . . and that sort of thing."

Shadde quickly challenged him. "How do you know? Been in there with them?" He didn't wait for Cavan's answer. "I'm not impressed with the photography story, Number One. Prefer to rely on my own observations."

"And jump to incorrect conclusions," said Cavan rashly.

Shadde's eyes narrowed and his mouth set in the hard line his officers knew so well. "May I ask how you know they're incorrect?"

"Anybody who knows Symington and Gracie knows they are." Cavan's voice had risen. He was getting angry and he knew that was unwise. With Shadde it was very unwise. He put his cigarette down and got up. The discussion was getting out of hand; he decided to say no more. Better to let the Captain do the talking.

Shadde was still sitting in the chair, shoulders stooped forward, hands on knees. There was a flicker of anger in his eyes and his voice was rough. "Now look here, Number One," he said, "I know you think you could command this submarine better than I do. Every first lieutenant thinks he knows more than his captain. But don't forget every captain's been a first lieutenant." He leaned back and paused to let the sally go home. "Now get this into your head—you've not been with me long, but if you want to do any good here you'd better understand this." He drew a deep breath. "While I'm in command, *Retaliate* is going to be run my way. That means that we're going to have discipline—discipline with a capital D. This isn't an 'S' boat—complement of thirty-five officers and men doing a huggery-muggery in compartments the size of our wardroom. Of course discipline has to be relaxed under those conditions; I concede that. But this is damn nearly a cruiser. Eight thousand tons of submerged displacement. Four hundred and twenty-five feet long. Three

36

decks. Officers' cabins. Air conditioning. A ruddy doctor. Cinema shows. One hundred and five officers and men. Separate messes for chiefs and P.O.'s—and all the rest of it."

The long recital put Shadde out of breath. He stopped speaking and just sat there, stretching and tensing his fingers. After a while he stood up and faced Cavan, his eyes smoldering. "You know the importance of this submarine. You know that our U.S. friends stung the British taxpayer close to thirty million for each Polaris boat we took over. That money wasn't spent for fun, you know. It's all in deadly earnest. If you think hard, it may even occur to you that we only did it because we want to survive. Or d'you prefer not to think of these sordid things?"

Sarcastic bastard, Cavan thought as he stared coldly at the Captain. I'd like to tell you what I think of you.

"It's necessary for me to talk like this, Number One, because you and others here don't seem to realize what's happening—to the discipline of this boat, for example. It's getting pretty sloppy, you know. Rather too palsy-walsy."

He lit another cigarette, throwing the match away with an exaggerated gesture. "And I'm not going to stand for it. This boat has a pretty important place in the scheme of things nowadays. What we do, and how we do it, can be vital to our side one of these fine days. And how we do it will depend on our discipline. *That*"—he shot the word at the first lieutenant—"is why I won't have my officers hobnobbing with chiefs and P.O.s ashore."

For a moment they stood looking at each other, locked in bitter, silent antagonism; then Shadde walked over to his desk and sat down. "And it's for that reason, too," he said, "that you'll always support me in future in matters of discipline, no matter what you think." He looked up at the first lieutenant. "Understand that? No matter what you think!"

Without waiting for a reply he turned his back and started to write.

37

"Is that all, sir?" There was a shade of sarcasm in Cavan's voice.

Shadde went on writing; he appeared not to have heard. Cavan waited for a moment and then left the cabin.

When the first lieutenant left, Shadde put down the pen and with a weary gesture stubbed out his cigarette. The depression of last night was still with him, and the discussion with Cavan had fanned the inner tensions and conflicts.

So the first lieutenant was siding with Symington and the Doctor—that was clear. But of course he'd do that. Smug bastard! Never put a foot wrong. King's Cadet at Dartmouth. Term Lieutenant. Rugby for the navy. Royal Yacht. It would be the Staff College next. Stolid, unimaginative oaf! I'll shake him up, thought Shadde, by God, I will!

But Symington was at the bottom of it all. No doubt about that. Why did they have to send him of all people? A burning surge of shame and injustice possessed him. It gave way to a desperate, choked sort of feeling. Like being caught up in a bad dream. God! What a bad dream.

That day they showed him the signal! It was burned into his brain: "Lieutenant G. A. F. Symington (N) to *Retaliate* for navigating and watch-keeping duties." Shadde had searched feverishly through the pages of the Navy List to see if it could be H.H.F.'s son. And there it was, "Symington, George Anthony Fitzhugh, Lieutenant, 16th January, 1960, *Dryad*." Perhaps he was only a cousin or a nephew— something more distant at least than a son. Pray God that was it. But the Fitzhugh was ominous.

When Symington came on board the first lieutenant brought him down to introduce him. An effeminate young man, pale and tall. Shadde looked hard at him. "Any relation of H. H. F. Symington?" he asked.

"Yes, sir, my father." Shadde couldn't help wincing at that. It was a dagger between the eyes, all right.

38

Symington added, "He asked me to give you his regards, sir."

Shadde thought he saw a flicker of amusement.

When Symington and the first lieutenant had gone, Shadde jumped to his feet and in a cold sweat paced furiously to and fro. There was no escape. It had happened. Tormented by his thoughts, he went back, fearfully, reluctantly to that night in *Sabre*. They had left their billet and were passing back through the Lombok Strait to Fremantle. They had sunk a schooner by gunfire a few days before, but otherwise it had been a quiet patrol. Too quiet for Shadde on his first wartime patrol. He wanted action. That's what he had joined for in Fremantle a few weeks before, a brand new sublieutenant. His first job as Third Hand. But he would never never forget that night. In an agony of recollection he pressed his knuckles into his forehead. From his bunk in the wardroom he had heard the insistent call: "Captain on the bridge!" Within seconds the klaxon sounded for a crash dive. The officer of the watch and the lookouts came bundling down the conning tower into the control room as the Captain raced in from the wardroom.

They leveled off at two hundred feet, reduced speed to two knots, stopped all fans and went into silent routine. Then the first chilling report from the asdic operator: "H.E.* closing rapidly—bearing Red one-six-zero, sir!" Moments later Shadde heard the propeller noises himself. They increased steadily and passed with a roar overhead. Seconds later *Sabre* was shaken by shattering blows. She thrashed and vibrated like a kicked drum. He heard the noise of breaking glass and of loose gear falling about. The lights went out and then the emergency lighting came on. The hull plating whipped and squeezed and bounced, and men were

* *H.E. Hydrophone Effect—the noise made by a ship's propellers as heard on underwater listening devices.*

thrown off their feet. He had never known depth charging before. It was fantastically terrifying, beyond all imagination. They were hunted for six hours. Six indescribable, shattering hours. Towards the end he realized his nerve was going. He couldn't stand it any longer. For what seemed the hundredth time he heard the report, "H.E. closing rapidly, sir! Bearing Red four-five, sir!" He knew with awful certainty what would follow. The sound of propeller noises increased steadily as the destroyer came in to the attack. What could he do? He was trapped! There was no way to get out of it. Without knowing what he was doing, he started to scream. He saw the astonishment on the faces of the men near him. Then the Captain's voice, urgent, imperative: "Stop him, Number One!" As in a ghastly dream he saw Grierson, the first lieutenant, coming towards him. Unbelievably, Grierson had struck him full in the face. At that Shadde stopped screaming and fell to his knees. There he slumped, sobbing, for the rest of the attack, broken and humiliated.

Afterwards they had repaired the worst of the damage and had continued to Fremantle. No one in *Sabre* ever mentioned the incident. When he left her on decommissioning at the end of the war, the Captain said, "You're the best Third Hand I've ever had."

But Shadde could never forget the Lombok Strait. Those scars would never heal. By every standard he respected he had failed. He knew that others had broken down under great stress, but that couldn't make up for his humiliation or the loss of his self-respect.

That was why when Symington and the first lieutenant left him, Shadde buried his head in his hands and sobbed. Why in God's name had the Admiralty sent Symington's son to *Retaliate?* That supercilious smile and patronizing manner—and behind it the knowledge of Shadde's shame. And of course Symington had spread the story in the wardroom. That explained why his officers were against him. No matter what he'd done since, what amends he had made since, he was being crucified for that night in the Lombok Strait.

When Dwight Gallagher and Keely came in, the ward-room was full. Noon had just struck and most of the submarine's officers were already there. Target kept popping in and out of the pantry with pink gins and horses' necks, and the air was filled with inconsequential chatter.

The conversation turned to the party at Skansen the night before. Symington looked at the sublieutenant thoughtfully. "Peter, tell us about your popsy last night. Did you return her safely to store?"

Keely put down his newspaper and raised his eyebrows. "Why d'you want to know?"

The Doctor shook a finger at him. "Not so touchy, my boy. We were in the party too, you know. We're interested."

"About what?"

"What happened?"

"Nothing happened." The sublieutenant went back to his newspaper.

Dwight Gallagher spun the glass he was holding. "How was this dame?"

Symington looked at him with a friendly eye. "Her mind, Dwight, or her vital statistics?"

The American scratched his nose. "Well, bodywise, I guess. I assume Keely is a man of simple tastes."

Symington nodded. "She was rather a sweety. About thirty-eight, twenty-two, thirty, I'd say."

Gallagher whistled. "Is that so? Thirty-eight's a lot to carry on top of twenty-two. What was wrong with her ass? Thirty doesn't seem right under thirty-eight."

The Doctor shook his head. "We don't know. We never really got around to that sort of thing."

"Did Peter blow the trumpet?"

"No. There was this girl, you see."

41

"Of course. I'd forgotten."

A signalman came into the wardroom with his cap under his arm. "Lieutenant Commander Gallagher, sir. Signal."

Shadde's spirits rose as the morning wore on, and he shook off the depression of the night before. They were due to sail for Copenhagen after lunch, and the prospect of getting to sea again filled him with a sense of well-being. In his cabin he could hear the hum of the submarine's auxiliary machinery, and writing at his desk he felt the trembling vibrations. They made *Retaliate* vital and alive. These were sounds and movements he knew and understood: the sedatives of all sailors.

At noon he sent for Keely and gave him a signal for enciphering. It was to the Flag Officer Submarines, repeated to the Admiralty and to *Massive*, another Polaris submarine, at sea off Göteborg. The signal gave notice of Shadde's intention to sail from Stockholm at two o'clock that afternoon. It would be followed by a diving signal in the evening when they had cleared Sandhamn. When *Massive* read the second signal and knew that *Retaliate* was at sea in the Baltic, she would enter Göteborg.

At half past twelve the British Naval Attaché came on board. Shadde handed him two reports for forwarding to the Admiralty by diplomatic bag. They drank a glass of sherry together in Shadde's cabin, and after a brief exchange of pleasantries, Shadde saw him over the side into the launch and watched it make its way back to Skeppsholm.

For some minutes he stayed on the casing enjoying the sunlight, then he went down to the wardroom. The officers stood up as he walked in, but he waved them down and told Target to bring a sherry. He dropped into an armchair and sat sideways, one long leg thrust over the arm of the chair, the other stretched out in front. It was evident that he was in a good humor, and Cavan and the Doctor exchanged knowing glances. How long would it last? You never could tell with this strange, unpredictable man; the switches were too sudden. But for the moment he was all right and seemed to have forgotten last night.

Shadde held his glass of sherry to the light and peered at it with one eye closed. "You chaps are lucky. Lovely day for the run down to Sandhamn. Came up in the dark, so you don't know what you missed. One of the most beautiful passages in the world." He looked around impersonally. "Islands, trees, castles, blue water. It's fabulous. Judge for yourselves."

Dwight Gallagher and Cavan had both made the journey in daylight but they said nothing. It would only annoy Shadde, or he would ignore them. He liked to do the talking.

Shadde sipped the sherry. "Pity it isn't Sunday or you'd see the water between here and Sandhamn stiff with sailing craft. Every Swede's a sailor. Never known a place where people take to the water like this one. Lot of ruddy ducks." He pulled up a trouser leg and scratched at a hairy shin. "I always wonder how they can afford it. They moan about their taxation, but they do pretty well. Nice houses. Cars, yachts. Must be lots of money about. Average Swede must be a damn sight better off than the average Englishman." When he paused and held his glass up to the light and squinted at it with one eye, Symington and the Doctor winked at each other. They knew he'd ramble on like this till the cows came home and that it didn't pay to interrupt. He wasn't addressing anyone in particular, just thinking aloud, jumping from one thing to the other, and talking so fast and inconsequentially that you couldn't always follow. If you jumped in on one of his pauses he'd look up at you as if you weren't there—a glassy sort of look—then would go on.

Now Shadde turned to the first lieutenant. "Any news of Kyle?"

"No, sir. The patrol's back but they didn't find him. The Embassy's trying police stations and hospitals."

"Postman back yet?"

Cavan pulled his ear. "Not yet. He's coming off at thirteen hundred."

Shadde frowned for a moment, pushing his legs out in front of him and leaning far back in his chair, while he examined his shoes. "Hope he has a letter for me." It was said quietly, almost an aside.

"I guess no news is good news, Captain." Dwight Gallagher was trying to cheer him up.

Shadde looked past him with that glassy stare. "I wouldn't know," he said softly.

Gallagher tried another tack. "Taking a pilot down to Sandhamn, Captain?"

The question annoyed Shadde. Was this oaf of an American making a veiled illusion to the pilotage money Shadde would collect if he didn't take a pilot? If it wasn't that, why had he raised the subject? With a slow heave he pulled himself up in the chair and turned to look at the American.

"No," he said curtly. "Didn't need one in the dark coming up. Why should I now?"

"That's right. Of course. I only asked because in the U.S. Navy in the same situation we'd take one."

Shadde looked at him coolly. "Yes, I suppose you would."

There was a long, embarrassed silence. Gallagher was well liked in the wardroom. Shadde stared at him. Now he would get his own back. "Reminds me. Perhaps you can tell me something I've always wanted to know?"

"Fire ahead. I'll help if I can."

"Why do U.S. destroyers always make such a business of picking up a buoy?"

"Do they? I don't follow."

"Well, surely you have noticed. Ours go up to it pretty smartly. Bit of a flourish, you know. Plenty of way on, and then a good hefty kick astern. Nice test of seamanship. Something we're rather proud of."

Gallagher saw the drift now and his face tightened. "That's fine. And the point is?"

"That's the point, you see. A rather nice test of seamanship. Like not taking a pilot. That's why I've wondered . . . about U.S. destroyers—you know. They do it dead slow. Like a Hong Kong scow doing hearse at a sea burial." The analogy rather pleased Shadde; he smiled, a quiet, self-assured smile. "A sad sight, I always think."

For a moment Gallagher saw red; then he shrugged his shoulders. He wasn't looking for any quarrels. That wasn't why he was there. "Maybe you're right, Captain. Maybe," he said slowly.

After lunch Shadde went off to his cabin. The postman was back, but there was no letter from Elizabeth. He tried to shrug off his disappointment, but it didn't work. Down in the pit of his stomach there was a gnawing apprehension. Why didn't she write? Where was she? What was she doing? When her letter came, what would it say?

The telephone buzzer sounded; it was Rhys Evans reporting main engines ready for sea. Shadde put on his cap, slung binoculars around his neck and went up to the bridge. Cavan and Symington and the leading signalman were there.

Symington reported, "Steering gear tested and correct, sir. All main vents cottered."

From the control room the coxswain's voice came up the voice-pipe: "Coxswain on the wheel, sir. Main engines ready."

"Very good," said Shadde.

The early afternoon was warm and crisp, and Stockholm lay bathed in sunlight under a clear blue sky: a pleasant jumble of modern and medieval, of warm reds and browns, and here and there the green mold of copper spires and domes. The streets along the waterfront were crowded with traffic, and these and the ships at the quays and the bridges were mirrored in the blue waters of the Strömmen.

Shadde looked at his watch and then at the first lieutenant. "Ready to slip?"

"Ready to slip, sir."

Cavan raised his right arm and looked forward along the fore-casing. Allistair was standing near the bow, facing the bridge; a party of seamen was behind him.

Shadde called, "Starboard twenty; slow ahead."

The submarine began to gather way. "Stop—midships," he ordered. Then in a louder voice: "Slip!"

Cavan repeated the order and dropped his right arm. Up in the bow a seaman knocked off the slip, and the slip-rope whipped clear of the buoy. The men on the fore-casing hauled it inboard.

"Port twenty—slow astern," the Captain called. The submarine trembled and her bow began to pay off slowly to starboard. When she was headed east down the Strömmen he stopped both engines and corrected the swing. Then he ordered, "Midships—slow ahead," and soon afterwards gave the coxswain the course to steer. The submarine gathered speed and began the passage down past the ships lying alongside the quays at Stadsgarten.

Ahead of *Retaliate* a small pleasure steamer was coming up towards the harbor, with her passengers lining the side to look at the big submarine. Watching them Shadde failed to notice the slow, at first barely noticeable swing of *Retaliate*'s bow to port until he heard Symington's warning.

In a flash he was at the voice-pipe. "Starboard twenty!" he ordered sharply.

The coxswain immediately repeated the order, but

46

the bow continued to swing towards the Swedish pleasure steamer.

Shadde's voice was like a lash. "Wheel amidships!" And as soon as it was repeated, "Hard astarboard!" But it was too late. Things were happening very quickly.

The coxswain's voice came up urgently to the bridge. "She won't answer, sir! Pressure's gone!" At the same moment the Swedish ship sounded a single urgent blast indicating that she was altering course to starboard. Shadde winced. Had she altered to port they might have cleared each other. He roared down the voice-pipe, "Full astern!" And then to the first lieutenant, "The hatches—quick!"

But that couldn't help now. The Swede's stern and the submarine's bows were swinging towards each other. Symington heard the cries of alarm from the passengers, followed by the screech of metal as the bow struck the pleasure steamer well aft and scraped down the side. The submarine rolled to starboard as she struck, but it was an oblique blow and this lessened the impact. Seconds later the steamer had swung clear again and Symington had a vivid picture of her captain standing on the wing of the bridge shaking his fist and shouting.

In the meantime the first lieutenant had raced down the conning tower to the control room, closing the hatches behind him. He jumped across to the ship's broadcast, pressed the call push and shouted: "Collision stations! Close all watertight doors!" With feverish haste he got through to Rhys Evans on the engine-room voice-pipe and told him to send an E.R.A. to the steering compartment at the double to see what had happened. Then he ordered all compartments to report if there was any flooding. Shortly afterwards the forward torpedo room reported a minor leak in the pressure hull. The point of collision had been the port bow of the submarine. This was fortunate because the buoyancy tanks

47

lay further aft. Had they been holed, *Retaliate* would have been in serious trouble.

Rhys Evans reported back that the tiller head was locked in the hard-aport position; the telemotor system which actuated the steering gear had apparently broken down. It wasn't yet clear what the trouble was, but it was obvious that there had been a pressure failure on the port ram cylinder.

On the bridge Shadde was maneuvering the submarine with the main engines. He had reported the collision to the port authorities by radio telephone, and very soon two tugs appeared. One went alongside the pleasure steamer and nudged her off down the channel towards Nybroviken. Shadde shouted to the other by loud hailer to lay off, and then proceeded to give a remarkable display of seamanship by returning to *Retaliate's* original buoy and picking up moorings without the assistance of the tug.

But it was a seething, grim and white-faced Shadde; and Symington knew that the trembling hands, the tight-shut mouth and the protruding veins at the temples were the portents of a storm that would soon break.

As soon as they had secured to the buoy, Shadde sent signals to the Swedish Naval authorities asking for the services of a launch, divers and dockyard officials to examine and report on *Retaliate's* underwater damage. Allistair was landed by the tug with orders to report what had happened to the Naval Attaché at the British Embassy. "Tell him I'll see him later," said Shadde grimly.

Signals were sent to Flag Officer Submarines, repeated to *Massive* at sea in the Kattegat, reporting the delay in sailing and promising further information soon.

All that done, Shadde went down to his cabin and flung his cap onto the bunk with a fierce gesture of despair. Then he sent for the first lieutenant.

When Cavan arrived the Captain was pacing up and

down the small cabin smoking furiously, hands thrust into the pockets of his monkey jacket. From under black, bushy eyebrows he shot one scowling glance at the first lieutenant; his voice shook when he spoke.

"There'll be no shore leave. Double up sentries fore and aft. Swedish naval divers and dockyard officials are coming off. Apart from them there's to be no communication with the shore."

The pacing stopped as he went over to the desk and rang for the messenger. There was a knock on the door and the seaman came in.

"Tell the engineer officer I'd like to see him at once."

"Aye, aye, sir." The messenger doubled off.

While they waited Shadde resumed his pacing, but he said no more to the first lieutenant. Normally, thought Cavan, he'd ask me to sit down. Nothing normal about this though. Why's he in such a flap? The collision wasn't his fault. He had done everything possible on the bridge. You had to admit that about Shadde. A first-class seaman if ever there was one. But what on earth had happened to the steering gear? The whole incident had taken less than a minute. It was difficult to sort out now what had happened.

There was a knock on the door, and Rhys Evans came into the cabin. "You sent for me, sir?"

Shadde went on with his pacing. Before any words came from him, they could see his jaw muscles working. Suddenly he stopped. "What the bloody hell happened to that steering engine?" The words exploded out of him, a mixture of recrimination and despair.

The Welshman looked hurt. "It was a failure in the hydraulics, sir."

"A failure!" stormed Shadde. "That's a fine bloody understatement. Damn nearly wrote us off." He spluttered with anger, head thrust forward, eyes piercing the engineer officer.

49

"We are making an examination now, sir. Should know the trouble soon, but—"

"Who told you to make an examination? Stop it at once! This thing's going to be done properly. I'm going to have an official inquiry into that steering engine. Today. Soon as I've seen the Naval Attaché. Stop the examination right away. Get everybody out of the steering compartment and have it locked. This moment, d'you understand?" He looked at them darkly, his eyes staring. "You know what this is, don't you? It's sabotage, my friends. I've been expecting something like this." He seemed lost in thought for a moment. Then he looked up, frowning angrily. "What are you waiting for? You've heard my orders. Get on with them," he barked.

|| 5 ||

The collision delayed *Retaliate* in Stockholm for three days, and during that time many things happened.

The underwater damage was not very serious; a buckled plate near the bow was found to be responsible for the leak in the forward torpedo room. But it was in the pressure hull, so the submarine was put into dry dock. Working around the clock, the Swedish dockyard staff made good the damage in forty-eight hours, and the integrity of the pressure hull was restored.

Then there was all the business of making depositions, taking statements and preparing reports for the port authorities and Flag Officer Submarines. There would be a court of inquiry in Portsmouth on their return; Lloyds was interested on behalf of the Swedish ship, which had suffered some damage of a minor nature, and civil proceedings were possible if the matter could not be settled satisfactorily between the owners and the Admiralty. This wasn't likely to be as simple as it seemed, for though the failure of the submarine's steering gear was the *prima facie* cause of the accident, it might well be shown that there would have been no collision had the Swedish captain altered course to port and not to starboard when the collision was imminent.

The inquiry into the failure of the steering gear was held in the wardroom late in the afternoon of the collision, with Shadde presiding.

Before it started he went to the steering compartment, unlocked the watertight door and had a look around. He wanted to refresh his mind on the detail of the telemotor system and steering gear. Sure enough, there was the tiller head jammed hard aport, and all over the steel deck on that side was a large mess of sticky liquid—the mixture of water and glycerine which provided the pressure for the hydraulic system. There must have been a major leak somewhere on that side; that would explain why the coxswain had reported that there was no pressure. But there was much else that couldn't be so easily explained, thought Shadde. Like what had caused the leak? And *who* was responsible for it?

As he looked around the steering compartment he experienced a sense of relief that he had sent the signal to Flag Officer Submarines. Burton, the Naval Attaché, had suggested waiting until *Retaliate* was back in Portsmouth.

"You'll be there in eight days. By then there'll have been time to sort this thing out. What went wrong with the steering, et cetera."

"I'll have that settled by this evening. I want DNI to send somebody here right away—while the scent's still hot. This is sabotage, Burton, make no mistake."

"How can you be so certain, old chap?"

Shadde shook his head vigorously. "Don't tell me you belong to the 'it-can't-happen-here brigade.' I've had a bellyful of that since I commissioned *Retaliate*."

"Really, what d'you mean?"

"This is the third effort. First was soon after we'd finished working up. We came back to Portsmouth with trouble in the low-pressure stage of our main turbines. Stripped them down and found steel filings in the rotors. There was a court of inquiry. Sat for three days and then didn't know the answer. Found that the possibility of dirty work couldn't be excluded, but that it was unlikely."

"What did they think it might have been?"

"Oh! Some cock or other. Workmen might have left the stuff there through carelessness when the turbines were first assembled. You know how we hate to admit anyone might have it in for us."

Burton cocked his head on one side as if he were confronted with a new aspect of Shadde. "The second effort?"

"At Queensferry, months later. Steam explosion in the heat exchanger. Wad of cotton waste had been put into a steam pipe on the intake side. Someone who knew all about our nuclear plant set-up. There was another court of inquiry. Same wishy-washy findings! Probably negligence on the part of some person or persons. . . . Yes! They always put that in. Very careful about their grammar."

Shadde looked lost for a moment. With a weary sigh, he drew his hand over his eyes. "Where was I?"

"You were giving the court's finding."

"Yes. Of course. '. . . on the part of some person or persons unknown. The court finds, however, that the possibility of malicious intent cannot be excluded.' Malicious intent! I ask you! Why beat about the bush? Sabotage, that was what it was. It was sabotage at Portsmouth and Queensferry, and it's sabotage right here in Stockholm. That's why I'm sending that signal to FOS."

Burton had looked at him quizzically then and shrugged his shoulders. "It's your boat and your problem, Shadde. Do whatever you think best."

So the signal had gone, and through the Embassy for security reasons; Shadde didn't want any of the ship's company to know what was taking place. It was strongly worded because he wanted quick action. First he had referred to the earlier signal that day reporting the collision, and then gone on to say that there were strong grounds for suspecting sabotage. He concluded with an urgent request to Flag Officer Submarines to arrange with the Director of Naval Intelligence for the immediate despatch of an investigator.

The man should come incognito, Shadde insisted, and take passage with them back to Portsmouth. That would provide every opportunity for completing the investigations *in situ*. Shadde was rather pleased with that tag. The tail of the signal passed the buck fairly and squarely to FOS/M: "Unless this is done, I shall be unable to accept responsibility for further occurrences."

When the Naval Attaché saw that, he shook his head. "Most unwise, Shadde. You're looking for trouble. Senior officers don't like threats."

But Shadde was adamant. "Looking for trouble? My dear chap, I've got loads of it. I'm not changing that signal. Last two occasions I told them it was sabotage and they smiled politely. Now they can bloody well carry the baby themselves." The intense dark eyes flashed. "I know FOS and he knows me. He knows damn well I wouldn't put that into a signal unless it was justified."

So the signal had been enciphered and sent off—threat and all.

Just before he left the steering compartment, Shadde made an interesting find. Stuck away behind a cluster of pipes which ran down the port afterside of the compartment, he found a piece of oil-smeared gray silk, half the size of a man's handkerchief. Three sides were scissor-cut and the third was torn. He hadn't been looking for anything;

it was just that a corner of the material sticking out caught his eye. He went over and pulled it out, and then something dropped onto the steel desk with a metallic clang. It was a brass lock nut with a reverse thread, about an inch in diameter and half an inch long. Shadde's eyes glistened as he wrapped it up in the gray silk and slipped the small bundle into his pocket. Instinct told him that he had blundered onto something of importance; it also told him to say nothing about his find for the time being. Locking the door of the compartment behind him, he went through the stoker's mess to the control room.

When he got there he was approached by the first lieutenant, who held up a message sheet. "They've found Kyle, sir. He's in the police station at Värtahamnen. Petty Officer Farrell's landing with a patrol at seventeen hundred to collect him."

So much had happened in the last two hours that Shadde had quite forgotten about Kyle. Now, with a start, he wondered if there were any connection between Kyle and the failure of the steering gear? Why hadn't he thought of that before? Perhaps because he had mentally pigeon-holed the engineering mechanic as a rating who had gone adrift and missed the boat on sailing. But what if he were a deserter? What more likely than desertion if you knew that at any moment the submarine's steering might pack up, especially during the tricky passage down to Sandhamn through the Swedish Archipelago? But he said only, "Good. Put him in the cells, with a sentry, until I've seen him."

Cavan's voice was a mixture of doubt and surprise. "Cells and sentry, sir?"

"Cells" referred to the submarine's one tiny compartment which wasn't normally in use. It was, in fact, an emergency storeroom for exceptionally long patrols; but among the various uses to which it had been put was that of locking up libertymen who had come off too much the

55

worse for liquor. To the ship's company it was "the cooler."

Shadde's eyes flashed. He was not accustomed to having his orders questioned. "Yes! Cells and sentry!" he snapped, and walked on through the wardroom to his cabin. Cavan followed him with his eyes. Extraordinary devil! Cells and a sentry for a rating who'd gone adrift and missed his boat? What next? The collision must have rattled the Captain more than he had suspected.

The inquiry into the steering failure began at 1745 in *Retaliate*'s wardroom. Miller and Target had been banished from the pantry and the watertight door into the control room was shut. Shadde presided at the head of the table, with the first lieutenant, the engineer officer, Lieutenant Commander Goss the electronics officer, Lieutenant Weddy the gunnery officer, and Lieutenants Allistair and Symington, the torpedo and navigating officers, along its sides. Lieutenant Musgrove, second in command of the engine room, was notetaker.

For an hour and a half Shadde examined and cross-examined all who could throw any light on what had occurred. The coxswain testified to what had happened while he was at the wheel, and that when the steering gear had been tested at 1345 shortly before they slipped from the buoy it had worked perfectly. Symington, who had been on the bridge at the time, confirmed this. The wheel had been put hard astarboard and then hard aport; everything had functioned normally and correctly. Chief E.R.A. Shepherd was called next and he explained how the steering gear and telemotor system were maintained. It appeared that only the day before sailing he had carried out some routine maintenance, assisted by two stokers. On completion they had tested the system and it had worked perfectly.

Shepherd also testified about what he had found when

sent by the engineer officer to investigate immediately after the collision: the tiller head jammed in the hard-aport position and the deck on the port side of the steering compartment flooded with liquid from the hydraulic system. Later, the engineer officer had sent him back with a working party to try and find out what the trouble was, but they had not been there long when they were told to leave the steering compartment and to lock it. He had done this and given the key to Lieutenant Musgrove.

"But," said Shepherd—and this was the first Shadde had heard of it—"by then we knew what the trouble was, sir. The hydraulic liquid in the telemotor system had drained out through the plug hole on the port ram cylinder."

Shadde's face was suddenly alert and aggressive. "Why wasn't I told this?" he snapped.

"Nobody asked me, sir." Shepherd's voice was aggrieved. "I was told to get my party out of the steering compartment and to lock it up. That was just after sixteen hundred. At seventeen thirty I was told to stand by for an inquiry in the wardroom, and here I am, sir." The steady gray eyes regarded the Captain with silent reproach.

"I see," said Shadde thoughtfully. "So the liquid drained out through the plug hole." He leaned over the table, his strong face thrust forward purposefully. "How was that possible?"

"The drain plug had come out, sir. We found it lying on the deck where it had dropped."

"Dropped," said Shadde with a trace of sarcasm. "What makes you think it dropped?"

"Must have, sir. It was lying there."

Shadde turned to the engineer officer. "What would make a drain plug *drop?*" He emphasized the word heavily, menacingly.

Rhys Evans shook his head. "Indeed, this is news to me, sir. First I have heard of it."

Shadde turned back to Shepherd. "How do you think it came to drop off?" Again that tinge of sarcasm.

With a slow shake of his head, Shepherd said, "That's what's got me beat, sir. Impossible for it to drop off."

"Ah!" said Shadde. "Now we're getting somewhere. Perhaps you'll tell us why it's impossible."

"Well, there's a lock nut, sir. It's reverse threaded. So long's that's on, the drain plug can't come away."

Shadde leaned forward, his hands clasped together in front of him. "So that on this occasion the impossible happened?"

Shepherd paused for a moment, his good-natured face puzzled. "There's something funny about it, sir. You see, we couldn't find the lock nut afterwards. I mean when we went there to see why the steering had failed."

"Perhaps it was never on?" suggested Shadde.

"It was on all right, sir."

"How d'you know?"

"It was there yesterday, sir. When we did the maintenance routine."

"You sure of that?"

"Definitely, sir. We had to remove the drain plug and drain the cylinders. I put the drain plug back myself."

"Yes, but it's the lock nut we're talking about."

"I know, sir. That's how I know. I put it on myself."

For a moment Shadde sat there thinking. Then he said, "Can you prove this?" and he gave Shepherd a hard, searching look.

"Yes, sir. Engineering Mechanic Finney, sir. He'll bear me out. When I'd put the lock nut on, it was him who brought it up tight."

Finney was called, and he corroborated all that Shepherd had said. After the chief E.R.A. had put the lock nut on and given it a few turns he'd ordered Finney to bring it up tight.

58

"Then," explained Finney, "I put me spanner on an' brought it up tight. Could'nt've moved after that, sir," he said, "'cepting someone put a spanner on it again."

There was a gleam in Shadde's eyes as he looked around the table at his officers. He didn't need to say "I told you so," because it was written across his face as large as life.

"One final question, Shepherd." Shadde almost seemed to be licking his lips. "You haven't told us who your working parties were yesterday when you did the maintenance and this afternoon when you made the examination."

Shepherd thought for a moment. "Yesterday it was me and Finney and Kyle, and today it was me and Finney and Stokes, sir." He paused for a moment. "Would've been Kyle again today, sir, but he's adrift."

Shadde's eyes glinted. "Yes," he said, "I know." Then his jaw set like a steel trap.

When Petty Officer Farrell and his four-man patrol got to the police station at Värtahamnen they found a tired, dirty and unshaven Kyle. A lump on his right temple was covered with plaster and there were blood marks on his jumper.

Petty Officer Farrell was a short stocky man with a bird-like face. He shook his head disapprovingly as he looked at Kyle. "Fine advert for the Royal Navy, I must say," he said.

Kyle looked bored and ignored the remark.

"Anyway, wot 'it you, cock?" inquired Farrell sharply.

"Swedish bloke," said Kyle. He yawned; this was not a subject he wished to pursue. The recollection of it was too recent and embarrassing.

The petty officer sniffed with contempt. "S'pose you were drunk."

"Not me," said Kyle vehemently. "Flipping robbery and violence it was."

"All right, me lad, come back to the boat an' tell that to the duty officer. 'E might believe you—I won't." Petty Officer Farrell thanked the Swedish police sergeant, signed for the prisoner and marched him off with the patrol.

Back on board Kyle was brought before Lieutenant Allistair, the duty officer. Kyle told him his story, and Allistair put him in the Captain's report for being absent without leave, missing the boat and for disorderly behavior ashore. Then he sent him to Surgeon Lieutenant O'Shea.

The first lieutenant reported to Shadde that Kyle had returned on board and that he had a head injury which was being attended to by the Doctor. Shadde told him he wanted to see the Doctor as soon as he had finished with Kyle.

Half an hour later O'Shea came to the Captain's cabin. "You sent for me, sir?"

Shadde was sitting in an easy chair, reading. He put down the book.

"Ah, yes, O'Shea. Come and sit down."

The Doctor felt stiff and ill-at-ease. The Captain's outburst at Skansen was still fresh in his mind. Now Shadde leaned forward in his chair and his dark penetrating eyes fixed on the Doctor. "I gather you've examined Kyle?"

"Yes, sir."

"What's his condition?"

"Nothing much to worry about. Bad bruise on the temple, and the skin's split. I've stitched it. Nothing serious. Nothing that a good rest won't put right."

"Did he tell you how he got the injury?" Shadde's eyes narrowed. Before the Doctor could reply, he added, "Could the blow have been self-inflicted?"

The Doctor shook his head. "Possible but most unlikely."

"How d'you know?"

"Because I've heard his story, sir."

"What is it?" Shadde's gruff voice didn't conceal his disappointment.

"He got tight in a pub yesterday evening. Apparently started drinking in the late afternoon, and must have had a skinful. Near midnight a pimp put a prostitute onto him, and she took Kyle to her room somewhere near the free harbor. Later on the accomplice turned up and caught them"— O'Shea paused—"in flagrante delicto."

Shadde frowned. "Why don't you use English, O'Shea? I've no time for these wordy affectations."

The Doctor shrugged his shoulders. "I don't think I know an appropriate English phrase, sir."

"Good heavens, man! You're English. Aren't 'in the act' or 'on the job' good enough?"

For a moment O'Shea was tempted to point out that he was Irish, but he thought better of it. Shadde never spoke of the British or the Scots or the Irish. It was always "the English."

"Well anyway, sir, the accomplice turned up and coshed Kyle."

"Motive?" Shadde's voice was full of doubt.

"Robbery. They took his watch, and wallet, with about ten pounds in it."

"Lot for a stoker to go ashore with."

"It was money he was saving to get his mother a present."

"Very touching," said Shadde sarcastically. "What happened then?"

"When Kyle came to, he found himself in a large shed and it was daylight. Apparently he had a lot of pain, and retched violently. Then he slept again. Sometime this afternoon he attracted attention by banging on the door and shouting. When he was let out he gave himself up to the police. Petty Officer Farrell and the patrol collected him from them soon after eighteen hundred."

The Doctor cleared his throat. "Mind if I smoke, sir?"

61

"No! No! Of course not." Shadde was already smoking; he waved his hand impatiently. "Go ahead.

"Tell me, O'Shea, d'you believe that story?" Shadde's dark eyes searched the Doctor's.

"Yes, sir, I do."

"D'you know that Shepherd regards him as a bad hat?"

The Doctor met Shadde's piercing glance steadily. "I wouldn't say that, sir."

Shadde looked at him quickly. "Why not, may I ask?"

"I got him talking. Found out a good deal about him."

"Such as?"

"He comes from a poor home. Despises his father, who drinks and who occasionally assaults his mother." O'Shea puffed at his cigarette. "Kyle's devoted to her, but it's the father who's done the damage. Not only does he misuse the boy's mother, but I gather his attitude to Kyle is a mixture of spoiling and bullying, depending on how much he's drunk."

"How very interesting."

The Doctor failed to detect the sarcasm in Shadde's voice. "Yes, it is," O'Shea agreed. "You see, children look for an authority figure. With boys it's usually the father. If that breaks down they become confused. That's because children try to find security in well-defined limits of behavior. But in a hopelessly irrational environment they can't. Then confusion inhibits and destroys their drives. In Kyle's case, his father's behavior has resulted in the son's lack of normal social drives. He suffers from a strong sense of personal inadequacy and tries to compensate for this by—"

"That'll do, thank you," snapped the Captain.

O'Shea looked startled. Engrossed in his subject, he had not noticed the signs of disapproval—the deep frown and drumming fingers. Now Shadde was standing up, fussing with the clock on the bulkhead. His back was to the Doctor, but when he spoke it was evident that he was struggling with his emotions.

62

"I haven't the faintest idea what you're talking about," he said impatiently. "I have my own theories about Kyle. They may not sound as highfalutin as yours, but they're at least more intelligible, even if I didn't dabble in psychology in Dublin."

With a shock, O'Shea realized that he had upset the Captain. He stood up, embarrassed and uncertain and at a loss to deal with the new situation. "I was only trying to explain in simple terms what I think's wrong with Kyle, sir." The tone was apologetic. "You told me Shepherd said he's a bad hat. I was trying to say that he displays the symptoms of a badly adjusted young man. He's sick. Mentally sick. And his experience last night won't have helped his adjustment problem either. He needs help, not punishment."

Shadde closed the glass of the bulkhead clock with a snap and spun around to the Doctor. A wave of anger swept through him and his mouth set in a hard, tight line. "Do you really think so?" His voice was withering. "I'd like you to know, O'Shea, that I'm not the least bit interested in your psychiatrical claptrap or any other mumbo jumbo. It's got no place in one of Her Majesty's ships, and as far as I am concerned it's . . ." Frowning, he hunted for the words he wanted. "It's a threat and an affront to naval discipline." He sat down with his back to the Doctor and started to write.

"You may go," he called over his shoulder. The voice was hard and peremptory.

During the next two days little was seen of Shadde. Most of the time he spent in the seclusion of his cabin, dealing only with matters so urgent that they could not be postponed. It was known in the wardroom that he was in one of his depressed moods, more or less unapproachable.

On the morning of the second day the first lieutenant reminded the Captain that Kyle was still in cells. Shadde

63

said, "I'm well aware of that." But he didn't snap as he usually did; he sounded tired.

"Aren't you going to have him brought up as a defaulter, sir?"

Shadde's voice was blank. His thoughts seemed elsewhere. "I suppose so."

"D'you think you'll be able to see him before we get to sea, sir?"

The only light switched on in Shadde's cabin was the small reading lamp over the bunk, and its illumination scarcely reached to where he sat in the easy chair, his face in shadow, head sunk forward and arms drooping over the sides of the chair. The first lieutenant was standing just inside the cabin door, cap under arm; Shadde had not invited him to sit down, nor had he lifted the dark eyes staring at the feet thrust out in front of him.

Now he turned his head and looked at the first lieutenant as if he were seeing him for the first time. Cavan was shocked by the red-rimmed eyes set in dark shadows, and the dull, listless stare. Poor sod, he thought, he's worrying about the court of inquiry in Portsmouth and his promotion. That day, he knew, Shadde had seen the marine surveyor's report on the damage to the pleasure steamer, and it had not been cheerful reading.

"I don't know," said Shadde wearily. "I'll let you know when I'm ready for him."

The Captain's steward had fared no better. Every attempt he made to break through Shadde's mood of depression failed. No, he didn't want anything to eat. No, not even a cup of tea. No, he didn't want the bunk turned back. No, he would not be dining in the wardroom. Eventually Miller gave up. But Shadde never objected to the silver salver with the soda siphon and the whisky bottle on it, and Miller saw the level in the bottle fall steadily. All this worried him, because he'd been with Shadde a long time, far longer than any other man in the submarine, and he was attached to the Captain in a strange way which he could never explain. Nor could he explain what had happened to the Captain in recent months—but whatever it was he didn't like it.

The Flag Officer Submarines was not pleased when he read Shadde's signal.

"Most peculiar," he said to Treadwell, the chief staff officer. "He's threatening me. I don't like it." He shook his head. "Of course, he's had this bee in his bonnet about sabotage for some time. And I don't suppose the collision's done him any good."

But FOS/M knew he'd have to send an investigator after Shadde's signal. Threat or no threat, it would be tempting fate not to. And, of course, there was always the outside chance that Shadde's hunch might be right. Still, FOS/M didn't like the signal. It struck him as queer, and it came on top of rumors that all was not well with Shadde's marriage. And now there was this collision in Stockholm. He would keep an open mind about the matter until the report arrived, but it was a worrying thing. It meant a court of inquiry and a lot of juggling with the *Missile*-class boats. Two of them always had to be at sea and *Retaliate*'s delay in Stockholm meant sailing *Deterrent* from Loch Ewe, putting *Missile* onto short notice and recalling one of her watches from leave. It meant a lot of fuss and bother. He hoped for Shadde's sake that the captain of the pleasure steamer could be saddled with a fair share of the responsibility. FOS/M had plans for bringing Shadde ashore later in the year. He wondered if he should accelerate them.

Mr. Buddington came on board just before they sailed from Stockholm. They saw him coming off in the launch, a strange, bleak little man in a dark suit and a bowler hat,

65

an umbrella in one hand, a worn leather suitcase in the other and a black leather box slung over his shoulder. Weddy, the duty officer, met him on the casing and took him down to the Captain.

Mr. Buddington was expected. It was known on board that Shadde had received a signal from FOS/M about an official from the Director of Naval Construction's office who would take passage in *Retaliate* to make observations connected with research into air-conditioning and humidity problems in the *Missile*-class boats.

Before the signal arrived Shadde had been told by the Naval Attaché that the "official" would be Clarence Henry Buddington, a civilian investigator from the Director of Naval Intelligence's office. Down in his cabin Shadde lost no time in briefing the little man, who soon knew exactly why sabotage was suspected and why Kyle was thought to be the man responsible. Mr. Buddington was the only other man in the submarine who knew about Shadde's find in the steering compartment, for the Captain gave him the oil-stained gray silk and the brass lock nut and explained their significance.

To only two men on board did Shadde reveal the real identity and purpose of Mr. Buddington. They were the first lieutenant and the engineer officer.

|| 6 ||

All her damage made good, *Retaliate* sailed for Copenhagen from Stockholm at 1400 on the afternoon of the third day.

Three hours later the pilot was dropped off at the Revengegrundet buoy and the submarine proceeded on a course of 124 degrees. Soon afterwards the diving signal to the Flag Officer Submarines was made. Then they dived to catch a trim, surfacing again ten minutes later when speed was increased to 16½ knots. At 1920 the course was altered to 210 degrees; it was Shadde's intention to pass south on the surface between Öland and Gotland during the night.

It was at 0116, some six hours later, that the Captain had gone up to the bridge in response to Symington's report that Great Karlsö light was in sight, bearing 168 degrees, 5 miles distant, through the mist and rain of a dark and cheerless night.

After the trouble on the bridge with Symington, Shadde went back to his cabin. He lay on the bunk with the light off,

67

his mind too active for sleep. An endless succession of images floated before him, each a sharply defined picture of his many problems. There was the moment of the collision, with the black hull of the pleasure steamer almost on top of him, and the oily piece of gray silk and the shine of the brass lock nut. Then he imagined Kyle crouching down by the port ram cylinder, easing off the lock nut, wrapping it in the gray silk, hiding it away. Then the tiller head locked over to port, and the sticky mess of the hydraulic fluid. Next he saw the Flag Officer Submarines at Blockhouse reading the report of the collision, and the dismal summary of damage prepared by the marine surveyor. That picture soon gave way to one of Mr. Buddington—the bleak little face, the deferential lift of the eyebrows. He didn't think much of Mr. Buddington's chances of finding out anything.

The parade moved on; now it was the Doctor's serious, ugly face, tousled red hair and protruding ears. Shadde remembered the conversation that morning, the absurd analysis of Kyle's troubles. Any fool could see what was wrong with Kyle. Chip on the shoulder. Bloody saboteur! Nasty piece of work; dirty little crook; that was what was wrong with him. What on earth was a doctor doing in a submarine? All that damned psychiatric nonsense! As if there was any mystery about Kyle! Nowadays there had to be an explanation for everything. A murderer wasn't a murderer any more. Oh, no! He was maladjusted, mentally sick. You had to be sorry for him; give him treatment, not punishment. Too bad about the victim. He couldn't get treatment.

And who was this pushing himself into the picture? Tall, slim, elegant—that supercilious, well-bred smile. Symington, of course. The muscles in Shadde's stomach contracted into a tight, painful knot. Symington always had that effect on him. His physical discomfort was acute. Why did it happen? It worried him. First he would feel a sudden surge of

68

apprehension, then the stomach ache would come. More than an ache really—a sort of knot.

And here was somebody else—the best of the bunch! Rhys Evans. Good old Chiefy! Kind, trustworthy, loyal. No frills. First class at his job, a sound disciplinarian. That was a happy picture and Shadde's mind dwelt on it. Then the procession started again—there'd be no peace tonight. Here was the first lieutenant, square-headed prig. So damned determined never to put a foot wrong. Awkward bugger. Doesn't like me. Knows I can see through him. Pro-Symington, of course. So God-damn smug! Knows all about the Lombok Strait, no doubt. That recollection pressed agonizingly on Shadde's mind. A dagger in the brain, white, hot, turning and twisting.

He wrenched clear, and other pictures came: Goss and Weddy, and Dwight Gallagher. In the dark, Shadde's mouth tightened, and he choked with resentment. Why did one of Her Majesty's submarines have to carry a U.S. naval officer? Who had thought up that humiliation? Nuclear weapons control officer, indeed! A U.S. officer controlling the main armament of one of Her Majesty's ships. A dirty political trick thought up by the politicians. Gutless lot of parasites. First they had let England be talked into taking over six Polaris boats, and then they'd allowed her to be stung thirty million quid apiece for them. Bloody robbery! And after that the deadly insult—a U.S. naval officer on board to have the final say about firing. Shadde's fingernails dug into the palms of his hands and his tightly shut eyes burned. His breath came faster. In his ears he could hear the fast pulse beat. Thud, thud, thud—like a bloody drum. How could he sleep with that? Why couldn't he sleep? Just one long night of sleep. Oh, God! Just one.

Who was this? Elizabeth? Yes, of course! Pale, sad and remote, that permanent question mark in the dark eyes. Sentence by sentence he reconstructed her devastating letter. He'd read it a dozen times, knew every word by heart. But he concentrated furiously on the sentences as they raced across the front of his mind. Perhaps he had missed something, misconstrued her meaning. The concentration made his temples ache. A throbbing, nerve-jabbing ache. Must get away from that. He got off the bunk and slid back the cabin door. Now he could see into the wardroom; beyond it lay the control room. He tried to concentrate on the sounds coming from there. Reports to and from the bridge; reports from the asdic and radar operators; reports from the engine and reactor control rooms; reports from the missile attack center. Endless bloody reports! What was it all about anyway? They'd drive him mad with reports. You could stand so much. After that . . . ?

No good standing here trembling. Get back onto the bunk. Voices? What were they saying? Ah! Helmsman and telegraphman. What was the thumping? Feet, of course. Feet on the corticine deck in the control room; feet on the ladders; feet on the bridge deck. What was that whirring noise? The motors turning the radar aerials. And that other noise? The crackling. Ah, yes. Transmitting in the W/T office! Behind it all the steady hum of the main turbines. No mistaking that. Good homespun sound. Knew where you were with that one. Like the slow lift and plunge and the creaks and the groans when the hull worked. Knew where you were with them. Must keep a grip on yourself, though. And now, please God . . . sleep! Look out, here they are again! Kyle, Symington, Cavan, the Doctor, the party at Skansen, the collision, the gray silk and the lock nut. And Elizabeth . . . Elizabeth . . . Elizabeth.

Hopelessly he tried to shut his mind against these intruders, but they wouldn't go. They wouldn't leave him alone. Suddenly there was the shattering "birr-birr" of the voice-pipe buzzer next to his head. The first lieutenant was reporting the bearing and distance of the light at Hoburgen Reef—reporting the alteration of course—reporting—reporting. Shadde turned on the light above the bunk and looked at the cabin clock. Five minutes to three—an hour and a half since he'd left Symington on the bridge. He looked next at the course and speed tell-tales—20 knots, 236 degrees. No use trying to sleep. He slid off the bunk and pulled on uniform trousers over his pyjamas, then the white submarine jersey, the monkey jacket and the duffel coat. Now the ankle-length sea boots, cap, binoculars. Thank God for the interruption.

He walked through the wardroom into the control room. For minutes he concentrated on the radar display, making a mental note of the ranges and bearings of the points of light on the PPI, the ships within radar range. Against the chart he checked the luminous depiction of the coastline far away on the starboard quarter, as each sweep of the radar scanner threw it into sharp relief. Next, at the fathometer, he watched the paper trace, comparing the depths with those on the chart.

As always Shadde didn't say a word to the men in the control room. Tight-lipped, remote, he walked to the conning-tower ladder and stood there for a moment looking up at the night sky wheeling and dipping with the pitch and roll. Faintly the noise of the wind and sea came down to him. The lights in the control room were red to protect night vision, but still it was hard to see when he stepped out through the upper hatch onto the bridge.

The rain had stopped and the wind from the southwest had freshened. Astern to port showed the first gray light of dawn. Looking ahead to the dark side of the horizon, Shadde saw the vague outline of the men on the bridge. He moved towards them and stood next to the tallest man.

"That you, Number One?"

71

"Yes, sir."

"Speed?"

"Making good nineteen knots, sir."

"Hoburgen light?"

"You can still see the loom, sir. About thirteen miles astern now." Cavan moved over to starboard and looked aft past the periscope standards.

"There it is now, sir," he called. "Period's about five seconds."

Shadde went over and stood next to the first lieutenant. The light loomed, and as it doused he started counting: "One, two, three, four, five . . ." On five it loomed again, barely visible against the dawn sky.

He went back to the fore-end of the bridge. Out on the port bow the clouds were scudding across a half-moon, low in the sky. The sea was short, and fine spray drove across the bridge as the submarine pushed into it.

There were many steaming lights in sight and Shadde examined them carefully with binoculars. Twelve had shown on the radar display but he could find only nine. Three must be beyond visual range, he concluded.

"Lot of traffic about." The remark was noncommittal.

Cavan was wary. "Yes, sir; mostly Baltic coasters, I imagine."

The Captain was silent, engrossed in his examination of the lights. At last he said, "Three are fishermen."

Cavan used his binoculars. "Two in sight a moment ago. You must've found a third, sir." Then, "Ah, yes, I've got it."

Shadde experienced a mild surge of pleasure. He'd found a light before the lookouts and the officers on the bridge. For the hundredth time he wondered why it was that C.O.s made sightings before their officers, and officers before their lookouts.

Cavan's voice broke in, "Like a cup of cocoa, sir?"

72

For a moment Shadde hesitated. "Yes, thank you."

In the half darkness he saw the control-room messenger at his side with tray and cups. He took one and its heat warmed his hands against the chill air of morning.

"When's sunrise?"

"O-three-twenty-nine, sir."

"Early, isn't it?"

"Yes, sir. Makes a long day."

Shadde put his head and shoulders into the chart table and switched on the light. He leaned his elbows on the table, sipping the cocoa and looking at the fixes: firmly drawn little circles with the lines of bearing intersecting at their centers, the time written neatly against each. Grudgingly Shadde acknowledged that the first lieutenant was a good naval officer: thorough, conscientious, capable. No doubt about that. The cocoa finished, he flicked off the light and went to the after end of the bridge. The early gray of morning was changing to pink, and with the coming of daylight Shadde's mood lifted. Dawn and the warm cocoa had brought a sense of well-being, and in the freshness of the wind and sea he forgot the anxieties and apprehensions of the night. These were the things he understood, the real, substantial things that a man could see and feel. Nothing hidden or evil about them. He went back to the forepart of the bridge and looked down on the casing, gleaming wetly in the half-light. Turning his back to the wind, he leaned against the bridge screen. The periscope standards and the wireless antennae were etched against the gray and pink layers of the sky. Above him the radar aerial turned and searched, and he heard the subdued roar and steady slap and churn of the sea as it raced along the casing.

He took a cigarette case from his duffel coat. "Like one, Number One?"

"Thank you, sir."

73

They stood for some time in silence. Then Shadde said, "What's the good of a bloody great monster like this if it's never used?"

"D'you mean this submarine?"

Shadde nodded.

"Isn't the fact that she exists enough? I mean isn't that the point . . . the deterrent? No one wants them to be used. I don't believe they ever will be."

"That's the trouble, isn't it? The tens of millions of pounds, this fantastic equipment, men trained to a high pitch of efficiency—yet everyone bloody-well determined that it'll never be used."

Shadde walked aft past the periscope standards and leaned on the rail looking astern. Then he came back to where Cavan stood. "D'you think the Russians would hesitate to use one of these if they thought their survival depended on it?" He gave a dry laugh. "Well . . . d'you think they would?" His voice was insistent and he peered into the distance as if he might find the answer somewhere out there. In the half-light Cavan looked at the gaunt figure of the Captain. There was a rocklike, compelling quality about him. Powerful forces seemed ever working in him. You could almost feel the tensions, the straining. You could not take him lightly or disregard what he said.

Cavan pulled at his ear, his voice was slow and hesitant. "No . . . I suppose—if it was survival—the Russians might. But would they? There wouldn't be any survival. Both sides know that."

Shadde flicked the butt end of the cigarette over the leeward side of the bridge and watched the glowing arc as it whipped down wind. Then he turned back.

"Number One," he said earnestly, "you're an Englishman. Wouldn't you"—he paused—"fight at any cost rather than submit to . . . those thugs?" He pointed astern. For a moment the gesture puzzled the first lieutenant. Then he realized that Shadde was indicating the general direction of Russia.

Without waiting for an answer the Captain switched to his Rover and the motoring holiday on the Continent he had planned for his next leave. The Rover had become an item of wardroom gossip. The Captain was understood to have no means outside his service pay, but lately his fortunes seemed to have changed. Notable in this respect was the Rover, bought second-hand but a recent model in excellent condition. When he first drove it down to the submarine at Portsmouth, the wardroom decided it must have cost a tidy sum of money.

Leaning against the bridge screen, Shadde said, "We've always wanted to do this trip. Talked about it often. Cross over to France by Silver City. Then drive down to the château country. Loire Valley, you know. Little French pubs; wonderful cooking. We'll make our headquarters at Chenonceau. Go and see Blois, Amboise, Chambord, Langeais, Chinon and the others. Went there with my people when I was a boy. After that we'll drift down to the Riviera. Bask in the sun. Then up the Rhône Valley, through Switzerland and on to Austria. Then Bavaria and up the Rhine to Cologne. We'll end up with the Ardennes and Brussels. After that, home."

The first lieutenant wasn't really interested but he had to say something. "How long'll that take, sir?"

"Do it in easy stages. Stop where we like it and that sort of thing. Three or four weeks, I suppose."

"Marvelous leave."

"Yes. Should be fun."

The sun was well above the horizon when Shadde left the bridge.

Mr. Buddington was an early riser. Soon after seven he closed the book he was reading and left his cabin to go to

75

the wardroom. There was a letter for his wife to go in the postbox. After that he would go to the bridge to take a look at the new day.

In the control room he stopped on the port side to examine the radar displays. Lieutenant Symington, the navigating officer, had explained them to him the night before. Mr. Buddington marveled at the detail of land and shipping they presented once the art of interpretation was mastered; something he flattered himself he'd already done. Finished with the displays, he turned forward towards the wardroom. As he reached the doorway he saw and heard in a fleeting second something which stopped him in his tracks.

Target and Miller were standing outside the pantry door less than eight feet away, their backs towards him. Target held something in front of him which Miller was craning his head sideways to see. He heard Miller's whisper. "In the victualing store in ten minutes, Bullseye. Too risky to give it the once over 'ere."

Mr. Buddington noted the time, 0708, cleared his throat and walked into the wardroom. With a mumbled "Good mornin' sir," the stewards moved apart, Dusty Miller thrusting his left hand behind his back. But the movement was not quite fast enough and Mr. Buddington saw the brown envelope. Then Miller stepped backwards into the wardroom pantry, closing the door, and began polishing the brass rail on the serving hatch, whistling softly as he worked. Mr. Buddington walked on into the wardroom, where he sat down in an armchair. Soon he was engrossed in *The Field.*

A few minutes later, Miller came out of the pantry and left the wardroom. Target followed soon afterwards. Mr. Buddington looked at his watch; it was 0713. *The Field* continued to engage his attention. At 0720 he moved quietly into the control room. Mr. Buddington always moved quietly. He was small and inconspicuous and wore rubber-soled shoes. Down the starboard ladder he went to the middle deck where the victualing store on the port side was shielded from him by the steel screen around the periscope well. Slowly he edged his way along the screen until he was immediately outside the entrance to the officers' quarters. He worked along the bulkhead until he was near the door of the store, opposite the notice-board, and his head was within two or three feet of the open door. There was a low hum of conversation.

Time was precious, for at any moment a member of the crew might walk along the alleyway and, in greeting him, give away his presence to the men inside. While he read the notices on the board he listened intently to the scraps of conversation from the open door. Target was talking in a low voice and Mr. Buddington could make out odd fragments: ". . . sure that stowage's O.K., Dusty? . . . put the tins on top . . . risky business . . . agents . . . two in Pompey . . . big prices for these prints . . ."

Then Miller spoke, but Mr. Buddington found him no easier to follow. ". . . see 'ere . . . blimey, what a weapon . . . dockyard police . . . nosey lot of buggers . . . worth it though . . . man's got to live, ain't 'e . . . see what we can do in Copenhagen . . ."

Mr. Buddington decided that he had heard enough for his immediate purposes. Quietly he worked his way back along the bulkhead, over to the starboard side and then into the alleyway of the officers' quarters. Once there, he walked boldly forward to his cabin. He went in, shutting and locking the door behind him.

At 0735, when the submarine was 23 miles south of Öland Reef, Shadde left his cabin and went to the control room. *Retaliate* was still running on the surface, steering 205 degrees, the course to which she had altered at 0620. The freshening southwesterly wind had kicked up a short, steep sea, and every now and then she shook and trembled as her bow was forced into it.

Weddy and Bagnall, the commissioned gunnery officer, were on watch. Away to starboard they could see the Swedish coast where it ran west and south about the Hanö Bight. From time to time a sheet of spray thrown up by the bow drove across the bridge, and the oilskins of the men there shone with moisture in the weak sunlight.

Shadde walked down the starboard side of the control room, past the men on the wheel- and engine-room telegraphs. He went first to the W/T office and then to the missile attack center. Then he crossed over to the port side and walked up forward, looking in on the A/S and radar compartments. Without a word to the men on duty, he examined the instrumentation before them. This occasioned no surprise; it was Shadde's custom at sea to wash and shave and then, immaculately turned out, start the day with a pre-breakfast stalk in tight-lipped silence, his dark, peering eyes searching everywhere. Yet Shadde's men had an immense respect for him. His remote aloofness and great skill as a submariner surrounded him with an aura of authority that was almost mystical.

From the A/S compartment the Captain went on to the radar displays, then to the ventilation control panel. He spent some time there before going over to the chart table. With a frown of concentration he studied the chart for a few minutes, after which he asked the A/S operator for a line of soundings from the fathometer. As these were called, Shadde compared them with those on the chart. Then he picked up a signal pad and wrote two messages on it. One he handed to Chief P. O. Telegraphist Gracie in the W/T office for immediate transmission. It was *Retaliate*'s diving signal, addressed to the Flag Officer Submarines; it gave the times at which she would dive and surface. Shadde folded the other sheet tightly and stood waiting with it in his hand. The sound of wireless transmissions came from the W/T office, and two minutes later Shadde gave the folded signal to a messenger and told him to deliver it at once to the officer of the watch. The helmsman called up the voice-pipe, "Permission for one man on the bridge," and then the messenger disappeared up the conning tower. Shadde went back to the radar displays.

The able seaman handed the folded paper to the officer of the watch. "Message from the Captain, sir."

Weddy opened the signal sheet. It read: For exercise repeat exercise order emergency dive Stop execute.

It took Weddy two seconds to reach the chart table and another two to check that the charted depths of water ahead of the submarine were in the thirty and forty fathom range. With one hand he grabbed the chart and with the other slammed the chart table shut into the recess on the side of the bridge.

Then he yelled, "Clear the bridge!" And as he did so he jumped to the voice-pipe and shouted, "Dive! dive! dive!" At the same moment he pressed the klaxon hooter button and instantly the harsh "ah-uu-uu-gah" of the alarm sounded throughout the submarine. In the control room the E.R.A. opened the main vents and the crew went automatically to diving stations. As the lookouts, the signalman and Bagnall bundled down the conning-tower ladder, Weddy took a last look around the bridge and then followed them, shutting off the voice-pipe, closing the upper hatch behind him with a slam and ramming home the clips. Then he was through the lower hatch and the signalman slammed it shut and fastened the clips.

As the crew hurried to their stations, a signalman collided with a seaman who fell against the coxswain seated at the hydroplanes. The coxswain growled, "Watch your step and stop that skylarking."

The seaman grinned. "Sorry, 'Swain. Accident."

"That's right," confirmed the signalman.

"Just—"

Shadde's angry voice froze them. "Stop that bloody chatter." Then he called, "Forty feet! Up periscope! *For exercise*, bring all tubes to the ready." A few seconds later he ordered, "Down periscope!" and snapped the handles closed. With a hiss the periscope sank into its well.

The submarine took on a bow-down angle and the short, pitching movement ceased as she left the turbulent surface water. Symington and the Doctor were at the plotting table and the "tick-tack" of its motor was the only sound. Allistair, the third hand, was on the attack computer, where instruments were feeding in the course, speed, and other data. The first lieutenant stood behind the seated planesmen, concentrating on the tell-tales and depth gauges, and giving pumping and flooding orders to get the trim right.

Now Shadde's voice was sharp, compelling. "Up periscope!" He made a rapid sweep of the horizon, bringing the periscope to rest on a cargo steamer a couple of miles away on the starboard bow.

"Down periscope! Start the attack!" He snapped the handles shut and stood back. "Starboard fifteen. Steer two-three-zero. Six knots." The helmsman and telegraphman repeated the orders and the hum of the main turbines took on a lower note as speed dropped. A few minutes later Shadde snapped, "Up periscope! Bearing is that! Range two thousand, seven hundred! Down periscope! I'm fifteen degrees on his starboard bow. Port twenty. Give me a course for a thirty track."

Behind Shadde a petty officer read off the bearings and called them to the third hand, who fed them into the attack computer. Within seconds Allistair reported, "Course one-eight-five, sir."

"Steer one-eight-five," from Shadde. The helmsman repeated the course. Then Shadde's voice again, cold, incisive. *"For exercise*—stand by all tubes." He added quickly, "What's the D.A.?"

Allistair was waiting for that. "D.A. Green Ten, sir."

Shadde had just repeated, "Green Ten," when there was a call on the engine-room telephone. An able seaman jumped forward to answer it, tripped against the coaming of a hatch and fell heavily. He tried to gather himself in a quick scrambling motion and slipped. He was a stocky man with a high color, and his exertions and embarrassment made him scarlet. Somewhere in the after end of the control room there was a titter of laughter, cut off by Shadde's furious "Down periscope! Break off the attack! Flood 'Q'! Hundred feet!"

There was the piercing hiss of compressed air escaping as the tank flooded, and in the control room the air pressure built up. Shadde left the periscope and looked quickly around the control room, his face contorted with anger. But there was no sign of the titterer; every man was absorbed in his duty as if nothing had happened, and the able seaman was at the telephone answering the call from the engine room.

The first lieutenant checked the submarine's dive at 100 feet; on the plot Symington noted the time—0750.

Shadde, still trembling with suppressed rage, increased speed to 15 knots and asked Symington for a course to pass south between Bornholm and the mainland. "Give me a least depth of twenty-five fathoms," he said through clenched teeth. Symington gave the course and Shadde ordered it to be steered. Then he turned to the first lieutenant. The shake in his voice betrayed his anger. "Remain closed up at diving stations. Plot inertial nav fixes every five minutes and run a continuous line of soundings. Report at once if the water shoals below twenty-five fathoms."

When he heard that, Cavan knew that the Captain intended to make life difficult. They would continue the passage submerged, comparatively close inshore and in water of no great depth; thus there was good reason for the navigational precautions. But this meant more work for more people, and no one realized that better than Shadde.

The helmsman reported that the submarine was steady on the new course. Shadde looked at the chart for a moment and then walked to the fore-end of the control room. He paused there and stood for a time in silence, legs apart, hands deep in the pockets of his monkey jacket, dark eyes glinting as he looked from one man to another. When he spoke, his voice was still angry. "We'll remain closed up at diving stations for a bit," he said. "Perhaps it'll remind those who need it that this isn't a Billy Butlin holiday camp." With a final glare he strode out of the control room.

When the Captain had gone Symington plotted the submarine's position on the chart and laid off the courses for the passage between Bornholm and the mainland, taking care they were within waters with a least depth of twenty-five fathoms. That done, he went to the W/T office. The chief P. O. telegraphist was writing up the W/T log.

"Hullo, Gracie."

"Morning, sir."

"Get that time signal?"

"Yes, sir."

"What's the error?"

"Still slow, sir." Gracie picked up the deck watch. "Here's the slip, sir. Twenty-six seconds slow."

Symington took the watch, put the slip in the box and snapped the lid shut. "Thanks." Cautiously he looked into the control room to see if Shadde was back. Then he put the deck watch down and leaned against the bulkhead. He smiled at Gracie in a faintly apologetic manner.

"Something rather unpleasant I must tell you." He paused.

Gracie looked up. "Something unpleasant, sir?"

"The Captain thinks we're too friendly."

"Too friendly? What's he mean?"

Symington told him of Shadde's outburst before the first lieutenant and the Doctor at Skansen.

"But where's the harm in you talking to me and Springer?"

"Probably it's not that. I was tactless." He hesitated. "Leaving his table when he was holding forth, not going straight back."

Gracie frowned. "Captain's always been good to me, sir. I think a lot of him. But—" He shook his head. "Don't like to say it, sir, but he's carried on a bit strange these last few weeks. Like that row in the control room just now. Just because somebody laughed at Purdoe. And now keeping us closed up at diving stations. Doesn't seem right. I suppose he's a lot on his mind. The collision and all that." He thought for a moment. "But surely it's not a crime to be friendly. You and me, I mean?"

Symington's embarrassment showed. "It's a bit more than that. Sounds incredible"—he laughed dryly—"but the Captain thinks our getting together now and then on photography is something else."

Gracie's brown eyes widened. "Something else? I don't follow."

Symington repeated what Cavan had told him of the Captain's suspicions.

When he got to his cabin Shadde rang for the messenger.

"Tell the first lieutenant I want to see him."

"Aye, aye, sir." The messenger went out, shutting the door carefully. He was sorry for the first lieutenant. The skipper was in one hell of a mood.

"You sent for me, sir?"

83

Shadde swung around. "Yes, I did. Shut that door."

The veins on Shadde's forehead were standing out, and in the long silence that followed Cavan watched them rather than meet the uncomfortable stare of the black eyes. When Shadde spoke, the words tumbled out angrily. "Fine bloody performance, wasn't it? Musical comedy. Or the Marx brothers, shall we say?"

Cavan thought, I'll say nothing. Let him talk. Anything can happen in this mood. Keep my yardarm clear.

Shadde glared, his mouth working. "So now we've reached the stage where I'm not permitted to carry out an exercise in my own submarine without the whole thing being treated as a lark. Ratings barging into each other. Able seamen falling flat on their faces. Titters from the bloody audience. The whole thing's a great joke, of course—the very idea that the Captain should want to exercise a torpedo attack. Wonder you're able to stand there without splitting your sides, it's so damned funny."

The first lieutenant's silence angered Shadde. "Told you yesterday what I thought of the discipline in this boat," he said thickly. "Now you know. I wasn't exaggerating. It's not bad—it's bloody bad! What d'you think this bunch'd be like in the real thing if they giggle like a lot of sloppy schoolgirls because a sailor slips and falls?" The dark eyes blazed and the fists were clenched, the flesh white and straining over the knuckles. "Well, what have you to say? You're the first lieutenant. You're supposed to run this boat. You'd better do something about it, instead of just standing there."

He's trying to bait me, the first lieutenant thought. Getting as near to insult as he can. Wants me to argue. Nothing he'd like better. Seen him in these moods before. Nothing quite like this, though. He's working up for something. Never seen him in a rage quite like this. Look at those veins! And all because Purdoe tripped and somebody laughed. God, what a man! The first lieutenant bit deep into his lip. He wouldn't give Shadde the opportunity he was looking for. He'd take this tirade. But though he didn't know it, his face was white with humiliation and resentment.

Shadde was pacing now; short jerky steps up and down the cabin, hands clenched behind his back, head stooped forward. The farthest he could go in one direction was twelve feet, so he would take a few paces one way and then turn abruptly and pace the other. Cavan thought he looked like something in a cage.

"And for a start," Shadde went on, darting a sideways glance at Cavan, "take a look at our late lamented exercise. Forty-nine seconds to make an emergency dive. Forty-nine seconds! For Christ's sake, who ever heard of a submarine taking that for a crash dive?" Now he stopped pacing and stared at the first lieutenant. "All that noise and chatter when we were closing up. Like a lot of bloody women at the market place. But that's not all. Oh, no! Asinine laughter in the middle of the attack." His voice rose in derision. "In the middle of an attack! Ye gods! In my boat." He started pacing again.

The first lieutenant knew that all this was wild exaggeration. The dive hadn't taken anything like forty-nine seconds, and there had been nothing wrong with the exercise except for the snigger of laughter when Purdoe fell. Even that was understandable—no harm in it. Nothing had happened to justify Shadde's frenzied anger. But he wasn't going to argue with the Captain. He said quietly, "I'll try and find out who laughed, sir."

"Try and find out," snorted Shadde. "You bloody well *will* find out, you mean." From under shaggy eyebrows he glared at the first lieutenant. "If that sort of thing ever happens again—" He stopped as if he'd forgotten something. "Now you can order patrol routine, except for those in

85

the control room. They can remain closed up until I give the word. It'll give them time to reflect that this submarine's not the huge bloody joke they think it is."

Cavan looked at the mole to the right of the cleft chin. It seemed bigger, more menacing than usual. "Is that all, sir?"

Shadde turned away, but his jaw muscles were working. Why couldn't this oaf of a first lieutenant look you straight in the face? "Yes, that is all. You may go."

He turned his back and started pacing again.

‖ 7 ‖

During the morning, *Retaliate* continued to the southwest making good 20 knots and maintaining a depth of 100 feet. At ten o'clock watch diving routine was resumed and on Shadde's orders the men in the control room, still closed up at diving stations, were told to secure. At half past ten, when the submarine was entering the waters between Hammaren and Bornholm, Kyle appeared before the Captain as a defaulter.

Earlier in the forenoon Shadde had asked Mr. Buddington about the weight of evidence linking Kyle with the sabotage attempt.

"There is no evidence, Captain," said Mr. Buddington in his mild, precise voice.

Shadde frowned, and the little man continued. "All that has been suggested against Kyle is either hearsay or circumstantial." He cleared his throat. "And what in fact does it amount to? That he was one of the three men who worked on the steering gear the day before sailing. That

87

Shepherd says he's got a chip on his shoulder. That he's unpopular in his mess and antisocial. He's also been heard to say he'd like to 'fix' Shepherd and this submarine." He paused. "Apparently he dislikes Shepherd, who he believes has got it in for him."

Shadde looked up. "You've learned quite a lot in your short time on board, haven't you?"

Mr. Buddington didn't know whether this was sarcasm or a compliment.

Shadde went on. "But there are one or two other points you might consider. For example, he's a stoker—or engineering mechanic if you like. He had access to the steering compartment. The other incidents involved our machinery. He could get at it, and he's got the know-how."

Mr. Buddington nodded politely. "So have forty or fifty other men on board, Captain."

"And," Shadde went on doggedly, "he was ashore at the time the steering jammed."

"That fact may yet prove that he had nothing to do with the steering trouble."

"What d'you mean?" Shadde looked up from under shaggy eyebrows, unbelieving.

"I'd prefer not to say at the moment."

Shadde shrugged his shoulders. "I've a hunch you're wrong, Mr. Buddington. But we'll see. Anyway, if it's not him, who d'you suspect?"

In his chair the little man raised a knee and clasped his hands around it. "I'm not a detective, Captain," he said apologetically. "I'm a civilian investigator on the staff of D.N.I. I try to avoid suspecting anyone. It destroys objectivity. Throws you off the scent, as it were." He rubbed the side of his nose with his forefinger, and the watery little eyes moved away from Shadde's challenging stare. "It's my job to observe, inquire and sift. That's the only way to solve a problem."

"Well, you haven't solved this one," retorted Shadde.

"Dear me! Perhaps I sounded rather boastful. I should have said 'try to solve.' You see, I sometimes fail."

Shadde regarded him coldly. "Yes . . . I imagine you do." He got up. "Mind if I make a suggestion?"

"Not at all."

"Find the owner of the gray silk and you've got your man."

Mr. Buddington regarded the Captain thoughtfully. "Perhaps," he said gently. "Perhaps."

When Shadde got to the control room, he went immediately to the small table at which the ritual of Captain's Defaulters was to be performed. Behind him and to one side stood the first lieutenant, the engineer officer, the doctor and Allistair, who had been duty officer when P.O. Farrell brought Kyle back on board. In front of Shadde, and to his left, stood Farrell, dapper and birdlike, his darting brown eyes never still.

The coxswain called the prisoner to the table. "Off caps!" he snapped, and Kyle removed his cap. Warily Shadde examined the pale, drawn face, the erupted skin and the dark rebellious eyes. There was a large bandage over the stoker's temple and above it, where smudges of mercurochrome showed, the hair had been cut away. He was a slight, forlorn figure.

The coxswain got on with the serious business of naval discipline. The words cracked out of his mouth in short sharp bursts like machine-gun fire, as he read from the charge sheet.

"Engineering Mechanic First Class Ernest Kyle, sir. One: that he conducted himself to the prejudice of good order and naval discipline in that he did on the eighth day of May, while the submarine was in Stockholm, remain ashore absent without leave from twenty-four hundred to seventeen thirty-five on the following day and did thereby miss his ship on sailing." The coxswain paused to look at Kyle with a baleful glare, then sucked his teeth and went on reading. "Two: that he conducted himself to the prejudice of good order and naval discipline in that he behaved ashore in a drunken and a disorderly fashion, leading to his apprehension and detention by the Swedish police, from whom his person was received by Petty Officer Farrell of the patrol at seventeen thirty-five on the ninth day of May."

Petty Officer Farrell then gave evidence of finding Kyle ashore. He was followed by Lieutenant Allistair who testified to Kyle's return on board. Finally, the Doctor reported on Kyle's injuries.

Standing behind the defaulters' table with his legs wide apart, Shadde looked bigger than ever in the confined space of the control room. His hands were thrust into the pockets of his monkey jacket and he leaned forward, shoulders hunched, dark eyes peering from under bushy eyebrows. He seemed to transfix the young stoker with that stare.

"Well, Kyle," he said, "What've you to say?"

The young man looked away and remained silent.

"Come on, Kyle, I'm waiting for your explanation."

"Sir, it wouldn't be no good if I did tell you. Nobody'll believe me anyhow."

"I'll decide that for myself, Kyle—when I've heard your story. Now what is it?"

In short, disjointed sentences Kyle told the story of his experiences ashore in Stockholm, skipping as delicately as he could over the events in Ingrid's apartment. When he had finished he fixed his eyes on an imaginary point somewhere over Shadde's left shoulder and gazed at it blankly.

Shadde looked at him with a puzzled frown. "Kyle," he said, "why do you forage about ashore on your own?

Why don't you keep with your messmates? An English sailor alone in a foreign port is always fair game. You've been in the service long enough to know that."

Kyle was silent. He continued to gaze into space with a blank, expressionless face.

Shadde didn't repeat the question. He turned to the engineer officer. "Lieutenant Commander Evans. This man is in your department. What can you tell me about him?"

Rhys Evans' kind, open face was distressed. "Indeed, he's a good man, sir. Diligent at his work and reliable."

Shadde gave the engineer officer a shrewd, comprehending glance. Dear old Chiefy, he thought, he's a heart of gold. Always puts in a good word for any of his people in trouble. But he doesn't understand what he's up against in Kyle. Then Shadde's eyes met the Doctor's. He knew at once what O'Shea was thinking, He needs help, not punishment. The recollection made Shadde's mind shut with a snap. This was the third time in six months that Kyle had been before him. That sort of thing didn't happen in submarines. He wasn't going to be influenced by any damned doctor dressed up in uniform. He wouldn't let any psychiatric humbug seduce him away from the sound and well-tried tenets of naval discipline. It was a system of discipline with centuries of tradition and experience behind it. The discipline of Drake and of Raleigh and of Nelson and his captains. A system which was a part of Shadde himself. In that moment he knew that what *Retaliate* needed was more discipline and less psychology. Kyle had not only been absent without leave, he'd missed his ship. That was a serious offense. What if Kyle's story was a pack of lies? What if it were desertion? A ruse to be out of *Retaliate* when the steering jammed? Let Buddington say what he liked. The whole thing was damned suspicious. Nasty smell about it. He was impressed by Shepherd's view. Shepherd knew Kyle a lot better than Buddington did. The young stoker was just the sort of little mixed-up type who might try his hand at sabotage. When they got back to their base at Fort Blockhouse, Kyle must be drafted ashore, whatever happened; it was dangerous to keep a man like him on board. In the meantime an example must be made of him.

Shadde looked hard at the stoker. "Kyle, you must pull yourself together. You come before me too often. There's no place in submarines for men who are not amenable to naval discipline. Men who don't know how to behave themselves ashore, particularly in a foreign country. If this sort of thing happens again you'll find yourself in serious trouble. As it is, I'm going to stop your leave for twenty-eight days."

Kyle's lower lip trembled. He knew the submarine would be back in Portsmouth within a week. He would still have another three weeks' stoppage of leave to go. That meant he wouldn't get the leave he and Mum had planned to spend together. As he contemplated the ruination of his plans and the bitterness of his mother's disappointment, his eyes filled with tears. But he said nothing.

"On caps! About turn! Double march!" snapped the coxswain. Ernie Kyle returned his cap to his head smartly, turned about and marched from the control room.

Later in the forenoon, Mr. Buddington handed Shadde a signal addressed to the Director of Naval Intelligence. It was in a private code which the little man had brought with him to *Retaliate*. Shadde promised to have the signal sent soon after midday, when *Retaliate* would go to periscope depth to transmit her noon position to the Flag Officer Submarines.

From the Captain's cabin Mr. Buddington went to see the Doctor. O'Shea was sitting at a desk writing. He smiled and put the pen down. "Hullo, Mr. B. Come in. You a patient, or is this social?"

"Oh, no," said Mr. Buddington apologetically, "not a patient."

"Well, sit down anyway."

Mr. Buddington sat down rather stiffly on the edge of the chair, hands folded on his lap, watery eyes blinking at the Doctor. There was a long pause. He cleared his throat. "Just came in for a chat," he explained. "Everybody seems busy or asleep."

"Yes, it's like that at sea."

"Very still now we've submerged, isn't it?"

"Great advantage of a submarine. You escape from the weather."

"Yes, quite." Mr. Buddington gazed absent-mindedly around the Doctor's cabin. "Hear you had a jolly party at Skansen the other night."

"Wasn't bad."

"I heard how you got a table." Mr. Buddington was looking at the titles of the books on the shelf near him.

The Doctor showed surprise. "You mean speaking Russian?"

"Yes. The headwaiter must have been furious afterwards. When he found you were all English."

The Doctor laughed. "Possibly. I was surprised it worked. My Russian's not awfully good nowadays."

Mr. Buddington scratched the side of his nose and watched the Doctor carefully. "It was good once, was it, Doctor?"

The Doctor looked up suddenly as if he were seeing Mr. Buddington for the first time. "My mother was Russian. She taught us to speak it. She hoped we'd visit Russia one day and meet her relations."

Mr. Buddington looked casually at his shoes and then

past the Doctor to the bookshelf. "Very interesting. When did she leave Russia?"

"She didn't. She'd never been there. Her parents were White Russians in exile. She was born in London."

"Does she live there now?"

"No. She died when we were children."

There was an awkward pause until the Doctor changed the subject. "Tell me, Mr. B., how are your investigations getting on?"

Mr. Buddington started. "My investigations, Doctor?"

"Yes. Air conditioning. Made any progress?"

"Ah, yes, of course. Yes, indeed. I started on them yesterday. Slow business, you know. Matter of collecting data just now. By the time we get to Portsmouth I'll have made some progress, I daresay."

"Complex subject—air conditioning?"

"Oh, very." Mr. Buddington's voice rang with conviction. "But interesting," he added, "most interesting."

"I'm sure it is," agreed O'Shea.

Mr. Buddington got up. "Thank you for the chat, Doctor." He smiled bleakly. "I must go along now. Lots to do, you know."

In his cabin Mr. Buddington took a notebook and the black leather box from the wardrobe. He opened the box and fingered the thermometers and hygrometers. Must get used to these, he thought. He opened the notebook and practiced entering temperature and humidity readings. Its previous owner had been very painstaking; the formulae, technical notes and sketches had been done with almost extravagant neatness. For a few minutes he looked through the air-conditioning manual. Must avoid technical discussions. The less you say, the more they think you know. Look wise, occasional nod or shake of the head, but keep your trap shut; that's the way to do it. He spent the next half-hour placing the test thermometers and hygrometers in the fore-ends, in the seamen's messdeck and in the reactor control room. Then he went to the missile attack center and read temperatures and humidities there, entering them in the notebook. Before leaving he took a pair of test instruments out of the black box and exchanged them with those on the bulkhead. Back in his cabin he hung the attack center set next to another test panel. Then he entered the readings in the notebook and wrote against them, "13/5/ 64—1052—panels in missile attack center removed for calibration."

Mr. Buddington's next move was to see the Captain again. He said he wanted to visit the victualing store and asked where he could get the key. It was important, he explained, that it should not be known that he was going there. When Shadde asked why, Mr. Buddington said he thought the store might yield some evidence. Among other things he would "test" temperature and humidity there, but he preferred at that stage to say no more.

Shadde respected this reticence, and an hour later the key was in Mr. Buddington's possession.

Shortly before noon Shadde invited the engineer officer to his cabin for a chat over a glass of sherry. The Captain seldom drank at sea, but occasionally he took a glass of sherry before lunch. Officially, he had sent for Rhys Evans to discuss the submarine's coming refit in Portsmouth; unofficially, because he was depressed and in need of company. Of his eleven officers, the only man he regarded as a friend was the Welshman.

They discussed various details of the refit, and then Shadde changed the subject to complain about events in the control room during the torpedo exercise earlier in the forenoon.

"It's damned serious you know, Chiefy. The discipline in this boat's bloody awful."

Rhys Evans cocked his head on one side. "Oh! Look here now. It's not that bad, sir. You're worrying too much these days. A good rest you need."

Shadde frowned and then with surprising vehemence said, "It *is* bad, Chiefy—it's bloody bad! I'm not exaggerating. This boat's not the fighting unit she should be. For one thing, too many of the officers are new."

"They'll be a good lot yet, sir."

"I doubt it. Look at that exercise. Absolute shambles."

"Do you really think it was so bad?"

"Bad!" snorted Shadde. "It was bloody awful." He leaned back wearily in the chair. "Trouble with a long peace. You can't get the crew to take things seriously. Everything's a ruddy exercise. They treat it all as a lark."

With a shock Rhys Evans noticed that Shadde's hair was beginning to go gray at the sides. He saw the Captain, almost daily, and yet this was the first time he'd noticed it.

"Yes," Shadde went on. "All a ruddy joke. Like playing charades. None of them believes the real thing will ever happen."

Rhys Evans held his sherry up to the light and examined it carefully, a habit he had learned from the Captain. "I'm not surprised at that."

Shadde shrugged his shoulders. "So even you don't take it seriously, Chiefy."

"Difficult thing to take seriously just now."

"I know. That's the danger. That's my problem. On the bridge this morning Number One said he couldn't believe we'd ever use *Retaliate* in earnest. The first lieutenant of this boat! See now what I mean? How dangerous it is. Like Pearl Harbor. It-can't-happen-to-us sort of idea." Shadde put the glass of sherry down and leaned forward, hands on knees, shoulders hunched. Intently, he searched the engineer officer's face. "Know what I think, Chiefy?"

"No, what's that?"

"*Retaliate will* be used one day—when we least expect it." He spoke slowly and with such earnestness that Rhys Evans was taken aback.

"Indeed, I'd be surprised," he said rather lamely.

If Shadde heard the remark he ignored it. Peering at the Welshman he said: "Yes, she'll be used. And d'you know what worries me?"

"Be the end of everything?"

Shadde frowned. "No, not that," he said irritably. "I'm afraid that unless our discipline bucks up, you'll find that when we're needed there'll be a ruddy argument. Probably find half the crew are ban-the-bomb rabble."

Embarrassed by the Captain's vehemence the engineer officer sipped at his sherry. Shadde frowned at him with bushy eyebrows. "Yes! And the Doctor'll explain that we're badly adjusted and need compensating."

Rhys Evans laughed, a small forced laugh. "You're joking, sir."

"By God, I'm not," said Shadde. "It's the last thing I'd ever joke about. Too bloody serious for that."

They sat in silence for some time, Shadde morose, distant, deeply engrossed. The Welshman decided to change the subject.

"You'll be taking leave in Portsmouth, sir?"

Shadde looked up gloomily. "Yes, I suppose so."

"Taking the little lady motoring in France, didn't you say?"

Shadde got up and made much of putting a book onto the bookshelf. "I don't think so," he said.

"Changed your plans, sir?"

"I haven't any plans."

"But only the other day you told me of them."

To Rhys Evans' astonishment Shadde turned around suddenly and barked, "Oh! For Christ's sake, stop prying into my private life." Anger blazed from his eyes; but then

97

he must have seen the look of hurt and astonishment on the Welshman's face, because he said thickly, "Sorry, Chiefy . . . point is . . . may not have a wife soon."

Rhys Evans' voice was full of anxiety. "She's not ill?"

Shadde looked away. "No, she's not ill." There was a long pause. "Perfectly well, as far as I know. She wants to leave me. That's all." Then his mouth shut in that final, implacable way and Rhys Evans knew the conversation was at an end. Shadde slid the door open, his eyes away from the engineer officer. "Well, Chiefy, I've work to do. See you later."

Rhys Evans said, "Aye, aye, sir," and his voice was sad. He was shocked. An old friend of Shadde's, he had often met his wife but never got to know her—probably because of her thinly veiled hostility which he attributed to social differences. It had never occurred to him that the Shaddes were anything but happily married. It was beyond his comprehension that a man of Shadde's character and authority could be a victim of anything so untidy as marital trouble. But he knew from Shadde's sudden outburst that the trouble must be pretty serious.

In the privacy of his cabin, Mr. Buddington was going through the personnel records of several members of *Retaliate*'s crew. After making some cryptic notes on a writing pad he put the papers away and transferred his attention to the piece of gray silk, which he examined with minute care. When he heard seven bells strike over the broadcast, he sighed deeply and locked away the papers and the silk. Once more he tried to interest himself in the manual on air-conditioning, but it was a deadly dull subject. That morning he had discussed a defect in the air-washing plant with Springer and Shepherd, and he recalled with embarrassment the polite lift of their eyebrows when he couldn't answer a comparatively simple question. Mr. Buddington hoped he'd covered up his blunder, but he didn't want the same sort of thing to happen again.

At five minutes to twelve he put the book down and went to the wardroom.

In the early afternoon *Retaliate* surfaced off Cape Arkona on the Pommern coast. A surfacing signal was made to the Admiralty and repeated to *Massive* in Göteborg. Then Shadde ordered a course of 262 degrees, speed 18 knots. During the forenoon the southwesterly wind had veered to the west, and the sky was heavily overcast. Frequent rain squalls reduced visibility to a few miles, and the wind across the north-going stream had piled up a short, confused sea which often broke over the submarine. The watch-keepers on the bridge were soon drenched. The motion was distinctly uncomfortable and at 1330, much to the relief of the crew, Shadde reduced speed to 12 knots.

Because of her deep draught Shadde deemed it inadvisable for *Retaliate* to approach Copenhagen from the south through the sound, and although they were now within seventy miles of their destination he set course for the west-about passage by way of the Great Belt, where a least depth of seven fathoms could be carried through, although a journey of some two hundred twenty sea miles was entailed.

For the first time in a long while, Shadde had fallen into a deep sleep; after a late lunch he had got onto his bunk fully dressed and dozed off. An hour later he stirred uneasily, wakened by an unfamiliar sound. He lay very still trying to sort things out. The clock on the bulkhead showed ten minutes past three; he had left the bridge more than an hour before. He rubbed his eyes and looked at the course and speed tell-tales, and then he heard the noise again. Faintly, from afar, the whine of a saxophone, and twined around that the husky voice of a woman crooning—so that's what had awakened him. Sodden with sleep his first thought was that there must be a party in the wardroom and women on board. Then the rolling and pitching of *Retaliate* reminded him they were at sea. Propped up on one elbow he listened intently; a man was singing now.

Suddenly he realized that the sound was coming from the wardroom and he stiffened with anger. It was forbidden to use the radiogram at sea except in the dogwatches. There wasn't an officer in *Retaliate* who didn't know this—and whoever was playing the radiogram knew it, for the volume was down. With a heave of his large body he was off the bunk and at the door, looking into the wardroom. But the only person visible was O'Shea, asleep in an easy chair; the radiogram was shut and the music wasn't coming from there.

Shadde went back to his desk and rang for the messenger. "Beneath this sky, for you, My love, I'll die, I'll die," the singer wailed; and the saxophone and a guitar echoed the misery. Waiting for the messenger, Shadde's anger began to choke up inside him. Whoever was responsible for this outrage would bloody soon regret it, but that such a thing could happen confirmed his belief that discipline in the submarine was crumbling. Back against the bunk, elbows on the bunk-board, he stood waiting like a boxer in the corner standing by for the gong. The long fingers were flexing, and the big head was thrust forward.

When the messenger arrived Shadde spoke with exaggerated calm, determined to keep a rein on himself. "Find out who is responsible for that—that filthy noise. Tell him to see me at once."

The able seaman stood still, puzzled, listening, his head on one side. "Mean the music, sir?"

Shadde's eyes bulged. "What the bloody hell else d'you think I mean?"

With a startled, "Aye, aye, sir," the young man fled from the cabin.

"Come back my heart, the spring is——" the husky crooner pleaded, and then suddenly, dramatically, she stopped. The messenger had delivered his message.

There was a knock on Shadde's door and Dwight Gallagher came in. "Understand you sent for me, Captain."

It had never occurred to Shadde that the heavy, gray-faced American could be responsible for this act of insubordination. He set his teeth and glared at Gallagher.

"Were you responsible for that filthy noise?" In spite of his attempt at calmness, he knew that his voice was giving him away.

Gallagher looked at him coolly. "D'you mean my record player, Captain?"

For a moment Shadde looked as if he would like to strike the American; then he turned away. "You've been in this boat for two months, Gallagher. I'd have thought you'd know by now that that sort of thing's forbidden except in the dogwatches."

"I know the wardroom radiogram can only be used in the dogwatches. This was in my cabin, not the wardroom." He smiled. "I was trying out a little transistorized job I bought in Stockholm. Had my door shut. Could you hear it in your cabin, Captain?"

Shadde struggled with his rage, standing still and tensed, the veins at his temples swollen.

Gallagher saw the signs and spread out his hands in a gesture of apology. "Certainly sorry if I disturbed you, Captain. Seems it was doing a better job on volume than I imagined."

This was too much for Shadde. "Look here, Gallagher," he choked, "I didn't send for you to discuss your——your bloody transistor or whatever it is. I——" He hesitated. "Understand this. While you serve in this boat you'll kindly observe the customs of the Royal Navy. One of them is consideration for men off watch." With an angry gesture he waved the American out of the cabin. As Gallagher went, Shadde added, "That may seem unnecessary in the United States Navy, but we attach some importance to it here." He slammed the door shut, and still trembling with rage he went back to the bunk.

But sleep wouldn't return. There was too much to think about now. Weary and exhausted, he lay there fighting with himself until his head ached to bursting. Then he went to the cupboard above the wash basin, filled the glass with water and washed down some of the white pills Elizabeth had given him when she first heard of his temple-splitting headaches. He started a letter to Elizabeth. He wrote two or three paragraphs, read them through and then tore them up with an exclamation of annoyance. For a few minutes he gazed moodily at the cabin bulkhead, then put his elbows on the desk and buried his face in his hands. For nearly ten minutes he sat like that. After long thought he decided to send for the chief petty officer telegraphist. When Gracie arrived, Shadde said, "Come in, Gracie. Close that door." He pointed to a chair. "Sit down."

Gracie was surprised. Never before had he been invited to sit down in the Captain's cabin. When he'd heard that Shadde wanted to see him he had imagined it was about Symington. He wondered what the Captain wanted him for.

Shadde looked at Gracie in silence for some moments before speaking, then he said, "Gracie, I need your help."

The chief petty officer looked surprised. "Yes, sir," he said.

"I'm worried, Gracie. This submarine isn't the efficient fighting unit she should be." The shaggy eyebrows bunched together in a frown as he peered at the telegraphist.

"What's wrong, then, sir?"

"A great deal," said Shadde darkly. "A great deal. That exercise this morning, for example. Trouble with a long peace is that everything's an exercise and the crew knows it. No reality. Nothing's taken seriously. Nobody believes this submarine'll ever fight. All a game." He shrugged his shoulders. "Result is we're damned slack. And that's dangerous."

Gracie wondered what on earth the Captain was leading up to. "How can I help, sir?"

Shadde smiled—a brief, mechanical smile. "I've a plan. That's why I sent for you. Gracie, we'll simulate the real thing. This ship's company's got to be shaken up in no mean fashion. It's got to be confronted suddenly with the real thing." He got up and leaned against the wardrobe. "Of course, it won't be, but they won't know that until after the exercise."

"Where do I come in, sir?"

Shadde's eyes narrowed. "You're going to receive two or three important W/T signals."

"Where from, sir?"

Shadde smiled again, humorlessly. "From you."

"I don't follow, sir."

"Simple. You'll transmit them and receive them."

"What sort of signals, sir?"

"Operational signals."

Gracie was bewildered. "Operational, sir?"

"Haven't worked out the details yet. Starting point might be a signal from Flag Officer Submarines ordering *Retaliate* to a certain position at a certain time."

"And then, sir?"

Shadde pursed his lips and placed the tips of his fingers together. "Then? Well, I don't quite know. Haven't made up my mind yet. Next signal might order us to adopt the first degree of missile readiness. That'd seem pretty realistic, wouldn't it?"

Gracie shook his head. "Couldn't do that, sir. It'd be top secret. Come in a cipher I don't know. Have to go to Mr. Keely for deciphering."

"Quite," said Shadde. "That presents no problem then, does it? I'll encipher the signals myself, and hand 'em to you for transmission." He ran his fingers through his dark hair and frowned. "Tell me this, Gracie: can you transmit a signal and simultaneously receive it through one of our receivers? So that the message comes in this end through the teletyper? You know, all the appearances of authenticity?"

Gracie thought for a moment. "Couldn't use the H.F., M.F. or L.F. channels, sir. Admiralty and other ships would read if I did." He frowned. "Don't see how it could be done, sir—unless . . ."

"Unless what, Gracie?"

"Unless I used the automatic transmitter. Put the message onto the tape first, feed it in and then let it transmit," he paused.

"On what frequency?" asked Shadde, lowering himself into the easy chair.

"No frequency, sir. I wouldn't actually transmit."

"I don't get you, Gracie."

"I'd close the circuit, sir. Feed the tape into the transmitter, and switch it on to transmit direct into the teleprinter. We do that when we check a punched tape against the original message. Signal would come out of the teleprinter just the same as if we'd been reading the Admiralty or any other station."

Shadde rubbed his hands together and beamed. "Capital, Gracie, capital! I thought you'd have the answer."

Gracie showed no signs of enthusiasm. Mournfully he said, "When d'you want this, sir?"

"Haven't yet decided," said Shadde. "But if and when I do, I'll let you know well in advance."

Gracie sensed from the Captain's tone that the interview was over. He got up. "Is that all, sir?"

"Not quite." Shadde fixed his dark eyes intently on the young man. "Gracie," he said, "absolute secrecy. D'you understand? *Absolute secrecy*. Not a word to anyone. Whole idea is surprise. Only surprise will create the atmosphere of the real thing. Not a word to anyone. You understand that, don't you, Gracie?"

"Yes, sir."

Shadde's eyes bored into him hypnotically. "Gracie," he said slowly, "I'm going to take you further into my confidence. There's a reason why secrecy is essential." His manner was conspiratorial as he waited for the words to sink in. "We've a saboteur on board. That collision. The jammed steering. Under certain conditions he'll give himself away. Don't ask me why. Have confidence in my judgment. D'you understand?"

"Yes, sir."

"Thank you, Gracie."

It must have been the discussion in the wardroom about marriage, or perhaps the tall dark girl at the Solliden restaurant. Something had triggered off the chain of thought. Lately he'd been thinking of Susan more often. And yet it was all years ago now—four, five; he couldn't remember exactly. Cavan turned uneasily in his bunk. He couldn't understand why he had such a conscience about her; it had only been a shipboard affair. Not his fault that she'd taken it so seriously. After all, they had only known each other for three weeks, as long as it took the mailboat from Durban down to Capetown and then on to Southampton. Anyway, she was married, and he was pretty certain it wasn't her first affair, although she swore it was. But that was a sort of technique women employed; they were always so anxious to convince you that it was the first time that anything of that sort had ever happened—probably to make you feel more responsible.

The night before Madeira they'd been dancing and then they went to the boat deck. But it was too cold there and after a bit she started to shiver. "It's freezing, Bengy," she said. "What time is it?"

His arms were around her and his nose was in her hair. "Four bells," he mumbled.

"What's that in proper time?"

"Two o'clock, my sweet."

She pushed him away and got up. "Come on, let's go." They went down below and he escorted her along the alleyway to her cabin. Then he followed her into the cabin and locked the door in spite of her protests. But they hadn't been very urgent protests, and anyway it couldn't have been a surprise to her, because he'd been threatening to do this for the last three nights. The only thing that had stopped him earlier had been the fear of being seen; but even that had not deterred him this night. Besides, it was very late and most unlikely that anybody would be about. He realized he'd have to be careful, however; there was an Admiral's wife on board, and if that sort of thing got about it wouldn't do him any good.

That was the night Susan told him how unhappily married she was; her husband was a good deal older and drank heavily. She was making the voyage to get away from him and think things over. Apparently the husband was devoted to her and wouldn't hear of a divorce, although there were no children. She hoped that when she got back things might improve, because her decision to go off on her own had shocked him and he had promised to pull himself together. It seemed she had ample means of her own and so her problem was not a financial one.

It was always at this stage of his recollection that Cavan

recalled uneasily the mistake he had made on that night. He knew that it was at the bottom of his uneasy conscience. In the darkness of the cabin she had clung to him and whispered, "Oh, darling, if only I had you always." And then like a chump he had said, "If ever you're free, Susan, you've only got to lift your little finger and you *will* have me always."

There was a moment's silence, and then she whispered, "D'you really love me, Bengy?"

"Of course I do," he replied thickly, his hands searching her body.

"Enough to marry me?"

"Of course. I'd be honored to be your husband." He thought it rather fine at the time, the way he'd said that. And obviously she had too, because she had held him even more tightly.

But that had been the trouble, all right. No doubt about it. It had been a stupid thing to do and he could never forgive himself for it. Ever since he'd gone to Dartmouth he had followed his father's advice religiously. "Always keep your yardarm clear, my boy, if you want to get on in the service."

He had not realized then exactly what that meant, but as the years went on he had understood and appreciated what wonderfully sound advice it was. He had seen what had happened to others who had not kept their yardarms clear, and he had seen himself forging ahead, one success after another, on the road to his ultimate goal of flag rank. Of one thing he was certain: it wouldn't be for want of trying if he didn't end up as Admiral Sir Benjamin Cavan. Once or twice he wrote it out to see what it looked like, and he had to admit that it looked good, very good indeed. But he always tore the scrap of paper into small pieces; that in itself was a part of keeping your yardarm clear.

But now, this afternoon, resting in his cabin in *Retaliate* and thinking about Susan, he realized what a near thing it had been and what an embarrassing situation he had landed himself in, all because for once he'd failed to keep his yard-arm clear.

Five months after that voyage a letter had arrived from her to say that she was now a free woman; after the voyage she had decided not to go back to her husband, "because I'd met you, Bengy. I couldn't after that," and he had eventually agreed to a divorce and really treated her rather well.

Cavan remembered his shock as he read the letter and the unambiguous ending, ". . . and so, Bengy darling, I'm yours for the asking."

For a week he groped with the problem, searching desperately for the answer. One half of him wanted to write back an ecstatic letter telling her to pack her bags and come; the other, the "keep your yardarm clear" half, said "no, you fool!" Again and again he martialed the facts, the pros and the cons. Studiously, thoroughly, he weighed the arguments as if he were preparing an appreciation of the situation for high naval authority.

The pros were pretty substantial, he thought. Susan was good-looking, she dressed well, she had an attractive personality, and last but not least, she had money of her own —a good deal, as far as he was able to judge. She was the right age and she seemed to get on well with people. These were all important considerations in a woman who might one day be the Commander in Chief's wife.

But then the cons had to be considered. There were really only two, but they were supremely important. Susan was divorced, and a divorcée was not the best choice of wife for an ambitious naval officer; indeed, divorce was a bar sinister. It was frowned on at the Palace and Their Lordships didn't like it, and that was surely enough. The other point that nagged at Benjamin Cavan was Susan's accent. There was something funny about it; of course, it could be excused on the grounds that she was a South African, but it would have been better if she'd not had it at all. He somehow couldn't imagine a C-in-C's wife talking that way.

It was these pros and cons which he assembled and re-assembled, marched and paraded unceasingly during that very difficult week of decision. At last, sadly and with a heavy heart, he had to acknowledge that the cons had carried the day; he was sad about it, because he was genuinely fond of Susan and he had a nasty feeling that she might think he was letting her down. He salved his conscience on this score, however, by reminding himself that she had placed him in a most invidious position by taking a shipboard affair too seriously. Nonetheless, the incident had served its purpose, because he resolved never again to forget his father's advice.

Perhaps his greatest regret about the whole affair was that he couldn't forget it. Somehow or other things were always happening to remind him of it; and wherever he went he found himself looking at tall dark women and measuring them against Susan. At least he liked to think that he was measuring them against her. He was still a bachelor and it was a romantic notion, and not for a moment would he acknowledge that what was really happening was that a defense mechanism within him was constantly on guard against a surprise meeting with Susan. That would be highly embarrassing, he knew, because when at the end of the week of decision the result had gone against Susan he had not had the courage to answer her letter. Well, it wasn't so much a matter of courage, he supposed, as a desire to spare her the hurt of learning why he had decided they couldn't marry. So her letter had gone unanswered; and then a month later another one had turned up in which she assumed with touching sincerity that the first letter had gone astray. In the second letter she wrote that she was coming to England and gave an address there. Like its predecessor the letter went unanswered, and ten days later Cavan left for the Mediterranean, where he spent the next eighteen months.

He had not heard from Susan after that, though he never forgot her. Some time afterwards he heard a vague rumor that she had married again, "rather well." On hearing the news his first emotion had been chagrin that she had put him out of her life; he almost succeeded in persuading himself that she had let him down. But when he got over the ruffling of his dignity, he breathed a sigh of relief and concluded that her remarriage had absolved him from an embarrassing debt of honor. It never occurred to him that it was a debt he had long ago repudiated.

Down in the steering compartment Mr. Buddington was stretched out at full length on the steel deck. Lying on his back alongside the port ram assembly he was absorbed in watching the steering gear at work. He must have spent the best part of an hour there before he got up and went back to his cabin, the black leather box slung over his shoulder.

Then he collared the engineer officer, and in the course of half an hour of questions and answers he learned a great deal about the telemotor system. What was more, he got Rhys Evans to agree to help him carry out some practical tests in the steering compartment when they reached Copenhagen.

|| 8 ||

The ticking noise was first heard in the fore-ends during the dogwatches. Nobody was quite sure who heard it first, but it became known officially at 1920 when C.P.O. McPherson reported to the bridge. By then *Retaliate* had made the passage through Langeland Belt and was heading up towards Halsskov Head and the outer reaches of the Great Belt. The wind was still blowing from the northeast, but they were in the lee of Sjælland and there was no sea to speak of.

Weddy was on watch with Bagnall, the commissioned gunnery officer, and as soon as he heard the report he went to the voice-pipe and called the Captain to the bridge. Shadde was there in a trice with a gruff "What's the trouble?"

Weddy pointed to the chief petty officer. "McPherson's reported a ticking noise in the fore-ends, sir."

Shadde spun round on the C.P.O. "What sort of ticking noise?"

"Sort of faint noise, sir. Mechanical, I'd say."

"How d'you mean mechanical?"

"Seems to be very regular, sir."

Shadde frowned. "Tried to trace it?"

McPherson nodded. "Had a good look round, sir. Nothing to be seen. Seems right up in the bows. Very faint. Could be port or starboard, sir."

For a moment Shadde was lost in thought. Then he said, "I'd like to hear it for myself." He went towards the conning-tower hatch. "Come along, McPherson, I'll need you," he called over his shoulder.

When they got to the foreward torpedo compartment the men there stood to one side as Shadde and McPherson went up to the tubes.

"May take you awhile before you pick it up, sir," said McPherson. "It's a wee bit of a noise."

Shadde put his finger to his lips and they stood listening. Then, very faintly, as if from far away, he heard it; an unmistakable slow "tick" . . . "tick" . . . "tick." He looked at the second hand of his watch. The time interval was exactly three seconds. His face set grimly. "It's mechanical, all right."

For a moment he stood there puzzled, deep in thought, and then suddenly in a flash of intuition he knew that it was sabotage. Somewhere in the fore-ends there was an explosive device. Easy to guess why the fore-ends had been chosen: there were twelve torpedoes there. Shadde realized he must act quickly. There wasn't a second to spare. The ticking noise had evidently started about ten minutes ago; it was obviously some form of time clock.

He swung round to the men standing behind him. "Get aft to the control room! Shut those watertight doors behind you! At the double!" he barked. "Not you, McPherson. You stay here and lend me a hand. We'll make a search."

For the next ten minutes they worked feverishly; every conceivable nook and cranny in the compartment was searched thoroughly, and all the time in the background they could hear that ominous, scarcely audible tick. McPherson, a taciturn man by nature, confessed afterwards that in those ten minutes in the fore-ends with the watertight doors shut on them he felt "chilled to the marrow of ma' bones listening to that wee tick."

But the search yielded nothing, and because every minute counted Shadde and the C.P.O. lost no time in leaving the fore-ends, shutting the watertight doors behind them.

On reaching the control room the Captain ordered speed to be reduced to three knots, enough to maintain steerage way, and then he went to the broadcast and pressed the call button. "This is the Captain," he said in a hard, incisive voice. "Be ready to act quickly, and keep cool. There's an untraced ticking noise in the fore-ends. It's regular and mechanical. I propose to assume that it's something which threatens the safety of the submarine. There's no need for alarm. We're not far off the land and I intend making for Korsör. In the meantime all watertight doors forward of the control room are to be shut and all forward compartments are to be cleared. As many men as possible are to go up top and assemble on the after-casing, where they will be under the charge of Mr. Bagnall. All hands, repeat all hands, are to wear life belts. Those orders are to be executed at once. That is all. Carry on."

The Captain's broadcast was followed by a buzz of excitement throughout the submarine, and men started to stream into the control room from the forward compartments, pulling on their life belts as they went. From the control room they went up through the conning tower to the bridge and then aft to the casing.

Shadde went back to the bridge where he found that the first lieutenant had already joined the officer of the watch. Course was altered for Korsör harbor and signals were sent to the Flag Officer Submarines and to Danish naval headquarters in Copenhagen, giving *Retaliate*'s position and reporting tersely that there was reason to suspect that an explosive de-

113

vice somewhere in the submarine's bows might detonate at any moment, and that sabotage was suspected. All possible steps were being taken to deal with the situation and further reports would be made as soon as possible. The signal ended with a request that a tug be sent out from Korsör to stand by.

On Shadde's orders rubber dinghies were brought up from below and laid out on the fore- and after-casings ready for inflation. Allistair was sent off with McPherson to make another visit to the forward torpedo room to check if the ticking noise could still be heard, and to report whether the time interval between ticks had changed.

Shadde believed that the interval would have changed. An idea was beginning to take shape. Since the ticks could only be heard very faintly in the fore-ends, and yet were not coming from any object there, they must be coming from outside the hull. In other words, it was an external noise and not an internal one as he had first suspected. Something had probably been fixed to the bow of the submarine. He realized that it must have happened in Stockholm. When they were in dry dock numbers of Swedish workmen had been busy on the bow plating night and day. In fact, the work had been finished during the night. What could have been easier than for one of them to have stuck a limpet charge or something of that sort onto the bow well below the water line? The ticking noise was almost certainly an arming device. The intervals between ticks had been three seconds when the submarine was doing twelve knots. Now that she was steaming at three knots he would expect it to have lengthened. They would soon know. But time was precious, vital; it could be a matter of life and death. He looked at his watch; 1933—thirteen minutes since the noise had first been reported to the bridge.

Sunset's not until after 2030 and there's a long twilight after that, thought Shadde, and he thanked his stars that all this was not happening in darkness. The sky was overcast, but the wind had dropped and was now no more than a light breeze, though there was still a short, choppy sea which lapped at the hull and sprayed the men hunched together on the after-casing. To starboard he could just see Korsör and beyond that Halsskov Head. Symington was down in the control room, and through the voice-pipe Shadde asked him for the distance to Korsör. Almost immediately the reply came back, "Five point three miles, sir."

Now Shadde realized what a wise thing he had done in reducing speed. If there were an arming device in the bow, the faster the submarine traveled through the water, the quicker it would arm itself. He looked forward over the bridge screen and up along the casing. Somewhere there, under the water, he knew there was deadly danger. He had a mental picture of the limpet and he could see the propeller of the arming device, spinning in the surge of water, in all its detail. At any moment the bow might erupt in a blinding flash of light. He realized suddenly that the nails of his clenched fingers were cutting into the palms of his hands. With a conscious effort, he extended his fingers and started beating a tattoo with them on the bridge screen.

Cold beads of perspiration rolled down the back of his neck, down his forehead and the bridge of his nose and past his eyes. It annoyed him intensely that the first lieutenant, leaning against the bridge screen near him, should look so calm and unruffled, almost bored. But that was typical of him: oafish, unimaginative, stolid, probably not thinking any further than his bunk.

As a matter of fact, the first lieutenant was at that moment conceding to himself that he felt distinctly windy, but he had no intention of showing it. There was nothing he would like less than to be blown up or to find himself swimming for it in the cold waters of the Great Belt, but he was first lieutenant and he was determined to set an example of calmness. He began to wonder what chance the men below would have if the forward torpedo room went up in smoke, and he wondered too what chance he'd have on the bridge. Probably get the full blast of the explosion, which wasn't likely to do him any good. He wished he wasn't there and he wished that Shadde would stop that senseless drumming with his fingers. It was a habit which the first lieutenant found intensely irritating.

These thoughts were interrupted by the return of Allistair, who reported to Shadde that the ticking noise could still be heard, and that the time interval was now two seconds. This puzzled Shadde; he had expected the opposite. He turned away from the bridge screen. "I'm going out on the fore-casing to see if anything's to be seen there," he said to the first lieutenant. "You look after the bridge, Number One."

Then he turned to Allistair. "You'd better come with me."

Allistair said, "Aye, aye, sir," and looked a bit unhappy. At any moment the fore-casing might go up in smoke; it was more or less awash at the bow, and it would be a wet uncomfortable job—one might even end up in the water. But he hadn't any option, so he followed the Captain down the steel ladder inside the bridge casing until they reached the pressure hull. There they stripped down to their underpants, shed their sea boots and stockings and retied their life belts. Then they knocked loose the clips on the port door and swung it inboard. Suddenly the sea seemed unpleasantly close as it lapped and gurgled along the hull below them. But the nearer the submarine got to the shore the calmer the water had become, and fortunately there was little more than a surface chop now. Shadde went out first, and Allistair followed close behind.

From the bridge the first lieutenant looked down on the scene with disapproval; while he acknowledged that the situation was extremely serious, he felt that Shadde was being undignified. The thing to do, he reflected, would be to send Allistair and McPherson out on the casing. They were perfectly capable of making the inspection; the Captain's place was on the bridge. And why strip down to underpants? Proper rig for the occasion would have been singlets and trousers, trouser ends tucked into the stockings. But this was like Shadde; the man couldn't help dramatizing everything he did. Sardonically, Cavan watched the two men move slowly forward; Shadde large and angular with those long hairy legs, and Allistair small, hairless, insignificant, and no doubt bursting with apprehension. It was not long before they had made their way as far as they could go, to the point where the casing sloped down to form the whalenose bow, and the sea was beginning to lap at them. Now Shadde was lying on the casing, leaning over first to starboard and then to port, with Allistair astride the hairy legs, acting as an anchor.

Damn funny, thought Cavan, if Allistair's not heavy enough and the shaggy bastard tips into the drink. He rather hoped it might happen; it would make Shadde ridiculous and give Cavan the kudos that goes with recovering your Captain from the water. Then he decided that these were rather shabby thoughts and he remembered that, incongruous though it might seem, the situation was a serious one, which Shadde was doing his best to deal with.

He saw Shadde leaning over the port side pointing to something in the water; a moment later Allistair changed places with the Captain and he now leaned over to port, apparently peering at something below the water line. So they had found something, after all?

At that moment the first lieutenant's attention was diverted to the after-casing from which he realized with a shock there came the sound of singing. He dashed to the after end of the bridge and saw that the thirty or forty men huddled on the casing, packed together like sardines, were having a sing-song. It was being done discreetly but, nonetheless, it was a sing-song. The commissioned gunner was standing among them gazing sadly at the bridge, and the first lieutenant beckoned to him violently. When he arrived Cavan said, "For God's sake stop that at once. The Skipper'll raise hell if he hears it. You should have known better," he added reproachfully.

Bagnall sighed. "They're cold, sir. Been there more than half an hour. Can't expect men to just sit there."

The first lieutenant made a gesture of annoyance. "Where would they rather be? In the fore-ends half way to kingdom come? Get them piped down double quick or you'll find yourself in serious trouble."

Soon after Bagnall got back to the men the singing stopped, and Cavan heard grumbling. A moment later Shadde was back on the bridge. His face was white. "Stop the engine!" he snapped. Then he had a quick look round; Korsör was right ahead and the distance between the submarine and the shore was closing steadily. There was a good deal of shipping about, mostly coasters and small sailing craft, but here and there a tanker and other large merchantmen.

"Slow astern!" Shadde called, and when the way was off the submarine he stopped the engine. After a quick look at the chart he said, "Any sign of the tug?"

Cavan looked towards Korsör. "Not yet, sir," he said. "Did you find anything?"

Shadde looked up somberly from under black, bunched eyebrows. "Yes, I did. An inch wire has fouled a shackle on an eye-plate below the water line. It leads aft into the water. Something heavy on the end. Can't see from the bows. God knows what it is."

He was still wearing nothing but underpants and they were wet and clinging now; above them his chest was a mass of tangled black hair. As he spoke he scratched it, and Cavan thought, My God! What an ape! Aloud he said, "What are you going to do, sir?"

Shadde's eyes pierced him. "Have a closer look, of course. Get a dinghy inflated on the after-casing. I'll take Allistair with me and go off from there. Shake it up!" he said sharply. "Every second counts."

A few minutes later the bright yellow dinghy was inflated and launched, and Shadde and Allistair, still wearing nothing but their underpants, paddled away from the crowded after-casing. As they drew level with the bridge, Weddy turned to the first lieutenant. "Incredible sight, isn't it? Never thought I'd live to see those two boating in the nude."

"Staggering," agreed the first lieutenant. "Have to hand it to the Skipper for keenness. I'd've sent someone else."

"Very keen type," said Weddy. "Could have been gunnery branch."

At that moment there was a high-pitched whistle from the after-casing, followed by a cry of, "Any more for the shore?" The first lieutenant had his eyes on the rubber dinghy when it happened, and he knew from the way Shadde's head jerked that he had heard it.

Once again Bagnall was summoned to the bridge. This time Cavan was really angry. "Who was responsible for that?" he hissed at the commissioned gunnery officer.

Bagnall shook his head. "Don't know, sir. Trying to find out when you sent for me."

"Well, find out and put him in my report. And when you get back pass the word that if there's any more skylarking every man there will have his leave stopped. The whole damned lot."

The rubber dinghy had reached the bow now and stopped under the port hydroplane. From the bridge Shadde and Allistair could be seen leaning over the side of the dinghy. They were talking and pointing, and then they

119

started pulling on something. The dinghy heeled over until it seemed it would capsize.

"They're hauling in a wire," said Weddy. "Hope there's nothing lethal on it."

The first lieutenant frowned. "Wonder what the hell it is?"

In the dinghy Shadde and Allistair were inching the wire home; they had already hauled in ten or twelve feet when Shadde said, "Steady, I think I can see something on the end now." He was peering into the water, his face close to the surface. But though they were in the lee of the submarine, it was difficult to see anything through the wind-rippled surface.

"Any idea what it is, sir?" Allistair sounded worried.

"Can't make it out. We'll have to haul it to the surface. Take it very easy," he cautioned. "Don't let it hit the side."

With the greatest care they hauled the wire up inch by inch until a dark, spherical object broke the surface.

For a few moments they looked at it. Finally Shadde broke the embarrassing silence. "Bloody dan-buoy sinker!" he said with disgust.

"Yes, sir." Allistair's relief was obvious. "We must have fouled a dan mooring put down by a fisherman."

"Yes," said Shadde in a flat voice. "That shackle must've been left by one of those workmen in Stockholm."

It took another fifteen minutes to get the mooring wire, and the shackle into which it had jammed, clear of the eye-plate. When they had finished they paddled back to the after-casing in silence. Allistair, relieved beyond belief that they had not had to grapple with an explosive device, tried one or two cheerful remarks, but Shadde, tight-lipped and forbidding, merely glowered.

On reaching the casing Shadde stepped out of the dinghy and without a word to anyone made his way through the crowd of men to the bridge, where he told Weddy to resume course and speed for the passage through the Great Belt. Then, ignoring the first lieutenant's, "What did you find, sir?" he went down to his cabin.

The dinghy was recovered and deflated, the forward watertight doors were opened and the men on the after-casing went below and back to their compartments.

When Weddy reported to the Captain that the tug had been sighted coming out from Korsör, Shadde said, "Tell him by signal that we don't want him." Then he added, "And thank him."

Later Shadde handed Keely a signal to the Flag Officer Submarines explaining what had happened, and that was the last any officer saw of the Captain until the forenoon of the next day. All reports made to him from the bridge were acknowledged with monosyllabic replies, but he never left his cabin.

It was twenty-seven minutes past four in the morning when Mr. Buddington decided that the moment had arrived to inspect the victualing store. He knew that the watches had changed at four o'clock, and it was still far too early for day dutymen to be about, so he dressed quickly and left the cabin. The galley and victualing store were on the same deck as the officers' quarters, immediately aft of them. When he reached the alleyway he saw with relief that it was clear, and in a moment he had opened the door of the store and gone in, locking it behind him. Then he switched on the light and had a good look around. What he saw looked like a cross between a grocer's shop and a huge pantry. The shelves were stacked with tinned foods, packaged foods, metal boxes, cardboard boxes, wooden boxes, bins and bags of flour, sugar, dried beans, dried peas and many other things. The only things there which weren't groceries were four silk lamp shades stowed away on an upper shelf, their bright colors conspicuous in that drab setting.

The victualing store struck Mr. Buddington as strangely domesticated and quite out of character. Somehow he felt that groceries in a nuclear submarine were incongruous. Surely the brains that had made possible the Polaris submarines should have been able to contrive that the men who manned them were sustained with something less prosaic than groceries. Then he remembered the fragments of conversation he'd overheard in the wardroom the day before: ". . . sure that stowage's O.K., Dusty? . . . put the tins on top . . ." What tins and on top of what? There were thousands of tins. Big tins and little tins, round ones and square ones. He looked at them in dismay and decided that the search would have to be a systematic one. Shelf by shelf and end to end. So he began in the middle of the after side, on the shelf which was at eye level, because he thought that would be the most logical place to start. And he was quite right, because after half an hour the search was rewarded. Although he was a calm little man, he could scarcely contain his pleasure when he found what he was looking for. Under the last of a pile of biscuit tins which he had lifted one by one was the brown, manilla envelope he had seen Dusty Miller clasping in the wardroom. He wondered whether he should take it back to his cabin or examine it there. He decided that to take it with him was too dangerous. The envelope was unsealed. He raised the flap, put his fingers in and brought out a number of photographic negatives. There were twelve in all. Mr. Buddington held them up to the light. "Dear me," he said. "How very stupid of me. I might have guessed."

Disappointed but intrigued, he looked at the buxom women and mustachioed men frozen by the camera in striking and erotic postures, to which their nakedness lent a ludicrous air of unreality, as if people couldn't possibly look like that without laughing. He recalled again the scraps of conversation he had overheard and silently acknowledged the correctness of Dusty Miller's, "Blimey, what a weapon!"

With a mild sigh Mr. Buddington replaced the negatives in the envelope, put it back on the shelf and stacked the tins on top of it.

Retaliate entered the Sejerö Deep a little before six o'clock, just about the time that Allistair took over the watch from Symington and Keely.

Shadde didn't come up, either for the passage between Sjælland Reef and the light vessel or for the alteration of course south of Schultzgrund. To all of Allistair's reports by voice-pipe he had replied with a toneless, "Very well. Carry on."

By nine o'clock they were in the Kattegat steaming east on the last leg of the passage round Sjælland; ahead of them lay the entrance to the Sound. There was a good deal of shipping in sight and the coast of Denmark was coming up to starboard as the submarine closed the land towards Gilbierg Head. It was a fine day and there was still no more than a light breeze as *Retaliate* creamed her way through the placid sea. Overhead the sun was shining from a blue sky scattered with wisps of cloud like pulled-out cotton.

They were due to arrive at Copenhagen at two o'clock in the afternoon. The expectation of this, coupled with the fine weather, was probably responsible for the good humor which abounded on the messdecks. By early in the forenoon it was evident that the incident off Korsör was to become a treasured recollection for the ship's company. Already a new phrase had been coined and such simple sallies as " 'Ow's yer tick-tocks this morning, Pincher?" caused gales of laughter on the messdecks.

Leading Steward Target whistled quietly as he stowed away the crockery in the wardroom pantry. It was after nine o'clock and the officers had finished breakfast. When he had put away the last plate he sat on the pantry stool, produced a cigarette from behind his ear and lit it. He was joined a few minutes later by the Captain's steward.

"Watcher, Target!"

"'ullo there, Dusty. 'Ow's tricks?'"

Dusty Miller threw his eyes to the ceiling. "Cor, strike a light. It's something awful this morning."

"What's awful? Skipper?"

"That's it."

"Chewed the ass off you?"

"Wish 'e had. At least that'd be 'im."

"What's it then, Dusty?"

"Nothing. That's the trouble."

"'Ow d'you mean?"

"Well, 'e just sits there. Sitting at 'is desk with 'is 'ead on 'is arms. Lights off, pitch dark. And 'e don't say a bleeding word. Not proper, anyhow."

Target picked at his teeth with a match. "I s'pose the poor old bastard's feeling a bit sore about that tick-tock business yesterday. Made 'imself a bit ridiculous, didn't 'e?"

"Wouldn't say that," said Miller loyally. "'E had to do something. There was that tick an' all. 'Ow'd 'e know what it was before 'e'd seen it?"

Target puffed at his cigarette. "You say 'e's acting strange this morning?"

"Kind of. When I says, 'Be taking your shower this morning, sir?' 'E just grunts. Then I come back later and I say, 'What'll you be having for breakfast, sir?' And 'e grunts again. Then I go back a few minutes ago and ask 'im again about the shower and breakfast, and d'you know what 'e says? And me trying to be kind like?"

"No. What'd 'e say, Dusty?"

"'E says to me, hoarse-like, 'e says, 'Miller, get to hell out of it and stop worrying me.'"

124

For a moment Target thought about this in silence; then he said, "Blimey! What d'you say, Dusty?"

"I didn't, I just got to hell out of it."

Target picked away at his teeth. He was searching back over his long years of naval experience for a parallel to the Captain's behavior, something he could impress Dusty with. But he couldn't think of anything. "Know what the trouble is, Dusty? 'E's chokka, that's what 'e is. 'E's been chokka ever since Stockholm. What with the collision, Kyley adrift, no letter from 'is old woman, and now this tick-tock business last night—'e's proper chokka, that's what 'e is."

In the wardroom Keely was busy with the cryptograph, deciphering a sheaf of W/T signals Gracie had brought him. He had finished the third signal when he gave a whistle of surprise; then he jumped out of his chair and capered about excitedly.

Symington, Allistair, Musgrove and the Doctor were sitting near him reading. Symington put down the paper and sighed. "Must be the sun."

"George, my boy. This is terrific! Look!" The sublieutenant thrust the signal in front of Symington. It was from the Admiralty, addressed to the Commanding Officer, *Retaliate,* repeated Flag Officer Submarines. Symington read it out aloud. "The following appointments are notified: Commander G. L. Straker to *Retaliate* in command, Vice Commander J. A. Shadde to *Dolphin* for duty as Staff Officer Operations to Flag Officer Submarines with effect from eighteenth May."

Symington raised his left eyebrow. "Good old Second Sea Lord. Never leaves his chums in the lurch."

Allistair picked up the signal. "Anyone know Straker?"

"Yes," said Symington. "Met him in Malta when he had *Advance.*"

"What's he like?"

"No idea really. He looked reasonable."

Keely sat down in front of the cryptograph. "Bound to be less of a shower than Shadde," he said in his deep voice.

"How long has the Skipper had *Retaliate?*" O'Shea asked.

Symington thought for a moment. "He commissioned her in the States."

"How long ago was that?"

"About ten months."

"Isn't a two-year commission normal?"

"Yes," said Symington. "But with all this new construction things are different. Shadde's the senior C.O. of this class. Knows a hell of a lot about them. Expect the Admiralty think he'd be more useful ashore."

"So do I," said Keely.

"Shut up," said Allistair in an undertone. "Not so loud. He might hear, even if the door is closed."

Keely looked across to the door of the Captain's cabin and lowered his voice. "Sorry. But this gives me a hell of a kick—I can't pretend it doesn't."

"Hadn't you better take it to him? After all, he's the addressee." Symington's voice was dry and practical.

Keely deciphered the last few signals and then clipped the originals together before going across to the door of the Captain's cabin. After his knock he heard Shadde's voice, but he couldn't make out what was said. He opened the door and went in. The cabin lights were off but in the reflected light from the wardroom he could see Shadde lying on the bunk, back to the door.

"What is it?" Shadde asked gruffly. He didn't turn around.

"Signals, sir. Just deciphered."

Shadde kept his back to the sublieutenant. "Leave them on the desk," he said.

Keely put them on the desk and left the cabin, sliding

126

the door shut after him. For a few minutes, Shadde lay on his bunk thinking. He hadn't slept at all during the night. His mind had been in a turmoil, worrying about what had happened off Korsör. But he would have to read the signals— there was no escaping that—so he got off his bunk and switched on the desk light and looked through them. When he came to the signal appointing Straker to *Retaliate*, he dropped the others and they fluttered down to the deck. When he had reread the signal he let it drop, too, and sat down heavily at the desk with his head on his outstretched arms.

His mind traveled back over the long years he'd been in the service—back to the very beginning when he had gone from his prep school to Dartmouth and then afterwards to sea. There had been no training cruiser for him because of the war. He'd done his midshipman's time in *Gambia* and *Rotherham*. Then back ashore for sublieutenant's courses and after that the decision to go into submarines. He remembered the time in the training flotilla at Rothesay, exciting days learning the trade in Inchmarnock water. After that had come the trip out in a trooper via the Cape to Fremantle, where he had joined *Sabre* as Third Hand. Again he winced at the recollection of *Sabre*; for him it could never be anything but a memory of that night in the Lombok Strait.

Shadde had stayed in submarines after the war and most of his service had been in the home fleet, except for a two-year commission with the Australian Navy. He remembered the thrill of his first command when he had been given *Amazon* at the age of twenty-seven. After that the staff course at Greenwich, and then war courses followed by promotion to Commander well ahead of the rest of his term. It was then that he had met and married Elizabeth. After two years ashore he'd gone back to sea and had two more years in command of submarines. Then, two years ago, the big moment had come. After a year in the *Dreadnought* class he had been sent over to the States to study the operation of the Polaris missile. Ten months later Britain had taken over six new Polaris boats and he had been given command of one of them. It was this more than anything that had given him the dedicated feeling of mission and destiny which had afterwards become a part of him. He felt that he had been put in command of *Retaliate* for some great but as yet hidden purpose.

Since he had taken *Retaliate* over in Groton, Connecticut, and commissioned her with a British crew, she had steamed twenty thousand miles under his command. The submarine had become a part of him and he a part of her, and now the Admiralty was going to stick him away behind some bloody desk in Blockhouse. The thought choked him.

He was thirty-eight, the oldest commanding officer in the submarine service. He supposed they thought he was too old now. Perhaps they'd tell him he was more valuable ashore than afloat, but whatever they said, he knew that once he was ashore his sea service was ended. This was his last command. He would spend the rest of his time in the navy rotting away in an office. They would be in Portsmouth in five days, so he had exactly five more days afloat. Not that he ever would have liked it, but a month ago the prospect of being stationed ashore wouldn't have been so devastating; he could have consoled himself with the thought of seeing Elizabeth. But now?

He wondered whether there would be a letter from her at Copenhagen. And if so, what would she say? He couldn't bear the uncertainty, the waiting, the fact that he couldn't talk to her, reason, persuade, convince her. Then he realized with a shock that if *Retaliate* were ever used in earnest now, he wouldn't be in command. He thought about George Straker. Straker was four years his junior. They had been together in *Sunfish*, when he was Number One and George was navigator. Shadde thought again about his sense of mission.

What about that now? The feeling had been immensely strong in him soon after he had commissioned *Retaliate*. The Cold War had started to warm up and he had believed the moment was approaching. Then it had cooled off again. Now there was talk of a new East-West rapprochement and the diplomats and the press on either side were billing and cooing. But the West was being taken for a ride; he knew that. Look what was happening in Africa and the East!

He moved from the desk and began to pace up and down the small cabin. Why couldn't they leave him alone? Why were they pulling him out of *Retaliate* after only ten months? Was it the collision? Was it Symington in some inexplicable way? Perhaps through his father, who was an old flotilla mate of the Flag Officer Submarines. Could it be that? Why didn't they leave him where he was? Could it be anything to do with his private life? Had FOS/M heard that Elizabeth might leave him? No, it couldn't be that. That was damn all to do with the navy.

Perhaps it was those signals he'd sent off Korsör, when they'd been investigating the ticking noise in the bows? But he had done the right thing. As it turned out it wasn't sabotage, but it might have been. It had been highly suspicious and it was his duty to let FOS/M know what was happening. Supposing it had been an explosive device and *Retaliate* had gone up in smoke? At least they would have had some idea at the Admiralty of the cause.

Miserable and depressed, he thought again about what had happened off Korsör. The messdecks would be treating it as a huge joke and there was sure to be lots of sly sniggering in the wardroom. And Dwight Gallagher would make the most of it in one of those reports he was always typing to his precious U.S. Navy superiors—that was certain.

But what would they have done if the responsibility had been theirs? Perhaps he had been too impetuous. Perhaps he shouldn't have cleared the forward compartments? Perhaps he shouldn't have told the crew what he suspected. But not to have done that would have been unthinkable. Perhaps he shouldn't have gone off in the rubber dinghy. Perhaps he should have sent others to do the dirty work. But at the time he had felt that risks had to be taken and he preferred to be there with those who had to take them. Besides, had it been what he thought it was, he wanted to be there himself to handle it, to make sure that whatever was done was properly done.

But what was the good of worrying about all that now? They were going to put him ashore, that was all that mattered now. He was to lose Elizabeth and *Retaliate*, the two most important things in his life. There wasn't much else if they went. Things had gone wrong in recent months, badly wrong—ever since Symington had joined. That had been the turning point. It was only after his arrival that the attitude of his officers seemed to change. It was then that the boat started getting slack. Of course Symington would have told them the story of that night in the Lombok Strait. But there were other things for which Symington couldn't be blamed; he had to admit that. Like the sabotage incidents, and Elizabeth's incredible letter. And now the dreary prospect of spending the rest of his naval career ashore. Or was Symington somehow responsible for that too?

His head ached fiercely. He had concentrated too hard. It always happened if he did: a sharp nagging pain at the temples, like somebody screwing in a gimlet. The long search back through memory had been an effort on top of the lack of sleep. An overwhelming feeling of depression and impotence in the face of all his problems settled on him. From the cupboard over the wash basin he took down the bottle of white pills Elizabeth had given him. He put three in his mouth and washed them down with water. Then he started pacing the cabin floor again. From the wardroom he heard the muffled sound of voices. He supposed they were discussing the signal. What would his officers and men think? It would be around the submarine in no time. They were probably gloating over it in the wardroom now.

In the chief petty officers' mess, discussion had ranged over a wide variety of subjects: the new rates of pay, the two days to be spent in Copenhagen, the refit in Portsmouth, leave arrangements, and, of course, the fun and games off Korsör the day before.

The coxswain clasped his hands behind his head. "Funny how certain the Skipper was that it was sabotage."

Shepherd lit his pipe and puffed hard at it until it drew. "I hear he thinks the steering jamming in Stockholm was sabotage too." McPherson looked up from the carpet he was making. "Maybe if you'd heard that wee ticking noise like we did you'd have thought it was sabotage. It was no' such a strange thought. There was that dead regular time interval and all."

"How d'you account for that?" asked Springer, the chief electrical artificer.

"I asked Lieutenant Allistair this morning. He said it's quite easy to explain. There was about fifteen feet of wire with the dan sinker on the end. As we went along, the pressure of sea water pushed it aft and upwards until it hit the side. Then the force of the blow would return it and it would swing back like a pendulum. Then the pressure of water would take it aft again and the whole process'd be repeated." McPherson paused for a moment. "When we reduced speed the time interval shortened. That was because there was less pressure of water against the sinker and that cut down the distance of the pendulum swing. That was why the ticking noise sounded as though it had speeded up."

With needle and thread Shepherd was putting the finishing touches to a gray silk lamp shade he was making. The coxswain looked at it with a critical eye. "How many this time out, Sheppy?"

"This is the fifth."

"What'll that lot fetch you?"

"Fifteen quid. Materials cost four."

"Not too bad. Nice hobby. Keeps the old lady in pin money and you out of mischief, I s'pose."

Shepherd frowned. "Money goes to the church," he said abruptly. Then he looked at Springer. "What d'you make of that little fellow Buddington?" he said.

"Creepy crawly sort of bloke. All over the boat all times of the night and day. Tell you one thing," Springer sniffed, "he may be a boffin and all that, but what he knows about the practical side of air conditioning is dangerous."

Shepherd looked up curiously. "Why d'you say that?"

"Remember that chat we had with him yesterday forenoon? About the air scrubbing plant? He didn't sound no expert then, did he?"

"That's true."

"You know," said Shepherd, "that jammed steering could have been sabotage. So could those other troubles in Portsmouth and Queensferry. What's more, when I look around our lot I don't have to think too hard who it might be."

The coxswain winked at the others. "Sheppy's on to Kyle again."

"Of course I am. And for good reason."

"Think 'e's a commy, Sheppy?"

"No, I don't. At least I don't know. But he's got a chip on his shoulder. Hates the boat and everybody in her. Got a permanent grudge against life. It's people like that who do senseless things like sabotaging machinery."

There was a discreet cough in the doorway, and the

132

conversation stopped. Mr. Buddington stood there blinking, the leather box slung over his shoulder. "May I come in, gentlemen? I'd like to read the temperatures and humidities."

The first lieutenant looked at Allistair and repeated the question. "But what did you make of the noise?"

"Same as the Skipper."

"Why?"

"I suppose because he'd already said over the broadcast what it was."

"Did it sound mechanical?"

Allistair nodded. "Quite definitely. It's easy now to explain it. Wasn't then."

"Arsed about a bit, didn't we," said Goss caustically. "Like to have seen FOS's face when he read the first signal."

The Doctor put down his book. "Skipper's very quick on this sabotage stuff, isn't he?"

"Got an obsession about it," said Goss. "I've an aunt like that. Always thinks she's got cancer. Gets a headache and says she's got a tumor on the brain. Pain in the arse and she reckons it's cancer of the anus."

"They say," said Symington, yawning, "that one attracts the things one fears."

Goss smiled at him, a slow, quizzical smile. He liked this casual elegant young man; most people did. He said, "Does one really, George." And the way he said it sounded like Symington speaking, and not at all like Goss.

The Doctor lit a cigarette. "I hear the Skipper's in a hell of a mood."

Goss cocked a leg over the arm of the easy chair. "Just for a change," he said sardonically.

Allistair sat down on the settee. "Strange bird, isn't he? Nothing but rage and gloom since Stockholm."

133

"Something gnawing at his vitals," said Symington.

Goss stood up, his hands plunged into his trouser pockets. "Queer sod. Either up in the clouds talking the hind leg off a donkey, or down in the dumps, making life a misery for everyone."

"For a few months he had moments of terrific form." Allistair laughed. "Remember the party at Oslo and the redhead?"

Weddy was lying on the settee in the corner, his legs over one arm. "Shall I ever forget it," he said.

"Before my time," said Symington. "But I'll believe you."

Weddy propped himself up on an elbow. "What causes this gloom and depression act?"

The Doctor shook his head. "It's no act. No fun for him, you know." He turned to Allistair. "Was he always like this?"

"Ask Goss. He's been here since we commissioned."

Goss shrugged his shoulders. "Always been a pretty strict, rigid sort of bloke. Very just, really. Seems to have changed in the last few months."

"In what way?" asked the Doctor.

"It's difficult to say. Been gayer and more talkative at times than he used to be. But then he's been much gloomier and more irritable at others. Seems to change his moods at the drop of a hat."

Symington got up from the settee. "I've been in this boat for four months. Seems like four years. The day I joined he was silent and glowering. When Number One introduced me you'd think it was Hamlet meeting the Ghost. Since then it's been mostly gloom and anger when I've been about." He yawned again. "Must confess I find it terribly boring."

Keely flicked three darts into the 20 sector. "He's an unutterable bastard. I'm bloody glad he's going."

Cavan was sitting in an armchair reading; he had taken no part in the conversation. Now he put his book down.

134

"Keely," he said abruptly. "Pipe down! I won't have the Captain discussed like that."

Keely looked defiant. "Sorry, sir, I was only saying what I thought."

"Well, don't. He's your commanding officer. You're one of his officers. Pretty junior one, too. Discipline and loyalty are both involved."

Symington sighed. "Don't you think Shadde tries them rather hard, Number One?"

As Symington said it, the door of the Captain's cabin slid open and Shadde walked into the wardroom. The effect was unintentionally dramatic. The officers stood up and there was an embarrassing silence. Nobody knew quite where to look. Shadde searched one face after the other with that intense smoldering stare his officers found so devastating. The dark eyes were red from lack of sleep, but he was freshly shaved and sprucely turned out.

Finally the stare ended on Symington. "What is it I try rather hard, Symington?" The Captain's voice was ice cold.

Symington looked him in the eye, but said nothing. Shadde, large and menacing, cleft chin thrust forward, moved a few paces towards him. The atmosphere was electric. "Come, come, Symington. You're not usually lost for words. Let's have it."

Symington's face was ashen. "It was a private discussion, sir."

"Surely it wasn't so private that I can't hear it? After all, it was about me."

"I'd prefer not to repeat it, sir."

There was a long, chilling silence. Shadde stood quite still, fingers flexing, his eyes fixed on Symington. Then he looked slowly from one officer to the other until he came to Cavan. "My first lieutenant," he said sardonically. "I might have known." He turned away and walked off into the control room.

As soon as Shadde got to the bridge the submarine's speed was increased to 16 knots. Half an hour later they entered the Sound and began the passage to the south between Helsingör and Hälsingborg. The sun continued to shine from a blue sky and the sea was a mirror with the lightest of breezes upon it.

Symington went to the bridge when they were off Landskrona. To his surprise Shadde was talkative and affable, for all the world as if the scene in the wardroom had never taken place. Symington decided that the man was utterly unpredictable. He hoped the new captain would be an improvement; he couldn't help but be.

Shadde ordered the W/T office to transmit a signal to the Flag Officer Submarines, repeated to the Admiralty and to *Massive* in Göteborg, notifying them of *Retaliate*'s intention to enter the harbor at 1400. Ahead of them Copenhagen was just visible against a pale horizon. Ahead and to port the forts of Middelgrunds and Flak stood out of the sea, and beyond them lay the city, a forest of towers and spires and roofs and gables glittering in the morning sun.

They exchanged signals with the pilot vessel off Middelgrunds Fort and shortly before two o'clock *Retaliate* was secured to a buoy in Yderhavn. A naval launch brought off the Danish officer of the guard, the British Naval Attaché, a representative of the mayor, two port officials, and a Danish naval postman with the submarine's mail.

Over on Langelinie the lilacs were in bloom, and below them Hans Andersen's Little Mermaid sat on her rock gazing serenely at the water.

The official visit to Copenhagen had begun; because of the delay in Stockholm it would be for two days instead of the five originally planned.

|| 9 ||

The postbag for *Retaliate* had in it surprises, disappoint-
ments, and for some the fulfilment of expectations.

It did not bring the letter from Elizabeth so eagerly
awaited by Shadde. The shock of disappointment gave way
to optimism; surely no letter meant indecision? There had
been more than time enough for her to write. He was filled
with fresh hope. Perhaps his Oslo letter had caused a change
of heart?

But the postbag did bring an unexpected letter. It was
from the Flag Officer Submarines.

My dear Shadde,
You will have had the Second Sea Lord's signal about
your appointment to my staff. It is now imperative to
have you at Blockhouse where your knowledge and experience of the *Missile* boats will be invaluable. I had intended to bring you ashore in September, but recent
events make it advisable to do so now.

Straker has completed a month in *Deterrent* where he has been understudying Peter Backer, so your turnover should be possible within 48 hours of *Retaliate's* return to Portsmouth.

I look forward to having you on my staff, to which you will be a most valuable addition.

Yours sincerely,
Tom Bannering

Mr. Buddington received a communication he had expected. It came in a large brown envelope, with the mark and seal of the Department of Naval Construction, and a label which gave the contents as "plans." In fact, it came from the office of the Director of Naval Intelligence, and in it was material asked for by Mr. Buddington in his coded signal sent after leaving Stockholm. Among other things in the envelope were the leave records of certain members of the submarine's crew and some additional background information about them.

The postbag also had in it a letter from Southsea for Engineering Mechanic Kyle. It was from his mother; a page of small news about the family and household led up to the important item that she had gone and "busted" some of her savings on a new hat and other "glad rags" for the trip to London. Before her letter Ernie Kyle had been depressed, but after it he gave way to a mood of rage and frustration. There was only one person in the world who meant something to him, and she meant everything.

There were also letters for Chief E. R. A. Shepherd from Dora and Win. Win was his sister-in-law, married to his wife's stepbrother, Arthur Hindle; Dora Shepherd was his wife. The Shepherds and Hindles lived near each other in Fratton; only two streets separated them, and there was much going and coming between the two households.

Dora Shepherd didn't really like Win Hindle; she mistrusted her. She was too smug, too anxious to tell you what was wrong with the world and how she would put everything to rights. On top of that she was always throwing her religion in Dora's face and sniffing at her because she was a poor churchgoer. But Dora had two small children to look after whereas Win had none, and small children made churchgoing difficult.

Dora Shepherd felt, too, that Win put on airs and graces and regarded herself as superior to the Shepherd and Hindle families, because she'd had a university education, was mistress in a county council school and a leading light on the local ban-the-bomb committee. She dominated poor Arthur Hindle, who had achieved no better than chief storeman at a small wholesale house in Portsmouth.

But most of all Dora disliked and mistrusted Win because of her friendship with Tom Shepherd, a friendship which she knew was based on their strong community of religious interest.

Tom was a regular churchgoer too, and the fact that he and Win and Arthur went off to church every Sunday while she had to mind the children was gall to Dora. One way and another there was no doubt that she was jealous of Tom's friendship with Win—not only jealous, but afraid of it. After living with Tom for close on twelve years Dora knew a lot about him—that he was an unworldly, easily led man, for example.

Win was a dominating personality, and Dora could see that under her influence Tom was developing a morbid preoccupation with religion. She feared this because it had changed him, and not, she felt, for the better. He had lost much of his good natured friendliness and easygoing humor, and he no longer seemed so interested in her or the children. Dora was well aware that Win Hindle was not only younger than she was, but better-looking. And of course, not having had any children, Win had kept her figure—even Dora had to concede that it was a good one.

Tom Shepherd, for his part, thought a great deal of Win. He admired her knowledge, her forthrightness, and her intellect, which he recognized as superior to his own. He liked, too, the way she talked about world affairs; unlike Dora, her conversation was not forever about the children and running the house and all those sort of wearying problems. He particularly respected her deep religious knowledge and the way in which she was able to interpret the Bible and the Will of God in a practical, down-to-earth manner. For him she had made these things something real and vital, and she had shown him ways in which he could assist his fellow men by carrying out the behests of the Almighty instead of just paying lip service to them.

Win had told him that religion was not just a series of "don'ts and mustn'ts"; it was a vital living thing which took into account the ordinary human frailties and insisted on the observance of the great humanities. As Win said, "It's not the little things God minds, Tom, like the individual erring sinner; it's the sum total of good and evil, the broad onward sweep of the human race, which concerns Him."

Often Tom Shepherd and Win sat up into the late hours and their discussions would range widely. Always for every doubt and fear that he might express Win had a plausible answer, a ready interpretation of the Will of God. Now, as he folded her letter and replaced it in the envelope, Shepherd thought of his coming leave and of the opportunities he would have to see Win. There was much he had to tell her. As always, thinking of her evoked mixed feelings of religious piety and physical anticipation, and left him with a gnawing sense of insecurity.

The fact that Shadde couldn't stand cocktail parties

didn't absolve him from going to them, and, in any case, this one at the British Embassy was a must because it had been laid on in honor of *Retaliate's* visit. But it got off to a creakingly slow start and he spent the first half-hour hating it and everybody there.

His mood of depression wasn't helped by overhearing Dwight Gallagher telling a group of locals about the Korsör business. Shadde couldn't hear much of what was said, but what he did hear was plain enough, especially when Gallagher said, ". . . that little tick certainly had the Captain worried!" It wasn't just the way he said it; he threw his head back and laughed with his nose all wrinkled and his teeth bared as if it were the funniest thing he'd ever heard. And, of course, his Danish listeners had to laugh too, and one tall woman with a folded, seamy sort of face laughed so hard that she had to put her hand over her mouth and discreetly edge her teeth back into place with a little finger. That gave Shadde a fierce moment of satisfaction, but he could have killed the American and he made a note to warn George Straker that the weapons control officer was not only disloyal but a bounder. Anyway, why did Gallagher always surround himself with admiring audiences at these parties? After all, they were given for the Royal Navy, not the U.S. Navy, and Gallagher was an interloper really. Surely he could see that.

Absorbed with these thoughts, Shadde stood in a small circle with the Ambassador, a Danish Admiral, the local Anglican curate and their wives. He took only a fleeting interest in the conversation because he didn't feel much like talking. It was less boring to look around the room discreetly and say "Quite" and "Of course." People thought you were a very good listener if you did that, and they liked you for it.

He saw Keely—with a pretty girl, of course—moving over to join the noisy mob around Gallagher. Over at the far end of the room where the bar table stood, he could see

Symington and the Doctor standing together, drinking and laughing. He wondered what they were laughing about? Korsör?

Bagnall, Allistair and Musgrove were in another group. There seemed to be a good deal of noise and laughter there too. Always this insane babble and laughter, that was what was so loathsome about cocktail parties. What was so funny, anyway? There seemed to be no sign of the first lieutenant, and just when he was wondering where the devil he'd got to, he saw him coming into the room at the far end with the Ambassador's wife. Trust him, thought Shadde; been looking at some art treasure or other and saying exactly the right thing, and conveniently bringing up the subject of the Royal Family so that it could lead up to the fact that he had served in *Britannia*. Then they would start swopping names and being astonished at how many distinguished people they both knew. The thought nauseated him.

As a matter of fact, Shadde was absolutely right, only he might have added that the Ambassador's wife found Cavan simply enchanting. She described him to her husband after the party. "Benjamin Cavan—their first lieutenant—is an enchanting young man, isn't he? He knows the Queen and Margaret and Philip and the children quite well, you know. He was in *Britannia*. Awfully good-looking, too, I thought."

"Probably be an Admiral," grunted the Ambassador, as he struggled with a sock. He had gotten indigestion and it was the devil, but he had to humor his wife or he would have a row and that would make the indigestion worse.

A moment later Shadde saw Rhys Evans and beckoned him over. The instant the Welshman joined them Shadde felt better. There was something about Evans; he was quiet and modest and intensely loyal and absolutely first class at his job. Here was one officer in the submarine about whom he could really enthuse when he handed over to George

Straker. Perhaps Goss and Weddy too; they were good, but not really in the same class as the Chief.

Shadde's eyes continued to search the room; Symington and the Doctor were still standing near the bar table and he saw them exchange their empty glasses for full ones from the tray of a passing waiter. He couldn't be sure but he thought they'd done that two or three times in the last half-hour. It irritated him that they were not moving about talking to people. That was their job; that was what they were there for—not to swill liquor. He supposed Symington felt it was all too much of a bore to be worth bothering about. He would have him on the carpet about it next morning.

Then the First Secretary came up with a good-looking young woman who turned out to be his Danish secretary and whose name was Margrethe. She had attractive, friendly eyes and a wonderfully infectious laugh, and Shadde liked her at once. She was easy to talk to and they got on like a house on fire. In five minutes he had that strange feeling of elation and all his bad humor had gone. This happened to him sometimes, often for no reason he knew of. But it was a wonderful experience—the sudden feeling of uplift, every care gone in a second, and then the surge of well-being and a sort of deep-down inward excitement. Whatever it was, it always transformed you: there was that tremendous zest for living; you wanted to be doing things, talking—especially talking. In these moods there was so much you wanted to say, one thing led so easily to another, and the ideas and the words simply came tumbling out of you.

Rhys Evans saw the change come over the Captain just as he had seen it many times before, and he blessed the Danish secretary for having turned up just then. Soon he left them together, talking so animatedly that they didn't even notice his going.

Over at the bar table Symington nudged the Doctor. "Do my eyes deceive me, Patrick?" He nodded towards the end of the room, where Shadde stood talking to Margrethe.

"You mean the Skipper and the piece of crumpet?"

Symington sipped at the schnappes. "Yes," he said. "Dirty old man. He's peeping down her plunge-line."

"Excellent!" said the Doctor. "Vive le sport!"

At that moment Shadde asked Margrethe to have dinner with him after the party.

"I'd love to," she said, and obviously meant it. "But I can't tonight."

A surge of disappointment swept through Shadde and he looked at her fingers—bare of any rings. "Boy friend?"

She laughed, a delicious tinkling laugh. "No. Old friend."

"Honest?"

"Honest!" She gave him an enchanting smile. "Do ask me some other time. You're my favorite submarine captain." Then she waved to him gaily and was gone. Shadde looked at his watch. He couldn't go yet; he would have to hang on a bit longer. But all the fun had gone out of the party now that she'd left. He liked everything about her: the gay laugh; the attractive accent; her fresh complexion and good figure and the eager compelling friendliness, as if she knew you would like her and as if she were tremendously and especially interested in you and everything about you. But now she had gone and he wondered when he would see her again —if he'd ever see her again. How old was she? Then guiltily he thought about Elizabeth and he realized with surprise that he had forgotten all about her while he was talking to Margrethe. This made him feel disloyal to her; he must forget about Margrethe. Just then Rhys Evans came up and tapped his watch and raised his eyebrows. But Shadde shook his head; out of the corner of his eye he saw the Danish Admiral coming over to them.

At that moment there was a crashing noise at the far end of the room and the tinkling of broken glass. When he looked over he saw a waiter on his knees and above him

Symington and the Doctor. They were struggling not to laugh, and they seemed to be apologizing. In a flash Shadde realized that they were somehow responsible for the accident. They had been standing near the bar table drinking ever since the party had started, and now he supposed they'd had too much and had tripped the waiter or something. He could tell from the smirks on their faces that they were involved in some way. By God, he thought, what a performance to put on at an Embassy party. And they were his officers. The whole room was looking at them. He burned with humiliation and his anger rose as he looked around for the first lieutenant. Where was the bloody man? Never about when he was wanted. Then he saw him and beckoned with a sharp flick of the hand. When Cavan reached him Shadde hissed, "Tell those two"—he pointed with his chin to Symington and the Doctor—"to return on board at once. I'll see them in the morning."

The first lieutenant looked puzzled. "Symington and the Doctor, sir?"

Shadde's eyes froze. "Yes. Who the hell else, d'you think?"

After the Embassy party Shadde and Rhys Evans stopped in at a restaurant for dinner. It was the Captain's idea but Rhys Evans was not keen. He knew that the business of the waiter's accident had upset Shadde and he had relapsed into one of those depressed moods of his. The Welshman tried to cheer him up, but it was an uphill struggle and Shadde's only response was to drink a good deal and complain that he had no appetite. The more he drank the more depressed he became, and at ten o'clock he yawned and complained that he was tired. "Sorry," he said, "but I didn't sleep last night. Been a hell of a long day."

"Sorry to hear that, sir," said Rhys Evans.

"Mind if we go back on board now, Chiefy?"

145

"Of course. Let's be doing that, sir."

At Nyhavn they found a launch waiting and when they got back on board Shadde insisted on a night cap. In his cabin he poured the drinks and they talked about the party, and he raged about how Symington and the Doctor must have been responsible in some way for the waiter's accident. When Rhys Evans said he thought they might not have had anything to do with it, Shadde disagreed fiercely. After a while he calmed down, and they talked about the refit and other things, until he suddenly became preoccupied. Twice he didn't answer the Welshman.

Finally he went over to the desk and took from a drawer the letter from the Flag Officer Submarines. He tossed it over to the engineer officer. "What d'you think of that?" he said.

Evans had heard that Shadde was leaving *Retaliate* and that a new Captain would join in Portsmouth. Everybody in the boat had heard it but he wasn't supposed to know officially, so he went to some trouble to look surprised.

"I'm sorry you're going, sir. But indeed it's understandable. They'd not leave a man with your experience afloat much longer."

Shadde's eyes narrowed and he looked at the Welshman intently. "Notice FOS doesn't say why he's bringing me ashore *earlier* than he intended? D'you see how he skates around that?"

"He'll be telling you, sir. No doubt there's a good reason."

Shadde shook his head. "No," he said emphatically. "You see, he says he's bringing me ashore earlier because of *recent events*." He leant forward. "What does he mean by that?"

"Could mean many things, sir. Changes in the construction program, for example."

Shadde gave a dark, knowing look. "I've a shrewd idea

it's something quite different. Anyway, what the hell! Let's forgot it. Have a drink?"

The engineer officer held up his half-empty glass. "Still going, thank you, sir."

Shadde poured himself another whisky and soda and sank back into the chair.

"You'll be glad to be ashore for a while, sir, won't you?" Evans suggested.

Shadde had been sitting back in the easy chair, hands in pockets, legs stretched out in front of him, his eyes half closed. But now he came bolt upright. "Glad?" he said incredulously. "Glad? I hate the bloody idea, Chief. D'you realize what it means? The end of my sea time. Rotting away behind some bloody desk in Blockhouse. The nearest I'll get to the boats will be chatting to their C.O.'s when they come to see the gilded staff. I loathe the bloody idea." He sat back again. "Why couldn't they leave me here? This is where I belong." He said it despondently, in a sort of sad, querulous aside.

There was a long silence and then he took a tin of cigarettes from the desk and offered one to the engineer officer. He emptied his glass and picked up the decanter. "Other half, Chiefy?"

"Not for me, sir. Bit late now."

Shadde ignored him and poured stiff tots into both glasses, squirted soda into them and passed one to Evans. He picked up his own. "Cheers," he said, and half emptied it. When he had put it down he looked at his companion challengingly. "Rejoicing on board . . . about my departure?" It was more a statement of fact than a question.

"Not true that, sir," said Rhys Evans.

"Oh, yes it is," said Shadde, and he told the Welshman what had happened in the wardroom that morning when he had overheard Symington's remark.

"Now, sir, you're taking these things too much to heart."

Shadde shook his head. "No, I'm not, Chiefy. I've no illusions about my officers. Look what happened tonight when I asked Number One to join us for dinner. I'll wager he hadn't got another date. Did you notice his embarrassment? No?" He paused. "The whole thing is, he can't stand me. I know that."

Rhys Evans sighed. "He's not a man I'm liking much myself," he said. "But I've never heard him say a word against you."

"He's too careful to make that mistake," said Shadde, and he shook his head vigorously. "The fact remains that I'm not liked by my officers, am I?" He shot an inquiring, almost hopeful glance at the engineer officer.

The Welshman looked at him unhappily. "Indeed, and that's not true, sir," he protested, but he knew that he didn't sound convincing and Shadde knew it too, because he shook his head again. "No! You can't bluff me, Chiefy. Nice of you to try. They hate my guts."

Rhys Evans could see that Shadde was torturing himself. He couldn't help him, but he had to do something. He said, "Sir!" in a pained sort of way.

Shadde leaned towards him confidentially. "They do, you know. I can feel it. Trouble is, I see everything that goes on. And d'you know what's at the bottom of it all?" He peered at the engineer officer, but Rhys Evans shook his head.

"Symington!" said Shadde triumphantly and sat back. "Since he joined the trouble started. And it's got worse—and, of course, I know why," he added.

"Now what is that, sir?"

Shadde sighed deeply. "Oh! That bloody business in *Sabre*."

"*Sabre*, sir?"

"Yes." The Captain's voice was weary. "You know—when his father was Captain and I was Third Hand."

The engineer officer was genuinely puzzled. "I don't know what you mean, sir?"

Shadde's look was half-annoyance and half-doubt. He gave a dry laugh. "Nice of you to put on that act, Chiefy. But you do know. The night in the Lombok Strait," he added significantly.

Rhys Evans shook his head. "You're talking Greek, sir. I know nothing about the Lombok Strait."

Shadde looked up quickly. "Then you're the only officer in the wardroom who doesn't." He frowned. "Just possible they wouldn't tell you. They know you're pretty close to me."

"What is it you're talking of, sir?"

Shadde looked at him for a long while. Then he poured himself another whisky and said, "I think I'd better tell you. Perhaps you'd understand."

In a disjointed, moving way Shadde told the story. He didn't spare himself, and Rhys Evans thought he was going to break down when he described how his nerve had cracked during the depth-charge attack. It was then that Shadde covered his face with his hands. "It was a bloody awful thing to do," he said hoarsely. "A cowardly thing. But I couldn't help it. I just couldn't help it, you know. I didn't want to scream. It just came. And when it did, I couldn't believe it was me."

There was a long silence in the cabin. Shadde sat hunched in the chair, head buried in his hands. Then he stood up and his eyes were red and he swayed a bit. He didn't look at Rhys Evans when he spoke. "And that's why my officers hate my guts. I'm sure Symington's not spoilt the story in the telling." He took a cigarette from the tin.

Rhys Evans shook his head. "Never heard that story before, sir. Indeed, I doubt if anybody here has. Anyway, there's not a man would hold it against you. Every submariner knows it's easy to lose your nerve when you're young and inexperienced. Many a time it's happened, and to many fine men too." There was a ring of sincerity in the Welshman's voice.

Shadde shrugged away the remark. "No good, Chiefy. I know what I'm talking about. I'll tell you something else," he said. "I wouldn't be surprised if FOS's putting me ashore hasn't something to do with Symington."

"With *Symington?*"

"Yes, Symington. His father's rich, influential. Knows the First Sea Lord. An old flotilla mate of FOS's. You can do these things if you know the top brass. How do I know what Symington's been writing to his father?" Shadde's eyes clouded with suspicion.

The engineer officer stood up and put his hand on the Captain's shoulder. All the little Welshman's concern and affection showed in his face. "It's sleep you're needing, sir. You're a tired man and it's playing funny tricks with you."

Shadde brushed away Evans' hand with an impatient gesture. "It's nothing to do with tiredness. I know I'm tired, but I don't imagine these things. They're facts."

Rhys Evans saw that he couldn't help. He went to the door. "I'll be getting along now. Have a good sleep, sir."

Shadde laughed mirthlessly. "Easier said than done. I don't sleep much these days." He sat down at the desk and, with a heavy hand, poured himself another whisky. Without looking around he waved casually towards the door. "Well, good night. Run along like a good little man."

|| 10 ||

The second day in Copenhagen broke fine and clear with a fresh crispness in the air after the early morning rain. Along the waterfront the sunlight shone back from the wet sides and upperworks of the ships at the quays. Out in the stream, *Retaliate* lay glistening at her buoy, a dark shape against the sleek white hull and tall masts of the sailing ship *Dannemark*.

Down in the submarine's wardroom the officers were busy with breakfast and the continental editions of the English newspapers. In his short time aboard Mr. Buddington had learned that conversation at breakfast was taboo. He was sorry about this because he was a sociable little man and he liked the thrust and parry of wardroom chatter. He felt that breakfast in the submarine was a wasted occasion. At the moment he had his back to the hatch of the wardroom pantry and was dividing his attention between eggs and bacon and a newspaper. But he found it difficult to concentrate because of the hoarsely whispered conversation which floated through the pantry hatch. Target and Miller were discussing their night ashore.

"Then she says to me, sweet-like, 'O.K. honey, hundred krone.' "

"Cor! That's five quid!"

"Then I says to 'er, cool-like, 'Blimey, I don't want to buy the flippin' thing, I wants to 'ire it.' "

Mr. Buddington didn't mean to eavesdrop, but now his curiosity was aroused. He wondered what it was that Target had wanted to hire. He waited, but the conversation faded to a lower, more confidential level. Then he heard Dusty Miller's quiet laugh. "Anyway," said the steward, "she 'ad a smashin' pair on 'er, didn't she?"

The postman returned on board soon after breakfast. Among the many letters in the postbag was one for the Captain. Shadde was in his cabin discussing the defects list with the engineer officer when Miller delivered the mail. When Shadde saw the writing on the envelope he felt that tight knot in his stomach. It was from Elizabeth. His normal calm deserted him. Tearing the envelope open, he took out the letter and said, "Sorry, Chief, must read this. It's from my missus."

He sat down at the desk and unfolded the letter, smoothing it flat in front of him. It read:

My dear John,

Your letter from Stockholm made me desperately undecided. That's why I've taken so long to write. I went down to Bournemouth to Winifred and tried to sort things out. Now I've made up my mind and I hope you're not going to be hurt too much. Yesterday I saw Tinkerton and Pillings and asked them how I should set about getting a divorce. I said I wanted to be the

guilty party. I gather it's all rather sordid and complicated, but I'm going ahead.

Your letter makes it clear that you haven't the faintest idea what life has been like for me during the last
two years. Most of the time I've been alone. If we'd had
children I expect I could have endured it, but I've never
been long enough in one place to make any real friends.
When we've been together you've usually been so absorbed in your work that I've often wondered if you
realized I was there. I know this sounds terribly bitter,
and I suppose I am bitter. At any rate, I'm terribly unhappy and my life seems to have got into a rather point-
less and wasted rut. I just can't face going on like this.
I wonder if you realize what your moods are like and
what they do to me. Do you remember your last leave at
home?

I've tried to help you over your fits of depression,
but you seem to resent that and you make me feel as if
I'm responsible. Then sometimes you go madly gay and
build terrific castles in the air and get all worked up
about things that never happen, like buying a house or
holidays abroad. They're things you can't afford, John,
and when I try and restrain you, you hate me for it.
Like buying the Rover.

I hate saying these things, but they've got to be
said, because your letter convinces me you don't realize
how serious they are, or what it's like for me to have to
put up with them.

I used to be very much in love with you, John, and
perhaps I still am. But I don't think it's possible to go on
loving someone you see very little of, particularly when
you're afraid of that person.

I'm still young enough—and so are you—to be able
to start again. I know I'm at fault too. I've failed to give

you children—I think they might've made all the difference. At any rate, whoever is right or wrong doesn't
really matter—I just can't bear to go on like this. I know
all this sounds hysterical and selfish, but I can't help it.

At the end of this month I'm going out to Sydney
to join Ruth and Edward, and I'll probably stay on in
Australia. Until then I'm going to Mother, but I won't be
going back to Petersfield.

I hope that you'll realize that what I'm doing is
best for both of us, though you may not agree now.

It's quite obvious that I've not succeeded in making
you happy. I'm sorry. Anyway, I do hope you find real
happiness in the future. There's not much point in life
without it.

Elizabeth

When he came to the end of the letter Shadde stared at
the bulkhead in front of him. He sat there for perhaps five
minutes. Then he got up, crumpled the letter into a tight
ball, threw it into the wastepaper basket and walked out of
the cabin without a word to Rhys Evans.

The Doctor and Symington hadn't the faintest idea why
they had been ordered to return on board from the cocktail
party. When the first lieutenant delivered the message and
they asked what it was all about, he shook his head and said,
"Haven't a clue. Says he'll see you in the morning."

"But what the hell about?" repeated O'Shea miserably.

"Don't ask me," Cavan shrugged his shoulders. "But I'll
tell you one thing . . ."

"What's that?"

"He's bloody angry about something. Expect you've
fouled your yardarm somehow or other."

When the first lieutenant had gone, Symington clutched
the Doctor's arm. "I could vomit when that man says that."

"Me too," said the Doctor. "Let's go. We're ordered off."

Next morning, still mystified, they waited miserably for the summons to the Captain's cabin. At noon, just before they had to leave the submarine for the burgomaster's lunch, the messenger came along and said the Captain wished to see them in his cabin.

They found him sitting at his desk, apparently deep in thought; he seemed unaware of their presence. Symington decided that this was being done for effect so he filled in the long silence by making up a rhyme which started off promisingly enough as "Fierce old Shaddy, in a frightful paddy . . ." But there he stuck and inspiration failed him. At that moment Shadde looked up and his dark eyes comprehended them slowly, as if he were having difficulty in focusing.

"Ah! You two . . . yes . . ." He stood up and leaned against the bunk. Because he was taller than they, he seemed to look down along his nose at them, menacingly, the Doctor thought.

"Now," said Shadde quietly. "Will you kindly tell me exactly what you were up to at that party last night?"

Starting off slowly, thought the Doctor. Good control so far, but what the hell's he talking about?

Symington looked as if he were thinking the same thing. "I'm not sure what you mean, sir," he said.

Shadde's head jerked towards him as if he were aiming his strong chin at the young man. "Please, Symington, don't put on that Christian-martyr act." His voice was calm but his eyes were cold. "It won't help in the least, you know."

The Doctor said, "I'm sorry, sir, but I don't know what you mean, either."

Slowly Shadde turned his head until he was glaring at the Doctor. "Don't you really," he said sarcastically. And then he added, "You bloody soon will." The remark sounded like a pistol shot. He moved nearer. "You spent most of your time at the Embassy standing next to the bar table, swilling drinks as if you were a couple of bargees on a run ashore . . . and then"—he stopped and glared again—"not content with that, you tripped a waiter and created the sort of scene one expects in a third-rate music hall. D'you understand now what I mean?"

Careful, thought the Doctor, look at those fingers; the gorge is rising. But Symington either hadn't seen the signs or was beyond caring. "We had nothing to do with the waiter's fall, sir, and I submit with respect that . . ."

Shadde's mouth snapped shut in a hard line, and he held up an imperious hand. "Stop that! I'm not here to listen to your respectful submissions or any other of that damned nonsense. You listen to me." He swung around on the Doctor. "And you, too!" He took a deep breath. "Please understand that when naval officers are invited to a party at a British Embassy they're not invited in their personal capacities but as representatives of their ship, in the first instance, and as representatives of the Royal Navy, in the second. It's their duty to move around among the other guests and to do all that they can—repeat, *all that they can*—to leave a good impression of the ship and the service. That's what they're there for, d'you understand?" He gave them another fierce glare. "Not to see how many free drinks they can swill and—" He stopped abruptly and waved towards the door. "That will do. You may go."

The Doctor saw that Symington was about to answer, and with his eyes he signaled to him furiously. Symington acknowledged the signal with an almost imperceptible shrug of his shoulders, and they left the cabin.

When they got to the wardroom the young man slumped into a chair and with both hands ruffled his hair in a wild gesture of despair. "My God! Thank Heavens we're losing him soon! Don't think I can stand much more of that."

The Doctor looked at him sympathetically. "I know how

you feel, but I think he's to be pitied, not us. Life must be hell for him."

"But that junk about tripping the waiter . . ." Symington threw out his hands.

"Perhaps from the other end of the room it looked as if we did. We were right next to him when it happened."

"But why doesn't the Skipper investigate the thing properly, if he really thinks that, instead of accusing us and then refusing to listen to our explanations?"

"Your 'I submit with respect' was superb, George, but it was a torch to ruddy gunpowder, you—"

The Doctor was interrupted by the quartermaster's voice on the broadcast announcing the arrival of the launch alongside.

The Doctor and the engineer officer each respected the special knowledge of the other. Apart from that, Rhys Evans liked the Doctor's warm kindliness, and the Doctor liked the Welshman's sincerity. But because the engineer officer couldn't understand why Shadde disliked the Doctor, and the Doctor couldn't understand why Rhys Evans liked Shadde, the one person they never discussed was the Captain. For this reason, the Doctor was surprised when the engineer officer came to his cabin and broached the subject of Shadde.

The Welshman came straight to the point. "Doctor, there's a matter I'd like to discuss with you." Evans looked very worried.

The Doctor stubbed out his cigarette. "What's the trouble, Chiefy?"

"It's the Captain," said Rhys Evans. "Known him a long time, Doctor. Always a strange man." He shook his head. "There's a man, now, that's hard but just." He said it defiantly, as if he expected to be contradicted.

"You like him, don't you?"

157

"Indeed. He's a fine man, but I'm worried about him."

"I know he's got a very good record," said the Doctor gently. "But why are you worried?"

The Welshman looked at him in silence for a few moments. "You'll not tell a soul, Doctor?"

"Of course I won't, Chiefy."

Then Rhys Evans leaned forward and lowered his voice confidentially. "He's a sick man these last months. Worrying too much. Too much on his mind, and it's doing strange things to him."

The Doctor lit a cigarette. "What's he worrying about?"

"Just about everything. Sabotage business, for one thing, but other things too."

"Such as?" prompted the Doctor.

The Welshman's eyes regarded him gloomily. "I'll have to be telling you the whole story."

"Not unless you want to, Chiefy."

The engineer officer shook his head. "It's better that you should know."

"Just as you like."

In the next ten minutes Evans told the Doctor all he knew. He started with Shadde's marital troubles and described the effect on Shadde of Elizabeth's letter. "The worst must have happened," he said unhappily. Then he told of Shadde's preoccupation with what had happened in the Lombok Strait, that the Captain believed Symington had spread the story among the officers, of Shadde's belief that his officers were all against him, and of his suspicions about FOS/M's motives in bringing him ashore.

The Doctor cupped his chin in his hand. "Lot on his mind, hasn't he, poor chap. I know he's got this bee in his bonnet about *Retaliate* being slack, and I know he can't stand Number One or Symington or me—but I didn't know all the other stuff." He paused. "Did you know about that Lombok Strait business?"

The Welshman shook his head. "Not till he told me last night."

"Nor me. I'm certain it's never been mentioned in the wardroom. I'd know if it had. Symington's a good friend of mine."

Rhys Evans lit a cigarette and puffed at it. "Skipper's a changed man these days. Told me last night he can't sleep. Too much to worry about, he says, and he doesn't care to eat either. He seems to brood."

With clouded eyes he watched the Doctor. "Can you not help him, Doctor?"

The Doctor got up and looked in the mirror. He pulled his tie straight. "He's a difficult man to help, Chiefy. He's proud, you know. Not easy to approach. And he loathes me."

"He needs advice, Doctor." The Welshman said it with soft insistence.

"Chiefy, I don't think Shadde takes advice. He's not that type. Besides, from what you say it'd be difficult to give."

"What d'you mean?"

"Well, I mean— You say his wife's clearing out. No medical answer to that one, is there?"

The engineer officer was silent.

The Doctor looked at his fingernails. "This thing about the Lombok Strait and Symington. Obviously he's got some sort of fixation about that. But I can't lie him on a couch and drag it out. He'd put me in irons. Anyway, I'm not a psychiatrist—and even if I were it wouldn't help. He doesn't like psychiatrists. In Stockholm I tried to tell him of Kyle's psycho problems. Shadde bloody nearly exploded. I thought he was going to hit me. Said it was 'psychiatric claptrap and mumbo jumbo.'" The Doctor mimicked Shadde. "A threat and an affront to naval discipline." He looked at Rhys Evans and shook his head. "Sorry, Chiefy, I don't want a second dose of that. Life's too short."

Rhys Evans got up. "So we can do nothing for him?"

159

" 'Fraid not. He must sort out his own problems. But don't take it too much to heart. We've all got them, you know. Perhaps he's got a bit of an overload at present, and that's getting him down. But nature's a good healer. We'll be in Portsmouth in a few days' time and he'll be leaving us. He doesn't like the idea now, but a staff job will mean a rest and a change. He'll have more men of his own age around him too. Won't be as lonely as he is here. That'll probably put him right."

Rhys Evans wasn't convinced. "Maybe you're right, Doctor. I hope so. I don't like to see a man suffer."

The Doctor's smile was warm and sympathetic. "He's got a good friend in you, Chiefy."

The Captain returned on board from the mayor's lunch at half past two. He went straight to his cabin and rang for Miller. When the steward appeared, Shadde said, "I intend to sleep this afternoon. I don't want to be disturbed. Pass the word to the duty officer."

"What time would you like a call, sir?"

"At no time," snapped Shadde. "I don't require a call."

As Dusty Miller left the cabin he heard the Captain lock the door. He couldn't recall that having happened before.

When Miller had gone Shadde started to work on his report to FOS/M about the Korsör incident. But it was difficult to concentrate, and after about ten minutes he got up from the desk. He felt very tired, so he lay on his bunk and tried to sleep, but his brain was too active. After a while he turned off the cabin lights and lay there in the darkness, his mind in a turmoil, thinking about Elizabeth's letter. He still couldn't believe that she was going to Australia. When he got back to Petersfield the house would be empty; he would be there alone. That's how he'd start life in the new job ashore. What had happened to Elizabeth? In the last two years she'd changed so; all the sparkle and gaiety gone. It was difficult to remember now how she used to be. Except her eyes, he could remember them: bright and lively, with little crow's-feet at the corners—not dull and mournful like now.

What was the *real* trouble? Because she couldn't have children? Must have been that. She'd become tense and frustrated, always on the defensive, ready to quarrel about anything. She was always restless. Couldn't leave him alone for a moment, even when he was worried and preoccupied. When he sat alone and tried to sort out things she'd always come along and try to break into his thoughts. She tried to be subtle about it, but he could see that she was prying, determined to get to the back of his mind; and it always infuriated him.

There were some things that couldn't be shared. Elizabeth never seemed able to realize that. How desperately you wanted to be left alone if you were depressed and worried.

She had asked in the letter if he remembered that last leave at home? Of course he did. How could he forget it? It never stopped raining, and she was always in tears, or trying to get him to go for walks or to pictures. But you didn't want to do that if you were worrying, and how could he have told her what was worrying him? She would never understand what Symington's arrival on board had done to him. What did she know about the Lombok Strait, and how could he ever tell her? She would only despise him if she knew.

And then when he made interesting plans and tried to get her out of the rut she'd slipped into, she always threw cold water on them. She had a phobia about money and debt, as if they were the only people who had ever owed anything.

But for all that, he knew he couldn't go on without

Elizabeth. She was closer to him than any human being had ever been, and immensely more important. She had been the only dependable person in his life: loyal, dutiful, attentive. And though she irritated him more often these days, she was always ready to help and encourage him, and what little security he could find in life was all centered in her.

It was six o'clock when he turned on the lights again, but he had not slept. For three throbbing hours he'd been lying there, and now his mouth was swollen and dry. He got up and took three of the white pills; looking at the bottle, he remembered the day Elizabeth had given it to him, and he thought he was going to break down. But that was something he had never permitted himself since that night in the Lombok Strait.

He couldn't stay in the cabin any longer. There was something prodding at him. If he stayed there those thoughts would get the better of him. He decided to go to the wardroom, but he was in no mood to see his officers. It would be better to go ashore. He thought of Margrethe and wondered if she were doing anything. "Do ask me again," she had said at the party. "You're my favorite submarine captain."

Not a submarine captain for much longer, he thought, and then tried to forget all that. He would go ashore right away and telephone her. If she couldn't make it he would go out on his own. One way or another he'd drown his sorrows. No sense moping about in the cabin.

He rang for the messenger and told him to have the launch alongside in ten minutes. Then he changed into a dark suit, filled his cigarette case and counted the money in his wallet. Up on the casing Weddy, the duty officer, saw him over the side into the launch. The bowman shoved off and they headed up the inner harbor towards Nyhavn.

At the first telephone booth Shadde put a call through to the Embassy. He had forgotten Margrethe's surname. The clerk on duty was quick on the uptake and Shadde soon had the telephone number of her flat.

When he spoke to her she sounded delighted. No, she was not doing anything tonight. Yes, she would love to meet him for dinner.

He asked her where they should dine. "In the Pavilion at Langelinie," she said enthusiastically. "The restaurant is very good, and I like very much to look out over the harbor and see the ships."

"So do I," agreed Shadde. "When will we meet and where?"

"What time is it now?"

He looked at his watch. "Six thirty-seven."

"We can dine at half past eight or nine."

Shadde was impatient. "That's a long way off. Can't I meet you now?" He heard her laugh, that tinkling refreshing laugh he liked so much.

"I must change," she said. "That will be quite a business. I don't often dine with British submarine captains."

That made him laugh, too. "All right. Let's meet at seven fifteen. But where?"

"Yes. Come here. I have a car. I will take you for a little drive before dinner. It's not dark until at least half past ten or eleven—and not properly even then. You will see how beautiful the country is outside Copenhagen."

"That sounds magnificent. I've got your address. I'll take a taxi."

Margrethe had done it again. Just by hearing her voice and laughter that inward excitement, the feeling of exhilaration had come back. He went into the Angleterre and ordered a double whisky and soda.

The band was playing and from their table they could see the harbor framed in lilac trees, heavy with bloom. Beyond the water, on the other side of the harbor, the gantries stood like sentinels over the unpainted steel hull of a partially built ship, and another, still a skeleton of ribs and stringers was taking shape nearby.

Almost opposite where they sat, *Retaliate* lay at her buoy, a long, low shape with the sail-like conning tower. The small dark figures of the sentries on the fore- and after-casing emphasized the bigness of the submarine.

"Like a huge whale with a sail on its back," said Margrethe.

Shadde smiled—a sad smile she thought. "And I'm its Jonah."

Margrethe shook her head vigorously. "Never. You are not Jonah. But you are something strange."

"Strange?"

"You look so fierce, but you are not really fierce. You are kind. I think you are lonely."

Shadde laughed. "Thank you. I doubt if my officers would agree about the kindness."

"Those at the party? They looked nice."

"Hm," he said noncommitally. The waiter came to the table. "Have a liqueur?"

He was enjoying himself. The drive before dinner had been a success. Margrethe was first-rate company, kind and sympathetic and sparkling, and she had this terrific effect of buoying him up and making him forget his troubles. The dinner had been a good one and it had turned out that they both liked the same things to eat and drink. Shadde knew something about wine and had taken trouble in choosing them, and for the first time in a long while he had an appetite. They had cold salmon with a white Côtes-du-Rhône Hermitage, and then a filet mignon with Grand Vin Clos de Vougeot. And later on, despite Margrethe's protests, he had ordered a Château-Yqem with the schaum torte she'd suggested.

"What's a schaum torte?" he had said.

164

"Ah! You shall see. It is delicious. Meringues that taste of almonds. It is a Danish speciality."

"I'm game. Let's wash it down with Château-Yqem. That'll insure its success."

"It will insure that you are bankrupt," said Margrethe.

"Couldn't care less," he said gaily.

The band was playing something very smooth and romantic which exactly fitted Shadde's mood. He looked at Margrethe. She's a terrific girl, he thought. Something special about her. It wasn't easy to define. She seemed to glow with charm and eagerness. A tremendous feeling of well-being took possession of him.

"What'll we do now?" he said.

"What time is it?"

"About ten."

She sipped her liqueur, holding her glass with both hands, her eyes on him. "Do you like to dance?"

He looked out over the harbor. "I've got a boat coming in to pick me up at Nyhavn at eleven-thirty. Doesn't leave much time."

"So?"

"It's a glorious night. Couldn't we go for a drive?"

There was the ghost of a smile in her eyes. "Yes, of course."

When they got to the car he said, "Can I drive?"

She looked at him doubtfully. "Do you know the little Morris?"

"Had one for years."

"Very well. Then you drive," she said and got into the passenger's seat.

"Where to, Margrethe?"

"We can go to Bellevue."

"What's that?"

"You shall see. It is by the Sound. Very nice. I will show you the way."

They moved off and turned right into Grönningen and then up Österbrogade. He found, as he always did on the Continent, that it was strange at first having to keep to the right, but he soon got used to it. It wasn't really dark, but the streets were brightly lit and still busy, in spite of the chill breeze which came in from the Sound.

His strange feeling of exhilaration persisted and he chatted gaily and inconsequentially to Margrethe while he drove. A cyclist cut in ahead and as they swerved, Shadde said, "Damn his eyes." But he laughed as he said it.

"Be watchful," she said anxiously. "You will be in trouble if you hit a cyclist."

"That, madam, will be the day," he said, and began to sing the chorus from the "Toreador Song." His pitch was too deep but it wasn't bad.

> "Toreador, e'er watchful be:
> Toreador, Toreador,
> Do not forget the brightest of eyes
> Now fondly thee await.
> And love is the prize,
> Yes, love's the prize awaits thee, Oh, Toreador."

He stopped. "Phew—I'm out of breath."

"Go on." She laughed. "I like it."

At that moment they reached the busy traffic junction at Trianglen and he began to turn left. "No! No!" she cried in sudden alarm. "Keep right!"

Instantly he turned the wheel to the right but it was too late. The screeching of tires was followed by a jarring crash as something hit the back of the Morris.

Shadde stopped at once and they got out. The driver of the other car was already in the street—a small, angry, excited man. Margrethe spoke to him in Danish but he brushed her aside and shrilled at Shadde in English. "Why did you turn to the left? It is not permitted. You cannot turn to the left. Then you swing right. No signals. Nothing. How can I know?" he demanded excitedly.

Shadde's eyes narrowed. "Don't shout at me," he said coldly, towering over the small man. "I'm not deaf. Why didn't you look where you were going?"

A small crowd had gathered, and a policeman appeared. The little man spat a torrent of words at him and the policeman listened patiently. Then he took out his notebook and questioned Shadde and Margrethe. Yes, it was her car. Yes, he was the driver. Yes, he was an English visitor. Yes, he had a license, an international one. No, it was not with him. Where was it? On board his ship in the harbor. What ship? *Retaliate.* The policeman looked up with new interest. The big British submarine? Yes, the big British submarine. There was a murmur from the crowd.

"Did you try to turn left?" asked the policeman.

"Yes, I did," said Shadde.

"It is not permitted to turn left here." The policeman pointed. "Look! There are the signs."

"Afraid I missed them," said Shadde. "I'm used to keeping to the left. I started to turn left through force of habit."

At this the little man bounced with indignation and waved his arms. "You see. It was his fault," he shouted.

Shadde looked at him with unconcealed contempt. "Kindly stop shouting," he said coldly.

This brought forth an impassioned protest in Danish.

The policeman looked at Shadde inquiringly. "Did you have anything to drink tonight?"

Shadde turned to Margrethe. "Can't you do something about this? It's most humiliating—I mean being quizzed in front of this crowd of yahoos, with that jack-in-the-box bobbing up and down in the background."

She and the policeman spoke to each other in Danish.

"He says we must go to the police station. Also, you must produce your driving license."

"How can I? We're sailing at eight-thirty tomorrow morning."

"I know. I told him. He says that makes no difference. You must produce it. The little man wishes to make trouble. He says you've been drinking."

"I have," said Shadde irritably. "But not the way he thinks. Anyway, let's go to the ruddy police station. It'll be better than performing in front of this lot."

The damage to the cars was slight—crumpled bumpers and fenders—and they were able to drive off. Margrethe took the wheel, Shadde sat next to her and the policeman got in behind. Still muttering with indignation, the little man climbed into his car and followed them doggedly. Shadde's high spirits had gone and in their place anxiety and depression had taken over. A wonderful night had been ruined, the situation in which he now found himself was stupid and humiliating, and he was worried about the con-sequences.

At the police station a surgeon took a specimen of blood from Shadde's forearm and explained that it would be used for the blood-alcohol test. An inspector told him that he must produce his driving license. Yes, it would be in order if it were sent up by messenger between seven and eight next morning. No, he could not say if there would be a prosecution. It would depend on the blood-alcohol test. Yes, the other man had laid a charge. Yes, they could go now but Commander Shadde might be required in court on the following day. Yes, he realized the Commander's sub-marine was to sail at eight-thirty the next day; it was unfortunate, but it made no difference. The law was the law.

From the police station they trailed off miserably to Margrethe's apartment, where she lived with her mother. On Margrethe's advice they telephoned the First Secretary and Shadde explained what had happened. Margrethe took the phone and confirmed his story. The First Secretary was concerned but understanding and helpful. "Wait there," he said, "until I ring you back." Twenty minutes later he rang back to say that Shadde wouldn't be required in court the next day and could sail in *Retaliate*. But the Embassy had been forced to promise that Shadde would return to Copenhagen to stand trial if summoned to appear.

"Does a minor collision justify all this fuss and bother?" asked Shadde icily.

"It's not that alone, unfortunately. Seems the blood-alcohol test wasn't too hot from your point of view."

At once Shadde protested that he was far from being tight; he explained what he had had to drink since coming ashore that evening: a double whisky, a single whisky, a martini, a sherry, five or six glasses of wine—or perhaps more, he was not quite sure—and an old brandy. Margrethe confirmed this.

"I'm sure you weren't," said the First Secretary sympathetically. "But you evidently dined and wined pretty well, and the Danes take their blood-alcohol tests rather seriously, particularly when a charge has been laid. But don't worry. We'll do what we can to put things right tomorrow and I hope they'll drop it. In the meantime," he went on, "they insist on seeing your license. So be a good chap and send it up in the morning."

Gloomily Shadde agreed, and thanked the First Secretary for his help.

"Don't mention it, my dear chap; these things happen in the best regulated families. Sorry you had such bad luck. Of course," he chuckled, "if you will go gadding with my pretty secretary you must expect this sort of thing."

Shadde was far from amused.

|| II ||

On that second afternoon in Copenhagen, the first lieutenant and Bagnall, the commissioned gunnery officer, were
the only members of *Retaliate*'s wardroom to watch the
soccer match between teams from the Danish naval base and
the submarine. Cavan was a rugger man who found soccer
boring to a degree, but he never missed a match in which *Retaliate* was playing. Early in his naval career he had learned
that this was one of the things which the successful naval
officer did, and so his tall figure on the sidelines and his booming "Come on, *Retaliates!*" became an indispensable part of
the team's effort. The men liked to have him there and
quietly admired his unwavering resolution.

After the match Cavan went back on board and changed
into uniform. Looking through the file of signals on his
desk he found one from *Massive* notifying her intention to
enter Oslo at 0900 the next day, and another from *Deterrent*
reporting her departure from Loch Ewe at 1630. Among
the domestic signals was one recording that leave for
Retaliate's ratings would expire at midnight and for officers

at 0200. He lit a cigarette and then settled down at the desk to write up his diary, a task which he took seriously and about which he was conscientious and meticulous. Then he wrote a letter to his mother, a conventional letter mostly about the places they had visited and about his health. Briefly and noncommittally he mentioned that he was finding the Captain a little difficult, but on rereading the letter he decided that this was a bit risky; mothers were apt to talk and it was unwise to have it known that you were not getting on with your captain. He crossed out the offending sentence with heavy strokes until it was illegible. Then he went to the wardroom, where he accepted the drink Weddy offered him.

"Where's Symington and the Sub?" he asked.

"On a run ashore with the Doctor and Gallagher."

"What're they after?"

"Wine, women and song."

"God forbid. Not another Oslo?"

"Could be," said Goss. "They went off in great style."

Just then Mr. Buddington came into the wardroom and said, "Good evening, gentlemen." His manner suggested that he feared someone might throw something at him.

Weddy smiled. "Hullo, Mr. B. What'll you have to drink?"

"That is very kind of you. A glass of sherry, please."

A telegraphist came in with a sheaf of W/T signals and showed them to Weddy and the first lieutenant.

Mr. Buddington cleared his throat. "What time are we sailing tomorrow?"

"O-eight-thirty," said the first lieutenant.

When Mr. Buddington's sherry arrived, the first lieutenant and Weddy said, "Cheers!" And the little man from the Admiralty blinked and said, "Your very good health, gentlemen."

Ten minutes later the wardroom had settled down to

its normal predinner routine, and Mr. Buddington and Goss were in a corner playing chess. It was their fourth encounter and it followed the pattern of its predecessors: Goss playing with fiery aggression and not much else, and Mr. Buddington playing thoughtfully and with care so that he soon had the upper hand. Musgrove was reading, one hand holding the book, the other plucking at his neat black beard, his forehead furrowed by a permanent frown. Goss leaned forward and moved the queen's bishop. Mr. Buddington looked at the board, then at Goss and said with mild surprise, "You lose your queen, I fear."

Goss's chin thrust forward and he looked at the board with fierce concentration. "Damn and blast it! So I do."

"Do have the move again," entreated Mr. Buddington.

"Never!" Goss said firmly. "The Goss's fight fair. I resign." He looked at Mr. Buddington's glass. "Have the other half?"

"No, no, thank you. I've had enough."

"Enough?" Goss boomed. "You wouldn't have beaten me if you had." He bundled the pieces into the wooden box.

From the settee next to him, Mr. Buddington picked up the *Daily Express* and pointed to a headline, "Commons Uproar on A-subs."

"Did you read it?" he asked Goss.

"Yes. Usual tripe about unauthorized firings. Raised every six months. First they went for the U.S. Navy. Now that we've got Polaris boats, it's us."

"I suppose those who bring this matter up in the House are reasonably well informed?" Mr. Buddington said deferentially.

Goss shook his head. "Lot of ignorant b's—take it from me. The penny hasn't dropped yet."

Mr. Buddington raised his eyebrows. "What does that mean?"

"Unauthorized firings are impossible."

"Impossible?" said Mr. Buddington.

"Yes, impossible. The security precautions look after that. You'd need collusion between too many different people in too many different places for an unauthorized firing."

"That's very reassuring," said Mr. Buddington. "What are the precautions, or is that a state secret?"

"They're well known in the service, and I've seen garbled versions in the press." Goss was looking at Mr. Buddington, summing him up. "You must have a high security rating or you wouldn't have been let loose here. Anyway, you won't repeat what I tell you?"

"Indeed, I will not," said Mr. Buddington primly, "I have been in the construction department for twenty years."

"Yes, of course," said Goss, "I'd forgotten that." He drained his glass, put it down on the table and lit a cigarette. "Anyway, there's no secret about the general procedure. There are checks and controls on firing at all stages. They start at NATO and run down through FOS operations room to the final control here."

"What happens at NATO?"

"Roughly this: there are always several senior staff officers on duty in the ops room representing the NATO chiefs of staff. In the case of the Polaris boats there's also a bloke representing the U.S. chiefs of staff. Our operational authority—Flag Officer Submarines—can only order us to fire if he's told to do so by NATO. Then there's another sort of tripartite control in FOS's ops room. NATO can only order them to fire by means of a special transmitter, and FOS can only order us to fire by the same means. The NATO transmitter won't work unless a number of NATO staff officers and the U.S. chap set the control dials with readings which only they know. FOS's transmitter to us won't work unless the NATO transmitter has actuated it first, and even then, three different people in FOS's ops room have to put special settings on their control dials."

173

Mr. Buddington wasn't altogether satisfied. "How would we know if an ordinary W/T transmitter had been used to send the firing signal to us?"

Goss nodded appreciatively. "Good point! Because the firing signal contains special address, prefix and target co-ordinate groups, which are top secret ciphers. Only NATO and the firing submarine have them."

"I see," said Mr. Buddington. "And what is the control here?"

Goss rang for the steward and pointed to his empty glass. "Another, please, Target." He looked at Mr. Buddington. "You too?"

The little man shrank back. "No, *thank* you."

"Well, first we must receive a signal with those special groups I've mentioned."

"What would happen if someone on board—you for example—decided to fire a missile? What could stop you?"

"Lots of things," said Goss, "Takes a lot of people to fire a Polaris—I'd have to get them to agree first. Then the firing circuits can't be actuated until our local control has approved the firing."

"And the local control is . . . ?" prompted Mr. Buddington.

"Firing signal has to be seen, and its import agreed upon, by the four different people on board who control our firing circuit. Unless each puts his own secret setting on a control dial, the missile can't be fired. It's mechanically and electrically impossible—no way around it."

Mr. Buddington nodded slowly, blinking at the lieutenant commander. "Remarkable. Who are the four people on board who do this?"

"Captain, first lieutenant, Weddy—our ballistics king—and Dwight Gallagher. He represents the United States chiefs of staffs. You know that they gave us these boats subject to their right to veto firings at all control levels. That's why we cart Dwight around the ocean with us."

"I see," said Mr. Buddington thoughtfully. "But if these facts are known in the Commons, why do they become so agitated about unauthorized firings?"

Goss shrugged his shoulders. "Don't ask me. They're politicians. When they're not talking nonsense about ballistic missiles they're belly-aching about something else. They've got to natter and make a stink—that's what they're paid for."

Mr. Buddington took off his glasses. "I see," he said. "I must confess I feel happier now. It's something I have always worried about. I expect most thinking people do." He paused. "D'you think the U.S. Air Force's atom bombers we read about—you know, they say a certain number are always in the air—d'you think they have the same sort of control?"

Goss lit another cigarette with a flourish and threw the match away. "Detail's probably different, but the overall picture's bound to be the same."

Target came in from the wardroom pantry. "Dinner's ready, sir," he said to the first lieutenant. "Care to 'ave it served now?"

The first lieutenant stood up, stretched his arms and yawned. "Yes, please, Target. Come on chaps. Once more to the trough."

At ten o'clock Dwight Gallagher suggested moving on.
"Where to?" asked Symington.
"Pelikan."
"What's it like?" The Doctor was being cautious.
"Cool," said Gallagher. "Really cool."
Keely's deep voice broke in. "Dancing girls?"
"Naturally," said Gallagher. "How not?"
"Let's go," said the Doctor.

Symington paid the bill and they left Faergekros. Outside in the street Gallagher put two fingers in his mouth and let out a high whistle. A taxi came up and they bundled in. The driver was a little hunched-up fellow and he jumped nervously when Gallagher touched him on the shoulder.

"You know the Pelikan?"

"I know all places," said the driver sourly.

Five minutes later the taxi stopped and they got out near a church. On the opposite side of the street a green and yellow neon sign flashed "Pelikan," and below it a flight of steps went down to a basement. Gallagher led the way, and they passed through swinging doors to a smoke-filled cellar crowded with people. The lights were low and the band was playing as they skirted around the packed floor. The headwaiter showed them to a table at the edge of the floor opposite the band, took their orders and disappeared. As their eyes became accustomed to the darkness, they saw the shadowy outline of men and women on high stools at a bar at the far end of the cellar.

Keely yawned. "I'm going over to the bar and see what gives," he said casually, and left the table.

"The eternal search," said the Doctor.

The band stopped, the lights went up and the floor emptied. Symington looked around the cellar and raised an eyebrow. "Very Left Bank, Dwight."

Gallagher nodded. "Wonderful, isn't it?"

"Been here before?"

"Three years ago. In a flattop. We had lots of fun. Conjurers, acrobats, strips, the lot."

"I see," said Symington. "Very high class."

The whirl of voices was drowned by the band as it crashed into life. The floor filled, the lights dimmed, the music hushed and a Negro stepped down from the dais and took over the rhythm with triumphant flourishes of his trumpet. The spotlight followed him as he moved among the dancers, its light reflected in his waving trumpet.

Peter Keely loomed up out of the darkness, twitching and shuffling to the music. He clapped his hands to the beat; opposite him a dark girl wiggled her hips and gyrated, her sloe eyes glued to his feet and her arms held like half-spread wings above the swirl of her skirt.

"Strictly clinically," said the Doctor, "they're beat drunk."

"Speaking of drunks," complained Gallagher. "Look at my glass." Symington poured a schnappes and passed the bottle.

When the band stopped Keely came back to the table.

"Where's the lady?" said Gallagher.

Keely looked across the floor. "Gone back to her husband." He sighed. "Why don't you people dance? Music's terrific."

Over on the dais the band put down their instruments and drifted off towards the bar. The Doctor took a deep draught of beer, put the glass on the table, wiped the froth from his lips and looked at his watch.

"Midnight," he said and jerked his head towards the deserted dais. "What say?"

Keely took his eyes away from the girl at the next table and raised his eyebrows at Symington. "What say, George?"

Symington laughed nervously and then gulped down his schnappes and spluttered. When he had recovered, he gasped, "Yes, let's."

They got up and moved slowly around the edge of the dance floor, stopping now and then by a table, Keely chatting to whoever happened to be about.

"Jesus!" said Gallagher. "They're not going to foul up this party?"

"Shouldn't think so," said the Doctor. "Have a drink and relax." With fatherly concern he filled Gallagher's glass.

The American pulled at his collar. "If there's fighting, I quit," he said firmly. "I'm aboard *Retaliate* to stop missile-happiness, not to give you fellows protection ashore." He paused, then added, "Anyways, I'm after promotion." And he meant it.

The Doctor kept his eyes on Symington and Keely. "No fights, Dwight, I promise. The word of an Irish gentleman."

Gallagher gave a hollow laugh. "You were the worst of the bunch in Oslo."

In the half-darkness the Doctor saw that Symington had reached the piano and Keely was stooping and that he had the trumpet in his hand as he came upright. It was any minute now. The sublieutenant moved to the front of the dais, put the trumpet to his lips, blew a high, piercing E, and swung into "A Love Is Born" to a small muted piano accompaniment from Symington.

At the first note of the trumpet the band leader came back quickly from the bar. He stood below the dais, listening uncertainly, and then went back to his seat. The spotlight came on and picked out Symington and Keely, and as the last note died from the trumpet, the cellar rang with applause and shouts of "bravo" and "encore." Keely laughed and shook his head, but he came down from the dais and stood at the mike, the spotlight following him. Behind him Symington crossed over from the piano to the drums. Keely held the mike in both hands and looked slowly around the cellar, smiling, his teeth brilliantly white in his flushed face. He held up a hand and there was silence, broken now and then by scattered laughter. "Thank you," he said. "Thank you very much. And now, may I introduce . . . Patriski! The Polish wonder boy!"

Symington rolled the drums and Keely flung his arm towards the center of the floor. The spotlight tracked across and picked up a male dancer frozen in a forward lunge, pointing at some distant horizon. He wore a white open-necked shirt, and his bare legs and feet stuck out like white pins below dark trousers turned up to the knees. The drums rolled again and the dancer leapt and spun and struck another pose, now facing the dais. His red hair was tousled and hung untidily above ears which stood out like sails. There was clapping and shouting and Keely went back to the dais, where Symington had moved across to the piano.

"Doc's bloody good, isn't he?" shouted Keely.

"Terrific," Symington agreed.

To the accompaniment of the piano and the drums, the Doctor swung into his act with fiery energy. He leapt and capered, somersaulted and pirouetted about the small floor in a wild burlesque of ballet and acrobatics. It went down very well with the customers. The fusing of alcohol with the blood of his Irish and Russian ancestors produced the most astonishing results, including a finale of handsprings and cartwheels to a roar of cheers. Above it Symington heard Gallagher's booming voice. "Olé, olé."

The Doctor stood in the glare of the spotlight making prancing, elfinlike bows. Over the mike Keely said, "That's all, ladies and gentlemen, thank you." And the applause started all over again.

When Keely and Symington got back to the table, the Doctor was already there, rolling down his trouser legs and panting with exhaustion while men and women stood around him laughing and talking. The sloe-eyed Danish girl came up and threw her arms around Keely's neck. "Peter," she cried. "You wair wandeefule."

The band started to play, and people drifted back to the floor and to their tables. The Doctor was busy with his tie and still breathless, but he looked at Gallagher and panted triumphantly, "See, Dwight, no fights."

"Yes, maybe I made a mistake." Then he turned to Keely. "Peter, that was some trumpet you blew."

"Mellifluous, wasn't it?" agreed Symington.

"You're all crazy as loons, but it was a great act."

The night wore on and the Japanese acrobats—small, sphinxlike little men, who did incredible things while their muscles rippled and trembled and knotted under nut-brown skins—came and went.

Then the compere took the mike. He spoke in Danish, French, English and German, and it seemed that he could have spoken in any other language that might have been necessary. "And now, folks, it's getting late," he said very smoothly, with an accent that didn't place him any more exactly than Western Europe. "There's a little lady here," he went on, "who's kinda tired and wants to go to bed." The band broke in appropriately, and the master of ceremonies continued, "And so she'd like to get ready for bed—*right here!*" The drums rolled majestically, and somewhere in the darkness a woman's brassy laugh cut off suddenly.

A girl stepped into the spotlight to a welcoming roar. She wore a sequin-studded, wine-colored gown, and around her shoulders was a fur stole. She had the authentic pinup girl curves and bulges, and that unamused, you-bore-me-to-hell, cheese-cake smile. When the clapping stopped she turned slowly on her heel and went around the floor showing off the gown and the stole and her body in the unreal, half-hurried, slightly self-conscious strut of a mannequin. When the parade was finished she returned to the middle of the floor, taking the spotlight with her. She put the back of her hand to her mouth and yawned, finishing off with a sigh, as she let the stole fall from her shoulders. The background music came up full and she kept time with the rhythm, moving around the floor, the spotlight always with her.

Then she started to loosen the fastenings on her gown in

an intimate, feminine sort of way. It slid to the floor, and after she had stepped out of it, she picked it up and threw it into the darkness beyond the spotlight, where shrieks of laughter and men's voices were calling out. The music went to a faster beat and she paraded again, keeping time to it, her hands caressing her body as she went. She stopped at a floorside table and looked hard at a gray-haired man sitting there. There was a lot of giggling around him and he looked half embarrassed and half pleased when she sat on his knee and ruffled his hair. The patrons roared their approval. When she got up the band started again, and as she undressed and paraded the oldest man at each table was the target for her affections.

Symington must have had an inkling of what was coming because he whispered, "So long, chaps," and disappeared into the darkness.

"Clot!" breathed Keely hoarsely. "He'll miss the *pièce de résistance.*"

"Not much resistance," said the Doctor.

The girl was now down to the smallest of brassieres and the skimpiest of panties, and the music stopped for the drums to beat a slow tattoo. Suddenly the girl had nothing on, and was making a show of outraged modesty as she tried to cover her breasts and thighs with hands and arms. But she didn't try very hard, and there was a lot of applause and shrill whistles before the band started up again. Now a girl in green came to the mike and crooned in a baby voice.

On the floor the nude girl and the spotlight were making the rounds again and there was laughter and giggling at each table she approached. Sometimes a man would make a grab at her and his partner would let out a shocked feminine squeal, but the girl knew her audience and swerved out of reach each time like a football player running for the line.

Suddenly the Doctor sensed that their table was the target. Until now the girl had seemed to ignore it, but here she was coming straight towards them. He shrank back into the darkness and thanked God that his chair was not on the dance floor, but Dwight Gallagher, plumb in the line of advance, seemed blissfully unaware of what was happening. As the girl reached the table, Keely said, "How ya, baby?" It earned him a dazzling smile but no more, because she dropped onto Gallagher's lap, took his face in her hands and sighed, "Honey man." She snuggled up to him, twining her arms around his neck, and threw in a long, very personal kiss, while she tousled his hair with her hands.

At heart, Dwight Gallagher was a modest man, a minder of his own business and an avoider of the limelight. Sitting there under the spotlight with a naked girl all over him and the customers shouting their heads off made him very unhappy. Twice he appealed to her unsuccessfully, finally he called out, "For Christ's sake, get this dame off me, will you?"

"Honey," she said, hugging him tighter, "don't be like that. I want . . ." But she never finished the sentence. Her back had been towards the Doctor and the pink round of her bottom within two or three inches of the cigarette in his left hand, and he had succumbed to the temptation. There was a shrill, piercing "Ow!" and she shot into the air as if propelled by some hidden force. In a flash she turned and slapped Gallagher's face. "You mean bastard!" she yelped, as she rubbed her bottom. "Whadya do that for?"

Suddenly there was a lot of noise and shouting, and the lights went up. Some of the band started to move over towards the table. "Let's get to hell out of here," shouted Gallagher, but he needn't have said it; the Doctor and Keely were making for the door so fast that he was left way behind. As he shot into the street, Symington raced up beside him. "Dwight," he laughed breathlessly, "What the hell did you do?"

At about half past ten that night Mr. Buddington went to his cabin and spent the next hour working on the papers from the Director of Naval Intelligence. Then he lay on the bunk reading until he could no longer trust himself to keep awake. He set his small traveling alarm clock, put it under his pillow and fell into a sound sleep.

It seemed only a moment later that he was jangled awake although his watch showed three-thirty. He went to the mirror, straightened his hair and then, with the black leather box over his shoulder, left the cabin. When he reached the victualing store he looked around to make sure the coast was clear before opening the door and locking it behind him. From the top shelf he took a silk lamp shade, and from his pocket a magnifying glass. With infinite care he compared the silk of the lamp shade with the small piece of gray silk that he took from his pocket. The blade marks on the cut edges were identical; the two pieces of silk had been cut with the same pair of scissors.

A few moments later Mr. Buddington was back in his cabin doing some hard thinking. Shadde had said, "Find the owner of the gray silk and you've got your man." And it was beginning to look as if Shadde were right. The case against Shepherd, weak and fanciful at first, was becoming substantial. He was the maker of the silk lamp shades; the scissors were his; he had been in charge of the men working in the steering compartment immediately before leaving Stockholm; the leave records sent by DNI showed that he had been on board on both occasions—in Portsmouth and Queensferry—when sabotage might have taken place; and he had access to the machinery and the technical knowledge necessary. Lastly, the confidential background material requested by Mr. Buddington, and received from DNI the day before, contained the ingredients of a motive, for it revealed that Shepherd was having a clandestine love affair with his sister-in-law, a Mrs. Winifred Hindle.

In itself that was no motive, of course, but DNI's report went on to say that Mrs. Hindle and Shepherd were staunch supporters of the same church, and that she was a prominent member of the ban-the-bomb movement in Portsmouth.

Mr. Buddington looked at himself in the mirror, laid his finger alongside his nose and reflected that there was no end to what people would do in the name of love and religion. But he was a careful man and never jumped to conclusions—particularly when the evidence was circumstantial. Besides, a great deal depended on the outcome of the tests still to be made in the steering compartment. There were others who might be implicated.

|| 12 ||

Chief E.R.A. Shepherd returned on board just before midnight. As soon as he reached the C.P.O.s' mess the duty E.R.A. reported to him. "We can't find Kyle. He was on watch in the engine room with Dobbin, but he's disappeared."

Shepherd's face tautened. "Disappeared? What d'you mean?"

"He disappeared about half an hour ago. Told Dobbin he was off to the heads. Fifteen minutes later he hadn't shown up, so Dobbin went looking for him in the stokers' mess. He wasn't there."

"Reported this to the Duty Officer yet?"

"No. Not had a proper search yet. I've checked on the machinery spaces. I was going off to do the forward compartments when you come down."

Shepherd thought for a moment. "O.K. You carry on forward. I'll do a double-check aft. If we don't find him chop chop we'll report to the duty officer. He may have gone over the side."

The search began. First Shepherd looked through the engine-room spaces, then in the stokers' mess, where those men on board who were not on duty were already asleep in their bunks. He noticed that although the watertight door between the messdeck and the steering compartment was shut, the clips were not secured. When he entered the lights were off and he sensed at once that something was wrong. He switched them on and there at the far end of the compartment was Kyle, sitting on a folded watchcoat with his back to the aftermost bulkhead. In his right hand he had a half-empty bottle which he was raising to his lips. He blinked at Shepherd with bleary, hostile eyes and waved the bottle feebly.

" 'Ullo, Mr. Bloody-nosey-parker-Shepherd," he said thickly. "What the flippin' 'ell d'you want?"

Shepherd moved towards him. "That'll do, Kyle," he said sharply. "You come along with me to the duty officer. You're supposed to be on watch."

Kyle hiccoughed. "Flip the flippin' duty officer." He raised the bottle to his lips and drank from it.

Shepherd hesitated for a moment. Then he snatched the bottle from Kyle's hand and looked at the label. It was Courvoisier. Kyle clambered laboriously to his feet and stood facing Shepherd, hands on his hips, body swaying, hair disheveled, the white face blotchy and erupted.

"Where did you get this brandy, Kyle?" Shepherd's voice rose to a higher pitch. "Looks like wardroom stock to me."

Kyle's face was twisted with contempt. "It does, does it? Well, you c'n shove it up, Chief," he said thickly. "That's what you c'n do—just shove it up."

Shepherd's anger was rising. He seized Kyle by the arm. "You come along with me, you dirty little runt," he said through clenched teeth. Kyle shook himself free and stepped back. "For Christ's sake! Take yer flippin' paws off me, yer bloody bastard!" he shrilled.

The blasphemy was too much for Shepherd; up to a

point he could stand insults from a drunk, but he wasn't prepared to have the Almighty's name coupled with them. He moved in swiftly, and as he came Kyle lashed out. It was a crude drunken blow, but Shepherd was not expecting it and it caught him full in the mouth. He stopped in his tracks, his eyes unbelieving, then he put down the bottle of brandy, squared his shoulders and hit Kyle twice in rapid succession. Shepherd was a strong man and the stoker went down like a felled ox.

Shepherd pulled him up and half carried, half dragged him to the messdeck, where he wakened two men and got them to help him carry the stoker to the control room. There he handed him over to the duty petty officer. "Keep him here while I go and report to the duty officer," he said.

The petty officer looked down at Kyle. "Don't look as if he needs much keepin' 'ere. He's in dreamland, all right. What hit 'im?"

"I did," said Shepherd grimly. "In self-defense." He pointed to his puffed and swollen mouth.

The petty officer's eyes went wide with surprise. "Blimey. Hit you did 'e, Chief? Well, I never. Nice state of affairs, I'll say. Striking a chief petty officer. Love a duck! What's the navy coming to?"

Shepherd went off to the wardroom. Weddy, the duty officer, was there and the chief E.R.A. reported at once what had happened.

Weddy whistled. "Struck you, did he, Chief? That's serious. I'll come along at once."

He followed Shepherd back into the control room. Kyle had recovered consciousness, but he was dazed and found difficulty in standing. It was clear that he was in no condition to take any interest in the proceedings. Weddy said to the duty petty officer, "Lock him up in the sick bay and let him cool off." He turned to Shepherd, "You'd better give him a hand, Shepherd. When you've done that, bring me the bottle. We'll have to investigate this in the morning and see how he got hold of it."

"Aye, aye, sir."

Weddy went back into the wardroom and knocked on the door of the first lieutenant's cabin. Cavan was sitting at the desk in his shirt sleeves, writing, when he came in. "Hullo, Weddy, what's the trouble?"

"There's been a hell of a shemozzle! Kyle's deserted his watch and he's been drinking. A bottle of our Courvoisier, I think. He's as drunk as a lord. Shepherd found him in the steering compartment, and when he tried to bring him along to the control room, Kyle struck him."

Cavan dropped his pen and spun around in his chair. "Good God! What've you done with him?"

"Locked him in the sick bay. No good seeing him now. He's too far gone."

Cavan nodded. "Good. Let him cool off there. Must be round the bend striking a chief P.O."

Weddy shook his head. "Deserted his watch. Stole wardroom liquor. Drunk on board. Struck a chief petty officer. Don't envy him when he comes up before the Skipper."

The first lieutenant's face was grim. "Nor do I," he said.

After the telephone conversation with the First Secretary, Shadde discussed with Margrethe the damage to her car and arranged that she send him the bill for repairs which, despite her protests, he insisted on settling. These arrangements made, he bade her an apologetic good night. At the corner he hailed a passing taxi and was soon at Nyhavn.

It was five minutes past midnight and the launch which had come in at eleven-thirty was still waiting for him. He apologized to the Danish coxswain, and they set off up the harbor.

Shadde was in a ferment of worry and anger. The night had ended disastrously, and now he was threatened with an appearance in the Danish courts on a charge of drunken driving. To travel back to Copenhagen from Portsmouth at his own expense, and to foot the bills for the damage to Margrethe's car and legal representation in court, would involve a good deal of money—much more than he could afford. But far worse than the expense was the humiliation of it all, and the possible consequences to his naval career. The Admiralty would know all about it, that he didn't doubt. The First Secretary would be bound to make a report, and if the case went to court the press would jump at it. It wasn't every day that the captain of a British nuclear submarine appeared in the Danish courts on a charge of drunken driving.

As the launch made its way across the harbor, Shadde looked ahead and saw the dark outline of *Retaliate* against the arc lights over the shipyards. When they neared her, the sentry on the after-casing hailed, "Boat ahoy." The Danish coxswain answered. *"Retaliate,"* and a few seconds later they were alongside. But there was no duty officer or petty officer to see him on board, and Shadde set his mouth grimly. Down in the control room he found a quartermaster, but no one else. Finally, in the wardroom he found Weddy and Shepherd looking at a bottle of liquor and laughing. They stood aside as he came in, but he ignored them, went into his cabin and slammed the door shut. They heard his bell ring and saw the quartermaster come in from the control room and go into the cabin.

"Tell the first lieutenant I wish to see him at once," snapped Shadde.

"Aye, aye, sir."

A moment later Shadde heard a knock on his door and Cavan came in. "You wanted me, sir?" The lieutenant saw at once that the Captain was in a raging temper. He

189

was standing with his back to the bunk, feet apart, his eyes flashing and his voice shaking with anger. "Why weren't the duty officer and duty petty officer on the casing to meet me when I came on board?" he demanded.

"They were down below, sir. The duty officer was—"

Shadde raised an imperious hand. "I'm perfectly well aware of that. I've just observed Weddy and Shepherd in the wardroom with a bottle." He paused and then added with heavy sarcasm. "Drinking my good health, no doubt."

"They weren't drinking, sir, they were—"

"Are you suggesting that I'm a liar, Number One?" interrupted Shadde.

"No, sir, I'm not. But Weddy and Shepherd are investigating a charge against Kyle, and the duty petty officer has . . ."

Again Shadde interrupted. "What charge?"

"He's drunk and he struck Chief E.R.A. Shepherd."

Shadde glared at him. His voice echoed his disbelief. "Drunk? How can he be drunk? He's not been ashore. He's under stoppage of leave."

"He must have pilfered a bottle of brandy from the wardroom."

Shadde turned away and picked up a sheaf of signals from the desk. "This is all most interesting," he said sarcastically, "but it doesn't explain why the duty officer didn't consider it necessary to meet me on the casing when the launch came alongside. Why wasn't he there?"

"I imagine because he was in the control room at that moment dealing with Kyle, sir. All this has happened within the last few minutes."

Shadde turned his head quickly and looked at the first lieutenant. "You *imagine* do you?" he mimicked. "Possibly you can also *imagine* why the duty petty officer, at least, was not on the casing?"

"He was assisting the duty officer. Guarding Kyle,

sir." The first lieutenant pulled at his ear, a habit which irritated Shadde intensely.

"I see," said Shadde. "Everybody was so bloody busy that it didn't matter a damn about the Captain coming off. After all," he added sarcastically, "he knows his way about the boat, so let him find his own way on board."

Cavan was beginning to have difficulty with his temper, but all the time he kept thinking, I must keep calm, he's baiting me, I must keep calm. He said quietly, "I can assure you, sir, that that was not the case."

Shadde picked up the sheaf of signals again and began to turn them one by one. "Anyone adrift?" His tone was ominously casual.

"Yes, sir. Holmes and Brown."

"Hm," said Shadde, "I'm not surprised. This boat's so bloody slack nothing surprises me."

Cavan said nothing, and this must have irritated Shadde because he glared at the first lieutenant. "You know, Cavan, I don't think you appreciate the seriousness of all this. You seem to have got into a sort of disciplinary rut, if I may say so. But I'm not used to arriving alongside without a duty officer to receive me on board."

The First Lieutenant stood quite still and Shadde flashed a look at him from under dark, bushy eyebrows. His voice was rising now and the veins on his temples were swollen. "No," he went on, "and I'm not used to boats where ratings help themselves to wardroom liquor and strike chief petty officers after drunken orgies." He started pacing up and down with his hands clasped behind his back. "I'm handing over in a few days to a new commanding officer. I can assure you I don't intend to hand over a slack boat. I haven't much time left but I intend to shake this boat up in no mean fashion." He stopped and his dark eyes pierced Cavan's. "D'you understand?"

The first lieutenant made no reply.

"For a start," Shadde went on, "you'll inform the duty officer that he's incurred my displeasure. For that I shall require him to be duty officer every day for the first ten days in Portsmouth."

At this Cavan looked him square in the face. "He's due to go on leave as soon as we reach Portsmouth, sir."

Shadde threw the sheaf of signals onto the desk and his voice shook with anger. "I don't give a damn what he's due for. You heard my orders. Carry them out."

Cavan felt that the Captain was behaving monstrously, but he realized that it would be dangerous to argue with him. Shadde was clearly beside himself with anger and beyond all reason. The first lieutenant was due for promotion to commander and he was going to keep his yardarm clear whatever it cost. He left the Captain's cabin without a word.

At five minutes past one, Shadde got onto his bunk and turned off the cabin lights. It seemed a long time now since he had enjoyed a really good night's rest. But though he was tired to the point of exhaustion he couldn't sleep. He lay there tormented by his thoughts: Elizabeth's letter, the collision in Stockholm, the end of his service afloat, and now the car accident and the dreadful indignities and humiliations it promised. He had drunk a good deal, he knew, but he had a considerable capacity for alcohol. No doubt the blood-alcohol test had painted a black picture because it couldn't show that, in spite of what he'd drunk, he was sober. A court case would put paid to his promotion prospects and wreck a career which had been full of promise. His world was collapsing; one by one its foundations were crumbling. What future could he look forward to now?

He thought about his difficulties with his officers, and this made his fingers clench. Weddy's failure to see him on board, the row about it afterwards with Cavan, the behavior of Symington and the Doctor at the Embassy party, the row with Gallagher about the record player. They were all against him except Rhys Evans. Why? Then the slim, sinister figure of Symington re-entered his thoughts, and he felt the muscles deep in his stomach knot into a tight, painful ball, and his head ached until the pain seemed unbearable. Almost hysterically he said aloud, "I must sleep! I can't go on like this!"

But sleep wouldn't come. He turned on the cabin lights again and saw that it was just after three. He rang for the quartermaster and told him that he wanted to see the Doctor.

"The Doctor, sir? *Now*, sir?" The quartermaster sounded doubtful.

Shadde glared at him. "Yes. Get on with it."

A few minutes later the Doctor arrived, a raincoat over his pajamas, hair tousled and eyes bleary with sleep. The Captain was at the desk in a dressing gown.

"You sent for me, sir?"

"Yes," said Shadde brusquely. "I can't sleep. Can't do my job properly without sleep."

"Have you been sleeping badly for some time, sir?"

"It's become very bad. My mind's too active."

"How's your appetite, sir?"

"Poor. Don't feel like food much."

"And your bowels, sir?"

Shadde glowered from under beetled brows. He disliked the Doctor intensely and the question struck him as too personal. "What about them?" he said coldly.

"Are they functioning regularly?"

"What the hell's that got to do with it?"

"A good deal, sir. I'm trying to help you."

"They're very irregular," said Shadde awkwardly.

"Headaches, sir?"

Shadde looked up at him. "Yes. Acute ones. Got one now. Always have when I can't sleep."

The Doctor felt a sudden sympathy for the Captain. In

that moment he thought he saw something of the suffering of this aloof, highly complex man. "When we get back to Haslar, you should see a Fleet specialist, sir."

Shadde's eyes narrowed and his mouth set grimly, "What specialist, may I ask?" His voice was chilly.

"A physician, sir, someone who specializes in diagnosis." The Doctor would have liked to have said a psychiatrist, but he dared not.

Shadde stood up and looked at the Doctor with cold, implacable eyes. "I sent for you, O'Shea, because I can't sleep. We go to sea at o-eight-thirty. I want to sleep *now*, do you understand? I can't wait for Haslar and your quack friends. I want to sleep *now*."

The Doctor's face was grave. "I could give you sedatives, sir. But it's after three. It's too late. You'd feel drugged at o-eight-thirty."

Shadde watched him in silence. Then he turned away. "Thank you," he said icily. "I see you're not anxious to help. You know," he went on, "you're like so many of the officers in this boat, O'Shea—full of facile explanations, never lost for a word. You've all got a great deal to say, but when it comes to doing things you're not an impressive bunch." Then he turned around again. "I put it to you, O'Shea, you don't really know what's the trouble, do you?"

The Doctor hesitated. He couldn't tell the Captain what Rhys Evans had said to him that morning so he said, "I *can* tell you, sir, that your nerves are in bad shape."

At that Shadde went white. The word "nerves" meant *Sabre* and the Lombok Strait. So this filthy little medico was trying to get at that, was he? He moved quickly to the door and slid it open.

"Get out," he shouted. "Get out before I throw you out."

As soon as the Doctor had gone Shadde sent for Gracie. When the C.P.O. telegraphist entered, he found the Captain, hollow-eyed and disheveled, sitting at his desk. Shadde pointed to a chair. "Sit down, Gracie." Then he started pacing the cabin floor. "You remember our discussion the other day about those signals."

Gracie nodded. "Yes, sir."

Shadde stopped for a moment and watched him closely. "I shall want them today, Gracie."

"Now, sir?"

"No. Later. When we're at sea. I'll work out the details and send for you later."

Shadde started pacing again and Gracie rose; it was awkward sitting there while the Captain was standing. "Since you first mentioned it, sir, I've thought of some snags," he said uneasily.

Shadde stopped again. "Snags? Snags?"

"Like this, sir. Signals dealing with missile states-of-readiness and firings are top secret. I don't know the address groups and prefixes."

Shadde gave him a dry, preoccupied smile. "Don't worry about that. I do. They're in my S.P.* I'll prepare the signals. All you do is transmit them on that closed circuit you told me about and get 'em through your teleprinter."

Gracie's forehead puckered. "Another snag, sir. A firing signal would give the target coordinates if it was to look genuine. I don't have them. They're top secret, too."

Shadde went on pacing, head thrust forward, hands clasped behind his back. "Don't worry about that. They're in the S.P. too. I'll look after that."

There was a long silence, broken eventually by Gracie. "Anything else, sir?"

The Captain didn't answer; he seemed deeply preoccupied, and Gracie wondered if he ought to repeat the question. Then Shadde stood still; he seemed to be listening to something far away. "Anything more?" he said, as if he

* S.P. *A highly confidential signal publication.*

were trying to remember something. "No! There's nothing more. Except"—he turned towards Gracie and his dark red-rimmed eyes seemed to bore into the telegraphist—"not a word of this to anyone. If you're asked, say we've been discussing the W/T channels you're guarding in harbor. Other than that, not a word. D'you understand?"

"Aye, aye, sir."

"Good," said Shadde. "Very good."

|| 13 ||

Ten minutes before the submarine sailed from Copenhagen, the engineer officer and Mr. Buddington went into the steering compartment and shut the watertight door behind them. During the next hour they devoted their whole attention to the port ram cylinder, constantly loosening and tightening, and sometimes just observing the drain plug and the brass lock nut which secured it. They did these things not once, but dozens of times—while the steering gear was at rest; while it was moving; while it was being tested hard aport and hard astarboard; while the submarine was slipping from her buoy in Yderhavn, and then again while she was turning; and finally as she made her way out of the harbor into the sound.

At last Mr. Buddington said, "Well, thank you very much. That will do very nicely."

The engineer officer scratched his head. "Indeed, and I have no idea what you're after, but I hope it will help you."

"Oh! It will," said Mr. Buddington with unusual enthusiasm. "In fact, it has already. You know I spent some time in here between Stockholm and Copenhagen, and it was then that I had this idea. And now these tests you've so kindly helped me with have really given me what I was looking for."

The engineer officer darted a keen look at him. "Not trying to poke my nose in, but . . . d'you think you've got your man?"

"No, no!" said Mr. Buddington hastily. "But I've got a useful line to work on."

Then a most curious thing happened. As they were leaving the steering compartment Rhys Evans noticed a dark object lying on the deck on the far side of the steering gear. It was particularly noticeable to him because the steering compartment was always kept spotlessly clean and nothing was ever left lying around. But here was this dark thing on the deck at the foot of the bulkhead.

"Just a minute," he said to Mr. Buddington. He went across and saw that it was a folded watchcoat. He picked it up and looked at the name tab.

"Kyle's," he explained to Mr. Buddington. "Must have left it here when he was on the drunk last night. Been using it as a seat, I see."

But Mr. Buddington was seeing something else: a piece of oil-smeared gray silk, with one side torn, hanging out of a pocket.

By nine o'clock *Retaliate* was northward bound up the sound, running on the surface at seventeen knots in a gray sea, with the sun shining weakly through the overcast. She was on the last lap of her voyage, homeward bound, and the crew's spirits were high. In two days' time, at eleven o'clock in the morning, they would be steaming into Portsmouth, and Portsmouth meant leave, wives, girl friends and families. In every compartment of the submarine, men were exchanging grins and light-heartedly chaffing each other. Another patrol was coming to an end; another round of visits to foreign ports was behind them, and England, home and beauty lay ahead.

A chill breeze blew in from the northwest, barely enough to ruffle the surface of the sound as it rose and fell to a gentle ground swell. There was a constant stream of shipping, and to port and starboard the coasts of Denmark and Sweden looked like the distant banks of a river, lush and green in the weak morning sun.

Down in the wardroom pantry Dusty Miller was confiding some astonishing information to Bullseye Target, and the Doctor, sitting in the wardroom, could not help overhearing.

"Skipper rings for me at half past seven and says, 'Miller, take this driving license up to the police station and show it to Inspector Jensen. Make it sharp,' 'e says. 'We're sailing at o-eight-thirty. Take a taxi on my account. And Miller,' 'e says, 'I would appreciate your treating this matter as confidential!'"

Target was impressed. "Blimey, Dusty, what's the old man been up to?"

Miller cleared his throat importantly. "'Old on a minute and I'll tell you. Ain't 'eard the 'alf of it yet. When I get there I find this Inspector Jensen and shows 'im the license, and 'e looks at it and writes something in a logbook. Then 'e hands the license back to me, and we have a little chat, and 'e asks me about our missile lot and what my job on board is. I told 'im I don't know nothing about missiles because I'm the Captain's steward, and then 'e says, quietlike, "Tell me, does your Captain drink much?"

"What did you say?"

"I said, 'Well the old man likes a snort now and then

like any naval officer.' Then this bloke looks serious and says, 'What's a snort?' So I says, 'A snort's a drop of tipple.' Then he says, quite nasty, 'How many drinks does your Captain 'ave in one go?' "

"Stone the crows," said Target. "Nosey parker."

" 'E was and all. Anyway I closed up then and said, 'The Captain's a man what's very moderate with 'is drink. Never known 'im have more than a couple at one session.' "

Target's tone was congratulatory. "Goodo, Dusty. Flippin' foreigners. Artful lot."

"I don't 'appen to like coppers," said Dusty in deprecatory tones.

"But what's 'is lordship been up to?"

"Ah," replied Miller. "I knew you'd ask that one, Bullseye. I said to the Inspector casual-like, 'Captain asked me to ask you what's going to 'appen?' "

"What'd 'e say?"

"Wait for it, Bullseye, wait for it! 'E said, 'Tell him the charge ain't framed yet but it'll probably be something like reckless and negligent driving while under the influence of alcohol.' "

There was a shocked silence in the pantry, broken eventually by Bullseye. "Cor, strike a light." His breath came heavily. "Skipper up for drunken driving. Where'd 'e get the flipping car?"

"Ah!" said Miller triumphantly. "Thought you'd ask that one. Inspector told me it belongs to a young Danish lady. And know what?"

"No. Go on!"

"When the Skipper 'ad the accident—collided with a Danish bloke—she was in the car with 'im!"

Target chortled hoarsely. "Skipper with a piece of foreign skirt. That takes some beating. Blimey, if the *Daily Mirror* gets hold of that lot! Can't you see the 'eadlines, Dusty? 'Atom-sub Captain drunk in car smash with Danish model.'

If that one's printed, Skipper'll hear from his old woman sharp enough."

After the alteration of course off Hälsingborg, Shadde left the bridge and went down to his cabin. Soon afterwards Mr. Buddington came in, the leather box hanging from his shoulder. Shadde beckoned to a seat and the little man sat down, prim and erect, feet and knees together. From his pocket he produced two pieces of gray silk.

"Ah!" said Shadde. "Rhys Evans told me of your find. What's the verdict?"

"It's the other half of the piece you found in the steering compartment in Stockholm."

"Is it, by Jove! So Shepherd was right. And it was in Kyle's watchcoat. We've got him now, haven't we?"

Mr. Buddington put his hand to his mouth and coughed. "I'm afraid we haven't, Captain."

"What do you mean?"

"It's not as easy as that. I admit that the presence of the gray silk in his watchcoat looks damning, but there are other factors which suggest it's unlikely to be him."

"Such as?" said Shadde dryly.

Mr. Buddington blinked for a few moments before answering. "At this stage, sir, I'd prefer to refer to only one of them."

"What's that?"

"Let's accept that the same man was responsible for all three incidents of suspected sabotage—Portsmouth, Queensferry and Stockholm. It's a reasonable assumption. The pattern's the same. Damage to the submarine's machinery by a person with reasonably sound knowledge of it and access to it. Do you accept that?"

Shadde nodded.

"Well, it may interest you to know, Captain, that on the two previous occasions—Portsmouth and Queensferry—

Kyle was on leave, and had been on leave for at least ten days when the incidents occurred. He couldn't possibly have been responsible for either of them."

"How do you know this?" asked Shadde.

"From the leave records."

After a moment's thought Shadde said, "Let us agree that Kyle was not responsible for the Portsmouth and Queensferry incidents. That doesn't necessarily clear him of the Stockholm business. Surely that gray silk in his watchcoat is damning evidence? And his outbursts on the messdeck about fixing this boat?"

Mr. Buddington's watery eyes avoided the Captain's, but his voice was firm and confident. "No, Captain, it's not damning evidence. I admit that I'm very puzzled, but I somehow don't think Kyle is the man."

Shadde was displeased. He sat there with his fingers drumming on the desk and a black look on his face. "See here," he said at last. "I don't want to be rude, but I think you're trying to make this thing sound unnecessarily complicated. Somebody put that lock nut in one half of that piece of gray silk and hid it behind those pipes in the steering compartment, where I found it in Stockholm. D'you accept that?"

"I do," said Mr. Buddington.

"And this morning you found the other half of the silk in Kyle's watchcoat, and there were traces of hydraulic fluid on it. Is that correct?"

"It is," Mr. Buddington agreed.

"And Kyle was one of the men who worked on the steering the day before sailing?"

"He was."

Shadde twisted around until he was glaring straight at Mr. Buddington. "And you say it's unlikely to be Kyle!"

"That is correct, Captain."

"Then how did he come by the silk?"

"Ah!" said the little man from the Admiralty. "That's what I'd like to know."

The Captain yawned, leaned back in his chair and stretched his arms. "You soon will," he said. "I propose to ask him when he comes up before me this morning. Any objections?"

"None at all. Indeed, it is essential that we should know."

The Captain slammed a drawer shut with his knee. "Would you like to be present when he comes up?"

Mr. Buddington's eyebrows arched in surprise. "Oh, dear me no, Captain. What would an air-conditioning expert be doing at such an investigation?"

Shadde frowned. "Of course. Stupid of me!"

C.P.O. Telegraphist Gracie wasn't as gay as might have been expected of a man homeward bound on such a fine day. He sat in the wireless office checking the W/T log and chatting to the telegraphist on watch, but his thoughts were far away. Since the Captain had sent for him in the early hours of that morning he'd had little sleep. He had been landed fairly and squarely on the horns of a dilemma. His training and instinct revolted against the idea that the submarine's complicated communications system should be used to produce make-believe signals, no matter what their purpose. The sort of signals the Captain had suggested might compromise the security measures on real missile firings. He didn't really know what these measures were, but he had a pretty shrewd idea about the communications side of them.

On the other hand, long years of naval training and discipline and his personal loyalty to the Captain left him with no option but to obey his wishes. He wondered if his compulsion about this was due to fear of Shadde or respect for him. He wasn't sure. Anyway, how could he, a young chief petty officer, tell the Captain that he wasn't prepared to cooperate? The Captain had far more naval experience than he, and knew much more about what could be done and what couldn't, and, of course, he had much greater authority and would be the last person to jeopardize security measures. Shadde had said that the boat was slack and wanted shaking up. Gracie didn't think that the boat was slack, but the Captain should know—after all, he was widely regarded as one of the most able submarine captains in the Royal Navy.

There was another thing. The Captain had said that the signals would create a realistic atmosphere which could help to find the saboteur. Gracie didn't know how or why, or how Shadde knew that the steering trouble was sabotage, but the man must know what he was doing; he was nobody's fool. Gracie wished that there was somebody he could talk to about all this, somebody who could settle his doubts for him. The more he thought about it, the more certain he became that he must get advice. The Captain had told him to keep it to himself, but he just couldn't. There was one man on board he could speak to, who had never let him down—the navigating officer. Lieutenant Symington was a good officer, well thought of on board, and his advice would be really worth having. Gracie decided to go to him at once. He would have to be careful, though, because it wouldn't do for Shadde to see them together after what Symington had told him about the Captain's suspicions.

The cabin Symington shared with Keely and Allistair was in the officers' quarters, on the deck below the control room and the Captain's cabin. Gracie had seen Shadde come into the control room and go up through the conning tower a few minutes before, so he knew the coast was clear. Without appearing to hurry he went down to the officers' quarters and looked through the open doorway into the small cabin. Keely was there but not the navigating officer.

"Hullo, Gracie," said the sublieutenant.

"Morning, sir. Have you seen the navigating officer?"

"He's down in the gyro room."

When Gracie came into the gyro room he found Symington writing up the gyro log. Without wasting any time he told him about the discussions with the Captain and of his own doubts and fears. At the end he said, "D'you see the trouble, sir? I mean, I don't quite like it."

Symington had been listening with his head cocked on one side. "I do, Gracie." He nodded. "It's a bit odd, I must say."

The navigating officer leaned against the bulkhead, arms folded across his chest, head bowed. He did some hard thinking, then looked at Gracie. "You'll have to do what he wants, Gracie. The responsibility's entirely his. After all, he's the Captain, isn't he?"

The C.P.O. telegraphist looked relieved. "Thank you, sir. That's what I thought, but I feel better now that you say the same thing."

Symington looked at him for a moment. "If the Captain hands you those signals for transmission, you must tell me *at once*. Before you put them onto your teleprinter."

Gracie nodded. "I'll do that, sir. You won't breathe a word, will you, sir? It'll ruin the Skipper's plan for a realistic exercise if it gets around, and he'll know it was me."

Symington smiled sympathetically. "I won't let you down, Gracie."

On the Captain's orders, the wardroom was cleared at half past nine. Shadde was seated at the head of the wardroom table, with the first lieutenant on his right and the engineer officer and Weddy, who had been duty officer at the time of Kyle's insubordination, on his left. Shadde had decided that the investigation would deal only with how the gray silk had come into Kyle's possession. The charges against him of being drunk on board, pilfering wardroom liquor and striking a chief petty officer were to be dealt with in Portsmouth. Until then he was under close arrest.

The young stoker came into the wardroom followed by the coxswain. A black eye and a swollen bruise on his right cheek where the skin was broken had given his face an odd twist. Under his dark, tousled hair he was pallid and dejected.

"Engineering Mechanic Kyle, sir," reported the coxswain.

Shadde motioned them to sit at the far end of the table; then he stared at Kyle. "Hm," he said. "You don't look in very good shape."

Kyle was silent. The Captain went on, "I've had you brought before me, Kyle, to answer questions about a matter of some importance." He paused and his dark eyes fixed on the young man. "In your own interests I want you to realize how important it is that you tell the truth. You may be in serious trouble if you don't."

Kyle's battered face showed no emotion.

From under the table Shadde produced a watchcoat and pushed it across to him. "Is that yours?"

Kyle opened it and looked inside. "Yes, sir."

"Ah!" said Shadde. "And when did you last use it?"

The battered face was expressionless. " 'Ad it with me in the steering compartment last night, sir."

"I see. And before that?"

Kyle thought for a few moments. "Took it ashore on me last liberty in Stock'olm, sir. Night I was coshed."

"Where was the coat kept between that night and last night?"

"In me locker, sir."

"In that case," said Shadde, and there was a note of triumph in his voice, "you may be able to explain how this" —he pulled out a piece of oil-stained gray silk and threw it across to Kyle—"came to be in the pocket?" Shadde's head thrust forward and his dark eyes gleamed.

For a moment Kyle looked at the silk, then he turned back to the Captain. "Yes, sir: I put it there."

"And can you tell me when you did this?"

"In Stock'olm, sir. Day before sailing."

Shadde's head thrust even further forward, as if he were trying to reach the stoker with it. "Ah," he said. "And where were you at the time?"

"In the steering compartment, sir." There was a deathly silence in the wardroom and Shadde gave Rhys Evans a quick I-told-you-so look. Then he said to Kyle, very softly, "And what were you doing there, Kyle?"

"Working on the port ram cylinder with Chief Shepherd and Finney, sir. Draining the 'ydraulic."

From the way Shadde put the next question, Rhys Evans knew he was closing in for the kill; he suddenly became casual and leaned back, as if the discussion were at an end. "Thank you, Kyle," he said. "That's been very helpful. Just one thing before you go—where did you get that gray silk?" He asked it quickly in a matter-of-fact voice, as if it weren't really very important, but his eyes betrayed him.

"From Chief Shepherd, sir," said Kyle. "He gave it to me to wipe my hands with. We'd forgotten to bring along any cotton waste."

The first lieutenant could see the shock of disappointment on Shadde's face. That's floored the old buzzard, he thought.

Kyle was taken away then, and Shadde sent for Shepherd, who confirmed Kyle's story in every detail. The investigation was over. When Shepherd had gone Shadde shook his head. "This thing's got me beat. But Buddington was right. He said it was unlikely to be Kyle."

"Who does he think it might be then, sir?" asked Rhys Evans.

"I don't know. But he says the tests this morning have given him a useful line."

"Yes, he told me that too."

"One thing's certain," said Shadde gloomily. "That piece of gray silk and the lock nut didn't hide themselves. Somebody put them behind those pipes where I found them. The thing is, who?"

Symington was working at the chart table in the control room, plotting the courses to be steered once they had cleared The Kullen. A volume of the *Baltic Pilot* lay open on the chart table, and he pushed it clear of the parallel rulers as he transferred a course from the compass rose to the chart. Around him the sea dutymen were at their stations, dim figures here and there in the red glow of lamps, surrounded by dials, scopes, valves, gauges and a mass of other instruments.

Symington was so used to the noise that he scarcely noticed the background of continuous sound: an intricate, delicate pattern made up of the tick-tock and whirr of the plotting and training devices, the toc-a-toc-a of gyro repeaters, the whush-whush of trace arms, the faint scratch of styluses, the high whine of small electric motors, and the low, deep note of the ventilating fans. But stronger and more purposeful than any of these was the steady hum of the main turbines, above which the sound of voices rose and fell as the crew made and answered reports.

The submarine pitched slowly in a long gentle swell coming in from the Kattegat. Except for that and for the vibration of the main engines, the men in the control room might not have known they were at sea.

Symington was still busy at the chart table when he became aware of someone at his side. It was the Captain. "Going to be long, Symington?" he asked.

"No, sir. I've almost finished."

"Good. I'd like to have a look at the charts." Shadde started to hum a tune, his fingers beating a tattoo on the chart table. Symington finished what he was doing and went over to the plot. Out of the corner of his eye he saw that the Captain was using the parallel rulers and dividers. Checking my courses, thought the navigating officer. Then he saw Shadde make some notes and put the sheets in his pocket. Next he looked at the *Nautical Almanac* and the *Baltic Pilot*.

When Shadde had finished, he went to his cabin and put the notes in his desk drawer. Then he unlocked the safe under the bunk and took out a ring-bound book in a black, plastic cover. For the next ten minutes he studied the book and made notes from it. When he had finished he locked it back in the safe.

The more he thought about what Gracie had told him, the more convinced Symington was that he should tell the first lieutenant. This was not a secret he wanted to keep to himself; it was something outside his experience and he didn't know what to make of it. Having made the decision, he spent a frustrating fifteen minutes trying to get Cavan alone. First he found him in the wardroom discussing Kyle's case with the engineer officer; five minutes later he went to the first lieutenant's cabin, only to find the coxswain there. After another interval of five minutes, he found him in the forward torpedo room talking to a chief petty officer. Finally he ran him to earth in the control room. Symington went up and stood next to him, making a pretense of looking at the air-conditioning control panel. "Number One," he said in a low voice. "Can I see you *alone, now!*" Without lifting his eyes from the panel the first lieutenant said, "Of course. In my cabin in two minutes." And he walked off. Two minutes later Symington followed.

Cavan shut the door and looked at Symington curiously. "Very mysterious, George. What's the score?"

Symington told him of the conversation with Gracie in the gyro room. At first Cavan was skeptical, but the navigating officer soon convinced him that Gracie was not making the story up.

"Incredible isn't it? A bogus signal from FOS to start a ruddy exercise."

The first lieutenant nodded. "Incredible's the word. Do you realize that it could compromise the security measures?"

Symington sat on the corner of the desk. "I know. He must be round the bend. Surely Their Lordships wouldn't approve?"

Cavan shrugged his shoulders. "Who knows?"

"I imagine they'd give him a first-class bottle."

The first lieutenant waved a hand irritably. "Stop nattering, George. I'm trying to think."

"Sorry," said Symington.

There was a long silence. "I suppose you'll tell Gallagher, won't you?" prompted Symington.

The first lieutenant thought about that for a moment, then shook his head. "Not Gallagher. He's U.S.N. and this is our affair. Anyway, he'd go and have it out with Shadde at once—quite rightly too. But then the cat would be out of the bag. Shadde would know that Gracie had talked. There'd be hell to pay."

Symington nodded. "Couldn't agree more. Must protect Gracie at all costs. If Shadde knows he's spilt the beans, he'll hammer him."

The first lieutenant shot him a glance. "And you, my boy. The whole story would come out and all hell would break loose." He was silent again for a moment, and then he said, "In some ways, I'd like to tell the Chief. He's a sound little chap. But it wouldn't do. He's too close to Shadde, and he doesn't really approve of me. If I told him he'd go straight to the Captain."

Symington shifted his weight from one side of his bottom to the other and draped his long legs over the corner of the desk. "What are you going to do?"

Cavan looked at him quickly. "You mean what are *you* going to do? It's your problem, you know. Gracie confided in you, not me. But of course I'll give you all the help I can."

Symington darted a curious, searching look at him. "I see," he said slowly. "That's very decent of you, Number One."

The first lieutenant patted him on the shoulder. "You can count on me. I won't let you down. Just one thing though—"

"What's that?"

"I'll help you on one condition. It's this: officially this discussion hasn't taken place. You haven't made any report to me. No one—and that includes Gracie—is to know that you've spoken to me. O.K.?"

The navigating officer looked puzzled. "Not really. What's the point?"

"The point is," said the first lieutenant, "that I'm not going to put myself in a position where I can be charged with conniving against the skipper if anything goes wrong. Got that?"

"Yes, I see what you're driving at," Symington said tightly. But his tone didn't seem to worry the first lieutenant.

"So you accept my condition?" he asked.

Symington shrugged his shoulders. "Of course. I've no option."

"Good," said the first lieutenant. "Now I'll have to put my thinking cap on."

‖ 14 ‖

The Doctor was lying on his bunk dressed, looking as though he had just woken up.

"Sleeping late, Doc?" Cavan said.

O'Shea rose, yawning and stretching. "Had my head down for about ten minutes when you knocked."

"Sorry. Didn't expect to find you asleep."

The Doctor rubbed his eyes. "Looks bad, doesn't it? We gave it rather a bang last night."

"So I heard," said Cavan. "Mind if I sit down?"

"Please do." The Doctor pointed to the chair. "What's the trouble?"

Cavan gave him a long, searching look. "I want your advice, Doc—your medical advice."

"Something wrong?"

"Before I tell you, I want your solemn word."

"About what?"

"That you'll not repeat a word of this discussion, unless I ask you to?"

The Doctor frowned. "Is this a medical matter?"

"Yes. In a way."

"Then it's quite unnecessary to ask for my word."

"This is a little different, Doc. It's not my health. It's somebody else's. Well?"

"Of course," said the Doctor, in a way that made it clear it wasn't necessary.

Cavan came straight to the point. "It's the Skipper. There's a strange state of affairs. I want your help."

The Doctor ran his fingers through his tousled red hair. "I'll do my best."

"What I want to know, Doc, is this: Can Shadde be going round the bend?"

The Doctor's eyebrows lifted. "Going round the bend? Are you serious?"

"Yes."

"Why do you want to know? What's all this about?"

The first lieutenant told him about the signals Shadde wanted from Gracie. When he had finished he leaned back in the chair, hands clasped behind his head, eyes half closed. "I know it sounds damned silly but"—he paused—"to put it at its worst, Doc, when he's received those bogus signals, what's to stop him firing a Polaris? What's the answer to that one?"

"*You*," said the Doctor promptly. "You're the answer. *You* can stop him. The thing can't be launched without your consent and until you've set the control dial. You'll know the signal's bogus. Gracie will have warned Symington, so you refuse to approve the firing. Where's the problem?"

Cavan shook his head. "Not as easy as that. I wish it were. The firing drill requires us to put on our settings *before* the Captain uses the firing plunger. In an exercise, nothing happens when he depresses the plunger, because the circuit's dead. The control dials are never set in an exercise. But he's told Gracie he wants to simulate the real thing. That's what the signals are for. So if a bogus firing signal arrives the control dials *will be used*, and we must presume that in that case Shadde won't use the firing plunger. But if

214

he were round the bend, who could guarantee that he wouldn't? You say I can stop him. How can I tell Shadde, *before* the control dials are set, that I know the signals are bogus?"

"Why not?" challenged the Doctor.

"Because he'd know at once that Gracie had talked. There'd be hell to pay. But that's chicken feed compared to what else. What about me? I'd have refused to obey an order. Challenged the commanding officer's authority, integrity, sanity—the lot. It would be the end of my naval career. I'd be court-martialed."

"Would you?" said the Doctor doubtfully.

"Of course I would. He's the commanding officer. If he decides to start an exercise with a bogus signal, who am I to say he can't? *I* reckon he shouldn't. But Their Lordships might take another view. They've never been keen on officers who disobey their Captain's orders—particularly first lieutenants. There's a nasty word for that—it's called mutiny. Imagine the situation in the control room if I were to disobey Shadde's order to put my setting on the dial? What would I say? 'I'm not going to play, sir, because I know the signals aren't genuine and I think you may be mad.' He'd put me under arrest pronto. After that, how could I or anyone else convince a court-martial that he *was* going to launch a missile? We ourselves wouldn't *know* that he was. Don't you see, Doc? The thing's extremely complicated. No easy way out of this one."

"Couldn't you put the wrong setting on your dial?"

"No. Shadde would know at once, because Weddy and Gallagher, who follow me, wouldn't be able to move their dials at all if I did that—they'd remain locked."

"So what d'you propose to do?"

Cavan looked worried. "It's a hell of a problem, actually. It's one of those cases where whatever's done may be wrong. Very difficult to know how to keep one's yardarm clear." He looked at the Doctor unhappily. "You see, I'm pretty sure it's an exercise, all right. It's the sort of odd, unpredictable thing Shadde does. It's just the nagging thought that it mightn't be. That he might really press the button."

The Doctor looked at him doubtfully. "Isn't that rather far-fetched?"

Cavan nodded. "It is. But isn't it rather far-fetched for the captain of a Polaris submarine to get together with his chief petty officer telegraphist and connive bogus signals about missile states-of-readiness? That's what sticks in my gizzard."

The Doctor shifted his position and sat with his elbow on his knee, his hand supporting his chin. "Aren't Shadde's motives plausible enough? He wants a realistic exercise, because he thinks the ship's company needs it and because he thinks it may somehow help solve his pet sabotage problem. Allowing for his complex about that, isn't that reasonable?"

Cavan shook his head. "Surely you don't compromise top security precautions on missile firings just to shake up the crew and in the remote hope that you might catch a saboteur. Surely you don't do that—unless you're a very odd type."

"Shadde is an odd type," said the Doctor. "You said so a moment ago. He's not the ordinary run-of-the-mill naval officer."

"You may be right," admitted the first lieutenant grudgingly. "Basically that's what I feel myself. But there's this nasty nagging doubt."

The Doctor brushed imaginary cobwebs from his forehead. "I think it's rather a fantastic one. Anyway, what would he fire a missile at?"

Cavan threw his legs over the arm of the chair and looked up at the Doctor. "I know it sounds crazy, Doc, but if he's off his rocker—just suppose he is—he might fire it at a Russian target. You've heard him nattering about the West being taken for a ride by the Russians, and how we're hamstrung because our sort of democracy can't start a preventive war, and time's on the side of the Russians and all that bilge. Remember he was at it again at Skansen? Then on the bridge just after Stockholm, he tackled me about it again. Asked me if I didn't think it better to risk the consequences of a nuclear war rather than submit to Russia. He called them "those thugs." You see, it's on his mind. If he thinks and talks about it when he's normal, mightn't he try and do something about it if he were crackers?"

The Doctor pursed his lips. "I don't think he's crackers, Number One."

"You think he's perfectly normal, then?"

"No. Not necessarily normal. But you're suggesting he may be insane."

"Well, if he's not normal, what is he?" insisted Cavan.

The Doctor yawned. "He's a neurotic. There are plenty of sane, lucid people, carrying great responsibility, who are neurotics. But that's very different from being a psychotic."

The first lieutenant raised his arms in despair. "Those are just words to me. What d'you mean?"

"A neurotic's a person suffering from a minor nervous disorder; there's nothing seriously wrong with his perceptions and conceptions of reality. Outside the area of his symptoms, he's in normal touch with reality."

"And the . . . the other one?"

"The psychotic," said the Doctor, "is another kettle of fish. He's got an abnormal or pathological mental disorder. He's out of touch with his environment. He won't or can't distinguish between fantasy and reality, because his judgment's grossly impaired. In fact, he's insane."

The first lieutenant sighed. "Thanks, Doc, but I'm afraid I'm not very much wiser. What makes you think Shadde's a neurotic?"

The Doctor slid off the bunk and stood at the mirror,

brushing his hair. "Sharp mood swings. Frequent fits of depression, sometimes bordering on melancholia. Sudden outbursts of anger for comparatively trivial reasons. Call that extreme irritability if you like. Sleeplessness. Loss of appetite. Restlessness. Those are some of the symptoms."

The first lieutenant was thoughtful. "Yes. He's got most of those, only I didn't know he couldn't sleep or eat."

"He can eat, but he doesn't want to. That's loss of appetite."

"What's gnawing at him?"

The Doctor put down the brush and comb and peered at himself in the mirror. He wasn't very pleased with what he saw. "Basically fear, I suppose. That's what's at the root of most neuroses. In psychology it's called anxiety. Normal fear's a response to a present threat. Neurotic fear's a response to anticipated future trouble. Very complex thing."

The first lieutenant looked at him with fresh interest. "What's Shadde afraid of?"

"What most of us are," said the Doctor. "Insecurity."

The first lieutenant regarded him thoughtfully. "Why should he feel insecure? He's done damn well. Certain to be a flag officer, I'd say."

The Doctor shook his head. "For professional reasons I'd prefer not to go into that, Number One. But you can take it from me that Shadde's got some pretty weighty problems, real and imaginary. I'll tell you of just one, but you must keep it to yourself." He paused. "His marriage is on the rocks."

The first lieutenant's face was blank. "Poor chap," he said in a matter-of-fact voice. "I'd no idea." He got up. "So you think my fears are exaggerated?"

"I'm a G.P., not a psychiatrist," said the Doctor. "I've told you what I think. Maybe I'm wrong."

Cavan was halfway to the door; he turned round quickly.

"So you don't exclude the possibility that he's a . . . what's-its-name?"

"A psychotic," said the Doctor. "No. I can't absolutely exclude that possibility. All I can say is that his symptoms appear to me to be those of a neurotic."

The first lieutenant's eyes flickered faintly. "Thank you, Doc," he said. "Remember what you've just said. May be important later. In the meantime, this conversation has not taken place. O.K.?" Once more his eyes flickered and then he was gone.

Bagnall looked into the azimuth mirror and called the bearing. "Light vessel, two-six-three." Then, crouching, he swung the azimuth ring again and called, "Gilbierg Head, one-seven-eight."

Weddy plotted the bearings, then looked at his wrist watch and wrote "1027" against the fix on the chart. "Let me know when The Kullen's abeam."

Bagnall nodded. "Aye, aye, sir."

Weddy looked aft at the line of sea gulls following in the submarine's wake, and then at the Danish destroyer on the starboard quarter. She was about two miles astern and coming up fast, a feather of white at her stem where the bow-wave rose and fell. The plot gave her speed as twenty-eight knots. Weddy's thoughts were interrupted by the commissioned gunner. "The Kullen's abeam now, sir."

Weddy looked at his watch again. "Thank you, Guns." He went to the voice-pipe and pressed the call button.

Shadde's cold voice came back: "What is it?"

"The Kullen's abeam to starboard, sir. Five point three miles. Permission to alter to three-five-five."

"Very good. Carry on. I'm coming up."

When he got to the bridge, Shadde looked around with

his binoculars. "That Dane's coming up fast," he said. "What did you say her name was?"

"*Willemoes*, sir. We've spoken to her."

"Been using us as a radar and asdic target?"

"Yes, sir."

"The Danes are good seamen," said Shadde inconsequentially.

"Yes, sir."

"Pity Nelson had to take their pants down at Copenhagen. They've never forgiven us for that. Of course, they asked for it."

Weddy didn't altogether agree with the Captain's sentiments, but he was determined not to upset what appeared to be a good mood.

Shadde turned his head and peered at him. "Read much about the Copenhagen action?"

"Not much, sir. I've read Southey's narrative, of course."

"Dull reading that, Weddy. Dull reading. There are several better. Carola Oman's account is first rate. Simply splendid."

Shadde proceeded to talk so knowledgeably about the Copenhagen battle and about the characters of the senior officers involved that he made the whole action live again. Weddy was fascinated.

"Yes," Shadde said, and his eyes glistened, "some great pages of English history were written in these waters. Those were the days to be an Englishman."

"They were indeed," agreed Weddy.

Shadde sighed. "I'm afraid we've missed the bus, Weddy. Born too late. In those days warships fought warships. The Germans started the fashion of using submarines to destroy liners carrying women and children. And now"— he waved his hand fore and aft—"look at us. Designed to destroy cities and everybody in them. What a role for a naval officer."

"Inevitable, isn't it, sir?" said Weddy. "I mean things never stand still. There's always progress."

"Progress!" snorted Shadde. "Progress be damned. Would you say the British Empire has progressed? This is the age of liberal thought, my boy. The long-haired gents are in charge, busy giving away what they didn't build up. This is the era of the great unwashed. Russia, India, China, Africa. One man, one vote. Absolute tripe! Doesn't matter if they're all bloody imbeciles—one man, one vote."

The words came tumbling out, and Weddy thought, now that he's got going he'll never stop.

"The teeming millions must rule," Shadde went on, "even if they're cannibals, half-wits, still in the trees. Ability doesn't count any more. It's simple arithmetic now. Oh! You have several hundred millions, have you? Then step this way, sir, please! In the name of democracy, *please* take over." He turned his head and peered at Weddy. "See what I mean? See the idiocy of it all?"

Weddy nodded distantly.

Then Shadde switched the conversation and for the next ten minutes gave Weddy little opportunity to talk. To all intents and purposes it was a monologue. Eventually he broke off the conversation in the middle of a sentence and went over to the chart table. "I see we'll be in deep water at about seventeen hundred."

"Yes, sir."

Then without a word Shadde left the bridge. When he had gone, Weddy looked at Bagnall. "Hasn't been in a mood like that for a long time."

Bagnall rolled his eyes in mock gratitude. "Looking forward to his new job ashore, I suppose. Come to that, I wouldn't mind swallowing the anchor myself."

Weddy went over to the chart table. "You're getting old, Guns. That's your trouble."

.   .   .

Rhys Evans and Musgrove were putting the final touches to the defects lists with Chief E.R.A.s Shepherd and Abbott.

The engineer officer put the pencil behind his ear. "Now, men, is that the lot?"

"Seems complete, sir," said Shepherd.

"Anything more, Musgrove?"

Musgrove held a pencil in one hand and with the other plucked nervously at his beard while his eyes darted over the defects lists. "Seem complete to me, sir," he said.

They stood up. Musgrove looked quickly from the engineer officer to Abbott and then to Shepherd. "I hear the Captain thinks that the steering trouble in Stockholm was sabotage?" he said quietly.

The engineer officer frowned. "Where is it you were hearing that, Musgrove?"

The engineer lieutenant looked down at his feet, smiled sheepishly and licked his lips before he spoke. "Sorry, sir. It's all over the engine room. Everybody's talking about it." The engineer officer looked at him coldly. "Then why not stop them? There's nothing better than a silent tongue in a man's head."

There was an awkward silence as they all filed out of the cabin.

Dusty Miller lifted the pantry hatch and peered into the wardroom. "Lot of basking seals," he observed caustically. He moved away from the hatch and jerked his thumb towards it. " 'Ave a dekko, Bullseye."

Target picked at his teeth with a match while he looked through the hatch. "Blimey," he said. "Who wouldn't be a pig?" Keely and Symington were sprawled in armchairs; beyond them the Doctor was stretched out on the settee. All of them were asleep and breathing heavily. The only other occupant of the wardroom was Goss, who sat reading in an armchair. Suddenly he picked up a magazine and threw it at the sublieutenant, hitting him on the shoulder. Keely looked up sleepily. "What'sa matter?" he said and turned on his side.

"You're snoring like a pig. Stop it!" said Goss.

The sublieutenant mumbled, "Sorry, sir," and closed his eyes again.

Symington stirred uneasily. "Stop nattering. Chap can't sleep."

"Who the hell d'you think you're speaking to?" said Goss.

The Doctor sat up. "What's the hour?" Nobody answered, so he turned his head and looked at the wardroom clock. "Seven bells. Well, well. S'pose we must take some interest in the sea around us."

Keely rubbed his eyes. "When you've seen one wave, you've seen the lot." He yawned. "Can't think why my people sent me into the Navy."

"What's wrong with you chaps?" asked Goss irritably. "The ruddy day's just started and you're drugged with sleep."

"We're short of it," said the Doctor. "We had a run ashore last night."

"You look a clapped out lot. What was it? Women?"

Symington said, "Sir!" deprecatingly, and raised his eyebrows.

"We had a jolly at the Pelikan," said the Doctor. He looked around the wardroom. "Anyone seen the U.S. Navy?"

Just then Dwight Gallagher entered and said, "Hiya, gang."

"In excellent health. How are you?" Symington answered, but he didn't sound as if he meant it.

Gallagher sat down and put a hand to his forehead. "Terrible! Terrible!"

The sublieutenant looked at him severely. "Shame on you, sir!"

"Excuse me," said Gallagher. "What did you say?"

"I mean—that poor girl."

"The way she jumped," said the Doctor.

Gallagher's eyes narrowed. "She was crazy." He looked around the wardroom as if he wasn't sure whether he was among friends or enemies. "Or else some sonofabitch framed me."

The Doctor looked at his fingernails. "Like to believe you, Dwight, but . . ." He took a deep breath. "Let's forget it, shall we?"

"Yes," said Symington. "Let's."

"Why did she spring into the air with that sad cry?" said Keely.

The Doctor shook his head and frowned at him. "Perhaps she *was* sad."

Symington looked at Gallagher and shrugged his shoulders. "So young too."

"Drop dead!" said Gallagher.

Mr. Buddington was pleased and puzzled when Shadde told him the result of the investigation in the wardroom that morning. He had never really believed that Kyle was responsible for the steering gear trouble; the circumstantial evidence had been strong up to a point—but only up to a point. He was pleased to have his judgment confirmed, but he was puzzled that Shepherd had so readily confirmed Kyle's story about the gray silk, because it made the case against Shepherd all the blacker. He proceeded to do some very solid thinking about the two pieces of gray silk which had originally been one. One piece had been found in the steering compartment with the lock nut in it, the other in Kyle's watchcoat. Shepherd was the owner of the gray silk and he had admitted giving Kyle the one piece. What had he done with the other? Mr. Buddington discussed this problem with Rhys Evans, and it was agreed that the engineer officer would tackle Shepherd about it during the day.

The first lieutenant knew he would have to work quickly. It was already well into the forenoon and at any moment the Captain might hand Gracie the signals. It wasn't easy to sort this situation out because it was really two problems in one; if he was to keep his yardarm clear he would have to play it very safe. He must take the steps necessary to forestall the vague but unpleasant possibility that had nagged at him ever since Symington's report, and yet do it in such a way that if things went wrong he wasn't implicated. After all, it was actually the navigating officer's problem, and if anybody could afford to be implicated it was Symington, because he was madly rich and not really very interested in a service career. In fact, Symington had said several times that he was thinking of leaving the Navy and doing something or other ashore. One way and another, Cavan began to feel that he was really being rather decent in helping him with the problem at all.

Having settled the moral issue involved, he got busy with the technical problem. After a few moments he realized that this didn't present many difficulties either, because fortunately he remembered a lecture on the Polaris firing circuit when they were training in the States. The lecturer had made a supposedly humorous aside, and though it hadn't seemed very funny at the time it had stuck in his mind ever since.

Half an hour later Cavan had not only briefed Symington thoroughly on what to do; he had even undertaken to help him see that the coast was clear. "But," he said firmly, "make no mistake, George. If you're nabbed, I can't come to your assistance. I want to be terribly frank about this. Even under oath I'd have to deny that I'd any knowledge of what you were doing or that we'd ever had any discussions on the subject."

Symington looked at him in rather a bored way and said, "You're rather franker than you think, aren't you?"

Cavan didn't know what was meant by that, and he didn't really care as long as Symington understood the position. Nevertheless, he would have liked the navigating officer to have been a little more gracious and appreciative of the help he was getting.

Symington went from the control room into the missile attack center and found two men working on the equipment there. He stood chatting with them for a moment while his eyes followed the run of the cable from the pedestal up the bulkhead and across the deckhead to the point where it entered the airlock and the black and yellow tracing bands disappeared. Then he opened the watertight door and went through it into the missile control room, shutting the door behind him and securing the clips. As he had expected, it was empty, and he quickly looked through the observation port to make sure that there was nobody on the gantries in the launching compartment. Once again he traced the black and yellow bands before opening the airtight door and letting himself into the small space, six feet by four, which was the airlock between the missile control room and the launching compartment.

With great care Symington shut the door behind him and secured the clips. It was pitch dark in the airlock and he had to grope for the switch, but finally he found it and the lights went on. When he opened the junction box he saw that the black and yellow bands were on the third cable from the left. Slipping on the rubber gloves, he took some long-nosed pliers from his pocket. Within seconds he had turned the milled ring on the cable holder until it came clear. Then he jerked the cable out of its socket and bound the end back with insulating tape. As he replaced the inspection cover, he heard the clips moving on the after airtight door. A cold chill swept through him as he looked down and saw them turn. In a flash he switched off the light and pressed himself into a corner, waiting with bated breath in the darkness. He heard the noise of the other clips turning and then a creak as the door opened and the air pressure increased.

There was a soft thud as the door shut, and the noise of heavy breathing and the metallic squeak of the clips being pulled tight. In the confined space of the airlock Symington and the new arrival were almost touching each other, and he could hear every movement the man made—he could even feel the warmth of his body. He shrank back, fearful that the intruder might brush against him in the darkness. If the newcomer opened the foremost door and left the airlock without switching on the light, Symington knew that all would be well. With thumping heart he froze against the bulkhead and hoped for the best, but apprehension surged through him as he heard hands groping for the switch. Then there was a metallic click and the airlock was a blaze of light. Within inches of him stood the engineer officer, eyes wide with surprise as they traveled from the navigating officer's rubber-gloved hands, long-nosed pliers in one of them and insulating tape in the other, to the open junction box above his head.

The look of blank astonishment on the Welshman's face was quickly followed by suspicion. "What's this, Symington?" he said sharply.

From the way he said it the navigating officer knew that he was in a very dangerous position. He smiled unhappily and said, "It's a long story, Chief. Can't tell it to you here. Can I come to your cabin?"

Rhys Evans' eyes narrowed. "What is it you've done?"

227

Symington reached up and shut the inspection cover. "Broken the circuit on the firing plunger," he said, as he tightened the wing nuts.

The engineer officer said incredulously, "Wha-a-aa-t? You must be mad, man!"

Symington's composure was returning and his brain was beginning to work again. "I'll tell you the whole story in your cabin, Chief," he said. "Wait until you've heard it."

Tight-lipped and suspicious, the engineer officer sat stiffly in a chair while Symington told him his story. Rhys Evans was the last person on board he would have chosen to tell, because he felt that the Welshman was far too close to the Captain to be able to judge the matter on its merits. Symington had no doubt about Rhys Evans' honesty and integrity; they were beyond question, but the Welshman's relationship with the Captain made the situation exceptionally difficult.

Symington was counting on one person now—the Doctor. On the first lieutenant's advice he had gone to see O'Shea, and at this very dangerous moment he realized how sound Cavan's advice had been. The first lieutenant had even suggested the questions he should ask the Doctor. "But remember that I didn't send you to O'Shea," he had ended. "You went of your own accord because you were so damned worried!"

"Well, that's the position, Chief," Symington said wearily. "What I've done hasn't been for myself. I've taken a hell of a risk. Obviously I wouldn't do that unless something vital was at stake."

The Welshman's mouth tightened. "Or unless your story's a pack of lies. Maybe it's sabotage you're after? How should I know?"

Symington shrugged his shoulders. "Test the story for

228

yourself. Go and discuss it with the Doctor. Ask him what he told me this morning. But please, Chief, not a word to anyone else. Please! Don't you see? If the signals are only for an exercise, then no harm's done, because the firing plunger won't be used. Immediately after the exercise I'll reconnect it. You can come and do it with me if you like. The only way the Skipper could know that the circuit is broken would be if he used the firing plunger—and if he did that you'd all thank your stars I'd made it unserviceable."

Symington leaned back in the chair. "Don't you see? It's the only way. The responsibility's entirely mine. No one knows I've broken the circuit—except you. I accept full responsibility for what I've done."

But there was still a gleam of suspicion in Rhys Evans' eyes. "A bad business. Playing with fire. Better to mind your own affairs. If that signal story's the truth, then the Skipper has a good reason for what he's doing. He knows what he's about." Rhys Evans got up abruptly. "I'll have a talk with the Doctor and then decide." He eyed the navigating officer sharply. "You'll know what I'm about soon enough."

The Doctor was doubtful. "D'you really think that would be wise, Chief? I know you've got the Skipper's interests at heart, all right, but if you tell him about this now, are you doing the right thing?"

"I think so."

"But is it? Let's examine the situation carefully. If you tell Shadde you caught Symington red-handed, you'll have to tell him the rest of the story."

The engineer officer looked doubtful. "And what's that?"

"Symington's reasons for what he did. That he knew about the signals and had doubts about Shadde's sanity. What d'you think the Skipper will do when he hears that?"

"Deal with Symington at once, he will. And rightly too."

The Doctor nodded. "Yes! And you know what that means? A court-martial for Symington. He'll be defended, and ably defended. Make no mistake. And d'you realize what his defense will be?"

Rhys Evans shook his head. "No."

"He'll say he considered the bogus signals to be a gross irregularity, because they could compromise the security measures. He'll say that, as a result, he even had doubts about the Captain's sanity and that he consulted me. Then he'll say that on the strength of what I told him this morning he couldn't exclude the possibility that Shadde's sanity might be in question. You can be sure he'd call me as a witness. I'd have to confirm what I have told him and describe the Captain's symptoms and give my estimate of his mental health. I've no doubt an eminent psychiatrist would be called by the defense. Can you imagine what that might lead to?"

The engineer officer nodded his head, but his eyes showed his doubt. The Doctor went on. "I'm a G.P. and I've only dabbled in psychiatry, but I must be frank with you, Chiefy. On his symptoms I make Shadde a neurotic. He's certainly that. But while I think its unlikely, I can't guarantee that he's not a psychotic. An expert witness might say it could reasonably be inferred that he was. That would be equivalent to saying he was insane. D'you see the danger for Shadde now?"

The Welshman's silence encouraged the Doctor. "The court-martial would probably finish Symington's naval career, and Shadde might be cleared technically. But the mud would stick and he'd probably be finished too."

Rhys Evans' eyes widened. "Shadde finished? What are you saying?"

"Yes," said the Doctor. "Finished. At the very least he'd be passed over for promotion and retired early. The court-martial would be headline news for days and the Admiralty wouldn't dare take any chances with Shadde after that. Yes, he'd be a ruined man, all right."

With bowed head Rhys Evans brooded over this. "Never thought of these things," he said gloomily. "I'd do nothing that could harm the Captain, be sure of that."

The Doctor looked at him sympathetically. "Leave matters as they are, Chief. If the whole thing's just an exercise, Shadde will never know about the broken circuit. We'll be in Portsmouth the day after tomorrow and he'll go ashore to his new job. If it isn't an exercise and he does use the firing plunger . . ."

"You're talking nonsense, man," interrupted the engineer officer. "The Captain's as sane as I am."

The Doctor shrugged his shoulders. "Are you sure? Remember what you said the night before last? That he's a sick man? That he's worrying too much? That he has too much on his mind and it's doing strange things to him?"

Rhys Evans frowned. "Quite different, that was. I was never saying that he was out of his mind. It's just that he has too much to worry about."

"That can damage a man's mind," said the Doctor.

"He's as sane as I am," said Rhys Evans stubbornly.

"You may be right, Chief. But think of that court-martial. In his mind, or out of it, it's likely to be the end of him. I strongly advise you to leave matters as they are."

The engineer officer looked away from the Doctor's compelling eyes. "Very well. He has troubles enough just now, poor man. I'll not be adding to them."

There was a note of relief in the Doctor's voice. "Thank you, Chiefy. I'm certain your decision's the right one."

Rhys Evans turned to go. "But mind you one thing," he said fiercely.

"What's that?"

"When he's been proved wrong, that damned navigating officer will have to go down on his knees and beg the Lord's pardon."

The two men's eyes met for a moment, the Doctor's friendly and the Welshman's puzzled and uncertain.

|| 15 ||

At noon Symington and Keely came up to the bridge and took over the watch. A light wind was blowing from the northwest, and the sunlight played through heavy banks of cloud to make a patchwork of the land and water below. To starboard the coast of Sweden rose out of the sea, a long, low rampart running north and south; through binoculars Symington saw the beacon at Marsten and to the north of it Skrea Church. Broad on the starboard bow the lighthouse at Morup Tange poked up like a tiny finger into the sky.

There was much shipping about; Baltic coasters, cargo steamers, passenger ferries, tankers, and here and there, sprinkled about like thin confetti, the brown and white sails of fishing boats and yachts.

Symington found it difficult to concentrate on his watch-keeping duties. He was consumed with worry about what the engineer officer was doing; at any moment he expected a summons to the Captain's cabin. The engineer officer had said that he would go and see the Doctor before deciding

233

what to do. Symington prayed that O'Shea had succeeded in persuading the Welshman to let matters be.

Just before coming up to the bridge he had broken the news to the first lieutenant. Cavan had gone as white as a sheet. "My God!" he breathed. "Caught you in the act, did he? My God!" For a few moments his face seemed to fall apart and then he pulled himself together and clutched at Symington's arm. "You didn't let on that I knew, did you?" His voice was hoarse, insistent, half accusing.

"I did not," said Symington. "You needn't worry, Number One. Your yardarm's clear." There was contempt in his voice.

The first lieutenant looked relieved. "What's the Chief going to do?"

"Check my story with the Doctor and then decide."

"Good. That's one of the reasons why I told you to discuss Shadde with O'Shea. So that you'd have that to fall back on if you were nabbed."

"Very considerate of you," said Symington drily.

Now, standing on the bridge, filled with apprehension, Symington wondered why it all had to happen to him? Two more days and they would be back in Portsmouth and then a new captain would join and Shadde would leave them for good. Why had Shadde hit on that fantastic idea of the signals? Why did the pleasant routine of a summer patrol in the Baltic have to be spoilt by the dreadful rows and tensions of the last week? What wretched stroke of luck had put him in this boat with Shadde, and what was going to happen now? What on earth was going to happen? That was the burning question.

Just before lunch Shadde came into the wardroom, and it was soon evident that he was in high spirits. After he had ordered a glass of sherry he chatted affably to everyone and even laughed once or twice. But he was restless and kept

234

moving about the wardroom while he talked, monopolizing the conversation as he always did on these occasions. As he spoke, jumping inconsequentially from one subject to the other, his officers exchanged knowing glances, and Target winked at Miller, who was helping him prepare the table for lunch.

No one quite knew how the row started. Shadde had dealt with the London traffic problem and the test match at Lord's and somehow this had led him to coal mining and then on to nuclear power. Then he said something about how the English always led the world in fundamental research and that he supposed sooner or later they would find an even more revolutionary source of power. Dwight Gallagher said very quietly, "Or some people else, maybe?" It had been intended as an aside for the Doctor, but it coincided with one of those sudden pauses and everybody in the wardroom heard it. The thick-set, gray-faced American sat there looking highly embarrassed, and opposite him Shadde stood staring, tight-lipped and frozen, as if he couldn't believe his ears.

"What did you say?" His voice was ice cold.

Gallagher said, "Nothing really, Captain," and looked uncomfortable.

"Nothing?" said Shadde. "On the contrary, you said, 'Or some people else?' didn't you?"

Gallagher could see the row coming and he made one more effort to avoid it. "It was of no importance, Captain."

Shadde was breathing hard. "What you were implying, Gallagher, was that I was exaggerating the role of the English in fundamental research. Weren't you?"

Gallagher jerked his shoulders.

"I was not, sir, but have it that way if you like."

There was a deathly silence in the wardroom while Shadde thought about the remark and the meaning it might conceal. His fingers were flexing and the knuckle bones were white. When he spoke there was suppressed anger in his voice. "I'd like to remind you, Gallagher, that the English gave your country nuclear fission, the jet, radar, the angled flight deck, the steam catapult and a few other things for good measure. And what's more, we didn't charge for them." Shadde was talking fast now and his eyes were smoldering. All his dislike for the American and his deep resentment of the presence of a U.S. naval officer on board one of Her Majesty's submarines—with a final say in weapons control—boiled up in him now. He went on, "Unlike your Government, I may say, which gave us these Polaris boats and then stung us thirty million quid apiece." He stopped, jaw thrust forward, eyes blazing. "And when I say stung, I mean *stung*."

Behind Shadde's back the Doctor was signaling frantically to Gallagher not to reply, but the American's blood was up and there was a hard look in his eyes. "That remark is not only pretty unfair, Captain—it's not true." He said it slowly and quietly but in a way that didn't leave any doubt that he had no intention of backing down.

For a moment Shadde stood there with the veins on his temples looking as if they were going to burst. When he spoke his voice shook with anger. "When I want your opinion, Gallagher, I'll ask for it. Until then I suggest you keep it to yourself." He stalked into his cabin and slammed the door shut.

There was an embarrassed silence in the wardroom. Weddy looked at the Doctor. "And that was that," he sighed.

Rhys Evans shook his head. "Better not to have argued with him. He's a tired man. A lot on his mind."

The first lieutenant lit a cigarette. "Pity he's upset. He was in such good form." He looked across at the Doctor. O'Shea saw the question in his eyes, but shrugged his shoulders.

Dwight Gallagher's hands were shaking as he opened a pack of cigarettes, and his face was taut.

"Have a drink, Dwight," said the Doctor, "and relax." As he said it, they heard Shadde's bell ring in the wardroom pantry.

Miller slid the cabin door open and poked his head inside.

"You rang, sir?"

Over at his desk Shadde was adjusting the hands of the clock. "Yes," he said, "I shan't be lunching in the wardroom."

Miller had been expecting this because he had seen the row in the wardroom. But he wasn't pleased because the Captain had started the day in an unusually good frame of mind, and he had hoped it would continue.

"Have lunch in 'ere, sir?" he said.

Shadde shrugged his shoulders. "Not really hungry, Miller." He fidgeted with some things on the desk. "Bring me a cup of tea and some biscuits . . . and that Danish camembert."

A gleam of apprehension showed in the steward's eyes. "Aye, aye, sir." He slid the door shut and was gone.

Ten minutes later he was back with the tray. The Captain was sitting at the desk with the wardroom atlas open in front of him. He was humming to himself, and when he looked up Miller was surprised to see him smile.

"Hullo, Miller!" he said.

The steward put the tray on the edge of the desk and began to pull the small collapsible table out from the bulkhead.

"A great day, Miller."

"That so, sir?"

"Yes! The sixteenth of May. On this day in 1803 England declared war on France and her allies . . . on Napoleon . . . the arch tyrant . . . the despot. He held a dagger at the heart of England, Miller. He would have destroyed our people."

Miller was surprised. From time to time the Captain had been friendly, but he had never spoken to him like this before. He felt he ought to say something. "Ah! That's right, sir."

Shadde's fingers were drumming on the desk and he didn't look at Miller as he spoke. The steward had the unpleasant feeling that the Captain had forgotten he was there.

"Yes," said Shadde. "Those were the days of high resolve for Englishmen. The sixteenth of May, 1803. That declaration of war started a chain of events which led directly to Trafalgar. A man had arisen to save England. Nelson crippled the combined fleets of the French and Spanish . . . the threat to England was broken! For Napoleon it was the beginning of the end. Nelson was dead, but England was saved."

"Yes, sir," said Miller.

"Nelson," repeated Shadde absent-mindedly, and when he looked up at Miller his eyes were misty. "D'you know what Rowse said of him?"

"No, sir."

"He said, 'I can never hear the name of Nelson without tears coming into my eyes . . . such genius, such courage, so transcendent a fate.'"

Miller waited patiently for the Captain to finish. He couldn't walk out of the cabin while he was talking, but he hoped the Captain would pack it up soon because he had to get back to the wardroom to help with the lunch. Besides, he wanted to let Target know that the Skipper was in a remarkably good mood in spite of the row with Gallagher.

But the Captain was off again. "Yes, Napoleon's power was broken. Mahan describes it very well somewhere . . . I forget the exact words. Something about a thin white line of sail between Napoleon and the conquest of the world."

He drew his hand across his eyes and yawned. Then he looked up again as if he were seeing the steward for the first time. "Ah! Miller," he smiled. "I'm tired. Very tired. Not enough sleep, I dare say. But there's much to do." He stood up and yawned again. "You can carry on, Miller."

The steward was about to slide the door open when he heard Shadde say curtly, "What cheese is this?"

Miller turned towards the tray and looked sadly at the cheese. "Piece of fresh cheddar, sir," he said in a low voice.

Shadde glared suspiciously at the cheese and then at Miller. "That it's a cheddar is perfectly evident. Where's the Danish camembert you got for me on Wednesday?"

The steward shifted his weight from one leg to the other and cleared his throat. "Haven't got it no more, sir." His voice was low and anxious.

"Haven't got it?" said Shadde angrily. "What the hell d'you mean, you haven't got it?"

Miller lowered his eyes. "Gone, sir. Been eaten by mistake."

The Captain's mouth tightened and his eyes flashed. "Eaten by mistake? Whose mistake, may I ask?"

"Wardroom officers, sir." Miller almost whispered the words.

Shadde waved his arms in an excess of rage. "Eaten by mistake by the wardroom officers . . . *my* cheese! I've never heard such goddam poppycock in my life." He breathed heavily, his eyes burning into the steward's. "Eaten or not eaten, go and find that cheese and don't rest until you've bloody well found it." He took a step towards Miller, a towering, menacing figure. "And now get out!" he shouted. "D'you hear me? Get out!"

Back in the pantry Miller told Target what had happened.

"Blimey!" breathed the wardroom steward. "Who lifted the flippin' cheese?"

"Lieutenant Commander Gallagher, the Doctor, Lieutenant Symington and the Subby."

"Cor, love a duck! When?"

"Two o'clock this morning, when they come off shore."

" 'Ow d'you know, Dusty?"

"Mr. Symington told me before breakfast. Said 'e hoped I 'ad no objections. I told him it was 'is lordship's cheese."

"Cor! What did 'e say?"

" 'E blooming near fainted."

Target looked at the Captain's steward with a sympathetic eye. "Don't envy you, Dusty, I must say."

Miller took out his handkerchief and mopped his forehead. "Wish me mother'd never 'ad me," he said sadly.

After lunch Shadde and Rhys Evans spent half an hour discussing outstanding refit matters. Then Rhys Evans brought up the subject of Shadde's appointment to the staff at Blockhouse, and was delighted to find that the Captain now displayed a lively interest in the new job; indeed, he was almost enthusiastic.

"I've been thinking about it, Chiefy," he said, "and there are some quite pleasant compensations. For one thing, I'll be able to do various things I've always been keen on but not been able to tackle at sea."

Rhys Evans encouraged him. "That's right, sir."

Shadde blow a cloud of smoke and narrowed his eyes as it drifted past. "Writing, for one thing," he said. "Something I've always wanted to do. You know, I've so many ideas I want to get down on paper."

The engineer officer nodded. "You could do that well, sir."

Shadde waved a deprecatory hand. "Not really a question of doing it well. I've never tried. But it's just something that must come out." Pulling the ash tray towards him, he stubbed out the cigarette. "Then fishing . . . fly-fishing. That's another thing. I did a little when I was a youngster. I'd love to take it up again. And walking. I'm keen on walking and bird watching, and there should be plenty of opportunities for that."

"Didn't know you liked walking," said the engineer officer.

Shadde nodded; he leaned forward and peered at Rhys Evans, the dark eyes boring into the Welshman. "Walking's a wonderful thing. Walking alone, with your thoughts." He leaned back in the chair, feet stuck out in front of him, and laughed self-consciously. "Sounds conceited, I suppose, but —d'you know—I prefer my thoughts to other people's conversation."

When he came off watch at two o'clock Symington went at once to the Doctor's cabin.

"Has the Chief seen you?" he asked anxiously.

The Doctor looked at the pale, worried face and nodded. "Yes. Before lunch. Told me how he found you in the airlock."

"What's he going to do?"

"Keep it to himself."

"You mean he won't tell Shadde?"

The Doctor nodded again.

Symington dropped his arms to his side and sighed with relief. "Thank God for that!"

"I put the wind up him," said the Doctor. "Explained how a court-martial would probably finish Shadde."

The navigating officer looked puzzled. "Court-martial?"

"Yes—yours!" said O'Shea, and he told him of the discussion with Rhys Evans.

Symington smiled, a faint, weary smile. "Thank you, Doc. That was good of you."

Back in his cabin Symington tried to read a book but

soon gave it up. In spite of Rhys Evans' assurances to the Doctor, the navigating officer had a dreadful feeling of impending disaster. Somehow or other he felt sure that Shadde would learn about the airlock business, and when he thought of it he felt sick with worry.

It was three o'clock in the afternoon and the first lieutenant lay on his bunk. He was due to go on watch at four, but rest was out of the question now; he was far too worried. It had been a devastating shock to learn that Symington had been found in the airlock by the engineer officer. Although he had done everything he reasonably could to protect himself, Cavan wondered desperately if his complicity would leak out. Only one person knew about it and that was Symington, and he was certain that Symington would never go back on his word. But the Doctor might have his suspicions, and now Rhys Evans was to be reckoned with, although he had promised O'Shea he would do nothing. What Cavan didn't like about all this was that there were too many people involved, and that added to the chances of a leak. If Shadde is genuine about his exercise, he thought, and my part in the plunger business comes out, I've had it. Their Lordships will have no mercy on a first lieutenant who has conspired against his commanding officer. He turned uneasily on his bunk. Interference with the main armament of one of H.M.'s ships was a major offense, and that officers should be the culprits would be an aggravating factor.

Once again he railed inwardly against the rotten luck which had led Rhys Evans to the airlock at that fateful moment. But for that the whole thing would have gone undetected, no one would have known about the broken circuit and after the exercise Symington would have reconnected it. But now five people knew—and one of them was the engineer officer. In spite of what the Doctor had said, Cavan doubted if Rhys Evans could keep the matter to himself for any length of time. For a moment he contemplated getting Symington to go to Shadde's cabin to confront him with the whole thing. Perhaps Symington could do it politely and tactfully. "I just thought I'd mention, sir, that I know about the signals you want from Gracie. Don't you think, sir, that it's taking an unwarranted risk . . . I mean, security precautions and . . ." Cavan didn't trouble to finish the sentence. It was blotted out by a picture of Shadde, tall, dark and furious, towering over Symington: "May I ask precisely what you mean?"

And what was the risk? That Shadde might be mad? How could Symington tell him that? No! Confrontation would never do—it would be fatal. He'd be involved at once; in no time Shadde would learn who had incited Symington to interfere with the firing circuit, and that would result in Cavan's arrest and court-martial.

The last thing the first lieutenant wanted to let himself in for was a court-martial. Whatever the outcome, it left a nasty smear. But if it did come to that he'd have a plausible defense because he was pretty certain that Shadde was exceeding his authority in using bogus signals for an exercise. That would be the line to take. It might be a bit tricky explaining why he had not consulted Gallagher. But fortunately Gallagher was a quiet, good-natured fellow, not the sort to make difficulties. Anyway, that was a bridge to be crossed when and if it was reached. Nothing more could be done now. It was a matter of waiting and seeing. If Shadde was going to have his exercise, he'd have to have it fairly soon. If he didn't, then the only thing to do was to hope and pray that if Symington's interference with the firing circuit leaked out, Symington would have the decency not to implicate him. He consoled himself with the thought that the navigating officer was a man of high principle.

When Cavan got to the bridge at 1600 they were off

Marstrand Fjord, steering 354 degrees and steaming at 20 knots. Out of sight to port lay the Skaw, and ahead of them the deeper waters of the Skagerrak. The northwesterly wind had freshened and the submarine's movements were more lively under a darkening sky and heavy banks of cloud, which rode up from the west.

‖ 16 ‖

Gracie was in the W/T office when the messenger came in and told him the Captain wanted to see him.

Going through the control room, Gracie had a nasty feeling that Shadde had summoned him about those signals for the exercise. He knocked and heard the gruff, "Come in." With a sick feeling at the pit of his stomach he slid the door open.

Shadde was sitting at the desk with two official-looking black books in front of him. With a heave of his shoulders he swiveled the chair around until he was facing the telegraphist. Then he said, "Ah! Gracie, come in and sit down."

Gracie moistened his lips.

The Captain leaned forward, hands on knees, shoulders hunched, and the telegraphist had to look away from the dark eyes—they did something funny to him.

"What time are you on watch tonight, Gracie?"

"Eighteen hundred to twenty hundred, sir."

The Captain nodded approval. "Good," he said. "I thought so. Tell you more about that later."

With a gesture towards the books and papers on the desk he said, "I've been working on those signals."

Gracie's heart sank. "Yes, sir."

Shadde closed his eyes and started to speak quickly, as if there were little time. "I want the exercise to start at half past seven. I've penciled in under its date-time group the exact time you are to receive the first signal. That's on the signal marked 'A.' You'll see I've marked it 'emergency' precedence. I've put nineteen thirty-three as the time of receipt. We'll dive soon after it's received . . . be in deep water by then."

The C.P.O. telegraphist started to say something, but Shadde went on as if he had not heard him. "The first signal orders us to a position in the Skagerrak by midnight. To reach it we'll have to reverse our course."

The Captain smiled, an abstract impersonal smile, as if at some inward thought. Then he said, "I've added rather a clever little frill."

Gracie said, "Yes, sir," but he didn't sound very enthusiastic.

Shadde leaned towards the young man and spoke confidentially. "Yes," he said, "it orders *Massive* to leave Oslo before twenty thirty and to reach a position in Bohus Bay by midnight, to the north of us."

"I see," said Gracie cautiously.

Shadde went on quickly, his eyes never leaving Gracie's. "*Deterrent* left Loch Ewe yesterday afternoon—you saw the signal?"

The young man nodded.

"For the purposes of this exercise," went on Shadde, "we'll assume she's somewhere near the Shetlands now." With his left hand he smoothed back his hair. "I don't really know where she is. But, of course, it doesn't matter in the least. Anyway, signal 'A' alerts her as well." There was that same impersonal smile. "It orders her to be in a position off Ålesund by midnight. What do you think of that?"

Gracie shivered under the physical impact of the piercing black eyes. It was as if someone had walked over his grave.

Without waiting for the telegraphist's answer the Captain continued, "Whole object of the signal is to suggest an unusual situation—one that requires all available *Missile* boats to be alerted and ordered to special positions. That should impart a touch of realism to the proceedings, don't you think?"

But he didn't wait for Gracie's reply. "The second signal." He reached backwards and took it off the desk. "This one"—he held it up so that Gracie could see—"is marked 'B.' Got that?"

"Yes, sir," said Gracie.

"Of course, they're in cipher. It's been a long and laborious business."

He jerked his chin towards the books on the desk. "Had to use those S.P.'s. Long time since I've had anything to do with that sort of thing." For a moment he seemed lost in thought. "Ah, yes! where was I?"

"Signal 'B,' sir."

"Yes, yes! Signal 'B.'" Shadde held it up again. "This one. You receive it about two and a half hours before midnight. We'll go to periscope depth then. Time of receipt is on it." He looked at the signal. "Here it is—'emergency' precedence again. I want you to receive it at twenty-one twenty-nine. I've penciled that in below the date-time group. Got that?"

"I come off watch at twenty hundred, sir," said the telegraphist. "Cartwright will be on from twenty to twenty-two hundred."

Shadde nodded. "Glad you reminded me. I've thought

247

of that. You must tell Cartwright—once you've got the first signal—that you're going to remain on watch for the time being. Important occasion, you know. Tell him you'll send for him when you want to be relieved. D'you understand?" The young man nodded slowly. "Yes, sir."

"Good! Now, signal 'B': like signal 'A' it's addressed to *Retaliate, Massive* and *Deterrent*. It's commendably brief." There it was again, the cold impersonal smile. "It orders the first degree of missile readiness." Shadde leaned back in the chair, arms folded on his chest. Then he spoke so quickly that Gracie found it difficult to follow. "That'll impart a little more reality to the exercise. It'll be interesting to see how the crew react to what they believe to be the real thing. About time they had a shaking up. Buck up their ideas a bit."

Shadde drew his hand across his forehead, head sunk on chest, and lost himself in thought. Finally he jumped up, folded the signals and handed them to Gracie. "Put these in your pocket, Gracie. Mustn't be seen carrying them. You've been in here discussing W/T refit matters. Got that?"

Gracie nodded and put the signals in his pocket. "I understand, sir." He remembered Symington's advice: "You'll have to do what he wants, Gracie. The responsibility's entirely his. After all, he's the Captain, isn't he?" Then he remembered what Symington had said next: "If the Captain hands you those signals for transmission you *must* tell me *at once*." I'll do that, all right, he thought.

The Captain was speaking. "That'll be all for now, Gracie." His eyes held the young chief petty officer's. "Remember," he said sternly, "not a word to anyone! Absolute secrecy! Understand?"

"I understand, sir."

"One final thing, Gracie. When that first signal has been received and the word has got around the boat . . ." He paused, his eyes mysterious. "Keep a sharp lookout for odd behavior. See what I'm getting at?"

"Yes, sir."

From the Captain's cabin Gracie went back to the W/T office, where he spoke to the leading telegraphist for a few minutes before he went to look for Symington. He soon found him in the small cabin in the officers' quarters.

"So the exercise is tonight, is it?" Symington was thoughtful. "Jolly time we'll have."

The C.P.O. telegraphist looked worried. "I'll say, sir."

"First signal will arrive about nineteen thirty, and the next about twenty-one thirty?"

"That's right, sir."

"And we're to reach the position in the Skagerrak at midnight?"

"That's what the Captain said, sir." The telegraphist got ready to go. "One thing, sir."

Symington's left eyebrow lifted. "Yes, Gracie."

"Now that you know about the signals . . . what will you do?"

The navigating officer pursed his lips and shook his head. "Leave that to me. Don't worry."

After Gracie had gone, Symington went along to the wardroom. The afternoon was getting on and it was nearly five o'clock. He was extremely anxious to give the first lieutenant the latest news, but there would be lookouts and a signalman on the bridge and it wouldn't be possible to talk in front of them. He would have to get hold of the first lieutenant when he came off watch.

Shadde spent a restless afternoon. He was never still for long; in and out of his cabin, stalking around the control room looking at the instrumentation, visiting the bridge, he was forever on the move. He was cheerful and commu-

249

nicative and there was no trace of the black and gloomy fits of depression of recent weeks.

Soon after half past five he made another visit to the bridge. The coast of Sweden was out of sight now and they were well into the Skagerrak, pitching and rolling to the swell coming in from the northwest. Overhead there was a thick blanket of cloud, and to the west lightning played against the horizon.

Using binoculars, Shadde made a careful examination of everything in sight. Then, after studying the chart for some time, he said, "Ask the control room for a line of soundings."

"Aye, aye, sir."

The first lieutenant went to the voice-pipe and asked for the soundings while Shadde stood at the chart table, beating a tattoo with his fingers.

"What's the delay?" His voice was impatient. "Tell them to shake it up."

At that moment the control room reported that they were ready to give the soundings. "Stand by," said Cavan. He looked across at the Captain and Shadde nodded. The first lieutenant repeated the soundings as they were called up the voice-pipe: "122—120—123—126—126—128—130—"

"Right," said Shadde curtly. "That'll do." He compared the readings with those on the chart and then came back to the front of the bridge. "I see we're to alter course to the southwest at eighteen forty."

"Yes, sir."

"Who relieves you at eighteen hundred?"

"Weddy, sir."

There was a long pause and Cavan wondered what was coming next.

"Number One!" said Shadde.

"Sir?"

"On arrival in Portsmouth the new commanding officer —Commander Straker—will join."

"Yes, sir?"

The Captain thrust his hands into his monkey-jacket pockets. "No leave's to be granted until he's on board and we've discussed matters."

"Yes, sir."

"I want his agreement to the leave arrangements. He'll assume command forty-eight hours after our arrival. After that, *Retaliate* will be his kettle of fish. See my point?"

Cavan said, "Yes, sir." But all the time he was wondering if Shadde had forgotten about the exercise. During the row in Copenhagen the Captain had said, "I'm handing over in a few days' time to a new commanding officer. I can assure you I don't intend to hand over a slack boat. Not much time left, but I intend to shake this boat up in no mean fashion."

His thoughts were interrupted by Shadde's voice. "Lot of cloud about. Might be a storm."

"Yes, sir, looks like it."

"Glass is dropping slowly, but it doesn't make any odds." Shadde turned and looked aft, leaning against the bridge screen. "We're in deep water now. We'll dive at twenty hundred. I'm all for a quiet night."

Out of the corner of his eye Cavan looked at Shadde's rugged face. If he's acting, thought the first lieutenant, he's certainly shooting a hell of a convincing line.

The Captain spent another quarter of an hour on the bridge talking endlessly about all sorts of things, but Cavan saw that he was tense and restless and couldn't concentrate. From time to time he moved about the bridge, and wherever he was his fingers beat a nervous tattoo. But, at last, he went below and the rest of the watch passed quickly for the first lieutenant. At six o'clock Weddy came up to the bridge and took over.

"What's the Skipper's mood like?" he asked.

"Terrific! Never stops talking. He's excited about the new job in Portsmouth, I think."

"Not as excited as I am. Got over the lunch-time row?"

"You mean with Gallagher?"

"Yes!"

"Forgotten all about it, I expect."

Just then it started to rain, a fine soaking drizzle that seemed to pervade everything, and the first lieutenant was glad to go below.

When he got to his cabin Cavan took off his jersey and began to wash. Almost immediately there was a knock on the door and Symington came in.

"Hullo, what's the trouble?"

Symington looked at him coolly. "Skipper's handed the signals to Gracie."

The shock of this remark made Cavan stop suddenly in the middle of toweling his face. Why he was so surprised he couldn't imagine. He'd been expecting this all day, and yet the news hit him now like an open hand. Perhaps it was because of Shadde's remark on the bridge about diving for a quiet night.

"Good God!" he said to Symington. "He has, has he? Any details?"

When Symington had told him of Gracie's report Cavan said, "Very interesting. A stickler for realism, isn't he? Reversing our course for a few hours will cost the British taxpayer a quid or two."

"Odd business, isn't it?" Symington shook his head. "But he's an odd chap, let's face it."

"Where's he now?"

"In his cabin. But he's on the move a lot."

"I know."

From a drawer under the bunk Cavan took out a shirt

and struggled into it. "On the bridge this evening he never kept still. He's a damn good actor. You'd never have guessed that he'd handed over the signals."

"I asked Shepherd," said the engineer officer, "and he says he gave the other piece to Finney."

"Where and when?"

"In the steering compartment the day before sailing from Stockholm. Tore it in two and gave one piece to Kyle and the other to Finney. To wipe their hands."

Mr. Buddington rubbed his chin and looked thoughtful.

"Very interesting," he said. "Did Shepherd seem at all . . . er . . . put out when you asked him?"

"No, he did not."

"I think we're getting somewhere at last." The watery eyes turned away shyly. "Would you mind making another small inquiry for me?"

"Indeed, I'll do that. What is it?"

"Ask Finney what he did with his piece?"

"He comes on watch at eight o'clock. Can it wait till then?"

"Yes," said Mr. Buddington. "It can."

The metallic clatter of the teleprinter stopped for a moment and the carriage slid back to the left; then the keys rat-tat-tatted to life again and in their wake followed the date-time group.

Gracie took the end of the paper roll, pulled it towards him and then, with a quick sideways flick, tore it off against the cutter bar. Before logging the signal he looked again at the unfamiliar address and prefix groups and the precedence and security classifications. When he got to the wardroom the officers were at dinner, with the first lieutenant at the head of the table.

Gracie went up to him. "Beg your pardon, sir. Emergency signal for deciphering."

Keely got up and took it. "I'll whack it through, sir."

The first lieutenant's face was drawn. "Yes," he said. "Do that." Out of the corner of his eye he looked to see how Rhys Evans, Symington and O'Shea were taking it. None of them seemed happy. He wasn't surprised.

Keely got busy with the cryptograph. After a bit, he whistled softly. "Wonder what's cooking?"

"Fish," said Goss. "Smell it a mile."

Keely pushed the cryptograph aside and his eyes were bright. "NATO ops signal from FOS," he whispered. Then he knocked on the door and went into the Captain's cabin.

A tray with tea and toast was on the table next to Shadde's desk, but it was untouched.

"What is it?" snapped Shadde.

Keely gave him the signal, and as Shadde read it the bushy eyebrows lifted in surprise. Then he wrote something on a signal pad, tore off the sheet and put it in his pocket. "I'm going to the control room. Tell the navigating officer I want him there."

When Symington got to the chart table Shadde showed him the signal. "Read that," he said in a strained voice.

Big act, thought Symington, but he noticed that Shadde's hands were shaking. The signal was from FOS/M addressed to *Retaliate, Massive, Deterrent*, repeated SACLANT* and other NATO and Admiralty authorities. It read:

Retaliate to position 58° 30′ N: 09° 52′ E by midnight Stop *Massive* to clear Oslo by 2030 and to position 58° 50′ N: 10° 12′ E by midnight Stop *Deterrent* to position 62° 40′ N: 3° 00′ E by midnight Stop Proceed submerged and with dispatch Stop Execute

* Supreme Commander Atlantic, Norfolk, Virginia.

When he had finished reading, Symington said, "Very interesting, sir." He could not think of anything more appropriate to say.

Shadde looked up from the chart. "Give me the course and speed to reach that position by midnight."

Symington got busy with the dividers and parallel rulers, and Shadde switched on the fathometer. He watched the trace for a moment or so and then went to the W/T office and told Gracie to make a diving signal to FOS/M. "Diving time nineteen forty-one. Surfacing twenty-two hundred," he said, looking at his watch.

"Aye, aye, sir."

Shadde dropped his voice. "Did you go through the motions of acknowledging that FOS signal?"

"Yes, sir."

"Good man,"

With purposeful steps Shadde went back to the center of the control room. "Bridge!" he called into the voice-pipe.

Weddy's voice came back at once. "Control room!"

"Diving stations . . . clear the bridge!" Shadde barked the orders. "Open main vents!" The klaxon sounded throughout the submarine and the crew moved swiftly to their stations.

The lookouts and the signalman came down from the conning tower, their wet oilskins glittering in the glow of the control-room lights, and behind them there was a dull thud as the upper hatch shut. Then Weddy's muffled voice: "One clip on . . . both clips on." A moment later he came down the ladder, and the signalman shut the lower hatch and put on the clips.

In front of the hydroplane operators the needles on the depth gauges were moving . . . 15 . . . 18 . . . 20 . . . 22.

"Take her down to two hundred feet," snapped Shadde.

The first lieutenant was standing behind the hydroplane operators watching the depth gauges. "Two hundred feet, sir," he repeated.

The submarine's bow slanted down and the slow pitch and roll ceased as she dived to the calm water below the surface.

"What's that course, Symington?" Shadde was irritable.

The navigating officer looked up from the chart table. "Zero-five-one, sir," he said quietly.

The Captain looked at the coxswain: "What are you steering now?"

"Two-four-six, sir."

With jerky strides Shadde reached the chart table. He stood next to Symington, fidgeting. "Come on! For Christ's sake, shake it up! Speed?"

"About eight knots, sir. If we turn now."

Shadde checked the course and speed indicators above the chart table—245° and 20.3 knots. "What time's it dark?"

"Have to look that up, sir. Won't take a second."

While Symington consulted the *Nautical Almanac* Shadde stood by tapping impatiently with his fingers. "Sunset's at twenty forty, sir. Nautical twilight ends at twenty-three fifty-eight. It'll be dark then."

Shadde stared at him. "Dark at midnight. Good." He stood there frowning and thinking. "When should we alter course if we're to be forty miles from the midnight position two hours before dark." The words tumbled out as if he were in a hurry.

Symington regarded him thoughtfully. "Forty miles away, two hours before dark."

"Yes."

The navigating officer worked away at the chart, making penciled notes in the margin while Shadde watched everything with an eagle eye. In a moment Symington straightened up and pointed to a position on the chart. "There's the point of turn, sir, off Kristiansund. We'll reach it at twenty-one hundred."

Shadde bent over the chart, forehead puckered, the rugged face and bushy eyebrows strong in the glow of the chart-table lights.

"What's the course from there to the midnight position?"

Symington put the parallel ruler against the penciled course line and rolled it across to the compass rose. "Zero-six-one, sir."

"Good! We'll alter to zero-six-one at twenty-one hundred." With a pencil, Shadde noted the time and course on the chart and drew a neat circle around the figure. "Now," he said, leaning over the chart table. "How far is the nearest land from the midnight position?"

With one leg of the dividers on the midnight position, Symington swung the free leg until it just touched the Norwegian coast at Risör off Sandness Fjord. He transferred the dividers to the latitude scale and read off the distance. "A fraction under twenty-four miles, sir."

"I see," said Shadde. "And at two hours to darkness?"

Symington was puzzled. "Two hours to darkness?"

"Yes, yes," Shadde frowned. "Two hours before midnight. You know, forty miles away from the midnight position. How far off the land then?"

Symington measured again. "Here, sir. Thirteen point eight miles off the Homboro light."

Shade stabbed a finger at the chart. "What are those lights clustered there?"

Symington bent down to read the small print. "Reieskjer, Geslingerne and Homboro, sir."

"Hm. Good position for a radar fix."

"Yes, sir."

"Splendid. We'll surface off them at twenty-two hundred." He went over to the first lieutenant and saw that the

257

depth gauges were showing two hundred feet. "Trim all right, Number One?"

"Bang on, sir."

"Good!" With eyes shining, Shadde rubbed his hands together.

"We'll go to watch diving now. Got that? Set H.E. watch. Check carefully on any ships near us. We'll go to periscope depth at twenty hundred—and every half hour after that. For W/T reception."

"Aye, aye, sir." The first lieutenant looked across to the coxswain. "Watch diving, coxswain. Pass the word."

The coxswain pressed the call push on the broadcast. "Watch diving! Watch diving!" And the control room was soon cleared of all men other than those on watch.

Shadde beckoned to the first lieutenant. "Come to my cabin, Number One."

When they got there he shut the door. "Tell the officers to keep a sharp lookout for any odd behavior by anyone in the next few hours." His eyes held the first lieutenant's in a compelling stare. "Got that?"

"Yes, sir."

Shadde stood against the desk, drumming with his fingers on the steel surface. "I'll talk over the broadcast shortly. Our saboteur friend may feel a bit queasy then. Might give himself away."

Cavan looked at the strained face and the dark bags under the staring eyes. You poor bastard, he thought, always on the thrash. Why don't you give yourself a rest?

"I'm not infallible," went on Shadde, "but I've got a hunch about this. Now, kindly inform the officers." He looked at the clock over the desk. "I'll talk to the crew in ten minutes' time."

He rarely used the broadcast. It would be clear to all that these were very special circumstances.

In a few minutes the Captain's voice sounded throughout the submarine. "This is the Captain speaking. I want to tell you about a signal we've received from the Flag Officer Submarines. It's a NATO operational order and requires us to be at a position in Bohus Bay, off Sandness Fjord, by midnight. It also orders *Massive* to clear Oslo by twenty thirty and reach a position about twenty miles north of ours by midnight. Finally, it orders *Deterrent* to a position off Ålesund by midnight." The Captain spoke fast and he sounded tense. "NATO operational orders of this sort suggest that an unusual situation may be developing." He paused. "But there's nothing to be gained by conjecture, so don't indulge in it."

The Captain cleared his throat. "To arrive by midnight in the position assigned to us, we'll alter course to o-six-o at twenty-one hundred. That'll more or less reverse our present course. We'll continue at twenty knots, and we'll go to periscope depth for W/T purposes at half-hour intervals. At twenty-two hundred we'll surface for a few moments off the Homboro Light—that's on the Norwegian coast. I'll keep you informed of any further developments. That is all."

|| 17 ||

In the wardroom, in the messdecks, in the fore- and after-ends, in the galley and storerooms, wherever members of the crew were together, the Captain's broadcast was the burning topic of conversation.

Conjecture about what lay behind FOS/M's signal was rife, despite Shadde's advice. A theory which found a good deal of favor was that this was yet another NATO exercise—an impromptu one laid on by bored staffs at NATO headquarters anxious to justify their existence.

Another view, less widely held, was that an ultimatum of some sort was due to expire at midnight, that behind the scenes intense diplomatic activity was taking place between East and West, and that the stationing of the *Missile*-class submarines in the midnight positions was a precautionary measure in case the balloon went up. In the fore-ends it was firmly believed that the United States was about to execute a *tour de force* by recovering a man from space in the Skager-rak—a demonstration on Russia's front doorstep, so to speak, of U.S. rocketry skill. That was why, explained those in the fore-ends, *Retaliate* and *Massive* were to be stationed twenty miles apart at midnight.

An able seaman put it neatly: "Perishing astronaut'll ditch in the 'oggin at twenty-four 'undred, right between us and *Massive*, and we'll 'ave to fish 'im out."

But underlying this conjecture and rumor, there was a rumbling of displeasure because of the threat to leave arrangements, and the ears of FOS/M's and NATO's staffs would have burned had they heard what was said about them.

Soon after half past eight Symington and the first lieutenant met for a hurried consultation. It was their first opportunity since the Captain's broadcast. Cavan shut the door of his cabin.

"Have to make it snappy," he said. "Skipper's on the prowl tonight."

"Where is he now?" asked Symington.

"In his cabin."

"Well, what d'you make of it?" Symington looked nervous.

"Let's have a quick recap," suggested Cavan. "The Skipper's given two signals to Gracie. The first's been *received*"— he drawled the word—"and the second's due at about twenty-one thirty. So the exercise is launched. By the way," he added, "what did you think of the broadcast?"

Symington shrugged his shoulders. "Very good. And you?"

Cavan made a circle with his thumb and index finger. "Superb!"

"He sounded excited, I thought."

Cavan nodded. "Shed his usual frigidity, anyway." He thought for a moment. "Probably *is* exciting for him. Don't forget he's the principal actor in this little drama."

261

Symington folded his arms. "And his motives now, Number One?"

"Ah! The sixty-four-thousand-dollar question. But the basic situation remains unchanged. We know he intends to shake up the ship's company and that he knows that Kyle's not the saboteur. Apparently he believes the exercise may produce . . ."

Symington shook his head. "That's moonshine. Why would a saboteur give himself away because he's suddenly confronted with what Shadde calls the real thing? Doesn't begin to make sense."

The first lieutenant slid off the bunk and sat on the corner of the desk. "Couldn't agree more, George. Never reckoned it was very convincing, but everybody, including Shadde, keeps quoting it as one of his motives. Maybe it is."

Symington looked bored. "Maybe."

"Anyway, we've done the right thing."

"*We?*" said Symington drily. "That's rich."

The first lieutenant frowned. Symington was getting rather too big for his boots.

It was past nine o'clock that night when the engineer officer told Mr. Buddington that Finney said he had thrown the piece of silk over the side in Stockholm harbor soon after they had finished working in the steering compartment.

Mr. Buddington turned his watery eyes on the engineer officer. "Threw it over the side?" he said. "That's very interesting." His head was cocked on one side. "Could you take him down to the steering compartment? I'll be there waiting for you." The little man was eager now, like a terrier after the bone.

Rhys Evans looked puzzled. "How do I explain that you want to see him there?"

"Don't explain. Don't mention me. I'll do the talking."

262

For a moment Rhys Evans was uncertain; then he said, "Very well. No doubt you know what you're about."

Mr. Buddington was waiting for them when they got to the steering compartment. The engineer officer came in first, followed by a fresh-faced young man with blue eyes set wide apart. When he saw the air-conditioning man from the Admiralty, the blue eyes showed surprise.

The engineer officer was ill-at-ease. "This is Engineering Mechanic Finney," he said bleakly. He liked Finney and wasn't happy about the situation that seemed to be developing.

"Ah!" said Mr. Buddington, looking hard at the young man. "Perhaps he can help me."

"Indeed, and I'm sure he will," said Rhys Evans, turning to the stoker.

"Aye, sir. If I can," said Finney with a wan, puzzled smile.

Mr. Buddington produced the oil-stained gray silk. "It's about this," he said apologetically. "Have you seen it before?"

Finney looked at it for a moment. "Yes, sir. That's a piece of Chief Shepherd's gray silk." His eyes sought the engineer officer's. "Like the bit you asked me about just now, sir."

Rhys Evans nodded gloomily.

"There were two pieces, sir," the stoker explained to Mr. Buddington. "The Chief gave me one an' Kyle the other, sir. For wiping our hands. Threw me piece over the side in Stockholm, sir." He seemed quite happy and confident about it all, and Rhys Evans could see that the man from the Admiralty didn't quite know what to make of it.

Nobody said anything for a while and Mr. Buddington just stood there wiping his glasses with a silk handkerchief. When he had finished, he put them on again very slowly and carefully, and then he shook his head. "You're lying, you know, Finney, and that's a great pity."

263

The stoker smiled; and he looked very confident when he said, "It's no lie, sir. That's the truth."

"I wish it was," said Mr. Buddington mournfully. "It would make my task much easier. Now see here, Finney," he said, and his voice made it clear that he wasn't going to stand any nonsense. "Since you won't tell the truth, I'm going to tell it for you. If some of my detail's wrong you're welcome to correct it, but in the main you'll find my story's right."

The watery eyes traveled from Finney to Rhys Evans and then back to Finney. "The afternoon before sailing from Stockholm you and Kyle, with Chief E.R.A. Shepherd, were the working party which came down here and worked on the port ram of the steering gear. Is that right?"

"Yes, sir."

"And the day *Retaliate* sailed from Stockholm she was involved in a collision because her steering gear jammed in the hard-aport position. Is that correct?"

"Yes, sir."

"And immediately after that collision, Chief E.R.A. Shepherd was sent down here by the engineer officer with you and Engineering Mechanic Stokes to see what the trouble was?"

"That's right, sir."

"And when you got here you found that the steering gear had jammed because the hydraulic fluid had drained out of the port ram cylinder. Is that so?" Mr. Buddington darted a look at him.

"Yes, sir."

"You all knew that, because you all saw the fluid covering the deck on the port side and you saw the drain plug lying there. Am I right?"

"Quite right, sir," said Finney.

"But *you*, Finney, saw something else. Something which the others didn't see. You saw the brass lock nut lying there, the lock nut which you were supposed to have tightened the day before."

Mr. Buddington's voice softened. "Then you got a terrible fright, and I can understand why. You realized with a shock that you had forgotten to tighten the lock nut—that it had fallen off—that the drain plug had turned in its keyed slot as the steering gear worked, until it too fell off." There was a pause, and Mr. Buddington sighed. "For your information, Finney, it must have taken approximately ten minutes to do that. After that," Mr. Buddington went on, "the fluid was discharged onto the deck and the steering gear jammed in the hard-aport position. The collision took place a minute afterwards." Mr. Buddington blew his nose. "You realized all that in a flash, Finney, and then you did a very foolish thing. You picked up the lock nut and hid it in the gray silk you had in your hand. Your last act before leaving the compartment was to push the piece of silk behind the cluster of pipes on the port afterside—over there." He pointed to the place.

All the color had gone out of Finney's face, but he still shook his head. "Could be what might have happened, sir, but it wasn't me. I threw me piece of silk over the side. That bit there must've bin Kyle's, sir."

"No, Finney," Mr. Buddington shook his head. "It's not Kyle's. We have his piece here." He pulled it out of his pocket. "You see, the tear matches exactly here where Chief E.R.A. Shepherd tore it across. See? Now if your piece had been thrown over the side we'd only have one half, wouldn't we? And that, Finney"—Mr. Buddington's eyes were mournful—"is why I knew you were lying."

Finney's face collapsed then and he started to sob. To Rhys Evans' surprise Mr. Buddington went over and patted the young stoker on the shoulder and said, "Come, come, Finney. You did a foolish thing, but it's not the end of the world. You got a bad fright because your mistake had very serious consequences. Then you tried to protect yourself, but you did it the wrong way. It's always better to tell the truth. But never mind, lad. It won't go too badly with you."

Finney shook his head, his arm still over his eyes, but he didn't say anything.

"Carry on with your watch now, Finney," said the engineer officer. "We'll deal with this in the morning."

When the stoker had gone, Rhys Evans said, "One thing puzzles me, Mr. Buddington: that ten minutes. How did you know it took ten minutes for the drain plug to work off?"

Mr. Buddington blinked. "Two reasons," he said. "The log book shows that nine minutes after slipping from the buoy in Stockholm the collision took place. Allow two minutes for testing the steering—that's what it took this morning —and a minute between the steering jamming and the collision taking place. In our tests in Copenhagen this morning we took the lock nut off except for two turns of the thread. Remember?"

Rhys Evans nodded. "Indeed, yes."

"Well, with the steering active, the average time for the drain plug to turn in the keyed slot and work up to the lock nut was eight minutes—so there's your ten minutes."

"Didn't know you were timing that," said Rhys Evans with admiration.

Mr. Buddington patted his wrist watch. "Oh, dear yes. That was the object of the tests."

"One other thing," said Rhys Evans. "How did you know Finney made a mistake? That it wasn't deliberate?"

"Because he has an excellent record and because it's not the way saboteurs go about things. First of all, he was working under Shepherd, and Shepherd should have checked that the lock nut was tight. How could Finney know that Shepherd would forget to make that check? Secondly, the jamming wouldn't have been serious if there hadn't been another steamer in that position at that precise moment. Thirdly, Finney's motive in hiding the lock nut was to cover up his mistake by giving the impression that it *was* sabotage."

At nine o'clock the Captain went into the control room and course was altered to 061°. Two minutes later the submarine came to periscope depth, and after a careful sweep around the horizon Shadde reported rain and poor visibility. The laboring of the submarine showed that a fair sea was running.

Soon afterwards they returned to 200 feet, and Shadde watched Symington plot the SINS position and draw the new course line to the midnight position in Bohus Bay. "We've had a southerly set, sir," the navigating officer said. "We should steer o-five-nine."

"Very good," replied Shadde, and the new course was ordered.

When he had punched the second signal onto the tape, Gracie fed it into the automatic transmitter. Then he turned the switch from "antenna" to "teleprinter" and saw from the clock on the bulkhead that it was 2128. He could hear Shadde's orders in the control room as they came to periscope depth. After the final "Up periscope!" he looked at the clock again, and at 2129 he switched on the transmitter and watched the teleprinter type the incoming signal onto the moving roll of paper.

It was, as the Captain had said, commendably brief. The priority address and prefix groups were followed by only six cipher groups and then, in plain language, "acknowledge" and the date-time-group.

After he had logged the signal he took it through to the wardroom and handed it to Keely. "Signal for deciphering, sir. Same address and prefix groups as the last."

Keely jumped up out of the easy chair and almost snatched the signal from the telegraphist. "Thanks, Gracie. Have got."

In the control room Shadde was standing by the periscope well, and the first lieutenant was behind the hydroplane operators. The depth-gauge needles were moving . . . 140 . . . 150 . . . 165 . . . as they went deeper.

In the wardroom Keely pulled the signal out of the cryptograph. "Jesus," he muttered. "This is getting serious."

Symington raised his eyebrows; he didn't like blasphemy. "Indeed," he said coldly. Inwardly he trembled, but it wasn't because of the blasphemy.

At that moment Shadde came in from the control room, glanced absent-mindedly at the officers in the wardroom and went on into his cabin. Keely's face was flushed with excitement as he flourished the signal. "Assume first-degree missile readiness," he said in a hoarse whisper. Then he knocked on the door of the Captain's cabin and went in. "Signal, sir. Emergency—operational." He tried to sound casual, but his voice shook.

Without a word Shadde took the signal. Like its predecessor, it was addressed to *Retaliate, Massive, Deterrent,* SACLANT and other NATO and Admiralty authorities. It read: "Assume first-degree missile readiness. Stop. Guard this channel each half-hour. Stop. Execute. Stop. Acknowledge."

Keely noticed that Shadde's hands were shaking when he put the message down on the desk.

"Tell the first lieutenant and the gunnery officer to see me at once."

"Aye, aye, sir."

When they arrived, Shadde got up with a quick movement and passed the signal to Weddy. "Read that," he said, staring first at Cavan and then at Weddy.

The gunnery officer looked at the signal and his eye-

268

brows lifted in surprise. "Something serious on the go, sir?"

There was a steady one-two, one-two beat from Shadde's fingers on the desk. He nodded vigorously. "Looks like it. No point in speculating. Let's get on with the job." He frowned at Weddy. "Means four missiles to be ready at three minutes' notice, doesn't it?"

"Yes, sir."

"What does that involve?"

The gunnery officer's face was pale and thoughtful. "We'll have to prime one and two in the starboard bank, and fifteen and sixteen in the port bank, sir. Activate their inertial guidance systems, couple them to the fire control and establish basic data from SINS and the G.B. computer."

Shadde's tense face was working. "Anything else?"

"Yes, sir. We'll have to build up pressures in the launching tubes, and check the ignition and control circuits on the motors and on the warheads and launching gear."

He looked at Cavan. "And, of course, Number One will have to check the firing-plunger circuit."

Cavan's eyes flickered. "Of course," he said quickly.

The Captain closed his eyes for a moment. When he opened them they seemed to burn into Weddy. "How long'll that lot take?"

"Under ten minutes, sir."

Shadde went over to the door and slid it open. "Get cracking. Sooner the better," he said. His voice sounded dry and husky.

Weddy left and in a moment they heard his voice over the broadcast: "Missile launching parties, close up."

Shadde smiled at the first lieutenant, a humorless smile with a shade of malice in it. "So much for your judgment, Number One."

"What was that, sir?"

"You couldn't believe *Retaliate* would ever be used in earnest." There was a note of elation in Shadde's voice.

Cavan thought, Wait, my friend. We'll soon know whose judgment was at fault.

"Anything else, sir?" asked Cavan.

The Captain looked up from the desk as if he had just noticed him. "Yes. Keep a sharp lookout for peculiar behavior. I take it you've already spoken to the officers about that?"

Cavan nodded. "Yes, sir."

With quick strides Shadde went through to the control room. The first lieutenant followed him.

For the second time that night the crew heard the Captain's voice over the broadcast.

"We've just received a second NATO operational signal from FOS. It's very brief. It orders *Retaliate, Massive,* and *Deterrent* to assume the first degree of missile readiness. You've already heard the order to the missile parties to close up." There was suppressed excitement in the Captain's voice and he spoke quickly and with great urgency. "The first degree of readiness requires us to be ready to launch four missiles at three minutes' notice. The missile parties are now preparing numbers one and two and fifteen and sixteen."

Again there was that hard, dry cough, and then the voice resumed, "It's evident that our three boats wouldn't have received these orders unless a most unusual situation was developing. However, I would like to make it *very clear*" —he emphasized the words—"that the order to assume the first degree of readiness is normally a precautionary measure. It does not mean that we will launch missiles, although that's a possibility which can't be excluded."

Shadde paused for a moment. "Once again I must warn you against conjecture. We're here to carry out orders, not to speculate about the reasons for them. As I told you earlier, we'll surface for a few minutes at twenty-two hundred for navigational purposes. That will be in approximately twenty-three minutes' time. I'll keep you informed of any further developments. In the meantime, keep calm . . . don't listen to rumor-mongers . . . concentrate on your duties. . . . That is all."

While Shadde was speaking the first lieutenant had opened the test panel on the firing pedestal and gone through the motions of testing the circuit.

"Firing-plunger circuit tested and correct, sir," he reported.

"Very good," said Shadde.

A few minutes after the second broadcast the Doctor went to the Captain's cabin to report that Musgrove had collapsed in the reactor control room. The lieutenant had been taken to the cabin he shared with Goss and Weddy, and the Doctor had attended to him there. Evidently Musgrove had fainted towards the end of the Captain's broadcast; after reviving he had relapsed into a condition of weepy incoherence.

"What caused the collapse?" snapped Shadde.

The Doctor shrugged his shoulders. "Difficult to say, sir. He's badly shocked and suffering from hysteria."

"What's that mean?"

"He's had a shock to his nervous system. Your announcement about the missile state of readiness must have triggered it off. He probably collapsed from sheer fright . . . that's shock. When I revived him he was incoherent and babbling."

Shadde frowned. "Babbling about what?"

"His mother, I think."

Shadde paced up and down the small cabin, hands thrust into his trouser pockets, shoulders hunched forward. "My God! What an officer! If that made him pass out, what the hell would he do in real trouble? Incredible!" Something occurred to him and he stood still. "What have you done with him?"

"Given him a sedative. He'll sleep for a long time. Feel much better when he wakes up."

"Sure he's not putting on an act?"

The Doctor watched the Captain carefully to see the reaction. "Quite sure, sir. His nerve broke under stress."

There was a look in Shadde's eyes as if he had been slapped in the face. His chin went up and he gave the Doctor a furious stare. O'Shea saw the mouth set hard and the veins protrude, and he braced himself for the outburst. But it never came; instead Symington's voice crackled in the speaker above the bunk. "Captain to the control room. Twenty-two hundred, sir."

The anger in Shadde's eyes gave way to a gleam of excitement. "Very good, Symington," he called back. "I'm coming through."

Hurriedly he pulled on seaboots and an oilskin, slung binoculars around his neck and went through to the A/S compartment. He tapped the operator on the shoulder, and the petty officer lifted the earphones and turned his head.

"Anything near us, Sinclair?" asked Shadde.

"Large single screw on red one thirty, sir. Probably a tanker. About two miles away . . . opening rapidly, sir."

"Good," said Shadde. "Carry on the sweep."

He went over to the center of the control room and called, "Diving stations." The order was passed on the broadcast and the crew went quickly to stations.

"Forty feet!" rapped out Shadde.

The hydroplane operators turned their wheels and the forepart of the submarine began to lift. Then came Shadde's voice again, sharp, incisive, compelling: "Up periscope!" After a quick sweep around the horizon he snapped the handles shut. "Stand by to surface!"

"Stand by to surface! Shut main vents!" called the first lieutenant. There were muffled thuds as the vents were

272

closed, followed quickly by reports from the various compartments.

The outside E.R.A. reported, "All main vents shut, sir."

"Surface!" barked Shadde.

"Blow main ballast!" called the first lieutenant.

The hydroplanes were put to hard arise and there was the hissing roar of high-pressure air expanding into the ballast tanks. The signalman opened the clips on the lower hatch and Shadde lifted his big body up the conning-tower ladder.

The first lieutenant was calling the depths: "Thirty feet, sir. Fifteen feet, sir . . ."

The submarine began to move about in the seaway as she broke surface. Shadde released the clips on the upper hatch, swung it open and climbed out onto the bridge, followed by the lookouts, the signalman, and the officer of the watch.

"Start the blowers," Shadde called down the voice-pipe.

The northwesterly wind had increased and a steepish sea was running. Speed was reduced to 12 knots, but even so the plunging bow kept throwing spray back across the bridge; this and the rain and the lowering clouds which darkened the northern twilight made the visibility less than a mile. Above the men on the bridge, the radar scanner was searching the horizon, providing the control room with data for the reports of bearings and distances of ships and the land.

Lookouts were quickly posted, but on Shadde's orders the navigation lights were not switched on. During the next few minutes there was intense activity. Symington carried out a quick calibration of radar, loran and SINS positions; the plot was started and position data was checked and reestablished on the SINS and computers; lastly, a diving signal was made to FOS/M. Exactly six minutes after she had sur-

273

faced *Retaliate* was back at 200 feet. Speed was increased to 20 knots and course was set to reach the position in Bohus Bay.

One hour before midnight Gracie was called to the Captain's cabin. Shadde was pacing to and fro like a caged tiger. As soon as he saw the telegraphist he beamed. "Splendid! Gracie. You've done a magnificent job. Quite remarkable! The exercise is a roaring success!"

There was no doubt about Shadde's excitement. The dark hollow-ringed eyes were bright and lit up the drawn face. Still pacing he went on, "Thanks to you, Gracie, the most realistic conditions have been achieved. There's not a man on board who doesn't believe that a most serious situation is developing." He must have thought of something because he added quickly, "Except for us, of course." Then he picked up the thread of his thought and raced on, "Yes, yes! Here we are, then. The whole crew faced with what they think is the real thing. It's first-class experience for them. Magnificent training!"

He came to a sudden stop and faced Gracie, eyes staring. "D'you know it's been so realistic that Lieutenant Musgrove's collapsed with fright?" He waited for Gracie to digest this, and then he snorted, "Fine thing for an officer. Shows how necessary the exercise is." With short, swift steps he was off again.

In all this time Gracie hadn't said a word. He stood just inside the door waiting for the Captain to come to the point —to explain why he had sent for him.

Now Shadde was speaking again. "There's only one thing needed to complete the exercise." He gave Gracie a dark look. "Know what?"

"No, sir," said the telegraphist. What the devil's coming now, he thought.

"A third signal," said Shadde, his eyes flashing. "A third

274

signal. I've already enciphered it." He picked up a signal sheet from the desk. "Here it is. . . . You'll receive it at five minutes to midnight. You'll see I've marked the precedence 'flash' this time. We'll go to periscope depth just before twenty-three fifty-five."

There was a deep sigh, a bracing of the shoulders and an upward jerk of the Captain's head; then he was pacing again. "This third signal will crown a remarkable performance. It will end the exercise on a dramatic note. You know —benedictions before battle and that sort of thing!" Shadde laughed gaily. "After that"—he shrugged his shoulders— "we'll turn for home, and I'll tell the crew over the broadcast what it was all about."

He paused a moment and frowned. "Shan't leave it at that, though. I'll draw attention to the results achieved and the lessons learned." His face was somber. "And they'll be considerable, I can assure you. Now that's all, Gracie. Once again, congratulations on a first-class performance."

The telegraphist looked away from the staring eyes. "Thank you, sir," he said uneasily. Then he left the cabin, and went straight to Symington to tell him that the Captain had given him a third signal—to be received just before midnight, contents unknown.

|| 18 ||

At five minutes to midnight the submarine went once more to periscope depth, and down in the W/T office Gracie again turned the switch from "antenna" to "teleprinter." Then he sat with hunched shoulders and watched the third signal come through. When the teleprinter stopped he went through the motions of acknowledging the signal, then flicked the sheet across the cutter bar.

After he had logged the signal he went through to the control room. Shadde was at the periscope and near him stood Symington and Keely, who were about to take over the watch from Goss. Gracie answered the questioning lift of Symington's eyebrows with an almost imperceptible nod. Then he handed the signal to the sublieutenant.

Keely looked at it and his eyes bulged when he spoke to the Captain. "Signal, sir. 'Flash' precedence."

Shadde stiffened at that and the taut mouth line drooped for a moment. Then he said: "Decipher it at once."

The sublieutenant went quickly to the wardroom.

When the "flash" signal came out of the cryptograph Keely saw that this time the address groups did not include *Massive* and *Deterrent*. When he read the message he felt as if he'd been kicked in the pit of his stomach.

Execute Thunderbolt four repeat Thunderbolt four at 0010 repeat 0010 Stop Targets KPF 18/19 repeat KPF 18/19 Stop Thereafter retire into the North Sea Stop Guard this channel at each hour Stop Acknowledge

The wardroom clock showed that it was two minutes to midnight. Pale and excited, Keely ran back into the control room. As he got there he heard Shadde say, "Take her down to one hundred fifty feet."

Keely went up to the Captain and thrust the signal into his hands. "It's to execute Thunderbolt, sir," he said in a dry, husky voice.

For some reason Shadde frowned at the sublieutenant; then he took the signal and read it. There were dark shadows around the hollow of his eyes and the pink glow of the lights accentuated his hawk-like appearance as he went over to the broadcast and pressed the call push. "First Lieutenant and Lieutenant Commanders Gallagher and Weddy report at once to the Captain's cabin," he said.

There was a strange quiver of excitement in Shadde's voice when he spoke to the three officers in his cabin. "Gentlemen, read this quickly, please. There's little time to spare." He handed the signal to Gallagher, then opened the safe under the bunk and took from it the black covered S.P. while Weddy and Cavan peered over Gallagher's shoulders at the signal.

There was a tense silence, and then Gallagher said, "That's certainly something."

Weddy said nothing. He had been expecting this ever since *Retaliate* had been ordered to assume the first degree

277

of readiness. It was the natural sequence; but all the same he had a tight, dry feeling in his throat, and thoughts of his mother crowded out everything else. He hoped fervently that she wasn't in London, that for some strange reason he couldn't imagine, she might have gone to the country.

Shadde went quickly through the pages of the S.P. until he found the page he wanted. Then he turned to them abruptly. "Well, gentlemen? Do you agree the import of the signal? Four Polaris missiles to be launched at ten minutes past midnight?"

Weddy's mouth was dry and he felt slightly dazed, but he nodded with the others.

When Shadde picked up the S.P. to show them the open page, his hands were trembling. "Target coordinates, KPF eighteen and nineteen," he said. "Let's see what they are."

He ran his fingers across the table of coordinates and stopped. "Here they are: KPF eighteen—naval base and dockyard, Kronshtadt." He looked up. "Thank God it's a military target." Then his finger moved on. "KPF nineteen—industrial complex, Leningrad. See that, gentlemen? See that, do you? Those are our targets."

With quick, jerky movements he marked the target coordinates with a pencil, folded the page and handed the book to Weddy. "Two-sector spread on both, Weddy. You'll find all the data there." He waved him away with a flourish of his hand. "Look sharp! Time's short! Get that onto your computers right away." He swung around to look at the clock on the bulkhead. "My God! Midnight! We've got ten minutes! Sound off missile launching stations, Number One. Come on, gentlemen, there's no time to spare."

Weddy had already gone, and Shadde bustled out followed by the first lieutenant and Gallagher. When they got into the control room Cavan went to the alarm panel and turned the small wheel until the pointer stopped at "Missile

Launching Stations." The insistent clamor of the buzzers sounded throughout the submarine, and while they were still vibrating the crew hurried to their stations. Some men looked calm and normal, but most showed alarm and many of them fear.

On Shadde's orders the submarine was taken up to 90 feet, and a shift was made from automatic to hand steering and depth-keeping. The scene in the control room was one of intense activity, and reports poured in from the missile attack center and the missile control room and launching area within seconds after the men reached their stations.

The clock above the chart table showed 0002—two minutes past midnight. The sublieutenant spoke to the Captain. "The attack center wants the estimated firing position at o-o-ten, sir."

Shadde waved an imperious arm at Symington. "Plot the firing position at o-o-ten. Maintain this course, but average eight knots at o-o-eight-o. Got that?"

"Aye, aye, sir."

"Well, get on with it!"

In a minute Symington reported, "Firing position at o-o-ten plotted, sir."

Shadde jerked his head towards Keely. "Pass it to the attack center! Buck up, man, buck up!"

Shadde went over to the navigating officer. "Symington, con the boat to arrive in the firing position at o-o-ten." Then he was back at the broadcast, pressing the call push. When he spoke his voice was hoarse. "This is the Captain. We've just received a NATO flash message." He paused and there wasn't a sound except the crackling of the loud speaker and Shadde's labored breathing. "We're to launch four Polaris missiles at ten minutes past midnight. That's in about six minutes. The targets are Kronshtadt, Russia's principal naval base, and the industrial area around Leningrad. These are about twenty-five miles apart."

Shadde paused and cleared his throat. "Range from the firing position to the targets will be about seven hundred and fifty miles. That means our warheads should reach them about three minutes after firing. Immediately after launching we'll go deep, retire into the North Sea at maximum speed and await further orders."

Again he stopped, and his listeners wondered what there was left to say. There was a dreadful, numbing finality about what they had heard that left little to the imagination.

But the Captain went on, "I must exhort you to concentrate solely upon the execution of your duties. You must refrain from all speculation as to the why and wherefore of our orders." His voice rose and something crept into it which might have been excitement or even exultation. "I'd like to remind you that in these waters, not far from here, the Royal Navy once broke the power of a mighty alliance which threatened England. Nelson's victory at Copenhagen smashed the confederacy of Prussia, Denmark, Sweden and . . . Russia." There was hatred in his voice as he dragged out the last word.

"Today, not alone, but with powerful allies—NATO, the United States and the Commonwealth—Britain faces a far more deadly enemy: Communist Russia." The voice rose. "We're now about to do for England what Nelson did at Copenhagen." He paused for a moment. "May we do it as well. That is all. God bless you." This wasn't the cold, calm Shadde the crew was used to; there was no doubt the occasion had choked him with emotion.

Symington leaned over and tapped the Doctor on the shoulder. O'Shea turned from watching Shadde and saw Symington's eyebrows raised in silent question. He gave the slightest of shrugs, shook his head, then leaned over the plot again as if nothing had happened.

Though the broadcasts had prepared them for what was coming, there had been a good deal of dismay and alarm among the men in the different compartments of the submarine when the buzzers had sounded for missile launching stations a few minutes before. But expected or not, Shadde's last statement came as a profound shock to most of the crew. It was a nasty jolt of reality, an end to conjecture. This was it; the much talked about, much prepared for, "it-can't-happen-here" nuclear war with Russia had started. There were thoughts of wives and children and parents and girl friends, of homes in towns and villages and country-side. And crowding these were other thoughts—unspeakable, inadmissible—about what might already be happening in England. But there wasn't very much time for thinking. Every man had something to do—a station to go to, a duty to perform—and, in the few minutes left, too much was happening for clear, consecutive thought.

Keely touched the Captain on the arm. "Attack center reports missiles ready for launching, sir." The sublieutenant's face was bathed in perspiration and his eyes seemed larger that usual.

"Very good," said Shadde. "Confirm firing time—o-o-ten—six and a half minutes to go."

Symington's voice broke in. "We're astern of station, sir." Then he called, "Revolutions for twenty-two knots."

The able seaman at the telegraphs rang on the revolutions, and down in the engine room the chief E.R.A. opened the main steam valves a little wider.

The night's events had shattered Mr. Buddington. It was now unmistakably clear to this intelligent, friendly and unbelligerent little man that he was about to be caught up in the van of a nuclear war. To his logical, well-trained mind the sequence of events that night permitted no other conclusion.

When the Captain spoke over the broadcast for the third time, Mr. Buddington's worst fears were confirmed, and he had the greatest difficulty in remaining outwardly composed. His thoughts flew to the little house near the river at Richmond, where Mrs. Buddington and Annabelle and Rosemary lived. There, when he was not at the Admiralty or otherwise away, he had for many years spent his happiest hours. Life had been good to Mr. Buddington, and he was blessed with its greatest gift, contentment. He was utterly content with his wife, his daughters, his home, and his work. He believed these to be rewards far beyond his deserts, and he was humbly grateful. But now, in this submarine, he was confronted with the loss and destruction of everything that he held dear, and the starkness of it was shattering.

On hearing the Captain's first broadcast he had experienced a vague, unpleasant feeling of anxiety. The second announcement had suggested frightening probability and left him dazed and uncertain. But now, after the third broadcast, there was no more uncertainty—just a ghastly, terrifying realization that drained away all his courage and left no avenues of escape. In five minutes this submarine in which he was a passenger would fire four Polaris missiles on Russian targets, and he had no illusions about what that would mean.

Sick with anxiety and fearful for his family, Mr. Buddington sought the company of someone with whom he could discuss matters. He couldn't bear this silence—broken only by the staccato bark of orders he didn't understand—this absence of communication with his fellow men. One look into the control room, however, made it clear that nothing could be done there; every officer, petty officer and man was intensely busy. He supposed it would be the same in all other compartments. Then he thought of the engine room. The engineer officer would be there: Rhys Evans, calm, friendly, sound as a drum. With twinkling feet Mr. Buddington sped aft.

Sure enough, there was the engineer officer standing on the control platform in the fore-part of the engine room, surrounded by a maze of machinery, the main turbine purring away rhythmically below him. Mr. Buddington could see at once from the faces of Rhys Evans and the other engine-room staff that he was not the only person on board suffering from fear and apprehension. He went up to the engineer officer and said, "I'm sorry to worry you at a time like this, but I feel I must speak to someone." He had to raise his voice to be heard above the sound of the machinery.

Rhys Evans gave him a friendly nod. "Certainly, Mr. Buddington."

"You see," panted the little man, "I'm gravely concerned about my wife and children in London."

The engineer officer's worried eyes met his. "Indeed, and who is not worried, Mr. Buddington?"

Mr. Buddington twisted his fingers uneasily. "It means nuclear war with Russia," he stammered. "May already have started. You realize that?"

"Better not to think of it," said Rhys Evans.

"Impossible not to." Mr. Buddington's tone was desperate, and his eyes rolled. Then he thought of something. "What happens when a missile's fired? Is there a loud explosion?"

The engineer officer shook his head. "No explosion. It's fired from the launching tube by compressed air. No sound unless you're in the launching compartment. Rocket motor doesn't ignite until it's clear of the water. Nothing to be heard of that either, down here."

"So there's no noise?" Mr. Buddington said it with some relief.

"Little enough, anyway. When the launching tubes flood, just after the missiles have gone, you'll hear the roar of water and the hiss of escaping air. They're flooded automatically to keep the trim on the boat. We'd pop up like a cork otherwise."

"I see," said Mr. Buddington unhappily. "Anything else? Does the boat shake?"

"You'll feel the change in trim. Boat rises suddenly after the missile's gone, then settles back when the tubes and compensating tanks flood."

"I see." Mr. Buddington was not really listening now. There was a faraway look in his eyes. Annabelle and Rosemary were running down the garden path towards him. "Daddy! Daddy!" they were calling, breathless and excited.

With a heavy heart he turned away. "How dreadful that this should happen! How dreadful!" he said despairingly.

At missile launching stations Target and Miller made up the emergency pool. Their duty was to stand by in the wardroom, in sight of the control room, on immediate call. For them it was a deadly time of watching and waiting; at least the other members of the crew had duties to perform which distracted their attention.

The two stewards stood by the pantry hatch watching the quiet, intense activity in the control room. Target picked his teeth with a match, his eyes on the wardroom clock. "O-o-o-four," he said. "Six minutes to go."

Miller nodded. "Glad I ain't a flippin' steward serving gin in Kronshtadt."

Target eyed him doubtfully. "'Ave the commies got wardrooms?"

"Sure to 'ave. They got officers, ain't they?"

"That's one thing. Wardrooms is another."

"Must 'ave," said Miller with finality.

There was a long silence. Finally Miller said, "Kind of

strange standing 'ere waiting"—he jerked his thumb aft—
"for Guy Fawkes to begin."

" 'Tis, ain't it?" Target sucked at his teeth.

"Reminds me of that story of Alf and Bill and the lions.
Ever 'eard it?"

Target gave a bored shrug. "Yes. 'Alf a dozen ·times
this patrol."

Miller's eyebrows went up. "No call to take on nasty!
Just trying to pass the time."

Target pulled out a handkerchief and blew his nose.
He looked utterly miserable. "Bit of a cold," he explained.

"That's right," said Miller absently.

Another long pause was broken by Target. "These
Polaris jobs doesn't 'alf nip along. Hear what the Skipper
said? Seven 'undred and fifty miles in three minutes."

Miller sighed. "It'll be flippin' lights out in Kronshtadt
when they get there."

Target picked away with the match. "Flippin' lights out
for the 'ole world. Mark my words."

|| 19 ||

The clock over the chart table showed 0005: five minutes
past midnight. Tension in the control room was mounting.
In the red glow of the lights, the faces of the men at their
stations were strained and apprehensive. A constant stream
of reports flowed in and voices rose and fell above the hum
of the main turbines and the chattering of the instruments.

Petty Officer Sinclair reported urgently from the A/S
compartment: "H.E. dead ahead, sir! Fast twin screws!"

"Very good," said Shadde. "Let me know what it's doing
as soon as you can."

Ten seconds later Sinclair reported, "Range about two
miles! Closing at about twenty knots! Bearing steady, sir."

In a quick movement Shadde was at the plot. He
nudged Symington. "Bloody thing's on our firing course."
His voice was husky and anxious.

The navigating officer looked at the clock; it was just
after 0005. "Yes, it is, sir." He did some rapid mental arithmetic. "If our combined speeds are forty knots, we're closing

at the rate of a mile every one and a half minutes. In two or three minutes we'll meet. When we reach the firing position at o-o-ten we'll be about one and a half miles past him."

"Thank God for that," snapped Shadde.

"H.E. still dead ahead, sir! Closing rapidly! Range under two miles."

"Very good," said Shadde. "Watch it carefully. Maintain an all-around sweep." He hurried across to the chart table. "Soundings, Symington?"

"Aye, aye, sir." Symington went over to the fathometer and switched it on. When the trace appeared he started calling: "310—307—305—306—306 . . ."

"That'll do," snapped Shadde.

Keely reported. "Missile control wants to know what time the launching caps should be opened, sir."

Shadde looked at the clock. "In two and a half minutes' time."

"Steer zero-six-three. Revolutions for twenty-two and one-half knots," called Symington, and the coxswain and telegraphist repeated the orders.

With three quick steps Shadde was back at the plot. "Distance to the firing position?"

Symington was ready for the question. "Twenty-two hundred yards, sir."

Then Sinclair called again. "H.E. still dead ahead, sir. Range one and one-half miles. Closing rapidly."

"Very good," said Shadde. "Anything else close?"

"No, sir."

The clock above the chart table showed six and a half minutes past midnight.

"Distance to go fourteen hundred fifty yards, sir."

"Very good."

With an impatient flick of his hand Shadde snapped, "Wake up, Keely! Watch me! Never mind the rest."

"Aye, aye, sir."

"Give the attack center and missile control the three and one-half minute stand-by."

At the plot Symington and the Doctor kept a covert watch on Shadde. There was only one thought in their minds: Would he use the firing plunger? Normally his demeanor was calm and collected, but tonight he seemed restless and excited. All part of the act, the Doctor said to himself, and then his thoughts were interrupted by Symington's voice. "Eleven hundred yards to the firing position. Three minutes to go, sir."

Through his headphones Keely heard Goss's voice. "Inspection hatches on launching tubes shut."

The sublieutenant repeated the message to the Captain. "Good," said Shadde. "Revolutions for four knots," and his tone was sharp. The telegraph bells tinkled as the new speed was rung on, and instantly Shadde called, "Stand by to open launching caps!"

The sublieutenant repeated the order to missile control.

"Higgins!" Shadde's voice was urgent and angry. "Why isn't the launching-area speaker on? Switch the bloody thing on at once."

The messenger flicked the switch and a new pattern of noise filled the control room: the shrill whistle of high-frequency sound, the hiss of escaping air and the whirr of compressors. Bagnall's calm West-Country voice could be heard giving orders, and the voices of his men answering.

The sublieutenant spoke into the headset and then reported to the Captain, "Attack center reports all checks and line-ups complete, sir. Ready for launching."

"Very good," said Shadde.

"Seven hundred fifty yards to the firing position; two and a half minutes to go." Symington wondered how his voice could sound so calm and clear.

Shadde looked at the clock. "Give the attack center the two-and-a-half-minute stand-by."

288

Sinclair reported, "H.E. passing overhead, sir!"

"Good. Carry on with your sweep."

Bagnall's voice came through on the loudspeaker: "Clear the launching area!" Then they heard the metallic thuds of watertight doors shutting.

"Launching area cleared, sir. Watertight doors shut," said Keely.

From the plot, Symington reported, "Speed nine and a half knots, sir."

Shadde's voice was dry and hoarse. "Open launching caps," he said, and Keely repeated the order to missile control.

Standing by the trim control panel the first lieutenant tried to concentrate on the depth gauges, but all his senses were keyed to what Shadde was doing and saying.

"Revolutions for ten knots." Now Symington's voice sounded shrill. The note of the main turbines rose to a higher pitch.

"Four hundred twenty-five yards to the firing position, sir—one and a half minutes to go!"

Shadde's voice sounded peculiar; it had a sort of hoarse tremble in it. "Control officers to the firing pedestal."

The first lieutenant joined Gallagher at the pedestal. Through the perspex screen they saw Weddy take off his headset and climb down from the console seat; then he came through the door and over to the pedestal. With quick strides Shadde reached them. He opened the stainless-steel door on the pedestal and the four control dials reflected back the red glow of the lights.

Shadde leaned down and turned the top dial several times. When he straightened up, there was no mistaking the excitement in his voice as he said, "Put on your control settings."

Cavan quickly set the second dial, then Weddy the third, and finally Gallagher bent down. There was a slight delay while the American put his setting on the bottom dial with calm, unhurried concentration.

Shadde watched him, irritated and impatient. "Quickly please, Gallagher," he snapped.

The American said, "O.K., Captain. All settings on now," and stood up.

Weddy raced back to the attack center and Shadde crossed over to the plot. The first lieutenant was over at the trim control panel again, and Gallagher remained by the firing pedestal. The clock above the chart table showed nine minutes past midnight.

"Two hundred ninety-five yards to the firing position— one minute to go, sir!"

He's feeling the strain, the Doctor thought, as he listened to Symington's voice.

"H.E. bearing Green fifty-five, sir! Closing!"

"Range?" Shadde's face twisted with anxiety.

"About two miles, sir. Large, single screw." Shadde went to the plot and watched the moving stylus arm with burning eyes. Then he moved to the firing pedestal and stood next to Gallagher.

Symington jerked upright from the plot. "One hundred sixty-five yards to go . . . thirty seconds, sir!"

The Doctor looked across at the Captain. Beads of perspiration had run down Shadde's face, leaving wet streaks, red in the glow of the control-room lights. Beneath the dark sockets of the eyes and above the high cheekbones there were red patches of perspiration. The eyes were wide and staring and the facial muscles never stopped working. Above it all, the tousled black hair was moist with sweat. As O'Shea watched, Shadde shouted to Keely, "Start the telemeter count!" His voice was hoarse.

The first strike of the firing gong sounded, strident and chilling. The count had started. All eyes watched the repeater over the pedestal. At each second the gong struck and the figure in the repeater changed, showing the number of seconds to launching.

Gong! . . . 10
Gong! . . . 9
Gong! . . . 8

With a quick sideways thrust Shadde brushed Gallagher out of the way and put both hands on the T-piece of the firing plunger. He watched the repeater with fierce concentration, his jaw thrust upward.

How he's loving it, thought the first lieutenant. Every silly, overacted, dramatic bloody second of it!

But O'Shea was reacting differently. He was looking at Shadde's eyes and all he could think was, Those eyes! My God! Those eyes!

Gong! . . . 5
Gong! . . . 4
Gong! . . . 3
Gong! . . . 2

Symington's voice shrilled: "On! On! On!"

With a heave of his shoulders Shadde pushed the firing plunger away from him, away and across the full travel of the metal arc until the pointer came to a quivering stop under the word "Fire."

|| 20 ||

There was a stunned silence in the control room. From the launching area the loudspeaker relayed the same shrill whistle of high-frequency sound, the hiss of escaping air and the whirr of compressors. There was no change in trim, no sound of the flooding of the launching tubes; nothing had happened.

Frantically Shadde seized the plunger, wrenched it back across the arc to the "Off" position and then rammed it across to "Fire" again; but still nothing happened.

With wild eyes he turned to Keely. "What's the delay? What the hell's happened?" Lunging at the astonished sub-lieutenant he wrenched the headset away. "Give it to me, you dumb idiot!" Then he roared into it, "Weddy! Attack center! What's the delay? I've depressed the plunger twice! Order them to fire, man! Order them to fire!" There was hysteria in his voice and he waved his arms as he shouted.

The first lieutenant dashed past Shadde into the attack center. "Check! Check! Check!" he yelled to Weddy. The gunnery officer pulled off the headset and stared at him in amazement.

"David!" panted the first lieutenant. "There'll be no firing. Those NATO ops signals were bogus! Shadde's off his rocker!"

"But what . . . ? But why haven't they gone? He's depressed the firing plunger!" Weddy stammered.

"Forget that now. The whole thing's a fraud. I'm telling you, man! The signals were bogus! Order missile control to secure!"

Weddy couldn't have been more confused. "But what about the Captain?" He looked through the perspex screen into the control room, where Shadde was storming and gesticulating.

"He's round the bend! Mad as a hatter! I'm taking over command." With that the first lieutenant tore back into the control room.

Shadde had seen Cavan run through to the attack center and concluded that he had gone there to find out why the missiles hadn't been launched. "What is it, Number One?" he cried. "What's happened?" Perspiration poured from him and his voice cracked.

The first lieutenant stopped a foot away from Shadde and looked him squarely in the face. "Nothing's happened, sir. But there'll be no firing," he said firmly. "Those NATO signals were bogus."

For a moment Shadde's eyes seemed to leave their sockets, and then with a roar of rage he sprang at the first lieutenant with such violence that Cavan, big as he was, fell back against the chart table.

The Captain screamed, "You bloody traitor! How dare you! This is mutiny! You're under arrest!" He swung around to Allistair. "This officer's under arrest. He's to be confined to his cabin." He spun around again. "Coxswain! Give the wheel to Higgins! Assist Lieutenant Allistair!"

Shadde was still clutching Keely's headset, and now he shouted into it, "Weddy! Weddy! Goss! In the control room at once!" Then he turned back, and with flaming, incredulous eyes he saw Symington, the Doctor, Keely and Cavan slowly closing in on him. His face contorted with rage. "Keep off, d'you hear? You mutinous swine! Interfere with history in the making, would you?" He danced in an excess of rage. "Allistair! Coxswain! Arrest these officers at—"

Before Shadde could finish the sentence Keely made a flying tackle which brought him to the deck, legs pinned; and Cavan, the Doctor and Symington piled in.

The struggle was fierce and bloody; Shadde was powerful and he lashed out devastatingly with feet and fists. While they fought on the deck, he fumed and shouted. "You bloody traitors! Betray England, would you! Wait for the court-martial! Aah . . . aa!" he panted, and lay there gasping for breath.

The sublieutenant was down on the deck, arms locked about Shadde's legs; the first lieutenant sat astride the Captain's chest, and the Doctor and Symington each pinned an arm to the deck. Shadde turned his head to one side and saw Symington. His eyes rolled. "You . . . you . . . !" he exploded, and started to struggle again with fresh energy. "Unspeakable little cad! This is your doing . . . all yours . . ." With a groan he relaxed and began to babble incoherently. "Lombok Strait! . . . Fitzhugh Symington . . . dogged by that bloody family." For a moment he lay silent; then, his eyes wild and staring, he was off again. "Ah! Nelson . . . happy band of brothers! Forgive me, Nelson, forgive me!"

"Take it easy, sir." The first lieutenant's breathless voice was meant to be soothing, but it drove Shadde into another frenzy of rage and the struggle was on again.

"You're mad . . . all of you . . . wait for the court-martial! Call yourselves Englishmen! . . . My God! You've sold her . . . you've sold her, I tell you. Stupid swine! . . . I could have brought Russia to her knees . . . ended the threat once and for all! . . . You stopped me! *You stopped me!*" There was a shattering, chilling scream; then he lay back breathless, exhausted by his exertions.

By now others had come into the control room and were crowding around, their faces filled with dismay. Goss and Weddy were there and Mr. Buddington and the two stewards. The control-room messenger had taken the wheel and the coxswain and Gracie and Farrell were standing over the struggling men. The faces of the petty officers were agitated and perplexed.

From the beginning Gallagher had watched the astonishing performance with open-mouthed wonder, but he had taken no part in it. Now he pushed his way through the circle of men around Shadde. "What's going on?" he asked quietly.

Still sitting astride Shadde and panting for breath, the first lieutenant said, "That can wait." Then he spied Goss and Weddy. "Weddy, look after the boat! Watch the trim! Keep this course and speed." He stopped to regain his breath. "Goss! Close the launching caps. Pump out and get those Polaris run down as quick as you can."

The Doctor gasped, "If someone will take this arm over from me"—he jerked his head in the direction of Shadde's arm, held in a vicelike grip—"I'll get some morphia and . . ."

"How dare you!" Shadde interrupted with a shout, and he wrestled again furiously. "Filthy little medico! Don't you try your quackery on me!"

Then he went limp, but a moment later he gave a violent heave which nearly unseated the first lieutenant. "Gallagher! Allistair! Coxswain!" He summoned them all in hoarse desperation. "Lend a hand! Pull these men off! Arrest them! They're mutineers! This is . . . ," his voice trailed away again and he lay back groaning and gasping, as Goss took over from the Doctor the task of pinning down Shadde's left arm.

In a few moments O'Shea was back with a syringe. He bared the Captain's forearm and with a quick jab injected the morphia while Shadde shouted and groaned and struggled to free himself. But it was not long before the drug took effect, and in the middle of a fresh outburst of hysterical rambling he lost consciousness.

The first lieutenant, Keely and the two stewards carried the Captain to his cabin and laid him gently on the bunk. With Miller's help, the Doctor took off Shadde's uniform coat, shoes, collar and tie. Sadly, O'Shea looked at the unconscious man; he tried to smooth back the thick tangle of hair from the moist forehead. "Poor old chap," he said softly. "You've been through hell, all right." He looked at Miller. "See that he's kept warm. He'll be out for hours. We'll keep him that way until we get to Blockhouse. Then Haslar will take him over."

When the Doctor had gone Miller stood over the bunk looking at the strong pale face, blood-smeared and sweating. With a moist cloth he gently wiped the blood marks away; and then he stood listening for a while to the labored and irregular breathing, broken from time to time by sobs like those of a tired, sad child.

Miller put two blankets over the Captain, and then turned the lights out. At the door he stopped for a moment and looked back. "Blimey, sir," he whispered. "What've they done to you?"

When he got back to the control room, the first lieutenant went to the broadcast and pressed the call push. He was still breathless. "This is the first lieutenant. The exercise is complete. Secure missile launching stations. The Captain's had a breakdown and is now under the Doctor's care. I have assumed command.

"You can't have known that tonight's happenings were, in fact, just an exercise. The so-called NATO operational signals from FOS—which the Captain told you about—weren't real signals. They were his idea for an exercise under realistic conditions. But . . ." Whatever Cavan was going to say, he changed his mind. "You've all, I'm sure, been very worried and concerned. I can only say how sorry I am for that. I must ask you, out of loyalty to the Captain—and to the Service, not to mention this when you're ashore. It's a domestic matter—let's do all we can to keep it in this boat"—he cleared his throat—"or at least in the naval family.

"I'll inform FOS by signal of the Captain's illness, and we'll alter course for Portsmouth. We should arrive there on Sunday morning. That is all."

Twenty minutes after midnight, course was altered; and ten minutes later the submarine surfaced and steamed to the southwest at sixteen knots.

It had stopped raining, and the northwesterly wind and sea were now abaft the starboard beam. The steady rolling of *Retaliate*, the gusts of fresh air which blew down into the control room, and the noise of the sea washing along the casing and slapping against the conning tower reminded the men below how good it was to be alive in a world at peace.

|| 21 ||

There was no meeting planned in the wardroom next morning, but after breakfast, when the stewards were still clearing away, the first lieutenant told them to leave the wardroom and shut the watertight door behind them.

Everyone was present except for Allistair, who was on watch, and Musgrove, who was still in his cabin in what the Doctor described as a highly nervous condition.

When the stewards had gone the first lieutenant said, "There are one or two things about last night which I think we should discuss. Bound to be an inquiry in Portsmouth and we'd better tie up some of the ends now."

There was the sound of a nervous cough and Mr. Buddington said, "Would you like me to leave, Mr. Cavan?"

The first lieutenant winced at the "Mister." "Not at all—but I'd better tell them who you are."

The little man nodded and the first lieutenant explained who Mr. Buddington was and why he was on board. There were exclamations of surprise, and Goss said, "Well, I'm

298

damned! My old chess pal a sleuth! No wonder you always beat me."

Mr. Buddington smiled disarmingly. "I shall miss those games, Mr. Goss."

"Me too!"

"Any clues about the saboteur?" asked Weddy curiously.

"There isn't one, gentlemen." Mr. Buddington's watery gaze traveled around the wardroom. "There wasn't any sabotage, you see. It was . . . it was . . . " he stammered, "a powerful obsession with your Captain. Not that he wasn't perhaps entitled to . . . er . . . think that." He told them about Finney.

"How is the Skipper, poor man?" There was a mournful ring in Rhys Evans' voice.

"Still out. Fully sedated," said O'Shea. "We'll have to keep him like that until we get in."

The engineer officer shook his head. "Poor man! Poor man!"

Gallagher looked at the first lieutenant. "What d'you say we get on with that discussion you mentioned just now?"

Cavan nodded. "We'll do that." He moistened his lips. "Thing is, we must put the best possible face on this for the Skipper. Look after his interests, you know, but it's going to be difficult after last night."

"I'll say," agreed Gallagher, and he sounded pretty grim.

"I'd better tell you the thing from the beginning." Cavan looked around the table slowly, as if he were taking stock of his audience. "It started the second day out of Stockholm."

He told them how Shadde had sent for Gracie and first mentioned the bogus signals he wanted for an exercise; that in the early hours of the morning, before sailing from Copenhagen, he had again sent for him and said he wanted them that day; that Gracie, worried and unhappy about the whole idea, had gone to Symington; and, finally, that Symington had come to him.

"When Symington told me, I knew instinctively that this could be damned serious." He paused and looked around at the expectant faces. "The threat to the security measures was fantastic. Shadde's moods had been getting more and more peculiar and . . . well"—he held out his hands—"I knew something had to be done. So I put my thinking cap on and I had to think pretty hard and quick. It was a hell of a responsibility, I don't mind saying."

"Quite," said Symington, and he looked up at the deckhead. The first lieutenant gave him a shrewd look.

"I knew I had to play the thing damned carefully, because otherwise a number of innocent people were going to be in serious trouble. I had to make sure the security measures weren't defeated, and at the same time I had to protect Symington and Gracie. So I hit on this idea of disconnecting the firing circuit." He gave a deprecatory shrug of his shoulders, but his smugness was obvious to all.

Cavan went on to tell them that he had been to see the Doctor to get an opinion of Shadde's mental condition and that consequently he had briefed Symington about disconnecting the firing plunger and told him to go see the Doctor and make his own inquiries about Shadde.

"That stood him in good stead later when the Chief bumped into him in the airlock. Didn't it, Symington?" Cavan asked the question with a smile, but there was no amusement in it.

"Brilliant bit of forethought," said Symington drily.

Lastly, the first lieutenant told them how the Doctor had persuaded Rhys Evans to stay silent, and added, "Thank you, Chiefy, for playing ball." But the Welshman seemed not to have heard; he just sat there gloomily, head sunk on his chest.

"And that's about all there is to tell," said Cavan. "You know the rest, because you saw it happen."

Nobody said anything for a moment, until Gallagher turned around in his chair and screwed up his face as he spoke. "Why did you send Symington to break that circuit? Why didn't you do it yourself?"

Cavan nodded. "Good point. You see, if I'd gone and been caught out at it, I'd have had no one senior to myself to turn to. By sending Symington it was different. I was always in the background to protect him if it came to a showdown."

"I see," said the American slowly. "And perhaps—"

"What beats me," interrupted Goss, "is Shadde's motive. Fantastic bloody thing to do."

The first lieutenant looked at the Doctor. "Over to you, Doc."

The Doctor shook his head. "Nothing that we'd understand. I know I'm being wise after the event, but Shadde's insane. He's a manic-depressive—with a bit of the compulsive obsessive thrown in, I'd say."

"How d'you know?" It was Weddy's quiet, shocked voice.

"Symptoms. Behavior."

"What's a manic-depressive?" said the first lieutenant.

"Form of insanity, in the extreme condition. Develops on the basis of the so-called cyclothysive personality. Quite common. Often found in people of high ability. Goethe for example."

"What are the symptoms?"

"Rapid mood swings. Periods of depression alternating with excitement and elation. Rapid thinking . . . flight of ideas . . . jumping from one topic to the other . . . overactivity . . . overtalkativeness . . . sleeplessness. Lots of people have these, but Shadde's have reached psychotic dimensions. He's lost touch with reality. His judgment is gone."

Gallagher puffed a ring of smoke at the deckhead. "How did he get that way?"

"Difficult to say. Basic condition might be hereditary, or due to a childhood trauma. Severe father . . . bitchy stepmother could have done it. You'd have to know the family history." Then the Doctor told them all he knew about the Lombok Strait business and the Captain's other problems. "Shadde was obsessed with the idea that you'd spread that Lombok Strait story in the wardroom," he said, looking at Symington.

Symington was pale and tight-lipped. "My father never mentioned the Lombok Strait. He had the highest opinion of Shadde."

The Doctor nodded sympathetically. "There's no doubt his condition deteriorated after you joined. Then came the breakup of his marriage and all the other things I've told you about. The car accident was probably the breaking point." With a shrug of the shoulders he stubbed out his cigarette. "Anyway, that's how I see it." He looked towards the door of the Captain's cabin and shook his head. "Poor old Shadde. We'll never know the hell he's been through."

"What are his chances of recovery?" The first lieutenant's voice was matter-of-fact.

"Probably not too bad," said the Doctor.

Gallagher cut in with a quick question. "In your navy, can he be promoted now?"

The first lieutenant shook his head. "I'd say not. Afraid he's had it as far as the service is concerned. There'll be an inquiry and a very rigid view will be taken of what happened. Public opinion and Parliament are as sensitive as hell about Polaris—danger of unauthorized firings and that sort of thing. He'll be invalided from the navy on medical grounds, I imagine." He shook his head. "Couldn't be more sorry for him."

"What shakes me," said Weddy, "is what might have happened! All the *if's*."

"You mean . . . ?" The Doctor raised his eyebrows.

"For example, if Gracie hadn't told Symington. If Symington hadn't told you. If you'd reassured Number One beyond all possible doubt that Shadde was sane. And of course the big *if* . . . " He looked around the table. "If the firing plunger hadn't been disconnected. It's pretty frightening to think what might have happened by now."

"Nothing would have happened." Gallagher said it very quietly and simply, but if he had thrown a bomb into the wardroom it wouldn't have caused more surprise.

"Nothing?" said the first lieutenant. "What d'you mean?"

"Those missiles couldn't fly, anyway—broken circuit or no broken circuit."

Cavan's face was blank. "Are you serious?"

"I certainly am."

"Why couldn't they be fired?"

For a moment Gallagher sat there saying nothing, but they could see he was thinking hard. Then he said, "There's only one setting on that bottom dial that could make the firing circuit alive." He paused. "The odds against guessing it are seventeen million to one, in case any of you ever think of trying."

"So what?" said Weddy.

"I didn't put it on."

"But I saw you work the dial."

"I put a phony setting on it."

Goss broke the stunned silence. "What made you do that?"

"Because I knew that firing signal was phony as soon as I saw it."

There was a challenge in the first lieutenant's voice. "How?"

Gallagher looked at him coolly. "That's a United States secret. We still have a few, I guess." He took out a cigarette case.

The first lieutenant pulled at his ear. "Why didn't you say the signal was bogus when Shadde showed it to you? Might have saved that business last night."

"And the bloody fright everybody got," added Goss.

"Might have saved Shadde too." Rhys Evans' voice was censorious.

Gallagher's eyes narrowed. "D'you mind waiting a minute? When that firing signal came in on top of the others, I was very interested. I knew it was a phony, all right. It shouted it at me." He knocked the ash off his cigarette. "But I figured that this must be some fancy British idea for putting on a tough exercise. We wouldn't do it in our navy, but I thought . . . well you know, Royal Navy . . . the *oldest* navy . . . maybe *they can* do it that way. So I just sat and waited. Why spoil the play? And . . . well"—he shrugged his shoulders—"I knew those missiles couldn't go, anyway." He got up out of his chair then and his face looked a bit grayer than usual as he leaned against the pantry hatch with his arms folded across his chest.

They were all looking at him now, wondering about the odd look on his face, but he was watching only the first lieutenant, and when he spoke it was to Cavan. "If you're finished," he said, "there's a question I'd like to ask you?"

Cavan gave him a dry, unamused smile and said, "Go ahead."

"Why did you get Symington to cut that firing circuit instead of coming to me?" said Gallagher. "I'm the weapons control officer in this outfit. I'm assigned here for the express purpose of preventing unauthorized firings or any violations of the security measures. You know that as well as I do, and yet when this situation comes up you keep right away from me. Can you explain that?"

Cavan shoved back into his chair and they all looked at him; but except that his face was a bit paler than usual, he didn't show any concern.

"I don't much like your tone, Gallagher," he said, "but I can understand a bit of what you must feel; and since you've asked for an explanation I'll give it to you. When Symington came and saw me I thought of going to you. But then I realized this was an R.N. affair and we had to settle it our own way. I knew that once the circuit had been broken the missiles couldn't be fired, so there was no danger on that account.

"My problem was to make sure that nothing could go wrong, and at the same time handle things so that I could protect Gracie and Symington and"—he paused and took a deep breath—"and, of course, the Skipper." He looked past Gallagher at the wardroom clock. "If I'd come to you I'd have"—he smiled—"I'd have let the side down. Don't you see?"

Gallagher gave him a long, hard look, and then he came away from the pantry hatch and moved close to Cavan. "That's a very moving story, Cavan," he said, "but I'll tell you another one that's pretty sad, too, and it's about your Captain." He stopped and there wasn't a sound in the wardroom. "He's quite a man you know—or was. One of your top submariners. But he's been a pretty sick man lately. O'Shea's told us all about that and sort of filled in the gaps, but I guess we've all known for some time now that Shadde's been having a tough time. But—with the exception of Rhys Evans here—we haven't done a goddam thing about it . . . haven't tried to help him in any way or anything like that . . . have we?"

The American looked around the wardroom and then turned back to the first lieutenant. "But when you heard about those signals, Cavan, you had a pretty shrewd idea your Captain *was* a sick man . . . so shrewd that you went and explained to O'Shea why you reckoned Shadde might be out of his mind. And O'Shea wasn't prepared to guarantee that he wasn't.

"Now if you'd come to me then—as you should have—and told me about the signals and what was on your mind, I'd have told you how I could put on a phony setting—that is if you didn't already know, which perhaps you did."

"I certainly did not," said Cavan, and his face was ashen.

"Anyway," went on Gallagher. "We'd have put our heads together and worked out things so that we could have given your Captain the help he so badly needed. We knew he was leaving this boat for a shore job in two days' time. I could have handled this thing so there'd have been no scene in the control room, no humiliation of Shadde in front of his officers and men, no certainty of disgrace and dismissal from the service."

He stopped and looked around at the puzzled embarrassed faces. "I hope you gentlemen don't think that I'm presuming on your hospitality," he said. "I know I am, so to speak, a guest in this boat, but I've got a bit of a conscience about your Captain, and I want to get this off my chest. Hope you don't mind."

He turned back to the first lieutenant. "The thing is, you aimed to handle it rather differently, didn't you, Cavan? You aimed to play it dead safe on a heads-I-win—tails-Shadde-loses basis.

"So you fixed it that whichever way it broke you'd be O.K. If it had been an exercise, you were O.K. If Symington was caught on the job, you were O.K. If it wasn't an exercise —which it wasn't—you were O.K. What's more, you'd get the kudos for having prevented the worst—so you'd be very O.K. . . ." Cavan pushed back his chair and stood up, his face as white as a sheet, but Gallagher went on, " . . . which is why you've been polishing your marble so goddam hard in this wardroom for the last ten minutes." Gallagher's hand waved in an airy gesture of contempt. "Protecting Symington . . . protecting Gracie . . . protecting Shadde. You give me a pain in the ass! The only person you were protecting was Benjamin Cavan. You were at your old game, Cavan—keeping your yardarm clear. It's a religion with you . . . more than that . . . it's a goddam obsession. And what you've done is to push Shadde so deep in the goddam shit that, cure or no cure, he's a ruined man."

Gallagher stopped and there wasn't a sound in the wardroom except the hum of the turbines. "And in case you think what you've done is smart," he went on, "I'd like you to know that at the court of inquiry I'll be saying pretty much what I'm saying now."

Cavan was the bigger of the two men, and for a moment it appeared that he was going to hit the American. Gallagher must have thought so too, because he stood there waiting, tense and wary. But the first lieutenant just looked at him, then shrugged his shoulders and left the wardroom.

After a long silence the others departed in ones and twos. At the end Gallagher was left standing there alone.

|| 22 ||

Later in the forenoon Gallagher pushed back the desk chair in his cabin and reread the report he had just typed. Then he wrote the covering letter, pulled it out of his typewriter and clipped it onto the report. Before signing the letter he read it through once again.

TOP SECRET

FROM: Lieutenant Commander Dwight Gallagher, U.S.N. (Nuclear Weapons Control Officer, H.M. Submarine *Retaliate*).

TO: Supreme Commander, Atlantic, Norfolk, Virginia, U.S.A.

SUBJECT: Attempted violation, control measures, Polaris missiles.

ENCLOSURE: Report on events May 16/17, while on passage Copenhagen-Portsmouth.

1. In accordance with Navy Department Instructions NWC 18-431/7 (para. 3) enclosure is submitted for information and action.

2. It will be noted that omission from the firing signal of the U.S. Control Group (indicating prefix and 6-digit setting for combination dial of firing key) precluded implementation of the instruction by undersigned and testified to invalidity of the signal.

3. Even if the existence of the system of U.S. Control Groups had been known to the commanding officer of *Retaliate,* he would not have been able to validate the signal, since he did not have access to the Groups.

4. Attention is drawn to the failure of the executive officer, Lieutenant Commander B.W. Cavan, R.N. who had prior knowledge of the attempted violation, to inform the undersigned as was his clear duty.

5. In terms of sub-section (iv) of para. 3 of the reference instructions, undersigned observes that the control measures worked admirably under circumstances possibly never envisaged: namely, collusion between the commanding officer of the ship and the head of his communications department.

Dwight Gallagher

He folded the letter and report and put them into a top-secret envelope. He sealed it, then placed the envelope in another top-secret, pre-addressed envelope and sealed it too before locking it in the safe.

Just after midnight the Doctor went up to the bridge. He couldn't sleep and he longed for fresh air and an escape from the cramped environment of his tiny cabin.

The night was clear and crisp with a gentle breeze and

a calm sea. They were well into the Channel now, and to starboard a myriad lights along the coast between South Foreland and Dover twinkled and blinked like jeweled confetti. Here and there in the distance the steaming lights of ships shone cold, remote and anonymous. Occasionally the silence was broken by the noise of aircraft passing overhead.

Symington was officer of the watch, and O'Shea stood with him in the forepart of the bridge, looking out into the night.

The Doctor sighed. "I'm glad this patrol's nearly over."

"So am I," said Symington. "Too much alarm and despondency."

There was a long silence.

"Dreadful about Shadde, isn't it, Doc?"

"Yes . . . another war casualty, really."

"Have you ever thought about madness?"

"Sometimes."

"What d'you think he feels? I mean, is he conscious of it, d'you think?"

"Yes. Definitely. But no one ever really goes mad with joy, you know."

There was a call on the voice-pipe. Symington answered it, then returned to the bridge screen.

"That was Cavan," he said.

There was another long silence. Finally the Doctor said, "You know, there's a hell of a lot more to Dwight Gallagher than I realized."

"Good type," said Symington softly. "Very good type."

Beneath them the sea lapped and gurgled, and the forecasing shone wetly in the moonlight.

The room was littered with clothing. It was everywhere, on the bed, over the chairs, hanging over cupboard doors, and falling out of half-opened drawers. In the middle of the room there was a cluster of half-full suitcases with their lids open. But she was determined not to take anything that wasn't essential, and so she selected and discarded and the pile of things that were to be left behind got steadily bigger.

After a time she felt tired and sat on the edge of the bed. She drew her hand across her forehead and sighed. She had often packed, but there had never been anything like this that was so terribly final, that meant you weren't only leaving clothes behind—and England—but your life.

She sighed again. She was running away, no denying that. She kept thinking of that letter of his from Stockholm, so proud and yet so urgent, like a small boy who had been punished and wanted to make friends but was too stubborn to say "sorry." And for that matter, why should he say he was sorry? It was probably her fault as much as his. But what was the use of talking about whose fault it was; it was much too late for that. You did what something in you made you do, and try as you might you couldn't fight against it even if you hated doing it.

She was deserting him, no doubt about that. Of course he would find someone else. Someone who'd give him babies, and that would make all the difference, and they'd be madly happy. How she hoped he would be happy. It was the only thing she felt certain about now: that she wanted him to be happy. It would help her conscience, and it was the least that was necessary to justify her decision. And apart from all that, she wanted him to be happy because he'd had so little of it in his life.

The telephone was ringing downstairs and she heard her mother answering it. "Yes, certainly. I'll call her . . . Elizabeth! Telephone, dear. It's Portsmouth."

A thrill of excitement surged through her. Could it be him? Could it possibly be him? What would he say? And what could she say? But she must go, even if it were only to hear his voice once more.

She ran down the stairs and picked up the telephone.

311

For a moment she held it until she got back her breath, then said guardedly, "Elizabeth Shadde speaking." She tried to sound calm, but her heart was pounding.

"Who did you say? . . . Oh! Surgeon Lieutenant O'Shea —Yes! Yes! Yes, of course."

She caught her breath sharply. "In Haslar Hospital! Why? What's happened to him?"

As she listened her head started to swim, and from far away she heard O'Shea saying, "It's most important that you should see him. He keeps asking for you."

When she put the receiver down she felt weak and her body seemed to go limp. For a few moments she sat there in an agony of indecision; then she dialed a number. There was some delay before they found the clerk she wanted. For an instant she was tongue-tied, terrified that her voice would fail her, but she was surprised at its firmness when she said, "I've had to change my plans, I'm afraid. I shan't be needing those tickets after all." Then she put the telephone down and burst into tears.

About the Author

Born in Praetoria, South Africa, in 1906, Antony Trew first went to sea as a cadet in cargo ships at the age of fifteen. Later commissioned as an officer in the South African Naval Service, he left the navy in 1930 and held various jobs until he re-enlisted in September of 1939. In 1943 he was seconded to the Royal Navy as a Lieutenant Commander and was awarded the DSC for his conduct in action while commander of a destroyer employed principally in convoy duties to Murmansk.

After the war Mr. Trew returned to South Africa, where he is now Secretary-General of that country's Automobile Association. Mr. Trew says that he "started writing because I found I was going to bed too early and not sleeping well." Married and the father of three sons, he is now at work on his second novel.